Call Me Maggie

First Edition Copy Presented To:

From:

May you enjoy reading "Call Me Maggie"
as much as I enjoyed writing it.
Nelson Brooks

Call Me Maggie

Nelson Brooks

ISBN 1442168757
LCCN

Printed in the United States of America.

Preface

Kevin Kennedy is obsessed with meeting a strawberry blonde dancer who frequently appears on American Bandstand. Kevin borrows his older brother Norman's sports coat and convertible and drives to Philadelphia to meet the girl of his dreams. A former classmate, showoff and braggart Linda Reed has other plans for Kevin. Kevin gets a promise from the blonde to meet him after the show. The blonde's pimp, Vinnie Gambini who she teamed up with as a way out of the ghetto, heads up The Impala Gang and he has other plans for Kevin, Linda and the blonde, Mary Anne Johnson. A street fight develops ending with Mary Anne who prefers to be called Maggie leaving with Kevin and Linda after the fight ends. If Maggie goes home, the pimp will find her. Having to go to work later that evening, Kevin must find a solution to his and Maggie's problems. He calls on his brother Norman who takes Maggie to a policeman friend to find space for her in a safe house. Norman, an ambitious workaholic photographer takes her to his apartment while waiting for police paperwork to finish, shows her his portfolio and Maggie volunteers to pose for him, telling the policeman, "Thanks but no thanks, I feel safe with Norman."

He gives her a lead as a stewardess with an upstart charter airline and offers to move her away from her alcoholic mother and sister. Maggie rents an apartment and offers to model again in exchange his help, bluffs and lies and lands the position attending flesh grabbing vacationers going to warmer climates, government contractors, advisors, and American servicemen to Southeast Asia. Norman begins a thirteen-year relationship with Maggie lasting from 1962 through of the troubling Vietnam War era in an age of peaceniks verses warmongers and patriotic and moral disintegration of the 1960's and early 70's.

Maggie develops a friendship with Linda, three other stewardesses who idolizes her as well as with Norman's family, and in particular, his father who becomes her gardening mentor and father figure. Along the way, Kevin buys drag racer, Linda drives it, Vinnie reappears, and Maggie poses for Norman in old dresses or without clothes at the drop of a hat for an ongoing book of pictures.

In addition to photographing her, Norman documents life on the home front while Maggie flies frightened young men to Southeast Asia and brings home the survivors, the wounded and the dead while pursuing her own methods of protesting the war's toll on soldiers she calls her boys.

Dedication

This story is dedicated to all young Maggie Johnsons, Bobby Joe Montgomerys, Rooster Petersons, Vinnie Gambinis, and Joe Jobbes who went to Vietnam by ship or plane and were forever altered, and to the 58,252 men and eight women who never came home but are remembered on a black wall in Washington, D. C. plus the more than 1200 who were not forgotten by those who wore MIA bracelets inscribed with their names.

The 45 news gathering persons who died during the war and the 18 still listed as missing are remembered in the fictional character Lindsay Brown.

Acknowledgements

My thanks to the History Channel for keeping the hardships our young men and women endured during the 1960's and '70's fresh in our minds today although this story is not intended feature them so much as it was written to show admiration for the Maggies, Midges, and Leannes behind the battle fronts in Veterans Hospital across the country. Maggie's battle continues today as care givers treat the once young men who gave large parts of themselves when called upon.

Special thanks to my son Gregory for suggesting I start writing and taking pictures again after my disability and unexpected retirement in 2003. This is the result of three years when days were too wet or too cold to enjoy the Virginia mountains or the Delaware seashore.

Contents

1

Bandstand Blonde

Before Interstate 95 was built, a thirty-mile drive between Wilmington, Delaware and Philadelphia, Pennsylvania could take at least two hours, if no accidents or tie-ups were encountered. By the 1960's the main route between the two cities, U.S. 13, had outgrown its thirty year-old design and tie-ups were to be expected.

On this sunny afternoon in 1962, Kevin Kennedy was making the drive between the two cities in a borrowed sports coat and his older brother's four year-old Chevy convertible. During the hours between 11 p.m. and 7 a.m. Kevin drove a huge earthmover that picked up soil at the Minquadale quarry and carried it to the Christianna Marsh right of way to form the roadbed for the future highway. The Interstate and its spaghetti bowl junctions would cover much of the marsh with soil and concrete. Kevin himself had moved thousands of yards of soil and would move thousands more during the next eighteen months.

He had quit school seventeen months earlier to make his fortune in the heyday of 1960's home building boom. He had to promise his parents he would attend night school if they allowed him to drop out of school and go to work. Reminding them that his father quit after fifth grade and his mother dropped out after only three years clinched his plea.

1

Call Me Maggie

Kevin had moved to Wilmington a few years earlier as his family sought the life of the city over Alabama farming and starvation. At first, he took a job driving a tow truck. General Motors had an assembly plant that was within walking distance of his home. The truck and he would go anywhere on the East Coast to pick up disabled car carrier trucks that delivered new GM cars. Kevin had to lie about his age to get the job. He remembered the lie and his regrets as he drove. The regrets began on the Friday morning of December 22nd when he picked up a car carrier tractor and trailer in western North Carolina and headed home. A few miles into the return trip, his old and worn out tow truck decided to die on one a Carolina mountain. A friendly resident passing by sent the county's only tow truck to rescue Kevin. Three trips up the mountain and back were required to retrieve the tow truck, the tractor, and the car carrier to the local service station and country store. Kevin knew his truck needed major repairs and called his dispatcher.

"Sleep in the truck," was the dispatcher final offer.

Kevin informed his mother. His mother informed Norman, Kevin's oldest brother. Kevin hitched a few rides to the Asheville's Western Union office while Norman wired him bus fare home. Seventeen year-old Kevin Kennedy's truck driving career ended when he pushed the tow truck's keys through the dispatcher's door slot on Christmas Eve.

Kevin pumped gas at Tommy Donovan's Esso Station the rest of the winter. In the spring he carried lumber from a skid pallet near the street to construction crews building the little matchbox houses in the suburbs from 7 A.M. until dusk. At $1.50 an hour, his fortune had shortcomings, but his six-foot, three-inch frame strengthened in proportion to his occupational frustration.

"Speed it up, hillbilly," other workers yelled at Kevin. "You ain't laying around on the farm no more."

From the worksite of his construction job, Kevin could hear the roar of heavy equipment building the new super highway through the marsh across the river. When he carried lumber up to the upper floors of the future homes, he tried to catch glimpses of the equipment working.

One of his older brothers drove an earth moving dirt pan at the site. Within a few weeks, Kevin's home building career was finished and the eighteen-year-olds new career was that of dirt pan jockey. Changing careers doubled his salary and he opened a savings account at the Bank of Delaware. Driving the dirt pan an extra day each week promised to fulfill another of his dreams, but the little savings account at the bank was not yet large enough to buy a car of his own, so he made do with the family station wagon as his brothers had done.

He found that he enjoyed driving the large earthmover. He hoped he could drive earthmovers the rest of his life. In fact, he liked driving everything from his father's garden tractor, to his two older brother's cars, to the family station wagon. By taking the graveyard shift job Kevin could sleep all morning and spend the early evening with his friends. At the controls of the equipment, he was in a world of his own. No one yelled at him for not keeping up with other crewmembers. He simply drove to the quarry, scraped up a load of soil, drove to the drop site, hit the lever that opened the pan, dropped the load and drove back to the quarry for another load. He performed this task twice each hour. The only drawback was remembering to downshift before descending downhill grades inside and outside the quarry. The machine would over speed greatly if downshifting came too late as a few drivers learned, including his brother, Ernest, who ridden his runaway dirt pan down the grade and into the marsh.

However, on this sunny spring afternoon, Kevin's mind did not linger on his graveyard shift job as he and Norman drove toward three 12-story skyscrapers above the Wilmington skyline. Taking Alternate 13 would have averted the skyscrapers and the traffic downtown, but he had to drop off his oldest bother downtown. It was a necessary delay, but one that had to endure since it was the older brother's car that Kevin would be driving to Philadelphia this afternoon. He could have driven the family station wagon, but the convertible was more to his liking.

Kevin promised his himself he would not ask his parents to co-sign another automobile finance note. He would pay cash for his new car as his father did and not be like his two older brothers who some-times floated loans from their mother to make their monthly GMAC payments. Kevin was uncertain who was out of step, but this trip was one that none in his brothers had taken. Was it him or his brothers who marched to a different drummer, his sub-conscience questioned.

Their parents had insisted upon that son find work as soon as they could after moving to the city. Ernest and Norman had delivered newspapers and mowed lawns before getting working papers. All four had found work after school at age fourteen and went their separate ways, yet when they needed one another; they came back together, much like they did when they lived on a clay and stone farm back in Alabama. His father was now a millwright and avid gardener. His mother tanned and colored leather in a Wilmington factory. His three brothers

Call Me Maggie

worked evening shifts as well. Norman, the oldest, took pictures for the city's morning newspaper and Ernest, the second son, mounted a "dirt pan" shortly after 3 o'clock each afternoon. The youngest, fifteen year old Lionel worked in Donavan's Esso station, one block from home. His sister and her husband, parents to two young sons lived across the street.

"I'll be here at ten," Kevin promised as he dropped off Norman.

Timing his return to retrieve his brother was critical. Kevin would only make the day's trip if he could successfully, make all the connections, and be at the heavy equipment yard before 11 p.m. to relieve another driver and keep the highway project moving ahead, otherwise he would be looking for another career.

After the newspaper office stop, he headed east to Church Street, and crossed the Thirteenth Street Bridge. For about eight miles, he could enjoy views of the Delaware River from Governor Printz Boulevard and his brother's '58 Chevy convertible but his thoughts were on his destination.

Large pear shaped sunglasses covered Kevin's eyes protecting them from sun and wind. Kevin did not mind the wind blowing through his thick, wavy red hair. He had put enough Wildroot Cream Oil on his head to weather the fifty-five mile wind blowing in the car with its top lowered.

Soon the road jogged left into Claymont around a huge steel mill on the right and through the oil refineries of Marcus Hook, Chester, and South Philadelphia. Within forty minutes, the Philadelphia skyline was in view. Once Kevin crossed the Schuylkill River, city cityscapes replaced the factories and refineries. After 30 minutes in Philadelphia row house canyons, he reached his destination, a warehouse looking building with no windows. A line of youngsters stretched down the block and around the corner. Like Kevin, most had been in the line before. Many had been there since noon today. Others milled around cars parked at the curb. All knew the routine of this Monday through Friday ritual. Thirty of them would get in the building, the others would be disappointed, leave, and watch the event on Philadelphia's channel six.

The president with whom Kevin shared the same surname had opened many doors, set new goals, and given confidence for young people to build a "Great New Society." Kevin had met him once when he tagged along with Norman as he photographed the then senator on a campaign stopover at the Wilmington airport. As the senator approached with Kevin an outstretched hand, Kevin turned to Norman and asked, "What du I du?"

4

Bandstand Blonde

"Shake his hand. You came here to meet him," Norman had instructed his brother.

Today, Kevin would fulfill a promise he had made many months earlier, dance with and possible take home a strawberry blonde haired girl who had caught his eye.

"I'll save you a spot," a girl yelled from the line while up raised arms tighten her Banlon sweater across her ample bulges, but she wasn't the girl he drove an hour to meet.

Kevin recognized the caller and flashed thumbs up to the young female. From behind the aviator sunglasses, he gave most of the other girls in line a glance as the car crept down the street. Whistles and cat-calls marked their approval of the Chevy ragtop.

Was it him or the car that the crowd approved, Kevin asked himself while trying to check out the crowd, drive, and find a parking space, while Fats Domino's gravel voice blared from the car's radio, "I found my thrill on Blueberry Hill."

After he found a parking spot around the corner beyond the end of the line, an ever-present comb rearranged red waves viewed in a mirror clipped to the sun visor before he adjusted the sunglasses again

Girls in full crinoline skirts reaching half way down their calves tried to cover their lips and muffle their giggles as he strolled past them en route to his spot being saved near the front of the line. Others in the line kept their Catholic school uniforms and makeup in overnight bags at their feet. They wore garments that would be shameless in the eyes of their parochial teachers. .

"Save me a dance." bolder girls asked, as Kevin walked past after parking the car.

A few braced their shoulders back stretching their Banlon sweaters tight to their Playtex Living Bras. Almost every newspaper, magazine, and television set on the planet showed pictures of Jane Russell promising the undergarment would give females a figure like hers. Girls older than fourteen had at least one of the bras living in her dresser or on her breasts. From behind the sunglasses, he observed that Jane's promise had been kept for a few of the girls. Their dark lenses prevented the girls from knowing which he overlooked, and which he summoned would for a dance or a ride in the ragtop.

Rounding the corner, Kevin could see Linda Reed waving him to hurry to the place she was holding in line. The Reed girl and Kevin were classmates and became friends at Wilmington's Bayard Junior High School. Many times, she had volunteered to join Kevin on school

Call Me Maggie

projects or after school outings. She knew she could find him at the Greenhill Drive-In on almost any given Saturday evening if she missed him earlier at the weekly Wilmington Armory dance or the dance at the Saint Elizabeth's High School Gym. Often she and girlfriends would share a six-person booth at the Charcoal Pit with Kevin and his brothers or a couple of other boys. She knew she could count on Kevin for a ride home from either of their hangouts, but they never actually went out together on a real date. Kevin always had an evening job after school before driving the dirt pan, but he kept Saturday night for cruising and hanging out.

"You are almost too late!" she chastised Kevin.

Linda was one of the few Catholic girls in Wilmington who did not attend St. Elizabeth's, Saint Anthony's, or one of the half dozen Catholic schools in the city. She had attended St. Thomas Elementary School for girls in the Irish part of town known as Forty Acres. Growing up, Linda had learned that a high tempered Irish girl must get along in a parochial school. She would have preferred public elementary school and its co-ed education, a wish her parents finally granted in her seventh grade. Linda had no brothers or sisters, and envied Kevin and the stories he told about sibling experiences.

She soon learned the class work was much more fun with the boys and even more fun when she hung out with them after school. Now a senior at the co-ed Wilmington High School, cutting classes was her major rather than home-ec and business prep. Dancing in the gym at lunchtime was her sub-major. She was an excellent dancer, fluent and fluid, slow or fast. Most boys in the midday crowd were less accomplished dancers. This left her to dance with girls or not dance. She danced to every song played during the lunch hour or on Saturday night.

Kevin was usually included in the weekday school or social life during her last three school years. On summer Sunday afternoons, they could be found swimming at the sandpit or working on an engine in front of his father's garage. Occasionally she would be part of carload taking a Sunday ride to beaches in lower Delaware.

Unlike nice girls of The Gang, Linda used the telephone to call Kevin's home to learn of his plans. Linda would tell anyone, "Nice girls do call guys; otherwise they end up sitting home and missing a lot of fun."

Some of the gang thought Linda had the hots for him.

Marble sized points centered upon the peaks of Linda's Banlon sweater were quite evident when Kevin reached her. If she noticed him staring, he could not be sure. The glasses prevented her from knowing if he was staring at her or the strawberry blonde.

Linda gave him a few moments to check out the blonde and other girls in the line. He gave her the same liberty when she checked out other guys. Would the strawberry blonde be as easy to know as Linda, Kevin wondered as he looked her over from the waiting line. Would she join him at the Charcoal Pit, the Greenhill Drive-in, and the Armory dance or in the family garage fixing up a seven year-old Ford he and two brothers were preparing to drag race?

"Did you drive up here alone?" Linda asked, grasping his arm. "I'd have ridden up with you, if I knew you were coming,"

"Had to drop off Norman," Kevin responded.

"Maybe I can ride home with you?" Linda said as she pressed her bust to his arm.

"Maybe," was his noncommittal reply.

Kevin and Linda had decided to make the first trip together on the "Pennsy commuter" one night at the Charcoal Pit. She and two other girls agreed to show Kevin the way, if he borrowed a car. The nine-passenger station wagon made their second trip.

"I came up on the train and it took all my money for the tickets and trolley over here," Linda stated. "Maybe you could drop me off at the train station afterwards."

"Maybe," was his answer again.

Kevin's eye and attention remained on a strawberry blonde. The blonde-haired young woman also wore a Banlon, a not too tight pink Banlon. However, if strawberry blonde-haired person had points under her sweater, they were not as evident as Linda's were. The blonde had no overnight bag at her feet, nor did she wear crinolines under her full skirt. Her attention frequently shifted to one of four young men wearing black "Zuit Suits" with extremely tight pants above their Italian loafers milling around a 1962 black Impala parked at the curb. Each was a carbon copy the other and impersonator of youthful Hollywood actor and heartthrob Sal Mineo.

Farther back in the line of mostly adolescent girls, Kevin observed a few girls he had danced with on his earlier trips to Philadelphia prancing nervously and stealing quick glimpses at him, at the other boys, or at the young men around the black Impala. Most of the girls giggled behind hands on their mouths. Some were glancing at Kevin. Two of the boys near the Impala looking at Linda.

"We'll be going in soon," Linda said.

Call Me Maggie

"Yup," he affirmed.

"I wonder who they will have in person today."

"Don't know," was her answer from Kevin and his concealing sunglasses.

Thoughts of an evening at the Armory weeks earlier went through Linda's head. It had been a crowded night at the dance. The reason was a live appearance by Jan and Dean featuring their California beach songs. Youngsters not dancing to their "lip-synced" recorded songs crowded near the makeshift stage. Behind the gazing crowd, other young people danced. Few had celebrated their twenty-first birthday, or even their eighteenth.

On the night she was remembering, Kevin had wrapped his arms around her legs so tightly when he lifted her onto his shoulder to give her a better view of the singers, she could feel his heart beating. With his right hands on her calves barely below her hips, Kevin had given her a good view, and wonderful feeling. A few other times she had that feeling when their legs and hips touched as they shared a booth with other friends at the Charcoal pit, or when she rode shotgun as he drove her and their friends to the sandpits near Hockessin for an afternoon of swimming. Even now, she could feel his right hand and the sensation it aroused in her. There would be no replay of that today. Bleachers were inside the building they were waiting to enter and no lifting was needed or allowed. Sitting close would be the best they would experience this afternoon. With luck, she could slide over close to him to hear him better in the convertible during the drive home, and Linda hoped he would offer her that ride. If not, she would ask in her most convincing demeanor. Being an only child of working parents Linda grew up with fewer inhibitions than most of her seventeen-year-old friends, either girls or boys.

A gray steel door suddenly opened. Screams erupted from the crowd.

"Who wants to be on Bandstand today?" asked the man who opened the door.

The roar grew even louder. Members of the Impala gang went to the places in the line saved for them by four girls. The one Kevin had surmised to be the leader joined the strawberry blonde.

"Me! Me! I do," chorused the hundred and fifty voices.

Some of those in the line passed through the door. Those rejected milled about to the left of the door. No young man entered unless he wore a coat and tie. No young woman passed the man unless she filled all his criteria and filled her sweater. It was the moment of ultimate acceptance or rejection for the young crowd. In a few minutes, millions from Bangor to Burbank would envy those who entered.

Linda approached the door attendant as confident as fighting roosters she had heard Kevin describe. Her eyes sparkled full of anticipation. A smile crossed her face. She held her shoulders back even more than before and the sized peaks under her sweater reached a new high. Linda had the looks the door attendant wanted and wore clothes fitting Bandstand's fashion mold better than most.

"Okay, Sis," the door attendant approved as she approached.

"He's with me," she told him, then paused as the doorman eyed Kevin with scouring scrutiny.

Meeting his acceptance threshold, Linda and Kevin joined gathering inside the warehouse looking building.

The crowd to the left of the door grew to more than double the size of the one inside. Those left outside had failed the selection process. Linda and Kevin were again to be participants in the nationwide after school phenomena known as American Bandstand.

The time slot once occupied by the "Mickey Mouse Club" had been bumped back to 5 p.m., as Musketeers became adolescents that bought millions of 45-rpm records. The show's producers had foreseen a niche they could fill. At first only viewers in Philadelphia saw the radical new broadcast. Later it was added the American Broadcast Company's weekday schedule filling the 90 minutes from 3:30 to 5 p.m. Bandstand showcased the newest, hottest and most popular young singers in the nation and could make or break a recording artist. It was the most watched of all daytime TV shows.

The music of California's beach and surfing craze took land locked teen-agers into the fantasies of west coast culture and Philadelphia do-whoop to those in California, Iowa or Arizona. Philadelphia had a finger on the pulse of young people. The real mystery was how a third placed Philadelphia television station could overshadow New York and Hollywood network productions. Those questions never entered Kevin or Linda's mind as they waited for the cameras to be turned on.

A half dozen production people rushed about adjusting countless lights, prompters, and cameras to capture the phenomena and send it to other stations across the country. Workers rolled a small speaker's podium over a taped square on the floor a few feet to the right of unfolded bleachers for the attendees. A soundman checked the podium

Call Me Maggie

microphone and another at the end of a 25-foot cable. A clock on the center camera read 3:15. Everything seemed to be ready.

Bill Haley's "Rock Around the clock" and Chuck Berry's "Hot Rod Lincoln" kept the pre-broadcast tempo high. No slow songs played until the show went on the air. Research indicated four fast songs to one slow one was the best mix for the broadcasts Neilson ratings. Higher ratings meant higher charges for the program's commercials and more profit for the show's producer.

Her feet fumbled nervously on bleachers. Her hands twisted over each other.

"I'm so excited I could pee in my drawers," Linda said.

Kevin heard the statement, but gave no response. His thoughts were on the girl seated a few rows away.

At exactly 3:25 p.m. music from the studio speakers silenced. A suit-dressed production worker raised the cabled microphone to his lips and told the audience to "Take a seat in the bleachers and listen-up. We are going to start in a few minutes. First, I am going over some rules. Absolutely no dirty dancing. No lifting your partner over your shoulder. No sliding them between your legs. No check-to-check dancing will be allowed. No yelling will be permitted. Be yourself. Don't say 'hi' to your friends at home. Act like fine boys and girls. In addition, at no time do you approach Mr. Clark. If he comes to you, that is okay. He may want to interview you on camera. He will tell you, if he does. When you are on camera, keep your eyes on him, not the camera. Stay calm, stay relaxed, and smile a lot. Break these rules and we will send you back outside. Now put your sunglasses in your pockets and leave them there."

The rule man was looking squarely at Kevin when he finished. Kevin, a few other young men, a couple of girls and all of the Impala gang complied, Kevin a little slower that the others as he made one more sweep of the girls from behind his sunglasses.

Every youngster in the room who had listened to the instructions, raced to the upper benches. Regular on the show had had already taken lower seats or someone saved one for them. Kevin noticed the strawberry blonde had taken a seat on the front row earlier and saved a space for the Impala Gang leader.

Linda and twenty-five other girls freshened their lipstick while most of the boys gave their TC curls a final twist.

As 3:30 neared, Linda's Banlon budged more than ever and her hip could only get closer to Kevin's only if neither wore clothes.

Bandstand Blonde

"I can't wait!" she said.

The overhead red and white "On the Air" sign came on. An unseen man's voice came over the studio speakers saying, "Live from Philadelphia, Pennsylvania, it's television's favorite dance party, American Bandstand. And America's favorite party host, Dick Clark." Another sign flashed the word "Applause." With that remark, Dick Clark came through a slit in the heavy curtain, walked before one of three cameras, and waited for the ovation and applause light to die away.

Linda sighed deeply and covered her mouth with both hands.

A studio monitor faded from the program logo to the dimpled face of Mr. Music Maker, Dick Clark. Applause and the image in the monitor continued for an eternal twenty seconds. A profile view of Clark with hand clapping teen-agers behind him finally replaced the tight view of Clark, his dimples, and his perfect hair.

Clark's on-camera persona portrayed him as the world nicest human being. He could have easily been one of the sweeter than sugar ministers seen on early Sunday morning religious broadcasts. Off camera he was a serious, no nonsense individual with the charm of a bank loan officer. His tanned and wrinkle free face made it difficult to assess his age. He could be a late teen-ager, a college student, or even over thirty. An observer could not be sure. His perfectly combed air swept across his brow making a guess even more difficult.

"Good afternoon, everyone. Welcome to American Bandstand. I have a very special guest for you today, and we will be reviewing five new records. Five of you will vote on the songs." Clark began and soon introduced the first record of the day, "Surfer Girl," by some California brothers.

Jitterbugging youngsters from Philadelphia, Delaware and New Jersey filled the floor, including Kevin and Linda. They continued for the next ten minutes until a commercial break interrupted the orchestrated mayhem.

The host stood on a platform behind the podium allowing the cameras to capture him above the dancers on the floor. His on air persona demanded maximum on camera time and the production crew made sure he got it. He was in position to make or break any upcoming young singer or group. He allowed no no-talent singers on Bandstand who would impede the shows successful mileage. Only a few one-hit wonders got past his screening into Bandstand's spotlight. His contacts in the recording companies were without measure. Area artists who could appear on short notice made frequent appearances on Bandstand. Return appearances propelled their popularity leading to more live performances and higher income.

Some dancers changed partners after Clark introduced another song. The first slow song played, came second after the commercial. That, and guest appearances were Bandstand's success formula.

Kevin was in search of success also. At the moment, he sought success with the young woman he had seen in the little colorless TV set picture at home and during his first two trips to North Philadelphia. There were many seventeen and eighteen year-olds Kevin could ask to dance, but the blonde still headed his list.

Some of the girls were admiring him just as he admired them. He wanted to hide behind his dark glasses, but weighed wearing them against removal from the studio. The choice was easy and the sunglasses remained in his pocket.

Several times Linda left Kevin's side to dance with other boys. Many regulars remembered Linda's ability and asked her to dance, but if she saw a boy she wanted to dance with, she asked him, rather than chance he would not ask her.

Regulars were a dozen or so excellent dancers who appeared on the show almost every day who were featured for their knowledge of the latest dance fads and an appealing performance. It was often a question of which dancer needed a good partner rather than which boy was dating which girl. The boys on Bandstand were not nearly as shy as the ones at the Armory or at St. Elizabeth's. Linda used this to her advantage and gained excellent dance partners.

Aware of a wilting wallflower's fate, Kevin resorted to his second choices while waiting for the strawberry blonde to be free.

"I loved dancing with that guy over there," Linda said after she returned from a second invitation.

"Good." his brevity continued.

"You looked good dancing with the girl in the blue skirt." she went on as she and Kevin read the crowd.

"Think so?" Kevin questioned.

"Oh yeah."

Anther regular grabbed Linda as the next song began and took her in front of a camera panning the crowd as regulars could do. Kevin asked one regular to dance with him, but their slow start resulted in a second choice area of the dance floor. The next song would be slow. He had viewed the show enough to know the second song after a commercial was always slow, and he would be ready. He positioned himself for his move of the day with the strawberry blonde. Approaching her, Kevin commanded "Let's dance!"

With barely a trace of a smile, she followed him.

After a moment of silence, he asked her name.

"I am Mary Anne Johnson. But call me Maggie."

"I'm Kevin." he said with a twang as thick as ever.

"Have you been her many times?"

"Dis is my third time," Kevin twanged, knowing he was uneasy and he had failed to hide his heavy accident.

"I have been coming for over a year now."

Kevin had first noticed her during unemployment after the tow truck fiasco.

"Where are you from?" she asked.

"Wilmington. Auh, South Wilmington."

During on air interviews, Bandstand attendees always preceded Philadelphia with north, south or west and sometimes simply "South Philly." New Jersey youngsters declared "South Jersey" as their home. Kevin felt compelled to say "South Wilmington" even though it felt unnatural to him. No one proclaimed "East Philly." East Philly was the Delaware River.

"And before that?"

"Alabama." he replied, but she heard "Aller Bamer."

Maggie did not denounce her new acquaintance, a slow talking boy from the Deep South with an equally deep rooted accent as many others did. His twang fascinated her. She kept the conversation advancing as the two danced slowly.

"Nice car you drive."

"Thanks," Kevin answered without mentioning ownership, and then asked of her, "Where are you from?"

"Chester. Save me another slow dance if you want," she said emphasizing "you."

The freshman Bandstand dancer seemed to be advancing with the veteran, but, at the end the dance, she returned to her Impala's and he returned to Linda. His slow found courage left him with amazement, pride, wonder, and satisfaction mixing in his mind.

"Who was that you just danced with?" Linda asked.

"Just a girl from Chester," he answered.

Kevin positioned near Maggie to ask for the next slow dance. She agreed. The song began "On a day like today, we pass the time

Call Me Maggie

away writing love letters in the sand." They were dancing before Pat Boone reached "sand."

This time neither spoke during the song while she danced with her head on his shoulder. A quick glance at the studio monitor made Kevin aware of Maggie's stature. The top of her head reached his shoulder even in low heel shoes, allowing her to see past him. In a silent guess, he put her height at five feet, ten inches. It was a lucky break for a boy of his height. He had not noticed her height before. He did not know the color of her hair until his first visit to the studio a few weeks earlier. He knew his dream had come true. He was dancing with the strawberry blonde.

"Thanks for asking me again," Maggie said softly when the song ended.

"Glad to," Kevin replied as he tried to guess her age.

"What's your last name Kevin?"

"Kennedy."

"Do you have a middle name, Kevin Kennedy?"

"James," he complied with her request.

"Kevin James Kennedy, where do go to school, Wilmington High or P. S. DuPont?"

"Neither. I went to Brown Vocational, but quit about a year and a half ago. Now I'm a heavy equipment operator driving a dirt mover building the new interstate."

"Me too. I quit almost two years ago. I wanted to be a model, but no one wants me without experience and no one wanted to give me any experience. I was voted best model in school, but I haven't done any real modeling except for a photographer who put my picture on an Atlantic City post card. After I posed in a skimpy little bikini he wanted me to model naked for a skin magazine. I posed for a few, but all he wanted to shoot was pornographic. I don't pose for porno any longer."

Was Maggie was opening up to him, Kevin ask himself.

"My brother is a photographer," Kevin added, hoping to find a subject they would share and he could talk with her again during the next dance or after the broadcast ended.

"Right now I am waiting to get in airline stewardess school. You can't be a stewardess until you're twenty one, so I have to wait about two more years."

"Too bad! I could take you to meet my brother. He does quite a few fashion pictures for the newspaper in Wilmington. He is always looking for new models. Maybe he could use you in some of his pictures," Kevin volunteered and quickly added, "I doubt if he would want to shoot any pornographic shots of you."

Maggie gave no answer and remained silent for the remainder of the song.

Linda asked Kevin for the next dance and conversation slowed as the couple moved to the music's rhythm. Kevin became aware that her leg was now between his and their hips touched. He enjoyed the closeness of her body and the smell of her perfume as they swayed, but was unaware of the monitors displaying their waist-up bodies, or the glances from the Impala Gang leader.

"Are you hitting it off with Miss Chester?" Linda asked.

"Don't know yet."

Kevin's confidence increased as the clock approached 5 p.m. He became bold enough to dance with Maggie as Jerry Lee Lewis's "Whole Lot of Shaking" played. His boldness peaked when he asked her to join him for a milk shake after the show.

"Meet you at your car," she assured him after a quick glance at the Impala leader.

Kevin realized he had a small problem on his hands. He was meeting the strawberry blonde he wanted to meet for months and Linda had no way home or back to the train station. He wanted to drive her home and he wanted to meet with Maggie. Using confidence he gained dancing with Maggie, Kevin grabbed Linda at the end of the song. As they danced, he explained his freshly contrived plan to the one girl he had known the longest and he wasn't as shy talking to her as with others'

"I'm meeting that girl Maggie after the show," he began. "I can give you trolley fare or drive you home. If you ride with me, she will be coming with us. I'll take her home after I drop you off. Chester ain't that far from Wilmington and I've got five hours before I have to be at the equipment yard."

It was not the first time Linda needed a ride home from one of her impulsive adventures. Slipping out a bedroom window for a rendezvous or hitching hiking where ever and whenever she wanted was a common practice for Linda. He had learned of others during evenings spent in Charcoal Pit booths or in the station wagon parked at The Greenhill Drive-in Restaurant.

Only one offer had come her way today and it left her with potential problems that might prove difficult for her to handle alone. For that reason and one other, she announced quickly, "I'll ride with you and Miss Chester."

15

Call Me Maggie

He knew she could "one-up" the boldest girls and most of the young who challenged her courage, daring, or audacious behavior. Taking the train and trolley to Bandstand was but one example.

After the song finished, Dick Clark closed the show with his signature salute. Maggie and another Impala girl lingered with other regulars while laughter, giggles and screams filled the air from youngsters recounting the broadcast.

Kevin led Linda outside past the crowd swelled around the door, down the sidewalk, around the corner, and over to the red convertible parked across from the warehouse studio to wait for Maggie.

They sat together on the car's trunk having their first cigarette in two hours when Linda asked, "Do you think Miss Chester puts out?"

"Linda!" Kevin spoke out quickly and loudly.

"I know that why you've got the hots for her? You think she might put out."

"I don't think she would do that. I don't have the hots for her or for anyone else. She is just a girl I would like to know better. And she's a good dancer, almost as good as you."

"She might be good a good dancer but she looked at you like she might be good at something else. She might put out for you." Linda bluntly stated.

Her statement caught Kevin off guard. Linda was one of his gang and a friend during the five years since they met in middle school. He enjoyed having her in his crowd. He suspected Linda lived on the edge at times. He had read many things into her one up boasts made at the Charcoal Pit to gain an advantage. He knew she once spent most evenings and after school hours in her parent's sandwich shop serving sandwiches, doing homework or watching the shop's television set. Recently she had begun substituting escapades with her friends almost every evening for TV. Other evenings she came to his home and hung out with him working on cars before convincing him to knock off and take her cruising to one of the youthful nightspots until he went to work or take-in one of the dances. It was she who taught him and his friends their dance steps. Those escapades filled her bag of boastful tales and one-up man ship stories she told when with the guys. Linda's language was often profane. Kevin felt she used foul or vulgar language in order to be accepted as one of the guys in their group of friends. Nothing regarding her putting out ever come out of her bag of show off boasts or over emphasized accomplishments that often matched or exceeded those of the others in the gang the hung out with nor did Kevin regard his long time companion as a tomboy.

"A guy named Dominic asked me to dance. Said he would drive me home if I would put out for him. He said he only picked up girls that put-out for him," Linda added.

"What did you tell him?"

"I told him hell no."

"Good. That's one less story for the Charcoal Pit."

"Dominic said I could make lots of money putting out. If I put out, it's because I like the guy, not because he puts a twenty dollar bill in my drawers. There are guys I like and I don't put out for 'em. There are guys I like and I would put out for 'em. There are guys I wouldn't put out for no matter how much money they offered me. I have never put out for you or any of our friends. You are a great guy. I like you and I would put out for you, if you wanted me to. I would not put out for anybody just for the dough. I have got more to give a guy than just a piece of ass. I would be screwing every guy from the milkman to the bread man to the dime store clerk who is always asking me to go to the drive-in movies with him. When I put out for a guy, it is on my terms and my terms only, not just to jump in the back seat with him so he will ask me out again. I ain't no cheap slut looking for a one night stand and I for certain ain't no dammed whore putting out for money."

Kevin and Linda were puffing their third cigarette with feet resting on the convertible's rear bumper when the black Impala from around the corner stopped in front of the convertible. A second Impala pulled to their rear leaving a three-foot space between the two cars.

"That's him. The one who wants me to put out," Linda blurted as a gang member opened the passenger door and stepped out.

"You were messing with my woman, dude. You're not gonna get away with it. Now I'm gonna mess with you," yelled the gang leader as he slammed the driver's door.

The shot gunner yelled, "Yeah, we're gonna mess you and your woman up bad."

An Impala member got out of each side of the front car and began walking toward them. Kevin remained seated. Linda slid off to the sidewalk on the right of the car and moved back to a building wall. Kevin could now see two heads still in the first Impala, one had black hair, the other had strawberry blonde.

"I saw you gettin' it on with my woman Maggie," the Impala leader continued, waving a 6-inch knife blade.

Call Me Maggie

"So?" asked Kevin.

"So! I'm gonna mess you up. Nobody messes with Gambini girls," the leader said.

"Yeah Dude, he's gonna mess you up" the shot gunner injected.

"And I'm gonna mess up your little woman. She likes to tease, but she don't wanna to go all the way. Nobody likes a broad that teases and won't put out," the leader stated.

Linda slipped off the trunk onto the sidewalk. The butt of a piston rose above the shotgun rider's waist as he pranced about only a few feet from Linda.

"I just had a few dances with her. I didn't know Maggie was hitched up," Kevin said, knowing his word choice was wrong.

"Hitched up? What kind of talk is that? You sound like Davy Crocket. Are you from the woods, Davy Crocket?" the leader asked.

"You from the woods, Dude?" came an echo form the sidewalk. "Is that how they talk in the backwoods? You'll talk weirder after we mess you up."

"Where's your coonskin hat? You got it in the trunk? How come you don't have it hanging from the mirror?" the leader continued.

Three steps now separated Kevin and the leader.

The shot gunner leaned on both his hands grasping the windowsill. One boy and girl from the front Impala stood near each of its rear fenders. The black car still contained two heads. Kevin was encircled, but he remained sitting on the fender. He knew that the more time he gave the leader to talk, the more time he had to come up with a plan. The sight of the pistol meant he needed a good plan. Images of other fights flashed into Kevin's mind. Some of the images were of farm boys. Others were of city bullies and punks in Wilmington. One image, almost as fresh as this morning's milk, included a construction helper. None contained images of a pistol. The south in Kevin was rising for a skirmish in North Philadelphia, but Kevin restrained his short-fused temper.

"Davy Crocket wants my woman. Is that it woodsy boy? It ain't gonna happen, Dude," the leader continued.

"What your name, Dude? Is it Davy Crocket or Daniel Boone? Are you John Wayne? Where is your horse, John Wayne? The man wants some answers, Dude," demanded the boy behind Kevin.

"I'll bet your mother named you Bobby Joe, or Jim Bob. No, she named you Peggy Sue 'cause you ain't got no balls. Is that it, Dude? You ain't got no balls?" the leader asked, searching for a raw nerve to enrage Kevin.

18

Bandstand Blonde

Kevin continued stalling. He knew a little about head games when a fight was about to erupt. He also knew that with four to one odds, he would fare better if he kept calm as long as he could. He felt the odds were closer to three against once since the Impala gang member behind him probably had more mouth than muscle, so he and remained on the convertible's trunk.

"What's your name?" Vinnie said.

Kevin slid off the trunk slowly, and faced the leader.

"My name is Kevin Kennedy. I am from a farm and I may be a hillbilly, but I have more important things to do than listen to a Philly punk with a mouth full of cow patties. If you wanna mess with me, let's get started," he said, also looking for a nerve to ignite.

The leader looked upward into Kevin's eyes. He had to look up. Kevin was a good five inches taller that the leader. He also carried forty or fifty pounds of construction work muscle on his tall frame. If it were just Vinnie, there would be no contest. Even with four to one against him, Kevin would still be a handful for the Impala Gang.

"You've been messing with one of Vinnie Gambini's women and Vinnie don't like it. Not from an overgrown Peggy Sue with no balls," the leader said

Vinnie failed to find a quick nerve and enrage Kevin.

"So?" Kevin asked.

"You been messing with trouble, Gambini style," Vinnie came back pounding a fist into an open hand.

"So?" Kevin said again.

"So? Is so all you can say?" Vinnie asked.

"Yea, so?"

Kevin and Vinnie stood less than half a yard apart like two hockey centers in a face off. Kevin stared down. Vinnie had to look up. Neither could fully read the other's next move. Both needed more time to evaluate their rival. The other Impala gang held their linebacker positions. The shot gunner's echoes had stopped. The black headed girl had gotten out of Vinnie's Impala and came to its rear bumper where she remained stolidly as a statue. The strawberry blonde remained in the car. Vinnie looked over his reinforcements, but Kevin kept his eyes on him and the shot gunner with the pistol. If things worsened, it would start with Vinnie and it would end with Vinnie out of action.

The Impala girls were Vinnie's unknown element. Kevin could not fully read the girls or their role if any action began. He would deal with the girls after Vinnie and the three boys were dealt with.

19

Call Me Maggie

"Maggie says you got the hots for her, but I don't think you can get a hard on. She thinks you want her, but you don't have the ball to pull it off. You got the hots for her, Dude? Or does the broad against the wall have more than you can handle? Are you some kind of queer or a faggot?" Vinnie asked, turning toward Linda.

"Maggie is OK, but I don't have the hots for her," Kevin said.

"She better than your bitch," the shotgun fired out.

"Maggie. Here. Now," Vinnie's shouted.

Kevin's ears rang at the command.

Maggie came to Vinnie's side.

"Maggie's my woman. These girls are all mine. They don't piss unless I say so. Maggie doesn't go with you unless I say so," Vinnie boasted.

"Was this dude messing with you?" He demanded.

"We danced."

"Did he have a hard on for you?" Vinnie demanded again, moving intimidation attempts to the strawberry blonde.

"Maybe," she came back

"Did the backwoods boy ask you to go out with him?"

"Just for a shake." was her answer.

"Anything else?"

"No, Vinnie."

"Anything else?" Vinnie kept pressing Maggie.

"Just a shake. I told you."

"Peggy Sue wants my woman, but he ain't got the balls to come out and ask for more than taking you for a shake, is that it? He's hung up on the bitch against the wall," Vinnie pushed farther.

"No balls, no dough, no woman," the shotgun fired too soon for Vinnie's liking.

"Shut up, Dominic!" the leader commanded the shot gunner.

"He don't know, Vinnie," Maggie said.

"He don't know. Well let me lay it out for the hillbilly. Maggie is my woman. Kate, Connie, and Teresa are my women. These are my boys. They don't do shit 'till I say squat. The hillbilly is on this Gambini turf. Vinnie don't like hillbillies on his turf." Vinnie rolled on. "You want Maggie, you deal with me. Maggie's is worth a hundred a night. My other women, too. I get half of their take. My women don't mess with Vinnie Gambini and hillbillies don't mess with Vinnie's women unless they pay me first."

Kevin's stomach churned.

Bandstand Blonde

"Your woman don't put-out. Maggie does," Vinnie said.

"He didn't know. We just talked and danced," she said.

"Dancing with you is gonna get him messed up."

"Vinnie, don't mess with him anymore." Maggie yelled.

"You're a whore. He knows now," Vinnie screamed back.

"Vinnie, please. . .

"His woman is a dike. She don't put out. You do."

Linda's stomach revolted as she struggled with overflowing tears and a flood building inside her. She was sure her bladder would burst at any minute.

Vinnie raised a hand preparing to strike Maggie. Kevin exploded. His feet hit the sidewalk. He lifted a knee hard against Vinnie's crouch. As Vinnie folded forward, Kevin's clasped hands came down on the punk's neck. Vinnie doubled himself on the street clutching his groin. Another kick struck the closest gang member mid chest and he flew backwards on the hood of the black Impala. With one hand on the Chevy trunk, Kevin vaulted half circle across the car and landed both his feet in the shot gunner's face. The shot gunner flew backward into the bricks beside Linda. Slowly he slid down the wall to sit on the sidewalk. A line of fresh blood led downward to his head. A pistol lay at his feet. Kevin went for the fourth gang member and the girl sitting on the black Impala's fender filing her fingernails. The boy held up open hands.

"No more, Dude, no more," the fourth young man shouted.

Kevin had an internal fight deciding whether lay him out, too. The fourth Impala remained standing, but moved backwards. Two girls backed away with him. The black haired girl who had been closest to Maggie and Vinnie continued popping her gum. Linda picked up the gun and ordered the brunette to "Move the damned car!"

His arm brushed against Maggie's Banlon as he passed her to open the door for Linda.

"Take me with you," Maggie asked, then stood motionless staring at Kevin.

Kevin returned Maggie's stares after opening the driver side door. For a long moment, the two tried to read each other and summarize the situation. If he left her there, she would have hell to pay with Vinnie. If he took her, he would have hell to pay with him, and the odds against him winning would be greater next time.

"Okay! Hop in," he finally answered.

Maggie slid past the steering wheel. Linda passed the pistol she picked up from the shot gunner to Maggie. Maggie dropped in into her

21

Call Me Maggie

handbag. Kevin placed the aviator sunglasses over his eyes, not to block the sun, but conceal his eyes. Linda copied Kevin.

The black haired girl had moved the car blocking the convertible forward and was walking toward them, then stepped behind the Impala to avoid being struck by the convertible.

"Ain't you gonna help 'em?" she asked.

"Nope!" Kevin answered.

"Thanks for nuthin!" Linda muttered, as they past the car while her out-held keys put a white scratch down the entire side of the new car before she crawled into the back seat and lay across it.

Kevin, Linda, and his strawberry fantasy back tracked the Philadelphia canyons in silence. The Schuylkill River Bridge and U.S. 13 were clogged as the open top convertible crept south, its occupants deep into their individual thoughts and questions. They passed the airport. Chester lay just ahead and no decision had been made about what Kevin would do with Maggie. Would he drop her off on the way south or drive back up after taking Linda home? At ten o'clock he had to meet Norman and be ready to work by eleven. And, he had to change clothes. He could change at Norman's apartment or in equipment yard shack. At that time of night, he could change anywhere outdoors.

"I gotta pee bad," Linda announced from the back seat.

A mile later, they approached the Lucky 13 Diner. Kevin tapped the turn signal and guided the car into a head-in parking spot. Linda jumped over the rear windowsill and was headed for the diner door before the engine died. Maggie still had not spoken since her "take me" request, nor had Kevin.

"Want anything from inside?" He broke the silence for both he and Maggie.

"Maybe a drink."

"What kind?"

"A Seven-Up, if they have it."

"Let's go in and find out," Kevin suggested.

The couple left the car and found seats in the diner. While they waited for drinks and Linda, Kevin silently questioned whether Linda really need the restroom, or if she was giving him time alone with Maggie. He had not decided if he really wanted to be alone with Maggie or take her home on the drive through Chester, yet there was something else about the strawberry blonde he could not put a finger on just yet. Linda's statement, "She might be good at something else" bothered him, too. Linda read people better than he did.

Bandstand Blonde

"Would you take me straight home?" Linda asked once she rejoined them. "You and Maggie can be alone together."

"Is that OK with you, Maggie?" Kevin asked.

"Okay with me."

"Okay it is, then," Kevin addressed Linda.

When they finished their drinks, the convertible headed south on U.S. 13 again.

"I still can't believe that damned Dominic. Or Vinnie," Linda announced. "I wouldn't put out for him no matter what he said or did."

"They can be real bad at times," Maggie stated.

"I'll bet they can if they have their gang nearby," Kevin added.

"They follow him like rats," Maggie said.

"He called me a dike. I'd like to show him who's a dike," Linda said, shaking her head and fist.

"Wouldn't make any difference," Maggie advised her.

"Are you really his woman? Do you put out for money?"

"Yes. I'm one of . . . his whores . . . I was . . . until today. He went too far this time. He ain't gonna get nuthin' else from me after today . . . And I ain't gonna get nuthin' from him except a bad beating when he finds me . . . I gotta go some place . . . where he can't find me," Maggie felt a need to make explanations, but could not find the right words. The strain of her search was evident in her uneven and jagged enunciation as she confirmed Linda's suspicions and raised new questions for Kevin. Kevin figured he could learn more if he did not enter the girl's conversation. His strong suits were driving and listening, so he remained quiet and drove on.

"Where did you find that creep?" Linda asked.

"At Bandstand about two years ago," Maggie answered. "But he was nicer then and he wasn't into pimping yet. He's only had me and the girls whoring for him since last spring."

"Didn't you see it coming?"

"No. He was real nice to me at first. He bought me some nice clothes. He said he wanted to help me be a model. Vinnie said his mom was a model before she got married. He said she worked all the big shows and did some magazine work. He got me some photo jobs. One was a post card for Atlantic City. I wore a little bikini. The photographer gave me a couple of studio jobs. Sometimes I wore only the bikini bottom. Sometimes he had a baby doll pajamas outfit for me to wear. Then he wanted me to wear nothing. I did that a few times. When he wanted pictures of me making out with men and other women, I quit."

Call Me Maggie

"Was Vinnie your boyfriend then?"

"At first he was. I would do anything for him . . . and I did. He got some of the pictures . . . started showing them around. After that, he wouldn't take me anywhere . . . except to Bandstand. Then he would never dance with me. But, he liked showing the guys my pictures. After the pictures got around everything died off. He wanted no part of me for himself, just the money I brought in when he set me up to take care of his friends and guys in hotel rooms," Maggie continued.

Linda found a kinship with Vinnie's former woman, but it had nothing to with dike feelings. Maggie could easily be one of the gang in the mixed group of her friends, if Maggie did not put out for money.

"What did your parents think?"

"My dad was killed in Korea. My mom came apart, and has not got over it yet. She stays drunk most of the time till the pension check runs out. She might dry out for a few days if she doesn't pick up some guy who will put a drink on the bar or a bottle in the cabinet. She almost always finds someone."

"You have any brothers or sisters?"

"An identical twin sister. She is on Bandstand a lot too. She's a cheaper whore than I'll ever be. She'll jump in bed with any guy who takes her there or anyplace else or for a six pack."

"Are you really a whore?"

"Yes."

Linda rubbed her eyes holding back her tears.

Large tears fell on Maggie's blue skirt as she cried unrestrained. The strawberry blonde Kevin had wanted so badly was right next to him and he could not think of a word to say. He tried to imagine Maggie and her sister had being with the guys in the way she had described. Why had he been attracted to Maggie? Or was it her sister he had seen on Bandstand. He wasn't sure he still wanted see her again after what she revealed about herself. Kevin had never been with a girl. He had petted with a few other girls after dates or in the drive-in movie, but not with Linda. He was not attracted to Linda in the same way. Even in movies, girls always brought a girlfriend along for safety, whether he wanted them invited to join them or not. Linda said she would put out for him, but she was more like a sister or one of the guys in his group of friends. Maggie might put-out but it would cost him. Besides, he had to go to work and he wanted to know Maggie better, he told himself.

"Is Kevin driving you home after he drops me off?" Linda continued her inquiry.

Bandstand Blonde

"Not home. I'll try to work something out while he takes you home, if Kevin has the time or will let me ride with you two. Vinnie will probably come looking for me at home, if he can walk. You got him good, Kevin. And Dominic too,"

"They deserved that and more," Linda stated.

Kevin saw a satisfying glimmer in Maggie's cobalt eyes as he checked her face in the mirror. Linda now sat up and wore a smile. He smiled knowing that Linda could see him in the mirror, as well as he saw her.

"I can ask my folks if you can stay at our house."

Kevin's brow wrinkled as he wondered what Maggie's answer would be.

"No, I can call some friends Vinnie doesn't know."

Kevin smiled again, but Linda missed seeing it.

The car moved southward on the Governor Printz Boulevard as the girls watched the river and boats. Kevin stole a few glances at the river too, but mostly he drove and only occasionally glimpsed at the girls. The sun was getting low and his aviator glasses served their first purpose nicely. Soon he made a turn onto Fourth Street. Linda's home was less than five minutes away.

"Drop me at the sub shop, please. I don't want to go home yet," Linda said.

"Okay." Kevin would comply.

Maggie sat silently. Kevin and Linda sensed unanswered questions in relation to where she would go were the reason for the urgency in her voice. Each felt concern for their co-rider, but they had to let Maggie decide her own fate.

"This will be fine. I'll walk from here. See you 'round, Maggie. Thanks for bringing me home, Kevin. If you had dropped me at the train, the ride home would've been awful," Linda said from the side of the car.

This had been and unbelievable day Kevin thought to himself. He had met the girl he wanted meet since first seeing her on TV and Linda had said she would put out for him. Both girls had revealed amazing surprises. And there were more than four hours to go before mounting the dirt pan. Taking care of Maggie would take half that time, he guessed. He wanted to know more about her and the Impala gang in case Linda wanted to return to Bandstand.

Kevin watched Linda hurry toward her parent's sandwich shop, then made an improper left turn from the Fourth Street curb to south-

25

Call Me Maggie

bound Union Street. A small restaurant was in the third block and he headed to it.

"Let's go in. I need to use a restroom," he said to Maggie when the car stopped.

Without answering, she opened her door and headed for the Post House Restaurant entrance. Once inside, both headed directly to the matchbox rest rooms. Kevin had read the menu twice when Maggie joined him in a corner booth.

"What would you like? Everything is good, but it's not the Hotel DuPont."

Maggie glanced up giving him her first smile.

"Not the Green Room, eh?"

Her smile full blossomed.

"Was the smile real or one of her come-ons?" Kevin asked himself silently. A trick could have taken her to the four star restaurant off the lobby in the city's oldest skyscraper. He knew it was highly rated and had been in it for Linda's Prom.

Maggie studied the menu. "What are you having, Mister Kevin James Kennedy."

"Shrimp. We didn't raise them on the farm."

"I'd like living on a farm. My grandparents had one."

"You would like only if you like working long days in worn-out, soiled, dirty clothes, not having close neighbors or few friends, and waiting until the sunshine get's piped in."

"I guess you hated it."

"I was seven when we left, old enough to begin having chores.

"Does everyone in the country talk like you?"

"Just the ones on the south side of the hills."

"You are really cute. Uh, I mean funny."

Kevin smiled, but said nothing aloud.

"I've been called no-balls Peggy Sue, Davy Crocket, Woods Man, John Wayne, Dude, Hillbilly, and cute today. I wonder what she will call me next?" he questioned himself, silently.

"I should have said handsome."

"What do you want to eat?"

"Shrimp. We don't raise them in Chester, either. Not even in East Chester,"

Maggie's spunk brought another smile to Kevin's face.

"Have you always lived in Chester?"

"We had a nice house in Talleyville till mother drank it away."

Silence overcame her until the server took their order.

"What are you going to do after we eat? Go home?"

"I can't go home. That's the first place Vinnie will look for me. I would call some friends he doesn't know if I had any, so I guess I'll get a motel room or sleep on a bench at the train station? The ones I called a moment ago didn't answer. I know about train station benches. They are an awful place to spend the nights and the creeps who hang out aren't any better than Vinnie or the guys in his gang."

"Are there any girlfriends in Chester you can stay with?"

"No one. The only two there are in Vinnie's gang."

Kevin began eating as Maggie rubbed her chest.

"Thank you for taking me with you and Linda. I would be home in a tub of ice if you had left me with Vinnie and his gang. He gets his rocks of hurting people."

"Has he hurt you before today?"

"He beat me real bad and made me get it on with him the first time and has beaten me lots of times since unless I do what he wants, especially if I don't want to get it on with the guys he sets up."

Maggie continued rubbing her chest as she spoke.

"Well, kick him between his legs the next time you see him. I will too, if I run into him or any of his gang again."

Kevin suddenly remembered something his brother, Norman had mentioned.

"I have to make a call," he said, heading for the telephone. A few minutes later he said, "Let's go get Norman."

"Who is Norman?"

"He's my brother. He has friends who can help you."

Neither Maggie nor Kevin had much to say as they drove. He remained silent and assumed this would be the last he would see of her.

For as long as Kevin could remember, his oldest brother was always there to help when a problem popped up. Kevin had ridden on Norman's shoulder in play and in need back home on the farm. When he was too tired to walk, Norman's shoulder was there. If playing got too rough, Norman was there. If he had a problem with homework, he could go to Norman.

Kevin unconsciously rubbed his left arm above and below the elbow. He could not remember getting the scar but knew the cause. When he was just old enough to sit in a high chair, Norman had been serving coffee to their parents one morning when he tripped and scalded Kevin badly. The doctor was forty miles from the farm and there was no

Call Me Maggie

car. His parents had to treat the burn with homemade remedies; beef tallow and cheeses cloth bandages, but the scars were still tender eighteen years later. Norman had apologized countless times since. Was the scalding why Norman was always there for him, Kevin wondered as he drove toward the newspaper office?

He and Maggie had been parked less than five minutes in silence when a young man approached, threw a jacket on the seat, hopped over the rear windowsill, and sat behind Maggie with his feet behind Kevin. Both turned to see him. Maggie assumed he was Kevin's brother, Norman. But were they brothers? Under moonlight, she studied their features. Kevin was wide shouldered and strong. Norman was thin, very thin. A strap from his left shoulder held a camera just above Norman's waist. His thin arms were more like hers than the large, muscular ones on Kevin. She assessed his face to be about forty, but suspected he was younger. His already gray hair was almost white in the moonlight. Norman wore his hair long with a single wave sweeping diagonally from the left to the right. He had long side hair, almost white, too. It was combed back above his large ears. Black rimmed glasses made the hair appear even whiter. Every hair was in perfect place. Maggie assumed he used women's hair spray.

"Head for the equipment yard. I'll lay it out for you and your new girlfriend on the way," Norman ordered. "I called John Choma who is gonna call someone in charge of victim protection to get you a place for the night, Maggie. It is Maggie isn't it? I don't remember people's names unless I write them down. John should know something by the time we get back from the yard."

Norman had a plan. Kevin knew Norman could usually a come up with a plan on short notice.

Kevin went over to Market Street and turned right. Maggie sat sideways in the shotgun seat to see both brothers.

This time, Norman's hair blew in the wind, not hers, as he spoke.

"The police have some safe houses the city owns where they take people they want to protect. You know robbery or shooting witnesses, wives of wife beaters, children of home violence, or anybody else who needs their protection. If that guy has beaten you, you qualify. John is working on it now. He grew up in our old neighborhood. He's a good cop and he'll take care of you. The worse thing is the waiting while they set it up for you. I'll stay with you until they do. That's the problem with night work; too late to date, and too early to sleep."

Bandstand Blonde

The car turned right off the highway and into a floodlit field crammed with road-scrapers, bulldozers, dirt-packers, dump trucks and a dozen scraper dirt pans. It was 10:20 p.m., but it was just another number on the construction crew's twenty-four hour clock. Even by moonlight, the equipment had to be kept moving toward an opening date of November 1963. Kevin and his other brother Ernest came to the yard six times every week and sometimes seven. They mounted their dirt pans and drove eight, ten or twelve hours a day. Both had driving in their blood, whether they drove a tow truck, dirt pan, station wagon, or a riding lawnmower.

"Don't worry about your girlfriend. John and I will take care of her as if she were our sister. I want you to help me put a Continental kit on my car. I will pick you up a seven and we get it. It came in today. I'll bring you up to date on Maggie in the morning," Norman assured both Kevin and Maggie as he got behind the steering wheel.

With a single "Okay," Kevin answered Norman and questioned Maggie. He removed the sports coat he had worn and laid it with Norman's, lifted an army duffel bag from the trunk, and walked to the side of the car where Maggie sat.

"Good luck Maggie. You will be safe with Norman. If I don't see you around, I'll catch you on Bandstand some time," Kevin said, but doubted if he would ever see the strawberry blonde again as he threw the duffle bag over a shoulder, and headed for a windowless trailer under one of the countless floodlights.

The car headed north back toward the skyscrapers reflecting moonlight above the horizon. Maggie found herself enjoying the view Norman knew the view well; a photograph of it hung in his apartment.

"Do you guys always look out for each other?" were the first words she spoke to Norman since he got in the car.

"I guess so. 'Cept when we're fight'n."

Norman emphasized on the words "cept and fight'n." Maggie liked the drawl twang he and Kevin turned on for shock effect or when they were nervous.

"Do you fight much?" she asked again.

"No, not much. No more than other brothers, I guess."

"I don't have any brothers, so I don't know. Just a twin sister. We used to fight a lot."

"Too bad."

"Yes, it's really too bad."

"What did Kevin tell you about me?"

Call Me Maggie

"Just that he met a girl from Talleyville with a mean boyfriend and he brought you with him so you would not get another beating. He asked me if I would help you find a safe place for the night. He said you couldn't go home; the guy would come looking for you there. Any guy who beats girls ought to have his nuts cracked. Excuse my inappropriate language."

"Kevin did. He did it for me and his friend Linda, too. Put two others jerks down, too," she told Norman, assuming Kevin did not tell him about the fight in Philadelphia.

Norman put the car in a parking spot on the Tenth Street side of the Wilmington Police Station under a green lettered white sign that read: "30 Minute Parking 8 a.m. to 5 p.m." He went around to help Maggie out but she was already on the sidewalk and was sliding something under the seat. He led her to a door with heavy wire over window where they could see a police officer inside. Norman pushed a button, waited until a buzzer sounded, and then pulled the door open.

"Good evening Sergeant McCafferty," Norman said.

"John's in the Squad Room finishing his paperwork. Go on back, son. You know where it is," the desk officer said.

Norman tapped on a door twice and twisted the knob.

"Hey Norman! What's up, Cousin?"

"John, this is Maggie. Maggie, this is John Choma, the city's best paper work police officer. It costs somebody three dollars every time his pen touches paper."

"Sometimes more," John replied.

The two young men laughed. Maggie did not; just being in a police station made her nervous. She realized remembering to put the pistol under the seat had been a good idea.

"Hi Maggie. Shifts will change in about a half hour. I'll fill out a report and the graveyard guys will handle it when they come on. Norman, why don't you go down stairs and bring Maggie, me, and the sergeant some coffee and donuts," the officer instructed Norman in cop language for "This is police business."

Norman knew from previous visits John did not eat donuts.

Maggie was visible through the door from the seat he took in the hall. To his eye, she appeared frightened and momentarily imprisoned, but handled her fears and imprisonment with dignity. She sat erect with her hands still and knees together but with her feet crossed as the police officer interviewed her. Norman then noticed her hair. He seemed to always notice a person's hair. He believed hair could camouf-

30

lage or could compliment the person as much as clothes. Her hair color was somewhere between red and blonde; It was shinny, well combed and brushed. Some of it hung down her back, some draped over her shoulders down to her chest. The loose sweater she wore did not permit him to judge her breasts size, but he estimated they were ample. She was not too thin or too heavy. Her profile contained a pleasing nose under straight bangs almost to her eyebrows and light blue eyes. Her eyebrows were almost as light as her flesh tones and must not have been darkened. Her lips were well formed, not just a slit and yet, not massive.

"She would be a great model. I have to photograph her and that great hair." Norman said to himself as he studied her.

At ll:59 John opened the door and motioned for him to enter the Squad Room again.

"I've got her report on paper. She can stay here if she wants. But if I were you I would go to the Toddle House and order a midnight dinner. I will meet you there or call you at your apartment when paperwork's done. Okay?"

"We'll be at my apartment if it's okay with you?"

John and Maggie said "Okay," simultaneously. Both laughed momentarily, before Maggie said more formally, "Thank you, officer Choma. I would rather wait with Norman than to stay here.

"I'll take the T-Bone next time. And, I won't let you forget. Gotta run upstairs. Goodnight Cousin. Don't worry Maggie, Norman will take as good of care of you as you would get staying here."

Norman thanked John and led Maggie back past the sergeant.

"How did you do that?" Maggie asked as Norman opened the right side car door.

"John and I go way back. Being a newspaper photographer helps. He gets to see his picture in the paper a lot."

"I usually avoid policemen."

A few minutes later Norman parked along North Adams Street. Maggie pulled the pistol from under the seat and returned it to her purse as he unsnapped the tunneau cover, raised the top, latched it, and killed the engine.

"My place is not much, just two big rooms and a toilet on the third floor. You can stay until you and Kevin figure something out. I'll get up at six to go get Kevin, pick up the kit for my car at eight and take it to Dad's house. Kevin can get Dad's car so you two can do whatever you have to do. Okay?" Norman asked as they climbed the stairs.

"Okay," Maggie answered.

31

Call Me Maggie

She felt a sharp pain and clinched her teeth as Norman held her arm going inside. A sense of security came over her as she looked over the apartment while he hung his coat on rack made of plumber's pipe.

Everything was in the single room except the tub and toilet. Two walls contained only windows. A bed was against one side of the room with seashells, buoys and driftwood hanging from a tattered fish net forming a canopy. Two unmatched chairs sat under a small table near the cooking area. A sofa sat behind a makeshift coffee table of bricks supporting pieces of plate glass complete with a half-empty coffee mug beside a box camera. Photography, art books, a sketch pad, and two large black albums lay on the lower glass. Large photographs held by thumbtacks covered most of the windowless walls. Another picture covered an entire door. A tripod with a huge old camera on top rested at the end of the sofa.

Neither Vinnie nor any of his gang would trouble her tonight. Even Kevin and Linda did not know she was here, she told herself.

"What do you think for $45.00 a month?"

"Good as $45.00 a night rooms in Atlantic City."

"Never thought of it that way," Norman chuckled. "But it's better than some of the farmhouses we lived in. If I lived in those old barns, I can live in this a while. I'm putting most of my money in cameras, lenses, lights and my car. Someday the car will be a classic and I will make money when I get it fixed the way I want it. In the meanwhile, it's take more pictures to pay for my girl and photography equipment."

"It's a real bachelor's pad. You must be one of the beatniks I read about. Got an artistic girl friend that helps you decorate or poses for pictures like the one on the door?"

"Girlfriend, yes. Decorate, no. If she did, it would be done in hospital linens and medical posters, not my photos."

"I posed for a photographer once."

"Kevin didn't say you were a model. He doesn't say much anyway. My photographs are sometimes artistic; Andrew Wyeth type stuff. Plus a lot of seashore and flower subjects. Do you know Wyeth's work?"

"All I know is that he's from Chadds Ford and painted Christina's World. It's a beautiful picture and even more beautiful when you know about Christina. She is not the type of woman you would expect to be a model."

Norman found her modeling and knowledge Wyeth's painting intriguing. Finding something in common seemed to ease her stiffness as well as his own.

Bandstand Blonde

"Let me fix you a drink. Or a TV dinner, maybe?"

"Kevin and I had a shrimp dinner a while ago. That's something we don't grow in Chester."

"The closest we farm boys ever got to the seafood was crawfish." Norman tried to volley back to her.

He knew Kevin loved shrimp. He questioned the Chester part of her answer. He was sure Kevin had said "a girl from Talleyville."

"Will your girlfriend come by to see you, now that you are home? I will leave and wait at the police station, if she is."

"No, she won't be dropping in. She is the Philadelphia General Hospital. I'll go see her tomorrow evening."

"Oh no!" Maggie gasped.

"It's not what you think. She is a nursing student and she is up there for school. There are no accredited psychological hospitals in Delaware so she had to go up there. I go up there to see her; she doesn't come here."

"Are you engaged to her?"

"No. How about a drink?" he asked again. "I can make you a scotch and soda, scotch and water, scotch on the rocks, or scotch and scotch like I drink."

"Water, and water, and no scotch."

"Maggie. Don't you trust me? You are Kevin's friend. You as safe with me as my sister would be. I don't mess with his girlfriends. He doesn't mess with mine. Mine are too old for him." Norman said while maintaining eye contact rather than letting himself check out her figure.

Maggie remained silent studying the room again, especially a large print of a girl in old blue jeans and an unbuttoned baggy shirt. He returned with a bottle of scotch, two tumblers of water and a shot glass.

"I'll let you mix it the way you like it if you change your mind," he told Maggie and then waited for her to pour her own.

Each sat with their backs against an arm of the sofa pointing their knees to the other with their feet just off the sofa.

"To new friendships." he held his glass aloft in a toast.

"To Norman and Kevin, knights who rescue maidens from the dangers of big cities."

Both sipped, he from scotch, she from a tumbler of water without ice or scotch. Maggie studied Norman across the tumbler she moved back and forth across her lips. Wearing black rimmed glasses, he could pass for a schoolteacher or a young doctor. He could be a lawyer or young minister, she told herself.

Call Me Maggie

He scrutinized her taking note of her hair again and figure as she studied him.

"It's the glasses that make him look older,"

"So Maggie, tell me about yourself and the trouble with your boyfriend."

"Ex-boyfriend!"

"Okay, ex boyfriend. By the way, I still don't know your full name." Norman sought to learn more.

"Mary Anne Johnson; Maggie to my friends. About two years ago I started going to American Bandstand where I met him, Vinnie Gambini. I liked him right away. We danced together a lot. After a few more days on Bandstand, he asked me out. We dated a few times. We talked about our plans. Mine was to be a model and airline stewardess. He helped me get some modeling jobs. Mostly with some men he knew. I don't have to tell you what kind of pictures they were. Some were in bathing suits, some in negligees and some with me wearing nothing. Vinnie got some of the pictures and soon he got me to pose for him. One thing led to another and he wanted to do more than take pictures. When I refused he beat me and got what he wanted. He found he could make more money with me in the flesh than in pictures. Vinnie wouldn't come near me after that. One night he beat me and locked me in a room with one of the guys his gang. Dominic beat me too and forced himself on me. Vinnie beat me again for not giving in to Dominic right away. I was black all over for two weeks. Then he started selling me to friends, strangers, or anyone with fifty bucks. One night I took some poison. I woke up four days later locked up with one of his other whores guarding me. Within a week, he was selling me off again. He would come to my house each day and take me to a Philly flea trap where he and his gang sent their clients. He had three other girls working there with three guys pimping them, too. A stable, he called us. He got half the money and got rich. We got beat and bruised. Sometimes he took us back to Bandstand to take on the boys there. If we could not make a set up, he beat us again. I decided the pain wasn't worth it so I gave up and took on his clients. He was setting Linda up yesterday to do the same thing, but Kevin got in the way. Vinnie wanted Linda in his stable, too. Lucky for her, Kevin was there or she would have gotten raped too."

"What did Kevin do?" Norman had to know.

"Crushed Vinnie's balls; probably broke his neck. Excuse my language, please. And he put down two of Vinnie's gang as quick as that," Maggie stated as she snapped her fingers.

34

Bandstand Blonde

"Are Kevin and Linda OK?" Norman asked quickly.

"Oh yes, neither Kevin nor Linda took a lick."

"How did it start?" Norman had to know again.

"Vinnie brought me to Bandstand to land a trick. We do that when Vinnie wants more money. I was working on Kevin and a couple of others. Didn't make it with any of them. Vinnie thought I was soft on Kevin and that Kevin might be trying to take me away from him, so he decided to put Kevin down after Bandstand was over. He thought Linda and Kevin were a team hustling just like I was, so he put Dominic on Linda. We were supposed to take them to a motel where we usually take our tricks. He wanted to put all three of us down, but for sure he had bad plans for Kevin for wanting to take for a milkshake instead of to a motel," she explained.

"What do you mean by put down?"

"Beat us senseless. Maybe cripple us. For sure, it would have been the worst beating I ever got. Maybe he would have beaten Linda just as bad. I don't think Linda had any idea about what was going down. He might have raped her too."

"What are you going to do now?

"Go back to Chester early in the morning, pack a few clothes and go where Vinnie can't find me. Ever!"

"Where will you go?"

"Maybe work in Rehoboth for the summer. And after that, any where I can work until I'm old enough start stewardess school. A stewardess is what I really want to be. Travel the world. See to new places. Meet interesting people."

The phone rang. Maggie's heart raced. When Norman said the call was for her, she almost fainted, but took the call and said. "Hello, this is Mary Anne Johnson," then listened for at least two minutes and closed the call with "I feel safe with Norman. I will stay with him. Thank You," hung up the receiver and said, "They have a place if I want it. But I would rather stay here, if that's okay with you. I'll call him back if it's not."

"Sure you can stay here. I have already told you it's okay. I haven't had anyone to talk to with after work in a long time, unless I go out drinking. And I don't do that often," he said, as they returned to their earlier positions on the sofa.

"I don't either. I like to keep a clear head."

"I had an assignment today that I want to tell you about," Norman said. "A new charter airline is setting up headquarters in the old Air

Call Me Maggie

Force hangers. It's a big deal for the county; about 400 jobs. They're a charter airline for tourists and won a contract to take soldiers and equipment to Vietnam. They need about eighty stewardesses. As a charter service, they don't have to meet the same rules other airlines meet. They're setting up a stewardess school in the old Officer's Club. They will be recruiting from Delaware schools and colleges first. Nurses will be recruited too. I am going to tell Michele. Wanna give it a shot? It won't be a summer in Rehoboth with all night parties on the beach."

"Damn right I do. I mean, of course I do. How old must the new stewardesses be?" Maggie asked.

"High school graduates, eighteen I guess,"

"I'm in. I'm eighteen. I'm in, man. Give me directions to the airport and I'll go home, get some more clothes and see if they will hire me as a stewardess. I would rather do that than wait on tables or be a clerk in a dime store." she said fighting an urge to embrace him.

Norman felt the same urge.

They leaned slightly toward each other, and then withdrew themselves before they touched each other. Seeking a way to overcome, his embarrassment, he quickly raised his glass and said, "To Miss Mary Anne Johnson, soon to be an airline stewardess."

"You don't have to call me Miss Johnson. Call me Maggie if we are going to spend the night together."

"Maggie it'll be. Want to see some of my pictures. I don't have a television set."

"Kevin said you were a photographer. Would you like me to pose for you? I don't have any clothes with me but these. You can photograph me in them I can take them off and pose naked. I have done it before for other photographers."

"Perhaps another time."

"Are you sure? I don't mind."

"I'll give you my phone number and when you get settled in, call me. I'll shoot some then but with you dressed."

For more than fifteen minutes she studied the collection of photographs, each encased in the album's acetate pages. The first album contained general news pictures including one near the back of President John Kennedy and Kevin with eyes and mouth wide open in amazement. Obviously, he was looking at Norman and the camera, not the president. Maggie had many questions about the incident and the president while gazing at the photo. With other pictures, she had typical viewer questions; who? Where? When or how did he take the pictures? The second album contained pictures Norman had made on his "Women's Page" assignments. She gazed upon each picture at length.

One photograph was that of a young woman wearing a long dress walking through a field of dandelion heads. The skirt of the dress was elevated well above of the dandelion tops and showed most of the model's legs.

"This is an excellent picture of a girl out in the country. I wish that it were me in it!"

"It could be you."

"I doubt it. Photographers don't want a model without experience unless is for some sort of kinky, dirty picture."

Another photo, an extreme close-up of a girl wearing a very wide brimmed hat, came next. The quarter profile showed only her face and a portion of the hat brim. Norman had printed the picture emphasizing her facial features contrasted with the weave in the straw-hat making the picture looked more like an ink sketch than a photograph.

"That's my girlfriend," Norman said, solemnly. "She doesn't like having her picture taken and that's the only shot I have of her when her face is not in a book."

"It's an interesting picture of her. Do you see her often, or is it too late to date in Philly girl when you get off work?"

"I usually go up there on my days off; Tuesdays and Saturdays. She rarely comes down here, although she passes through on her way to Smyrna going to see her mother."

Maggie took a long time examining the book's pictures. Some models wore gowns, some street clothes, and some wore bathing suits. She rubbed he chest as she viewed a few wearing only bra and briefs. A couple of the pictures showed nude girls with a soap package, a perfume bottle or other consumer product aimed at women. Maggie turned the page to find a picture of a girl in a swimming pool situation. The camera had frozen the girl, her hair, and the water in a huge question mark shape as the model quickly hoisted her head and long hair out of the water. Back lighting made the water appear as ice.

After viewing all the pictures in the first album, she placed a second one in her lap and began inspecting the prints in it. Most were more glamorous than ones seen in the first album were. Some showed female subjects in elegant dresses and swim suits. Several showed a girl in positions similar to dance positions and another show a buxom dancer in revealing costumes. Maggie showed no surprise when she viewed some of the subjects posing without clothes.

Call Me Maggie

"Kevin said you don't shoot this kind of picture but I see you have made some. Where do you get your models? Is Linda one of them? I didn't recognize her in any in of your pictures." Maggie asked.

"Linda is not one of them. They're just ordinary people. One is a waitress, one dancer, another is a gymnast, and another is a professional artist and a model as well. One of the twins is librarian, the other an office worker. All approached me and volunteered to pose so I didn't have to embarrass myself by asking them. Linda never indicated that she wanted to model for me and I never asked her, but she would be a good subject. So would you," Norman explained.

"I thought I was going to be a model once. But I guess that won't come about." Maggie said as she returned the book to the shelf and wiped tears from her eyes with the back of her hand. "Photographers don't want models without experience and I can't get experience without modeling. I'll never see my picture in a book like that,"

"Sure it will. You have all the assets of a model. Your features are great. You have a good figure and an attractive face. You have no baby fat, no large beauty marks, or scars. In addition to that, you have great looking hair. Not too red; not too blonde. Do not cut it. We photographers are always looking for girls with long hair, especially me. Let a good photographer find you and he will do the rest. Soon your picture will be on the cover of magazines in at every grocery store and on every new stand in the country," Norman said, hoping to raise her confidence.

"If Vinnie finds me, I won't have a face worth photographing when he gets finished with me."

"Don't bet on it. You have the Kennedy brothers on your side. The past is past. Vinnie is history." Norman answered, still trying to comfort his houseguest.

"After Kevin finishes work in the morning, we'll go get Dad's station wagon, pick up your things, take you to the airport so you can check out that stewardess job and help you find a place to stay, but I have to do in the morning so I can be at work by two in the afternoon."

"We? What about your continental kit?" she asked.

"It can wait. You need help," he said.

"Do you Kennedy brothers help everyone you meet?"

"Oh yes ma'am, we surely do. We are movers, mechanics, towing specialists, gentlemen farmers, and all around good guys. We rescue young maidens in distress and help old ladies cross the street."

"I owe you and Kevin something for rescuing this one. How can I repay you?"

Bandstand Blonde

"You don't have to. Let us help you move, get a job, find an apartment, and tomorrow will be the first day of you new life."

"I hope today was,"

Tears filled her eyes as he said, "I hope it was, too."

Maggie smiled a forced smile. "Let me dry my eyes and I pose for you now. It's the least I can do unless you want to sleep with me."

"I would love to photograph you, but we won't be sleeping together. I'll take lots of you after you get settled into your new life, if you want some practice modeling. I'd like to shoot one your tears now."

"Kevin said you shoot a lot of fashion. He didn't say you took pictures of subjects balling their eyes out."

"Kevin only sees what is published in the newspaper. A good subject is not always happy and smiling. The first assignment I had at the paper was of a young boy crying. It was a great picture. I don't always shoot attractive girls in fine clothes or naked. Let your tears flow."

"Like I said before, I don't have fine clothes but I'll pose in what I have or you can take pictures of me naked. Besides I owe you something for letting me stay here tonight."

"You don't have to pose naked, but I would love to shoot a few of your tears, face, and hair, if you don't mind."

"I don't mind. After seeing the great pictures of girls in your portfolio books you don't seem to be the kind of photographer who gets girls to take their clothes of so he can shoot kinky pictures I have known a couple if those. They usually want more than pictures once they take a few. I'll pose any way you want so I can more experience modeling as long as it not kinky or vulgar."

"I won't take any like that."

"Then start shooting."

Norman raised the camera hanging from his shoulder and made a few picture of her face then said, "I could photograph you all night, but I'm getting up at six to go get Kevin and Dad's station wagon. If you feel safe staying here, you can sleep-in until I get back."

"I feel safe, but I don't want to be left here alone. I'm going with you when you get Kevin."

Norman assumed Maggie would get up early and go with him, no matter what he said.

" I'd like to take a long bath after the day I've had. You take the bathroom first and I'll wait until you are finished. You wouldn't have any bubble bath, would you?"

"I'm afraid I don't."

Call Me Maggie

"Ivory Liquid will do just as well. Have any of that?"

"That I have."

"I didn't bring any other clothes so I'll have to sleep in my birthday suit while these clothes dry."

"That won't be necessary. I have plenty of shirts that will cover you. I could even put some blankets in the studio and you sleep in there and not have to worry about having your privacy."

"I don't need privacy. Like I told Officer Choma, I feel safe with you. I'll curl up on the couch after my bubble bath."

Maggie began pulling her Banlon over her head and revealed several red contusions on her arms, chest, and back, but she made no attempt to hide them. Norman considered asking how she got them, but turned and walked to his closet when she began removing her bra. He returned with a sheet, blanket, pillow, and laid them on the sofa, then went to his homemade clothes rack, removed a long-sleeved shirt from its hanger, carried it to Maggie, held in front of her, and said, "Yep, long enough, but, I don't have any bottoms!"

2

Dirty Money

Norman awoke to the aroma of Ivory soap filling his nostrils. Maggie lay next to him with her head on his chest. He lay still for a moment not wanting to disturb her. Finally, he slowly slid away and rushed to the bathroom. Maggie's skirt, sweaters, and undergarments had to be moved from the shower rod before he showered. When he exited, she held the same position on the bed as she held when he had entered; her head resting on her outstretched right arm, her right hand open, and facing the ceiling. The morning light coming through the certain-less window lit her back, although her front remained in shadows and darkness. The sunbeams illuminated and emphasized the hand just as it did her uncovered back. The scene was as serene as any Norman had ever seen. He took a camera from his bag and made half dozen shots of her hand. For the final shot, he held the camera high above the bed pointed downward capturing the entire bed, its ruffled linens, the hand, and her naked figure.

Ten minutes later, the stranger he met the night before appeared in the bath room doorway with a towel covering only the discreet areas of her torso.

"Thank for letting me stay. I'm sure the safe-house would not have been so enjoyable or the people so nice," she said, as she lightly placed her bosom against Norman's back.

He said "You're welcome, but thanks aren't necessary," without turning or looking at Maggie.

"My clothes are still wet. Got any jeans and a shirt I can borrow?" she asked.

"I'm sure we can find something. They may be a little large, but they will cover you."

"I can't be choosey. I'll wear anything you offer,"

Call Me Maggie

"We don't have time for breakfast. I'll stop for something on the way," he told Maggie as she tied an old shirt around her waist. "My plan is to pick up Kevin, go get Dad's station wagon, grab Ernest, and go get your stuff. Between my car and the station wagon, we should be able to carry whatever belongings you need to haul. If you need anything else, you can call me at the newspaper office after two o'clock.

"The only things I'll bring are my clothes and my car."

As they left the apartment, Maggie wore one of his shirts and a pair of his blue jeans with legs rolled-up three folds.

"My clothes look better on you than they do on me," he commented aloud.

He pulled up to a drive-up service window at Eleventh and French streets near the skyscrapers and one block from the police station. Morning workers formed a line to a window and a sign reading "TAKE OUT."

"Mix us a dozen filled, three large coffees, cream, and sugar, unmixed, please," Norman ordered through the window.

Maggie fumbled with her purse as she said, "Let me get breakfast. It's the least I can do to repay you for letting me stay with you last night."

"You will need your money for a place to live later," he stated, then opened the lid of a box sitting on the car's floor between Maggie's feet and his, removed ten quarters, paid the waitress and drove away.

The lids on the coffee cups and tape on the donut box remained in place until they reached the trailer where they left Kevin the night before. Kevin was waiting under a flood light that still burned even though the sun had risen half an hour earlier. His long-sleeved shirt and jeans were covered with brown dust. He moved slowly as if he was one of the large, dusty machines, as he approached with the duffel bag hanging on his shoulder, and threw the bag in the trunk. The white ring around the mouth on a face that could have been that of a colored man opened at the sight of Norman's passenger. Maggie opened her door, pushed the seatback forward, and squeezed herself in the back seat. Kevin folded himself and took the seat she vacated.

"Mix me a coffee after you pass one to Maggie," Norman ordered. He did not intend it as an order, but the lifelong habit was well engrained and surfaced once more. "Maggie needs help getting her stuff out of her mom's house. John found a safe house, but she didn't want it. She has a lead on a job at the airport. Are you up for a ride to Chester and a little moving?" Norman asked.

Dirty Money

"Yup. How do you take your coffee, Maggie?" Kevin replied.

"Black."

"Kevin is Norman's shotgun today," Maggie told herself as Norman drove away. Why had she never met boys like these brothers, two young knights off to save a maiden from the jeopardy's of a concrete jungle? Both pleasant and unhappy memories of the afternoon and evening before smoldered inside her. Did they know trouble followed her everywhere? Kevin had samples of it yesterday. Would both get more today?

Soon they pulled up behind a red and white '55 Ford parked beside a picket fence surrounding a white house with gable windows.

Norman pulled the knob under the dash again. Kevin got out lifted the duffel bag from the trunk and walked to the front porch door as Norman headed toward a garage at the end of a 100-foot driveway where a 1950 Chevy station wagon had been backed up to a garage door. Two other young men were putting armloads of boxes in the vehicle. Within three minutes, more than a dozen cardboard boxes were in the station wagon. Then the three young men returned to Norman's car. Kevin came out of the house with a washed face and wearing clean clothes, but still wearing dirty boots.

From her seat in Norman's car, Maggie saw the four Kennedy brothers standing in front of the white fence. They all were more than twice the height of the fence. Three of them could make up half of a football line. Each of the three younger brothers could push the scale over 200, but Norman would barely reach 175 pounds, she guessed.

"Kevin, you drive the station wagon." Norman ordered again. "Maggie, this is Ernest, my oldest brother, and this is Lionel, my baby brother. Kevin and Ernest are taking the wagon. You and I will take my ragtop. Lionel, get the gate. Loraine is using the washing machine. Her boys will be out soon."

"Don't call me a baby! I'm going too," Lionel demanded.

Norman gestured with his hands raised in hopelessness.

"Anything else?" Norman asked, paused, and said, "Let's do it. Maggie and I will lead. You three bring up the rear and stay close behind. If things get nasty, make sure Maggie is well protected and comes home with us."

Norman and Kevin put aviator sunglasses over their eyes. Norman climbed in the convertible. The three would-be Eagles linemen headed for the station wagon with Lionel trailing his two older brothers.

Call Me Maggie

"Do you guys always work together like this?" Maggie asked after they got under way and her astonishment cleared.

"Guess so," Norman answered.

"My sister wouldn't throw a rope if I were drowning."

Norman winced and replied after a short hesitation "Too bad. Family helps family. Friends help friends."

"Well, as I see it, four great guys are on the road first thing in the morning to help a whore they don't know."

"Don't ever, ever say you are a whore again. You are just a girl who had more problems than she could handle." Norman said. "Get a grip. The past is done. This is the day you take charge for yourself. If we had helped Loraine when she needed us, she would not have two babies or expecting a third. We help her now. And the boys, too, when they need it. Her husband sure doesn't. All he wants to do is drink cheap bear and make more babies."

"Too bad. Sounds like my sister, except for the babies."

By now they were driving by the Wilmington Airport. A few four-engine planes stood between two buildings close to the highway and large Quonset hut structures farther from the road.

"Those are the buildings the airline is getting. The two large ones are for maintenance and the low ones for offices and the stewardess school."

Forming plans of her own, Maggie nodded.

Norman headed north on U.S.13 and soon took "13-A." through the east side of Wilmington to avoid downtown traffic, crossed the Church Street bridge, and then cruised up Governor Printz Boulevard, where Kevin had traveled the previous day. The sun was an hour over the horizon. Diamond sparkles came and went from the surface of the river. Maggie stared at the highway ahead. A near frown told Norman that she was in deep thoughts she was not ready to share. The plans had not completely formulated under her strawberry blonde hair now blowing in the wind. He took the camera off his left shoulder, made some adjustments, and pointed it toward Maggie, the sun and the river. He clicked off half a dozen shots and put the camera in the box with his remaining quarters. Maggie was unaware the pictures had been made, or the station wagon was never more than 100 feet behind the convertible.

"Maggie, you have to tell me where to go."

She stared at her lap. He wasn't sure if Maggie was catching up on sleep she had lost the night before or she was contemplating apprehensions she might encounter when they arrived.

Dirty Money

"Maggie, I'm gonna need some directions," Norman said as the car made the doglegged curves around the Claymont steel mill or Marcus Hook refinery. Both exuded odors that would awaken anyone with a sense of smell. Chester was only a few miles farther up the road and she must have gotten accustomed to the sulfur fumes that permeated the early morning air he told himself.

Within ten minutes, both cars pulled to the curb in front of a neglected Chester row house. All five carried boxes as they stepped onto the house's small portico.

"Kevin, Ernest, Lionel, wait here. Norman and I won't be long." Maggie said after eyeing cars parked in the street.

The four brothers took note she was now in charge, and the three younger ones remained on the porch while their older sibling followed her. Maggie led Norman through the unlocked door to a little room off a hallway. Inside she pulled clothes from a tiny closet and pushed them in a box he held, went to a dresser, opened the bottom drawer of a bureau, and then stuffed a second and a third box. Norman carried the filled boxes to the porch; Kevin took them to the station wagon while Ernest and Lionel paced the porch. Norman returned for more boxes as Maggie had emptied the top drawer then he took three more boxes to the porch and returned. All the dresser drawers were empty and open. Maggie crossed her arms and swept the room with her eyes then took a school-type photograph from the dresser top, ripped it and threw it on the un-made bed. She placed another framed photograph of a soldier against her chest, added a well-worn teddy bear, and scoured the room once more.

"That's it. Let go," Maggie said to Norman and departed.

If her sister and mother were inside, neither she nor he could be certain. In less than fifteen minutes after they first entered, she and Norman exited the house.

"Meet me at the Wilmington Airport Terminal parking lot," she instructed the four brothers, before going to a 1949 Nash Metropolitan parked in an alley next to the house, looked up to a second floor window, and opened her purse for keys.

She started the tiny car, glanced up again, and took her a place between Norman and Lionel in the ragtop and Kevin and Ernest in the station wagon.

Soon the three automobiles moved south on U.S. 13 opposing morning commuter traffic to Philadelphia. Within an hour, a billboard picturing a jetliner and the words "Fly the Friendly Skies of United"

Call Me Maggie

greeted each as they pulled into the Wilmington airport terminal and parked near the Dutch Pantry Restaurant.

Maggie took a long breath and went to the car's trunk.

"I need one more thing. Could I leave my stuff in the station wagon for a while? I have some things to do," she said when the brothers joined her.

"Sure," Kevin and Norman answered together.

"Good, now let's have some breakfast."

"No thanks. We have work to do on Norman's car this morning," Kevin replied.

"Are you sure?" Maggie asked. "It's on me."

"Yes," four voices answered.

Norman and Kevin stood shoulder to shoulder before her. Their brothers were slightly behind. Standing on her toes, Maggie put an arm around Kevin and Norman. Ernest and Lionel dropped their eyes to the asphalt when she whispered, "Thank you both very, very much,"

Maggie's eyes were tear-filled when she finally let go.

"Kevin, I need to talk you. Can you stay?" she with an almost pleading tone.

Offering Kevin and Maggie privacy, Norman said, "I'll take Ernest and Lionel back to Dad's house with me.

"Okay," Kevin agreed.

Norman and two brothers climbed into the convertible. Maggie and Kevin sat on the trunk of the little Nash. Both remembered a similar scene the day before.

"It should be Linda sitting here with you now, Kevin, not some slut you picked up yesterday," Maggie began. "You two have known each other for a long time. She came close to ending up like me yesterday. She was really scared. And she'll need you to look out for her if she goes back to Bandstand. Vinnie and his gang won't forget her or what you did to them. You need someone, too. Let it be Linda. I know I turned you on yesterday. I know how you looked at me the other times you were at Bandstand. But I am a whore. I was setting you up. I'm supposed to turn you on. I'm supposed make you want me. Get it in your beautiful head, I'm a whore. It's what I do."

"I can't believe that about you,"

"It's what I am or was until yesterday. Let me be your friend, if you to want an ex-whore for a friend. If you don't, I'll understand. You and Linda talk it over. Let me know when I come to get the stuff in your dad's car. OK?"

Dirty Money

"OK, but I wish you would change your mind."

"I won't. Now you go get some sleep and maybe I'll see you around six this evening. If I can't make it I'll call you, if you'll give me your number?" Maggie continued.

"999-1999," he rang off the number, although its ring was soft and solemn.

"Good. Norman gave me a lead on an airline job in those buildings over there. I'm gonna pull myself together and go over there. If I can't get into the stewardess school, I'll try for work as a waitress. Or spend the summer at the beach. The guys down there are always trying to pick up my kind of girls. I also need to find an apartment, or find a room to rent."

"I can come with you," Kevin said.

"No, you can't, Kevin. I have to do this by myself."

Comparisons of Maggie and Norman entered Kevin's mind. Norman usually took charge. Now she had taken charge. Both are quick thinkers. Both are a few years older and living on their own. But, Norman's got a job. Maggie doesn't. How will she make it? Will she continue to be a whore?

Inside his head he heard, "Please Vinnie, don't do this." pleading "Take me with you." in the street appeared. She was pleading differently with him now.

Norman's jeans slid up almost to her knees as Maggie slid off the of the little car,

"Hold the lid, please, Kevin," she said as she opened the trunk. A small suitcase lay inside. Next to it, a pair of women's dress shoes lay in their box. She unsnapped the suitcase. Kevin could see neatly folded women's clothes inside when she took the shoes and placed them in the suitcase.

"I've got to use the restroom and change clothes. Sure you couldn't eat some breakfast?" she asked as she closed it and removed it from the trunk.

"I prob'ly could," Kevin answered as he took the suitcase. Both went inside and directly to the restroom doors.

"I'll get a table and order. What do you want?"

"Orange juice and two eggs over well," Maggie answered, as she took the suitcase and entered the ladies' room.

Ten minutes later, she placed the suitcase, women's blazer, and a bag on a chair next to Kevin. She wore a light blue scarf tied inside the collar of white blouse with countless pleats that ran down from her

47

Call Me Maggie

shoulders to a gray flannel straight skirt. A two-inch belt pulled in her midriff. Nylon stockings and black patent leather shoes covered her legs and feet. Her damp strawberry blond hair lay on her shoulders and covered the pleats down to her chest. Each strand lay perfectly over her blouse.

"Wow!" formed on his lips before she had time to seat herself across from him.

"I'm gonna get that stewardess job Norman told me about and I'm gonna be the best stewardess they ever hired."

Kevin believed her. Maggie forced herself to believe it too.

"My cousin Janet works for the apartment complex just up the Route 13. Let's go up there and she what she's got available."

No answer came right away. She put a fork full of eggs to her lips and looked into Kevin's eyes for a moment, then said, "Alright. But after that I'm on my own. You need to go home and get some sleep."

With two more bites, the eggs were eaten. She drank the juice. She put four $1.00 bills on the table. They left and the Nash followed the station wagon back up U.S. 13 less than a mile. Inside the rental office, Kevin introduced Maggie to his cousin.

"Hello, Janet. Do you have any efficiencies open?"

"A corner unit for seventy-five and another for sixty, utilities included," Janet answered. "Would you like to see them?"

With a polite "No thank you," Maggie pulled bills from her purse, removed five $100.00 bills from the center and placed them on Janet's desk and added, "Eight months in the $60.00 one. I'll be studying to be a stewardess for Intercontinental Airlines at the airport."

Janet filled out the lease agreement a security deposit form and Maggie signed them, "M. A. Montgomery," took the $20.00 dollar bill and two keys Janet held before her, said "Thank you, Janet," and headed back to the cars. Kevin had not spoken since the introduction.

"I have to do the rest on my own. I have to on alone from here. Please understand. I'm sorry for what Vinnie and his gang did to you and Linda. If I had known you were the kind of person you are, I would have refused you the first time you asked me to dance. Say hi to Linda and thank Norman for me, too," Maggie said before rising on her toes and embracing him.

Kevin watched as she drove away, started the station wagon and followed her back down U.S. 13. Both turned west onto Basin Road. Linda turned left into the airport, Kevin continued west. Soon he was at the future Interstate 95 where he had spent the previous night and

Dirty Money

would spend many more thinking about her, the events of yesterday, earlier this morning and what she had said after Norman, Ernest and Lionel left.

"I still can't believe she's a whore," Kevin said aloud.

Maggie got directions to the airline office from a gate guard and drove on to the former Officers' Club building. For a few long moments she sat in the little Nash before asking herself, "What have I got to lose?"

Following a few deep breaths, the eighteen year old pointed her patent leather pumps toward the building and marched forward. At a reflection in the door, she adjusted her blouse, tightened her scarf, brushed her skirt downward, braced her shoulders back, held her head, took another long breath, opened the door, and marched to the reception desk as proud as a new chicken colonel.

Ninety minutes later she re-opened the door, stepped across the threshold, leaped as high as her skirt would allow, screamed. "You did it Maggie," marched to her car and drove less than two miles.

One of the keys Janet had given her opened the door marked A-300. Maggie entered the one room apartment that seemed only half as large as Norman's. Its bare walls smelled of fresh paint even though someone and opened the windows. Its floor was bare as well with and even stronger smell of Pine-Sol that grew more acrid in the kitchen and bathroom. Pebbled glass doors encased the combination tub and shower an upgrade from the free standing one she shared in the Chester row house. As she inspected the vanity, Maggie gave herself a two fisted thumbs up. Returning to her car, she brought in the few possessions he had brought from Chester. Opening what appeared to be a closet, she discovered it to be a full-sized Murphy bed minus its mattress. A telephone and telephone book lay on an island separating the kitchen from the living and bedroom area. A dial tone told Maggie she had service for a while. She opened the book to its yellow pages, scribbled a few addresses on the important numbers page, and left her new home.

About 4 p.m., she returned, unloaded her Nash Metropolitan, and began putting things in the kitchen cabinets and drawers. About five, she remembered to call Kevin so he could bring the things left in the station wagon. Within a few minutes, he and Linda arrived and unloaded the boxes from the station wagon. A little after 5:30, a knock interrupted their chores as two delivery men stood waiting to unload a sofa, a mattress, two chairs, a table and table lamp. For another hour they arranged apartment A-30 into livable, though less than modest con-

49

Call Me Maggie

ditions. When Maggie walked Kevin back to the station wagon, each of the three said goodbye as though they would never see each other again.

Five miles north, Norman was printing pictures and recalling the past 24 hours with the misfortunate girl Kevin had brought when he returned the convertible. He had considered submitting one of the pictures for publication, but had reservations because the subject in the picture was Maggie. When the pictures finished drying, Norman slipped two copies of them into envelopes, took a photo album from the supply cabinet added it to his camera bag, hung the bag on his shoulder, and left the newspaper building by the back door office nearly an hour later and headed for his car. The red Chevy was in its usual parking space smiled as he came within sight of it. Bits and pieces of light reflected from the abundant chrome on the car. He could barely see the fire engine red bumper pan and tire kit on the back of the trunk lid in the darkness, but the chrome ring surrounding the tire and rim sparkled with the brilliance and glitter of a Christmas tree ornament. A proud smile came to his face, while a lump of gratitude to his three brothers swelled in his throat. The four of installed the continental kit in the hours between moving Maggie and when Ernest and he reported to their jobs. Norman had reported in to the newspaper and Ernest to the highway site before three. At 11 P.M., Kevin would replace Ernest at the interstate project. Fourteen year old Lionel walked a block and a half to pump gas at Mr. Donovan's Esso Station from six to ten. All four brothers had worked for "Mister D" at some time, although Norman's tenure had been the shortest.

Norman and Ernest often returned to the family home to work on such projects. Kevin and Lionel still lived with their parents. They could usually be counted as extra hands. Kevin enjoyed working with his father's tools; most especially when he worked on an engine. Kevin possessed a knack for getting every last possible rpm from any engine, whether be on a garden tractor, his father's pickup truck or the family station wagon. When Kevin wasn't tweaking a car at the garage door, he was fine tuning a garden tractor or a neighbor's lawn mower. Lionel was usually there, at his side looking and learning when not in school or the Esso station. Kevin had spent two years high school auto shop before making his earlier career move while in the eleventh grade. Lionel was in "Auto Mechanics I" and had two years to go before graduation in 1964.

Back in the winter, Ernest bought the '55 Ford. Ernest, Kevin, and Lionel spent the coldest months of 1962 bringing the car to race

Dirty Money

condition. With a little more "tweaking" from Kevin, it would be contender at Maryland's Cecil County Dragway.

Depending on "pick-up money" earned from tune-ups and repairs on engines for friends or neighbors, the income Kevin earned wasn't reliable enough for him to make monthly payments on the car he wanted to purchase. His "dirt pan jockey" job salary and his occasional "pick-up job" earnings would speed his goal into a reality, but he had to purchase the car with cash, and use little of his future salary to tweak the new car. For now during most early mornings or early evenings, he could be found under a hood of some vehicle in front of the little garage earning an extra dollar whenever he could. The promise Kevin made to himself had proven harder to keep than it was to make.

Linda often joined Ernest's girlfriend and girls dating Ernest's friends in lawn chairs under a giant dogwood canopy near the boys hanging around the garage. Friends from old neighborhood in the city, new ones from "South Wilm'n'tn" plus their girl friends and of course three or four Kennedy boys often filled more than a dozen seats around the dogwood tree or would-be speed shop.

Norman had the same voluminous passion for using his hands. Cameras, lenses, and light meters were Norman's tools, not wrenches or tachometers dwell meters.

At the moment Norman wanted to do a little adolescent cruising and show off his new continental kit. Two drive-in restaurants in the suburbs would be the place to go this evening. The top was down and the tunneau snapped in place, as they were on most sunny days or rainless nights.

This was the third Chevrolet car he had owned since he was seventeen, all had been convertibles. Two were red, one green. But this one he favored with its big boxy look, Frenched-in headlights, three bullet-like tail lights, and now, a new glistening continental kit and it sparkling rim. Other than the reflections the car was sitting in darkness as he opened the door.

"Ohmygod!" Norman shouted and then took a startled step backward. The envelope fell to the asphalt pavement. He saw a human form on the rear seat when the courtesy lights came on.

"It's Maggie! It's Mary Anne Johnson."

Except for her legs, Norman could not see her clearly.

"What in the world? I almost wet myself."

"I'm sorry if I stunned you, but I had to see you," she stated with excitement overflowing from deep within her.

Call Me Maggie

"What happened? Did Vinnie find you? Are you okay?"

"You are looking at the newest stewardess on Intercontinental Airline. School starts in two weeks. I just had to tell you," she said, omitting to say it depended upon passing the physical exam as she climbed into the shotgun seat.

Norman sat behind the wheel with his mouth still open.

"And I got an apartment I want to show you."

"Great!"

"Got time to go there now?"

Inside she wondered if coming to see Norman was a mistake. As he overcame his scare, he began to share her excitement.

"What's it like?" he asked, picking up the envelope.

"Oh you know the usual first apartment stuff. Bare walls. Unfurnished. Plain poverty. But it will get better when I'm a stewardess and earn some honest money. Wanna follow me down there?" Maggie answered and asked.

"Sure! Where is it?"

"Near the airport. Kevin took me over to where your cousin Janet works. Rented it sight unseen. I could walk to school."

"Tell me the school part first."

"I get the job as a stewardess if I go through three months in their school. Other schools are six or more. I'll be in the air before Christmas. Gotta pass a physical though. Can't sweat that. I'm in good shape and tougher than most girls my age. Now let me show you my apartment, please, please, please."

"Right now?"

"Yes right now. Follow me."

"Lead the way. But keep your wheels on the ground." Norman assumed she had her car. He was truly happy for her.

Maggie led him to the Wilmington Manor Apartments. The key to A-300 opened the door again. Both stepped inside. Norman did not recognize the function of what he assumed was an armoire. A recently painted avocado colored dresser was nearby. No mirror hung above it. On the wall leading to the kitchen slightly tattered but new sofa sat where the one in his apartment sat. Before it stood a brass legged glass coffee table. He dropped his envelope on it and placed the Leica on top of the envelope. A well worn table and two chairs were in the dining area. The walls contained no pictures, posters, calendars, or art of any kind. It was obvious to him the apartment offered more space and freedom than the 9x12 foot bedroom in Chester.

Dirty Money

To Maggie, it was beautiful. It was her new home. The first home of her own. Holding his arm but not speaking, Maggie led him to the kitchen, opened a cabinet to reveal a set of all white Corelle. A drawer revealed white bone-handled flatware. Norman headed for the bath while Maggie stayed in the kitchen. In the bath, a pair of his blue jeans and a tee shirt hung over the shower door. After going back in the kitchen, Maggie held two tumblers half filled.

"To the airline stewardess, and to Norman Kennedy, the guy who convinced her to go for it," Maggie toasted.

"To Maggie, her new career and her new home," Norman toasted in return.

After they tapped glasses and each sipped, he asked, "How did you get this scotch. And it's J&B, too."

"Parked outside the liquor store. Begged a lot of customers until one gave in."

"I'm surprised. You said unfurnished earlier. How and where did you get the furniture since this morning?"

"Yellow pages. Salvation Army. Manor Used Furniture. Justis Brothers. That took some begging, too!"

"It's hard to believe. I'm proud of you, girl."

Resisting the urge to give her an embrace and he went to the coffee table, picked up the envelope, returned to the little kitchen table and handed it to her.

"I suppose you could say this is a house warming present for you and your new home."

Maggie accepted the album and viewed the top picture he held facing her, the shouted, "That's me!" leaving no doubt she was surprised.

She gazed at the picture, a silhouette of a woman with blowing hair backward away from her face. Sparkling water made up most of the background. A starburst replaced the sun over the water. Highlights formed the profile and blowing hair leaving her face in shadows.

"I said last night your modeling career wasn't over."

"It's beautiful. You did great. I didn't even notice you taking it. Let me give you a hug for taking it."

"You'd better look at the other one before you hug me."

Maggie stared at the silhouette until Norman handed her the album, then gave the first page in the album an intent look. It showed the picture of her taken with the camera high above her that morning. After a long moment, she held the album to her chest and cried while he taped picture on the refrigerator door. Norman cringed not knowing if

Call Me Maggie

she cried because she approved of the picture or if it upset her. After another moment and a few passes over her eyes with her hands, Maggie laid the book down and spoke.

"They are beautiful, Norman. I love them. You made something beautiful out of a very ugly situation. You could have taken advantage of the situation and I would have let you. Instead, you let me sleep and took a picture of me. It's more beautiful than the other. Thank you!" Maggie paused, and stared into his eyes. "Thank you for believing in me. I don't feel like a wh. . . . I don't feel cheap or dirty tonight. I can't believe how you, your brothers, helped work out my problems. I've got a big hug to give each of them when I see them"

"You did more for yourself than we did. We just moved some clothes for you."

Norman ran two glasses of water from the sink spigot and placed them on the table. Maggie gave him an embrace and an apology, and then motioned for him to be seated opposite her.

"Tell me the truth, now. You brought your brothers along for protection in case Vinnie showed up, didn't you?"

"Yes," he answered sheepishly.

"And what would you have done without them?"

"Done it anyway," was his answer.

"I'd bet you would have."

Maggie rose from the chair, stepped around the table and knelt beside Norman. She put her head on his chest and her arms with the album on his shoulders.

"Thank you, Mister Kennedy."

"Thank you, Miss Johnson."

"Call me Maggie. We are friends now and all my friends call me Maggie," she said placing her arms around him and drawing herself closer.

His hands reached up under her hair and rested on her shoulders. The soft hair felt good against his hands. Her head felt even better against his chest. Maggie kept it there for a few moments as she listened to his racing heart. Norman wanted the embrace to continue, but had a question compelling to be asked.

"Now, you tell me the truth, please Maggie," Norman said softly. "How did you get this place and furnishings? Where'd the money come from?"

"I used my Dad's dependent survivor's check money, but mostly I used the money I got from Vinnie. Before I couldn't spend Vinnie's

Dirty Money

money except sometimes for groceries for Madeline and my mother. Vinnie's money was dirty money until today. I spent most of it and I'm gonna finish spending the rest tomorrow. When it's gone, I'll be finished setting up my apartment. And finished with Vinnie. Everything else can wait until I finish the stewardess school. Until then I will get by on the survivor's check. The rent's paid for eight months. I'll stock the cabinets with basic foods and live like I did in Chester for the next three months," Maggie explained.

"You are one amazing lady, Mary Anne Johnson."

"There is nothing amazing about me. I'm just a little ole girl raised in Talleyville, USA. Please call me Maggie," she said, trying to mimic the Kennedy Alabama drawl. "I have done too many wrong things to be called amazing. But that's going to change now that I'm on my own."

Maggie withdrew from the embrace, rose, returned to her chair and entered a bastion he could not breach. For a long time she did speak and when she did she said, "I would interested in modeling for you. I'd pose for any pictures like the ones I saw in your albums. I would refuse to pose for any you wanted to take that were kinky or vulgar."

"When I take a shower the bathroom mirror steams up. I want a picture with someone's face in the steamed-up mirror. It would be a good one if it were you and your long hair. If you're willing, you could wrap a towel around yourself. The only thing that worries me is showing your face and having it seen in Philadelphia. Another shot is your face against the dry mirror forming two images of the same face. Another is a diffused silhouette shot through your shower door. You would have to be naked for that one. I can't ask you to pose for nude. There are hundreds of others I would like to shoot. I could go on all night telling you about them, but I won't," Norman explained.

"I'll take my chances, let's do some. You don't have to ask me to pose nude. You saw all me this morning. You can see it again tonight. There is the camera. Start shooting." she stated.

"I'd like a little more scotch first. It's been a while since I had a model as wiling as you," he said.

"How about coffee instead of scotch? We are going to be a while," she came back.

She made coffee in her new, used coffee pot. As the coffee was being made Norman removed a large case from behind his new continental kit on the car trunk lid. He carried the case into the apartment and laid it on the uncluttered floor.

Call Me Maggie

"Your neighbors will probably think I'm moving in with you," he said as he opened the light case.

Maggie finished brushing her hair beyond the open bathroom door, lay down the brush and went to avocado chest where the photograph of a soldier shared the top with the soiled teddy bear. She opened the top drawer and removed a small pouch, walked to Norman and knelt while she removed the bag and unzipped it. A single key lay against folded currency. Her hand removed the key and held it before Norman.

"This is for you. You can come here after work or in the morning before I go to school. Use it anytime! You don't have a girl to talk with at your place. After school starts, I won't be here long after you get up. You could stay and we'd have breakfast, and I'll be here when you finish work. We can do anything you want to do. I mean anything you want; talk, take pictures or make love. Call me if you like. My number is 627-9266. If you forget, dial MARYANN with no "e", okay?"

"I won't forget, Mary Anne with no "e". But it will be what we both want. How about some coffee with two "ee's?"

"Coming up," she answered.

Two cups of coffee, a quart of milk and four packets of sugar were placed on the table. She returned a second time with two napkins and two bone-handled spoons. Then she sat across from Norman again while he was adding milk and sugar into a white cup.

"When did you start taking pictures?" Maggie asked and then sipped unsweetened, black coffee while waiting for an answer.

"When I was thirteen or fourteen Mom got a box camera as a prize for selling perfume. She used every spare minute to help support her kids. She still does. And Dad, too. Anyway, I started taking pictures with the camera even though they didn't always turn out good. I even used the camera for the first two pictures the newspaper printed while working there as a copy boy after school. I got the photography bug real bad, took pictures of everything on that camera. One of the staff photographers at the paper sold me a better one and I took even more pictures. After high school graduation, which I almost didn't finish, they moved me to the photo lab. Still worked nights, but had days to shoot more and more pictures. Mostly I would just shoot and proof. They said it cost them too much to enlarge many of my shots. A year later they promoted me to being a real photographer. That was almost five years ago. It's been my life ever since, shooting and printing pictures," Norman said.

"From what I've seen in your albums, you are good. Mister Norman Kennedy," Maggie complimented.

Dirty Money

"It is not all me. There's a lot of luck. And a subject can make all the difference in the world. We have to work as a team with the same goal in mind, pictures. Good pictures."

Maggie went to the dresser again, returned the purse to the top drawer, opened the bottom one, removed a long sleeved blouse, half as long as the shirt Norman offered the night before, removed the Banlon she had been wearing, her bra, her shoes, her shorts and her panties, all the while her back was to Norman.

Maggie slipped her arms through the sleeves of the pink blouse and buttoned the two buttons closest to her breasts and returned to the table. Large bump pressed the fabric outward.

"My "B&P" lines will be gone in a few minutes. I'm sure the pictures won't be good if they show. If my nipples still show, let'em show. Got a middle name, Norman?" Maggie asked.

"David," he answered.

"Photographs by Norman David Kennedy. Someday I'm gonna see that on a book title lying on coffee tables everywhere," she said.

The photographer in Norman smiled as he sat silently.

"Do you use your subject's names with your pictures?"

"Usually. Well, most of the time," he answered.

"If you ever use one of mine, just print M.A. Montgomery. Montgomery was my dad's first name. No one will know but you and I. Could you do that?" Maggie asked.

"I could do that," he answered.

Many questions came to mind as he wondered about her reason for the request, but hiding from Vinnie ranked highest.

"Good, let's take some good pictures," Maggie ordered.

"Are you sure you want to do this? You barely know me! You can't be sure of what picture will be like. Some might be two raw! You don't have a chaperon. There's all the legal stuff to think about. How about model releases? You don't have an agent to represent you. What about your mother? She could sue me. If I shoot something you don't like, you sue me. Maggie, taking of you naked is not that simple," he warned.

"You didn't have a model release this morning. I never had one before. You made two great pictures of me and I didn't know it. Now I know, and we are going to make better pictures. I'm now over eighteen and legal. We will be a team. Norman David Kennedy, photographer and M. A. Montgomery, model."

"Young woman!" Norman interrupted.

Call Me Maggie

"Young woman, nothing! I'm your model. Look at me. Really look at me. What do you see? A high school dropout. A Bandstand dancer. A former nude model. A former wh. . . The only job I've had was selling my a. . . myself."

"Maggie. . ."

"Look at me and let me finish. I've got a good face. I've got a good body. You said so yourself. What I don't have is an education. If I don't make it as a stewardess, I'll have nothing left but the face and body. What then, show my ass and tits as a cocktail waitress, and hope enough tips come in to make a living. Most girls would give anything to have what I have and what I see in you. We could be good together. We could be a team. Teach me. Train me. Be my agent. Be my photographer. Believe in me the way I believe in you."

Tears were in her eyes again. Norman remained silent. Maggie continued crying with her head lowered.

"Maggie, I'll do it with one condition. That is if we a truly a team. A partnership. Trust each other implicitly when it comes to modeling and photography," Norman laid out conditions. "And no porno shots, no risqué picture, no pictures of your private area, not even your pubic hair or erotic display of your breast, just beautiful pictures of you. Are you sure you want to do this?"

"I already trust you. Let me clean my face and so we can get started," she said.

"No, don't dry your face. The picture will be better if you don't, believe me. Trust me. I should have said better in my opinion. You liked the ones from last night. I would like more before I try to shoot any of you nude," Norman said.

"I believe you, I trust you. Tell me what you want me to do."

"Nothing but look at the camera. I will be shooting you from the waist up. Later, you can rest your face on your arms, play with your hair, sip from your cup or do whatever you would be doing if did not have a camera in my hands," he said.

"If you didn't have the camera in your hands I would be snuggling in your arms" she said.

For half-an-hour Maggie posed, changing her poses and her clothes often. As the half hour became an hour, she abandoned her bra and allowed glimpses of her breasts beneath low cut tops and open blouses. Often her nipples pressed against her sweater, blouse, or chemise. Less often most of her breasts could be seen but not recorded by the camera.

Dirty Money

"Still want to do the mirror shot?" he asked.

"Sure. Want another cup of coffee first?"

Norman nodded, went to the case, and took three lights into the bathroom. Maggie made coffee while Norman used his hand as a model while adjusting the lights until they were positioned. After their coffee break, Maggie climbed on the chair and dropped the blouse to her feet before he had time to raise the camera to his eye. Once the camera raised, Norman saw two images in viewfinder; one real, one mirrored.

"Are you sure you want me to see you undressed?"

"Yes, I'm sure."

Norman reached out and put his hand over her closest breast, fluffed her long strawberry blonde hair until it covered her breast.

"Place your face lightly on the mirror facing toward me, please. Don't smile, please. Lower your eyes, please. Raise your eyes, please. Tip your head to the mirror, please. Look into the camera, please. Looks good. Great. Raise your eyes, please. Put your hand closest to me on the mirror, please."

Norman chattered his photographer's banter. With each please, the camera clicked. He had noticed that her nipple closest to him protruded through her hair. He took a deep breath before adjusting her hair. Again he brushed her nipple, but with the back of his hand this time as he pulled more hair over her breasts. He wanted the shot, so he kept shooting and the banter continued until the camera refused to click.

"Out of film. Need a new roll. That's it for this setup. Take a breather and we'll do more."

Maggie draped herself with the blouse. Norman noticed marble sized nipples protruded from each breast as he reloaded, then made a few shots of the scene with the pebbled glass door as a backdrop.

"Want to take a break?" Norman asked.

"I'm fine."

"We can do the shot with you behind glass door shot this time," he said as he sat up his lights to hit the back wall of the bath enclosure. Directing Maggie to enter the tub-shower, he closed door so the camera would shoot her silhouetted nude form diffused by pebbled glass.

"We are going pretend you're taking a shower. Don't turn on the water; just follow to my directions, please. You can't see what the camera sees and you'll have to trust me. I don't want to take any picture just because you're naked and showing your private areas. I want pictures that leaves hidden and unseen."

"I trust you. You don't have to hide my private areas."

Call Me Maggie

"Reach for the shower head, please. Put your hands on the back of your neck, please. Push your hips back, please. Put your shoulders back, please. Pull your stomach in, too, please. Turn to me a little more away from me, please."

Norman continued directing. Maggie continued following and posing. She became aware of the arousal within herself.

"Now turn facing me and press your body against the glass, please. Pull one side a way a little, please," the banter went on and the camera clicked on. Without prompting she sometimes made changes to her poses. They exposed another roll using the pebbled glass.

"What would you like to do next?"

"Steamy mirror shot, please."

"Would you like my hair wet or dry?"

"Wet, please."

"Then I'd like to shower, too. If that's okay?"

"Would you mind if I kept shooting while you do? I might get something I haven't thought of."

"I won't mind."

Maggie turned on the water. As she showered Norman made more pictures, but without directing Maggie. Soon she asked if he would shoot some with the door open. Norman finished the third roll photographing with the door open. Some were made as she dried herself. Norman had a fourth roll loaded when she finished. Maggie climbed back on the chair, moved close to the mirror, and waited for Norman's directions. The roll was half used when he asked her to stand at the edge of the door. He made a few more shots with long wet hair hanging down in front of her chest hidden behind the door.

"That's it I guess," Norman said as Maggie fluffed her hair with the towel. "Thank you. Miss Montgomery."

"Are you out of film? Because if you're not, shoot one more pose for me, please."

"Oh yes, I have lots more film."

Maggie lay on the open area of the hardwood floor. Norman began shooting the pose she suggested. Some were low angle views, some were high angles. Some used only light from the kitchen and bath; some were made with extra light from Norman's flash. In some she faced the light, in others she let the light fall only on her back. In all the pictures, the lines of the floor lead to and passed under Maggie's body, reminding Norman of Playboy's first cover. He guessed that she had seen the picture of Marilyn Monroe.

Dirty Money

"We can stop for tonight. How about breakfast?"

After answering yes, Norman packed his gear while Maggie prepared two bowls of cornflakes. Bananas, milk, and sugar packets were put on the table next to coffee cups.

"How did I do?" she asked before eating.

"You did fine, but we'll have wait until we see the proofs to be sure," he replied.

"We?" she questioned.

"Yes, we. You have some input to offer, I hope."

"I have got input I haven't begun to use." she boasted.

"I'll count on it," Norman came back.

"I am glad I met you. I am glad we made the pictures. You taught me a lot just now. I am glad you did. Yesterday you were hell-bent to help me. I thought it was for sex with me. But, when I came to you, you only held me. I slept with you expecting you to take me. To-night, when you found me in your car, you only asked about me. You stayed late printing picture of me. You are a different person than I first met. While taking the pictures you were tight and very formal. You treated me with respect and kindness. You must have two sides, one with the camera, one without. Last night and now you are a pleasure to be with in the middle of the night. You made me think about what I have to offer beside a frolic in the bed. You make me believe in myself. Now you make me laugh. You make me feel good. And it feels good to feel good. Do I make any sense or am I totally batty?"

"It makes sense. Last night I jumped in a car with a girl avoiding a beating. Tonight a different girl was in the same car telling me about how well she did for herself today. They were in the same body, but yet different. You shared yourself with me off camera. Sure, I can take a little credit for hiding you and helping you get out of Chester, but mostly it was you wanting more than the dead-end rut you were in. That took courage and guts. Everything I know about you since last night took courage. It rubbed off on me, too. Two days ago, I would never have brought you home with me or followed you home tonight. I photo-graphed you last night assuming I would never see you again. I saw loneliness, desperation, insecurity, and fear, but printed a set of pictures for you anyway. I photographed you overcome by darkness, yet willing to share yourself with me. I saw you full of despair but in spite of your despair you gave of yourself. This morning, I saw you bare as the day you were born and at peace. That picture was not a nude young woman modeling. It was your life as I saw it and I shot what I saw. Tonight, I

Call Me Maggie

found you again and photographed you again. Tonight it was a happier you. I hope I can take more pictures of you and your new life. It's going to be one worthy of every picture I shoot," Norman said as tears formed in his eyes.

Maggie's eyes overflowed again, yet they were locked on Norman. Her image of him was blurred yet his words rang clear. The blurred image had given her hope many times in last thirty hours.

"Let's finish our coffee on the sofa," Maggie suggested.

Norman stood and carried both cups to the coffee table. Maggie quickly moved the cereal bowls to the sink, gave them a quick rinse, flipped the light switch, followed Norman, removed his shoes pushed him against the sofas back and lay beside him with her hair on his chest.

"You can have me now if you want me. I owe you that much for getting me out of Chester and the beautiful pictures you gave me."

"You don't owe me for anything. I need a good model for the pictures I want to make. You want a photographer who will work with you, but I don't want you to feel you have to do that in exchange for anything we do. I would rather have you as a model, a friend, and partner, than as a conquest in the bed. I know that except for the last shot on the floor, you were modeling to repay me for last night and this morning. You don't need to do that. I will photograph you because you are wonderful person, a good subject, and a woman who that doesn't try to hide her assets from me and my camera. But, don't pose because you think you owe me something. It is I that is indebted to you."

"Is it because I have been with other men before you?"

"No, virgins are hard to find in this time of beatniks and free love. And it's not because I wouldn't like to make love to you. I would, but I can't make myself take advantage of you that way."

"You would not be taking advantage of me. No one ever will again. Could you hold me a little while, please?

"I would like it too. I would like it very much, but don't expect me to do anything but hold you," he answered, placing his arms around her waist.

"Thank you, partner."

Norman left Maggie's apartment that morning to do personal film in his home lab. He began developing the exposed film shot of Maggie. When he got to work a few yellow message slips were in a pigeonhole labeled "Kennedy." One contained a telephone number with a 212 area code. In the space marked "caller," the name Michele appeared.

"Dammit, last night was Tuesday night."

Dirty Money

Norman sat at the desk and lowered his head to his hands above his elbows on the desktop. His shoulders slumped. His mind raced.

"Can't do anything until tonight," he said out loud again.

Maggie did some shopping before reporting to a suburban doctor's office. After the medical exam, she did more shopping. She would fill her little Nash Metropolitan, return to the apartment, and unload several times before evening. Except for a single $100.00 bill, Vinnie's dirty money had been spent. The little apartment had everything she would need for the next eight months, except for occasional food staples such as milk, bread, eggs and meat.

School and shopping for a graduation filled most of the day for Linda. Instead of going to the Gravel Pit for swimming with her classmates, she wanted to be with Kevin. So she took a bus down Union Street and the Kirkwood Highway, got off a Newport Pike, walked two blocks and found Kevin under the hood of Ernest's drag racer. She began her visit telling him about a Tuesday evening run she and friends made to the Charcoal Pit, their last one as high school students. Evening approached and watching him fiddle with the car became a bore, she told Kevin wanted to see Maggie's new apartment and began begging him to drive her to visit Maggie. He gave in, cleaned himself, and drove her to the city's southeastern suburbs. She and Maggie set up the apartment mixing details of the stewardess school with directions on how Maggie wanted her treasures displayed although Linda had hoped to learn more of Maggie exploits of a personal and adult nature. That would have to wait until Kevin wasn't around. She insisted Maggie be at her graduation and party afterwards. Maybe she could ask her questions at the party?

Kevin helped by moving the few heavier items and offered only brief "yup's" and "nope's" when the girls asked him a question, until Linda left to use the bathroom. He moved close to Maggie, and stated softly, "I thought over what you said yesterday. It doesn't make any difference to me if you have gone all the way with other guys. I still want to see you as much as I did before I borrowed Norman's car and drove to Bandstand."

"That's very nice, Kevin. I'm flattered. If you mean dating, I am not ready to date anyone. I've got stewardess school and a lot of other things going on. When school is over, I'll call you for the milk shake you invited me to share, but don't expect anything more than that."

At nine, he left in time to drive Linda home before he went to work on the interstate.

Call Me Maggie

Norman knew the next few minutes would be difficult when he made a call to the 212 area code phone number shortly after nine. Michele wanted to know why he stood her up Tuesday evening. She reminded him he had always driven to Philadelphia on Tuesdays.

"I waited all evening. You didn't even call." she shouted.

"I could see you Saturday night or Sunday afternoon." Norman promised trying to make it up to her on the weekend.

"Saturday I'm going to my grandparents and I'll be with my mother for Mother's day. I won't be back until Sunday night," Diane snapped smartly at her boyfriend of two years.

"What was so important that you didn't come to see me or call me last night?"

"I did some processing and took some pictures."

"They must have been very special pictures."

"They were!" Norman answered, but offered no details.

Other altercations with Diane went through his mind as she continued.

"I hope so. You stood me up. You teed me off. And you didn't call for a whole day. I hope the pictures were worth it."

"I think they were"

"I have tests tomorrow and Friday. I have to study. I can't talk to you any longer."

"I told you I am going home this weekend. I will call you when I want to see you. Goodnight," Diane snapped.

Norman's mind wandered through the past twentyfour months. The relationship Norman had with Diane rarely included contact with her family or his. It also had no deep intimacy, but it had worked for nearly two years. Only an hour drive separated the two, but there was a distance between them that could not be measured in time or miles.

On the way to the newsroom for a last check with the editors, he questioned how he would spend the next few hours when it was too late to date, too early to sleep. The night's paper was being put to bed on time without incident. Barring any story that might break in the next two hours and there was little to do but go to the bar with the reporters or cruise the drive-in and that was not as attractive tonight as it had been on other nights before before last night.

"Go on home, Norman. I'm working on something special for you tomorrow, so rest-up!" the editor told his young photographer

Norman walked back to the photo-lab where the phone was ringing. "Photography Department, Norman Kennedy speaking."

Dirty Money

"Hi, Norman. I hope is alright to call you at work," asked a voice he recognized immediately.

"Yes, it's alright. Is everything all right with you, Maggie?" Norman questioned as he slid prints into an envelope. "Are you having any trouble?"

"Everything is fine, Norman. Just fine."

"That's good, but why did you call?"

"I wanted to know if your day was as good as mine."

"Was yours good? Good enough to talk about?"

"Oh yes. If you can come by, I'll share it with you."

"I can come over, but I may not be good company."

"Come anyway, you've seen me in the dumps. I can manage an evening with you feeling gloomy," she reassured him. "Besides, partners share everything fifty-fifty. Thirty minutes?"

"Thirty minutes," Norman answered.

Knowing he had a few minutes, he added contact viewers and pencils to his bag, walked down the hall, and spent those minutes washing, combing and re-spraying his hair. Soon he knocked on her door even though he had the key. Maggie slipped through the slightly open door into the hall, and took Norman's arm with the camera bag and the envelope and said, "Close your eyes, then I'll take you in."

He allowed himself to he led halfway across the apartment, until she stopped saying, "OK, Open them," and gave him a moment to examine the apartment.

Norman's mouth dropped open as his eyes moved around the room. She had been decorated the wall with the foldaway Murphy bed in a flower motif he mistook for an amoire. Old wall pots held white silk flowers. An antique potter's stand with well-worn paint held more pots and more white flowers. Old advertising signs hung on the wall opposite the sofa. From the sofa wall hung numerous Pennsylvania Dutch hex signs. A few wooden toys and farm tools surrounded a copy of Andrew Wyeth's "Christina's World." On the wall with the door hung bridles, riding crops, horseshoes, saddlebags, stirrups, and horse related objects.

Maggie removed the envelope he held, the camera on his shoulder, plus the bag he carried and put them on her coffee table, encircled his waist and drew Norman close to her and said, "Someday, I'm gonna get myself a horse too. Maybe a pair."

"Maggie it's beautiful. It's comfortable and country. It reminds me of homes and stores back in Alabama or boutique shops up here. I'm overwhelmed you did all this today. How?"

65

Call Me Maggie

"I shopped thrift stores. Linda and Kevin stopped by and wanted to help arrange things; so I let them," she answered, then led him to the kitchen area where several cast iron pots, splatter-wear utensils and a few pottery crocks filled open spaces. A strip of masking tape with hand printed letters reading, "Model: M. A. Montgomery" had been added to the picture of her was on the refrigerator.

Maggie led him back to the little table set for two. White plates held large boiled potatoes, a portion of broccoli and a steaming hamburger patty with a single red pansy blossom on top. Unmatched goblets held ice water with floating pansies. A bud vase held three yellow roses.

"Where did you find the flowers?" he asked while she adjusted yellow roses in a bud vase centered on the table.

"From the flower bed where I parked my car. I hope they didn't mind me taking them."

"You've come a long way in two days, Maggie!"

A sugar and creamer with tiny chips sat on the table. Maggie set the coffee pot down and seated herself opposite Norman, raised her water glass and said, "To Maggie, the stewardess. I passed the physical."

"To Maggie, one hellava girl," Norman toasted.

"Thank you Mister Kennedy," she replied. "I hope you're as hungry as I am. If you had not come tonight, I'd have eaten both plates."

"I have a question. Am I supposed to eat the pansy?" he asked.

"I do. It's good for my hair. Gives it its color."

"In that case I'll have a couple of dozen more. I haven't had color in mine for years," he retorted as he lifted the blossom off the paddie, made a questioning expression, sniffed it, put it in his mouth, and began chewing.

Maggie covered her mouth with both hands as she strained to prevent him hearing her laughter.

"Where did you learn to cook and decorate with flowers?" Norman asked after he deposited the blossom in the toilet bowl. His father grew flowers but never served them as food.

"Grandmother Johnson, I suppose. My sister and I used to spend summers with her before she died. There were always flowers in Grandmother's house. Flowers everywhere; on the tables, in the bathroom, in our bedroom, Daffodils were first in the spring. Then azalea cuttings. Later large white magnolia, or pink rhododendrons, and throughout the summer there were roses, lots and lots of roses. She grew them all, herself. At Christmas there was holly and cedar everywhere. My mother never even put up a Christmas tree."

Dirty Money

Halfway through dinner, Maggie lifted the flowers from her plate, placed them in the water glass, stirred them with her finger, and raised the stockade of silence around herself as she tried to prevent anyone reaching the real Mary Anne Johnson. Norman noticed the quietness and waited, giving her a few minutes as he wondered in silence if he had offended her by not eating the flowers or questioning her flower uses.

"It is her fortress and she must have used it often in the past two year. Perhaps all her life,' he said to himself as he waited for her to restart their conversation.

She not taken her eyes off the flowers spinning in glass as she spoke and kept them there for another short eternity after she finished, then she looked up in a cold daze. As she finished her journey back to the farm, a soft smile slowly replaced the stupor.

"Did I tell you Grandmother had a farm near Booth's Corner? She had a couple of cows, a few chicken and ducks, and one white horse. Really it was my grandfather's horse, but when he died, she could not sell that horse, even though many people wanted to buy him. I loved that farm. I found a lot good things shopping this afternoon like she had. I could have bought them all," Maggie said when she broke her silence.

"You did extremely well, Maggie. Your grandmother would be proud of her granddaughter's home," he assured her.

"I hope so. Norman, don't expect a lot from me. I need time. I have got to put a lot of distance between me and my past. Linda is trying hard to be a friend. Kevin wants to date me, but I told him Linda was better for him. And you, Norman, you helped me get on the right track. I am grateful. I don't feel dirty anymore. I feel warm and good. How can me thank you," she said and gently squeezed Norman's hand before placing it against her breast.

The response she expected from Norman never came. He dropped his eyes to their hand, and then moved his hand away with her still holding it. For another moment they stared at each other; he not sure she that she intended for him to hold her in such a private way and she wondering why he had moved his hand away, when so many other men put their on her chest without being encouraged or invited.

"So you approve of my place, do you? Most of everything is used. I had a tight budget. And now, it's all gone. But then, it's better than staying in Chester with my mother and my sister. I never had much to live for there and anything I do will be a step out of the slum they're still in. I hope she and my sister get out someday. I have been able to see how other people manage their lives. I may never be rich, but for damn

Call Me Maggie

sure I never going to act like I am poor again. In the next three months I am going to give it everything I have got. After stewardess school I will know. Kevin told me a little about the life you came from. I can read you and your brothers, a little bit. You are good people and I am going to become a good person, too. Like you said, I have a new life ahead."

Norman began removing the plates and serving dishes leaving the table desktop clear. She did not follow his lead, returning to her silence instead. Afterwards he took the bag and envelope from the coffee table and returned to the chair opposite Maggie. He removed two contact viewers from the bag and handed one to Maggie with its light on.

"Let's do some editing," he said as he removed a pair of red grease pencils and the contact prints from the envelope. "Look them all over, put a dot on the ones you like, then we'll go back and put a square on the best of the ones with dots. That the way I do it."

He laid his viewer on his first contact sheet. She copied his example. Conversations they held were held with their eyes glued to their viewers.

"What's the first thing you look for in a model, Norman?" Maggie asked while viewing proofs of the shots he had taken of her the night before.

"Usually it's the hair," Norman answered.

"Most people look at another person's eyes first."

"I do that too. But I look at their hair. The person doesn't have to be a model. They might be a blacksmith, or a bank officer. It could be a man, woman or child. The eyes may be the window into their sole but their hair tells me how they feel about themselves. It takes discipline to take of hair. It's the last thing we do when grooming ourselves. And in some cases, being last means being neglected. Well maintained hair usually means a well kept body. If the hair is haggard, the person is probably carefree and lazy unless they are in an occupation that abuses their hair. Use Kevin and Ernest for examples. In the dust all day. In and under old cars. They try but they can't keep their hair or bodies picture perfect all the time. And my sister is the opposite. She doesn't keep herself up for her husband. She gives herself to him, but she does not prepare herself before she does. She should make herself more desirable and less available."

"Who else are you talking about? Linda? Or me?"

"I was looking you over in the police station. In spite of all the crap and trouble you had that day, your hair was beautiful. In the bed picture the next morning, your hair was pleasant. You were at peace and

Dirty Money

so opposite the one with it windblown on the refrigerator. I had a great picture to take of you. Your hair made it even greater," he replied.

"Most guys would have seen an opportunity to make their move when they had a girl in their bed. Why didn't you?"

"I knew what led you to sleep in my bed. I knew I had a chance to one of a kind photograph to make and that I should take it and get your approval later. The picture could be of a baby and it would be a great picture. Seeing you lying there that way made me want to photograph you more than to seduce you. I wanted that picture more than I wanted to prove my virility. If you want, I will give the negative to you and you can destroy it and the print."

"You could have taken the picture and taken me too. I wouldn't have objected then, the first night, last night, or now."

"Would you regret it later? I have photographed models who thought I only wanted them to pose so I could take other advantages of them. I have known a few who let me photograph them because they wanted to take advantage of me more than they wanted me to take pictures of them."

Norman and Maggie continued studying the proofs.

"What do you see in me as a model?"

"Many things. Of course your beautiful hair. And a nice figure. But I see more, too. I see the face of all women in your face. And I see what all women see in themselves in your face. Not so beautiful as to intimidate them, and certainly not unattractive. Your face sets the tone or serves as proof that you are who you want me to think you are. It's an honest face. Sure your face is one of the tools you have just like the good mind you have. You may not have a piece of paper to say you are educated, but you are. Hell, you could pass an equivalence exam in a minute and still have brains left over. You have an uncanny knowledge of everything. You have style. It shows in your personality, your body language and your manners. It's not the style that nice clothes provide. Your style comes from within you. It's not something you put on each morning, it is already there. You don't have to wear tight sweaters and skirts to get attention. You could get attention in my blue jeans. It's the mind, not the clothes or figure that makes a lady more than just a woman. Style, brains, good looks, a great body, elegance, security, self-reliance, determination, amazement, eagerness, I see all that in you. Some models are face models and some are clothes mannequins. Face models have what you have, a face men love and women like. They can be too heavy for mannequin modeling but still make it very well with

Call Me Maggie

their face. Mannequins need the bones and body first, and the face second. Whether it's a face or a body she is modeling, a good model recognizes that she has what the photographer needs and trusts him to use her for the benefit of both."

"Am I a model or a mannequin?"

Norman paused and thought before answering.

"I know from looking at these pictures you can perform as a mannequin, and I see a good face for photography. I guess I would call you mannequin with a photogenic face. Six months from now you can be a stewardess with a modeling career as well."

"Where do you want your photography to take you?"

"I enjoy my work. It beats picking cotton, hoeing weeds or following a mule all day as we did on the farm."

"I mean do you want to remain a newspaper photographer or move in to another area of photography like Vogue, Playboy or one of the other magazines?"

"I could enjoy it for a while, but I would burn out doing it every day. The same subjects would become boring. I couldn't make eye catchers every day. I'm lucky if I can make one a week now. As long as I can make good pictures like these, I'll be happy working on the paper and doing pictures like these in my free time. Photographing you was a real treat for me."

"Someday you may burn out photographing me. Will you find someone else? Maybe Linda? Maybe one or two of the models you use in the newspaper or ones you used before we met?"

"If I ever photograph Linda, it won't be the way I photograph you. She's attractive enough, but she is very different from you. She is more like a little sister. I have watched her grow from a skinny little bean pole into a full-blown young woman. Maggie, you are a rare blossom. Other young women are only pretty flowers. You are going places in your life. You don't have the hang-ups other girls have. You are bold and you go for things that most other young women are afraid to think about attempting. I want to be there and record your attempts and accomplishments with my camera. I want photograph you in your classes, at home studying, and flying. And I want to take more than nudes of you. I also want to capture the other facets of you, too, whether it's walking along the beach, shopping in thrift shop or dozing on the sofa."

Norman had said many things about photography and gave Maggie many insights into him and into herself. She wanted to know more. She listened to his every word.

Dirty Money

It took them more than an hour to put dots on the sheets. Her eyes examined the composition of each image as though she were a seasoned editor, although her technical knowledge fell short of where she wanted it to be. She would increase her input in future sessions. And there would be future modeling sessions and discussions as long as Norman wanted to photograph her. As Maggie viewed the photographs, she saw pictures that included her bare body and the face everyone could see was hers, but she did not see herself. She saw images that included a beautiful young woman modeling who could have been any woman willing to trust a photographer who cared about his model as much as getting pictures without underlying motives.

"Are these first nudes you have taken?"

"No. They are my first I've taken in a long time."

"I suspected that last night was the first time for you. All you pleases and thank you made led me to think you were nervous. You should not be. You've photographed other girl's nude. You have seen me naked. It doesn't bother me that you see me again and it should not bother you. I am the same person naked that I am when I'm dressed. I want to be in those books you will publish some day, naked or not. You said I have the face, body, and hair you want for your pictures. Use me anytime you have a picture idea. It's not something you'll be forcing me to do. I want to model for you."

Norman sat staring at her for a moment saying nothing.

"Some guys think that once a model is naked, they can have her for other things, too. A girl can want a good picture taken of herself naked as much as the photographer wants to take the picture. Modeling nude is not an invitation for anything except picture taking."

"I know, but convincing a girl that's all I want is difficult and up until now, impossible."

"It's not impossible with me, Norman. Neither you nor I want to make any pictures that would be vulgar. I've had the chance and had to fight the guy off. It's not something I want to do again."

"You won't have to fight me off," he replied. "Some models pose and are ready to jump in bed whether the photographer wants to or not. A few I have known were that way. Mostly they just wanted to make love and forget about the pictures I was trying to get. That's not the kind of model I want to work with."

"After they drew squares on all the proofs, Maggie said, "If you want to make love tonight, we will make love. If we are making photographs, we will make photographs. Lovemaking will come later. Now

71

let's have some tea and sit on the sofa until you are ready to take more pictures, make love, or go home,"

"We won't be making love tonight."

Norman set Maggie thinking and questioning. He could have taken her, but instead he had planted an idea within her rather than defile her as other men had. Was it because of the other men had that he did not ravish her. He said it was not and she had believed him, now she was not so sure and new doubts had risen.

Maggie led him to the sofa, removed his shoes, and told him to lay down let her lay beside him, then snuggled close. When he tried to speak, she placed a finger over his lips. He wondered why he had never spent a night with Michele as had spent the last three with Maggie. Why had he never met anyone like Maggie before? She was so free, so unrestrained, and so trusting. She had trusted him more than the police safe house. She allowed him to bring her to his apartment. She had trusted him to photograph her, even without clothes. She trusted him again, allowing him to lay with her. Was she allowing him to lay with her hoping he would put his hand on her chest again? If that were the case, she would have removed her clothes. She said she slept nude. Should he put them on her breast and see if she left them there. And if she did not remove them, what would it mean? Would she still be interested in him and his photography when she became a stewardess? These questions were asked again, and again, before sleep overcame him.

Norman woke up before six. Maggie still lay snuggled in his arms. She had slept in her clothes. When tried to get up, she pulled him back down and asked, "Does it really not matter that I have made love to other men?"

"I told you it did not and it still does not."

"Do you have any ideas for pictures today?"

"At the moment only a hundred or so."

"When would you like to shoot them, now or after we have breakfast? If you want flowers on your pancakes, you'll have to run outside and pick some."

Norman lifted his camera and began photographing her. Later in the morning, they drove to a farm auction near St Georges, Delaware instead of taking a walk on the beach or touring thrift shops or second hand stores. As she found more articles to decorate her apartment, he found new facets of her for his camera to capture. He photographed her examining articles she found interesting, and the expressions on her face as she made her discoveries, and as she competed with others bidders.

Dirty Money

Maggie was particularly taken by a young white mare. He snapped candid pictures with as Maggie petted and hugged the horse. When an Amish man bought the horse led the mare away, Norman photographed the disappointment in her face, ran after the man, and wrote a few lines in the notepad he carried.

As they took her treasures to the car, Maggie said, "Save that note. Someday I may take that mare home with me, too."

After dropping Maggie off, Norman went home, freshened up and went to work. Crossing the newsroom, he met his picture editor.

"Come into my office after you drop your bag in the lab. I've got some things to go over with you,"

Within two minutes, Norman entered the office where dozens of photographs were spread on a table. File trays held stacks of type written pages. A coffee mug held sharpened lead pencils and several red grease markers. Two plastic cropping squares resembling large "L"s lay next to the mug. A three-part typed page lay over the photographs. A police radio monitor squealed and sputtered static.

"Let's go over your assignments together," the editor said, as he straightened himself from bending over the table.

Norman took a position alongside the editor and adjusted his eyeglasses. Another pair of thicker glasses lay on the three-part page. The editor lifted the glasses and the page, tore off the top sheet, and passed it to Norman.

"We have a lot going on the next few days. Here is what we need from you," the editor continued. "Can you work this Saturday?"

"Sure," Norman answered.

"Good. Let's get today and Friday out of the way first. I need half dozen shots of the old Greenbank Mill. The county officials are going to restore it and turn the area around it into an historical park. Need some shots of it inside and out, the land around it, the waterwheel and the raceway. Jack is putting together a map that will be used with the story and pictures. It will be the second news front lead on Saturday." his editor said.

"The water wheel is still there, but it's in pretty bad shape. And the raceway is full of tires and trash," Norman said, having seen the mill often since his father's home was just half mile from the mill.

"Get me a couple of eye catchers on the wheel so I can play it big," the editor said. "At 7 o'clock you and Judy Rawlins go to check out a safe house the police have set-up for crime victims. She's the best reporter for the story since most of the residents are women."

73

Call Me Maggie

"Don't let her hear you call her Judy. She wants to be called Judith." Norman chuckled as he reminded the editor of Judith's name preference.

"I know. She put me on notice a few days ago," the editor chuckled with Norman. "Any questions about today's jobs?"

"Yes, how about faces in the safe house. Are we shooting police people posing as victims or will they be real victims?"

"They will be victims. Keep them unidentified. Come up with some symbolic stuff, but no faces on this one, Norman. You know what I need," the editor said.

"I know." Norman did not mention his knowledge of the safe houses.

"For the next few days, get me some shots of the progress on the Interstate. We will be using that on Page One, Saturday. It is a big story. We will have a second larger feature on "95" for Memorial Day weekend. Shoot lots of film on that whenever you can between now and then. I'm asking the rest of the guys to shoot it too," the editor kept referring to his now two-part list. "Since you attended Wilmington High School, I'm assigning you to cover their graduation Friday afternoon at three and we will print that Saturday morning also. I am putting Bob and Robert on P.S DuPont, Claymont, New Castle and Newark. Get me a variety of shots. I want to feature them all, but you know how it works, the best pictures get published."

"You got it, Chief," Norman answered.

"Are you sure you want to work Saturday? I can send Robert or one of the others." the editor asked.

"I can make it."

"Good. Here is the way I see it. Pick up a plane Saturday morning. I have already reserved it for you. It's a Cessna 182, heavier and faster than those kites you usually rent. And I called John Choma. He needs the hours and will be your pilot. Photograph the Interstate from the Maryland line to the Pennsylvania line and all in between. You know, bridges, overpasses, interchanges, the toll booths and get me some shots as it goes through Wilmington. Get lots of Wilmington shots showing how the city will change when the interstate bisects it. While you're over the city, get a shot of Rodney Square facing the Hercules Tower going up behind the library. Lighting on that one will be tough. It faces north. There are two apartment buildings nearly as tall going up west of the interstate. Make a pass or two by them and show the way they look from the air," the editor said.

Dirty Money

"Anything else, Chief?"

"While you have the plane, fly on down to Rehoboth. Get me a shot of the U.S 13 bridge just north of Odessa and the intersection on the south side of Dover where "13-A" crosses U.S. 13. Then get me a few shots at the beach. There should have some people on them now that warm weather is here. After that, rent a car, got into Rehoboth Beach and get some shots of college students getting the town ready for summer. Dinner for you and John are on the tab. Eat light. I'm giving you the plane and a rent-a-car for the day. That should keep you and John out of trouble on Saturday."

The editor completed his list as Norman squirmed.

"Is a two pound Henlopen lobster light enough, Chief?" Norman asked with a grin.

"Get out of here and don't call me Chief.

The editor threatened Norman with a grease marker making an "X" sign in the air over the table of photographs.

Norman returned to the photo department, grabbed two bulk packs of film and was soon on his way to his mill assignment. The top on Norman's Chevy was down and music from four speakers filled the car. The song "I'm Moving On" was all Norman noticed.

A workman riding a lawn mower was cutting grass on the two acre lot surrounding the stone and mortar mill structure. Norman photographed the man in a wide panorama of the acreage. He made photographs of a dozen more views that including the raceway leaving and returning to Red Clay Creek. He spent another half hour photographing the water wheel. Norman tested the lock on the mill's door and found it unlocked. He entered the building. Inside, he saw and photographed long leather belts connecting various stones, sifters, and milling machinery to the shaft coming out of the wall from the water outside. Tools of all sorts hung from wooden pegs throughout the building. Norman remembered seeing his father and uncles using similar tools back in Alabama. His two uncles still used many old and worn-out implements today as they scraped and scratched, attempting hang on to their little farms as his father and grandfather had done as well.

Oblique sunlight beams shot down through dust and cobwebs onto a dustier floor. Some light beams ended on footprints in the floor. The scene was much the same on the second floor where burlap and linen bags sat waiting to be delivered for nearly a half a century. The metal roof had kept them dry all the years. As Norman made photographs of the bags, he remembered trips to the gristmill in Alabama that

Call Me Maggie

he visited Saturday afternoons with his father and Ernest where farmers would gather, share gossip and news while waiting for their corn to be ground into meal for their homemade cornbread. After ninety minutes Norman stepped back into the twentieth century and drove up the hill from the mill to his parent's home, half-a-mile away. Loraine's two sons were in the yard, almost hidden under the full-leafed umbrella of the dogwood tree standing in the lawn. He moved the Lexica from his shoulder and made photographs of the boys and the tree. Then he spent a few minutes with the boys and their Tonka trucks under the hemisphere of leaves reaching almost to the lawn. Kevin was tinkering and tweaking Ernest's racecar. A few more shots were made of Kevin's greasy face and hands as he continued working on the car before Norman asked, "Are going to Linda's graduation Friday?"

"I will be there and at the party for her a while that Mom is holding here before I go to work."

"I've got an assignment to photograph the graduation. I'll make sure to get a few shots in her cap and gown. Too bad you'll miss some of the party."

"Yep," Kevin came back.

"What's up? You seem to be down," Norman asked, sensing that his brother's spirit was low.

"I saw the picture on Maggie's refrigerator. Do you two have a thing starting?" Kevin asked without looking up.

"No, but I am taking pictures of her. I thought you had your eyes on her."

"I did, but she won't go out with me."

"That's too bad. Maybe she will change her mind."

"Maybe," Kevin answered in a slightly higher spirit.

"Look, little brother, I hope it works out. I'll probably see you at Linda's graduation. I'm going to miss the party too, unless I come after work. Right now I've got to process the film in my camera before going my evening assignments."

As he left, Norman sidestepped back to his nephews playing under the tree's canopy umbrella. He spent a few more minutes with the boys and hopped over the picket fence gate as he left. Before he reached the highway he was already wondering about the triangle of Maggie, Kevin and himself. Should he continue seeing Maggie and come between his brother and her or should he let Maggie handle Kevin in her own way? No matter which way the triangle broke up, he wanted to make more photographs of her.

Dirty Money

Norman took the Kirkwood Highway back to the city. At the intersection of Fourth and Union Streets Norman came upon an automobile accident. A white Pontiac convertible with temporary tags lay upside down in the intersection.

Rescuers had raised the convertible slightly to get inside. A Hurst tool, resembling giant oversized scissors was being used to pry a door open. Two rescue squad members removed contents of the vehicle while two others worked hastily with scissor-like tool nicknamed of "jaws-of-life." But they were too late. Three young people were removed and covered with sheets. Three red gowns and three white "mortar boards" lay in the same intersection where Kevin had turned south after dropping off Linda Monday night. Norman spied Linda in the spectator crowd as he photographed the wreck and rescuers, but she left before he could finish and say hello. She had heard the impact a half block away in her parents shop.

He added the accident film to his processing duties back at the photo lab, made proofs of each roll and delivered the contacts to his news editor. A few minutes later, Norman received the contact sheet containing the accident pictures with six frames surrounded by red grease marker. He opted to skip dinner and dialed "MARYANN" on the phone in the darkened print room. A cheerful hello told him she was home. The two talked about Maggie's day and Norman's mill pictures. The accident was not discussed.

"Why don't you drop by for coffee when you finish?"

"I have a job to photograph and process. It would be too late."

"Even if it's midnight, it won't be too late, Norman."

"We'll see, but I will be pretty late."

Norman and Judith Rawlins arrived at the safe house after a short drive in his car. Judith asked her journalistic battery of questions. He made a number of pictures always making sure the subject's face was obscure in some way. One of the final shots he made was of a sleeping girl in a worn and torn dress sleeping as an armed guard stood in the background. The photographer and reporter returned to office. She wrote of their assignment while he prepared a visual record and left in the Photo Editor's office.

In a final check, Norman told the editor he would like to leave and look for some night-time pictures of the interstate. The editor approved and suggested Norman take plenty of the new highly sensitive film in the supply cabinet. He packed ten rolls high speed film and 20 rolls of regular film in his bag, and spent the next 90 minutes making

Call Me Maggie

night shots along the construction route. He even made a couple of shots of Kevin and a grease truck operator preparing Kevin's dirt pan for a night's hauling on the graveyard shift. The grease man's presence kept Norman from a conversation he yearned to finish with Kevin. By midnight he was on his way northward on U.S. 13 to the city and saw the light in Maggie's kitchen was still burning.

"She's too frugal to leave a light on, she's still up. I should call first, but I'll stop in anyway," he told himself.

A quick turn and a moment later, he was knocking on door A-300 and shocked when Linda opened the door and said "Hi Norman. Not too late for a date, eah?"

"Not too late for coffee with two lovely girls," Norman said recovering quickly.

Maggie heard Linda greet him and then quartered the sandwiches she prepared for two. A moment later she brought three plates to the table, each with pansy blossoms along the edge and three glasses with rose petals floating in each.

"Hi Norman. I told you midnight wasn't too late."

A little before 1 A.M., Linda said "If one of you will drive me home, shakes are on me at The Greenhill Drive-In,"

"I will," Maggie and Norman answered at the same time.

In a flash the three cruised into the Greenhill Drive-in restaurant in Newport. Norman's red ragtop longer by two feet and the continental caught the late night cruising crowd's eyes. Having Linda riding shotgun and Maggie in the middle, Norman's post mid-night cruise uplifted his spirits dramatically.

Many of the drive-in customers, including Linda, seemed to know everyone in every car. Most of the celebrants would receive their high school diplomas the next day. Linda lingered at several cars, and waved at others cruising through with horns blowing and radios blasting. Norman and Maggie sipped their milkshakes and watched the crowd. A few crowd members came by to ask questions and have close-up looks at Norman's car

On the way back to Maggie's apartment, he suggested they walk along the Delaware River before taking her home. Maggie agreed. They parked on an old ferry boat pier in New Castle and walked about in Battery Park. Norman asked Maggie if she had ever seen submarine races in the river near Chester or Philadelphia. She said no. Submarine races were held only under a full moon even though many young people came to park on other nights even if the moon was not seen, he ex-

78

plained, straining to hold his laughter after none appeared. He promised to bring her back to the park on the June full moon for races just off the pier. She said yes and promised she would hold him to a return visit with or without a full moon.

A low flying plane inbound to the Philadelphia airport gave Norman another idea to present to Maggie. He pondered the thought only an instant before asking, "Miss Johnson, will you come flying with me Saturday morning,?"

"I love to. But I have got to warn you, I have never been in an airplane before."

"Starting stewardess school in two weeks and you've never flown. You gotta be kidding me."

"No, it's true. Not even been in one on the ground. It never occurred to me even though I have wanted to be a stewardess for years."

"We'll do something about that Saturday. And bring a bathing suit! You'll have time for a little sunbathing while I'm doing shots of the summer workers getting the town ready for summer."

"Count me in."

Norman asked if she would reload for him during the flight. Using his Leica, he gave her quick instructions on loading the camera. After a few tries, she had the knack. The two walked and talked until the sun rose over the river providing Norman another picture of his new model.

Norman reported the office early, one third short of his usual six hours sleep. He located a copy of the morning's paper featuring a short, wide photograph, caption and headline appeared across the bottom of page one. "Three Students Die in Auto Accident," was the headline. In the picture, rescuers were loading a stretcher into an ambulance, other rescuers were removing a student from the overturned automobile, caps and gowns lay in the foreground. Linda could be seen among the crowd in the picture's background. For a few moments Norman relived emotions he felt the previous day at the accident scene knowing that Kevin used the same intersection going to and from Linda's home.

Kevin read the newspaper's account before tinkering, tweaking, and sleeping.

A phone call to John Choma assured John that an afternoon and dinner in Rehoboth would make points with his wife, Carmella. Norman insisted John bring her. John gave Norman a maybe and Norman gave John a quick itinerary for Saturday's assignments and fight destinations

Call Me Maggie

Norman arrived at Linda's graduation ceremony early enough to photograph proud parents primping the graduates and posing for family snapshots. He found Linda and her parents, and he photographed them performing the graduation rituals. One frame contained their three heads pulled tight together by Linda's arms over each parents shoulder. Linda eyes looked upward to the tassel on the mortarboard. Norman made another "tight shot" of Linda and Kevin's heads. Maggie was giving Linda's cap a slight tilt in the shot Norman made of the two young women. Delaware's Governor stepped behind a black ribboned podium for his featured speaker address in the somber ceremony. Three empty chair backs on the stage had matching ribbons above folded red gowns topped by white mortar boards. Norman finished the assignment with shots of three pairs of parents receiving diplomas their children had earned plus the caps and gowns from the ribbon crossed chairs. His final photograph contained 312 mortarboards sailing over the Wilmington High School class of 1962.

Driving back to the office Norman noticed a particularly interesting cloud formation in the rear-view mirror of the car. He parked the car and photographed the steeple of a church against the clouds reflected in his car mirror. At the office he went through the ritual of processing, proofing, and printing his record of the day's events. Once the needs of Saturday morning paper were met, he made prints of the grease penciled images of personal pictures of Linda's graduation, then made prints of Kevin's oil covered face hands. The final exposure Norman enlarged slowly turned from all white to an image of his nephews under the dogwood leafed umbrella.

The Kennedy clan's party for Linda was still going on when he opened the white picket gate as Norman had hoped. Long tables along the side fence of Kennedy yard held sandwich from the Reed shop, vegetables from the garden and a few of Pop Pop Kennedy's early roses. Numerous chairs filled the lawn near the dogwood tree. Farm lanterns and kerosene lamps flickered from several locations. Norman greeted everyone including his nephews. He passed out envelopes containing pictures to his parents and Linda's parents. Then he gave Kevin, Maggie, and Loraine envelopes as he circulated through the crowd on his parent's lawn.

By 9:30, Norman still had not found the right moment to talk to Kevin when he left the celebration for his dirt pan driving duties nor had Linda found an opportunity for her girl talk with Maggie. The older Reeds asked Maggie for a ride back to town in her two person one seat

Dirty Money

Nash, but Norman interceded. He, Maggie, Linda and her parents cruised into town in the convertible with the top down.

"We never thought we would live to see this day," Mr. Reed stated. "Linda was a blessed event we received very late in our lives. Now she's all grown up and out of school."

As Norman returned Maggie to her car, she said "I wish it had been me instead of Linda graduating today. Well that's not right. I wish I were graduating today also."

"It's not too late. Most schools have night classes for students who have dropped out."

"I know and I have been thinking about it recently. I have stewardess school to worry about first."

"Maggie, you can do anything. By the way, you might want to bring a dinner dress tomorrow. We can have dinner in Rehoboth with John Coma and his wife, Carmella."

"Follow me home and I'll show you what I have."

"Okay, but I won't stay long. The plane's reserved for eight o'clock in the morning."

He lead the way, Maggie followed. As they traveled east on Basin Road between Newport and the airport, Norman suddenly pulled off the road and Maggie followed. He used the car's trunk as support while he made pictures of a dirt pan dropping its load on the roadbed with the skyline on the background horizon. Within a half hour they were in Maggie's apartment. She held dresses pulled from her clothes rack before herself and ask which Norman liked. He clicked shots of each as he answered. Soon a small suitcase with clothes, shoes, and a small grooming kit for the next day was packed.

"Take me back to your place with you, please Norman."

"Alright, Maggie."

Shortly after they entered his apartment, Norman interrupted his packing to set an alarm clock. When his clothes on hangers had been hung with Maggie's, his camera bags and shoes set at the rack's feet, he took his spot on the sofa and pointed his knees to Maggie. Her shoes joined Norman's and she pointed her knees to him.

"I enjoyed the ceremony and the party your parents gave for Linda. It's too bad you missed most of it. It was a nice party. You would have enjoyed it."

"Working nights, I go to a lot of parties, but I always seem to miss out on the most important ones in my own life, the ones given for birthdays and anniversaries."

Call Me Maggie

"I think her parents were pleased. Of course they could have decorated the sandwich shop and held it there, but it would not have been the same. It's a shame Kevin could not spend more time with her. Linda has it all out for him. She practically said so tonight before you came. Kevin was quiet and withdrawn all evening. I think I made him as uncomfortable as I make Lionel."

"I've been trying to have a talk with Kevin for a couple of days. Maybe I'll catch up with him on Sunday. I wanted to today but I was rushed and he was working on the racecar. I'm going over there for Mother's Day. Maybe we can talk then."

"What do you want to talk to him about?"

"About this triangle between the three of us, he wants to date you but he thinks you want to date me and I don't know where I stand with you or with Michele. It's a situation that could hurt each of us."

"I have told him where I stand with him. What did you tell him about you and me?" Maggie continued her questions.

"I haven't actually told him anything about us. But I believe he thinks you and I are an item. He saw the picture on your refrigerator and I told him I was shooting more of you."

"Are we an item? I thought you and Michele were an item."

"We were, but I think it's over. I stood her up Tuesday night and she was not a happy camper."

"I'm sorry I caused you to miss seeing her. Did you mention anything about me to her?"

"Not a word was mentioned about you or the pictures we made."

"Do you think it will get better with you and Michele?"

"I don't know. I know I'd rather spend evenings with you than with her."

"I like my evenings with you too, Norman. But I want what's best for everybody. I don't want to come between you and Michele or between Linda and Kevin."

"She has liked him for years, but he couldn't see her except as one of the guys. She really cares for him."

"Where does that put you and me, Norman?"

"Monday night I met you when you were coming out of an ugly situation. Tuesday night I photographed beautiful pictures of you baring your body and yourself to me. Wednesday we went over proofs of that session and talked more. Last night we talked all night and I finally became at ease with you. It's the same tonight. I am glad you are here. Tomorrow I want you to see me doing my photography in other ways. Each time we're together, it's not time spent bragging and bantering. It's quality time. I don't really know how to be with a girl except to make pictures or discuss medicine or photography. I have had real conversations with you. Maggie I don't know where I stand with you except when I photograph you. I don't want to see you just to photograph you or go over the proofs. I want to share more with you than just photography. But on the other hand, I don't want you to be with me for the usual guy and girl reasons. You have more to offer than that. You have a new lease on life. You got yourself into school and I don't want to get in the way. Don't let me or anyone else steer you away from that. Yet I can't walk away from you. I guess that's where I stand."

"Norman, you are an inspiration to me. You encourage me. You support me and my dream. You are kind and considerate to me. I don't feel like a mannequin for your pictures or a partner for your bed. I left an ugly life this week and found a beautiful new one. You are a large part of that new one. I won't let you interfere in my schooling, but I won't leave you out of my new life either. I want you to have a large part of it and if you want me, you can have me too."

"We have talked about that before. I want you as a friend and as a model more than a lover. When your classes start, you won't have time for either."

"I'll make time."

"Not with me if it interferes with your lesson and training. I have waited years to find a model like you. Three more months won't make much difference."

"Then let's make the most of the time I have before my classes begin. Keep lots of film on hand and your cameras close by."

Call Me Maggie

3

City Girl, Farm Boy

John was making the pre-flight check when Norman and Maggie approached the ramp at the Wilmington Airport. Carmella carried two bags to the plane. One was marked St. Elizabeth High School. The other was marked Salesanium Academy. Norman assumed they brought dinner clothes and a bathing suit in their old schoolbags. Maggie carried her overnight case plus a hanging bag. Norman carried two camera bags plus a gym bag.

Maggie could not tell if Carmella knew of John's previous introduction to her and greeted Johns wife cautiously when greetings were exchanged between the foursome.

John put the hanging clothes and bags in the plane's luggage compartment while Norman placed one camera bag on floor in front and another between the seats. The two long time friends had flown many times so Norman knew the routine.

"I'll try to keep it right side up for you, Maggie," John kidded after learning this was her first light.

With a few more checks, the women climbed in back before Norman and John boarded the plane. Soon they were in the air flying parallel to the interstate headed south-bound. Maggie felt and uncomfortable ear pressure and began trying to get relief rubbing them. Carmella gave Maggie chewing gum. Norman made exposures of various points: two large interchanges plus the tollbooth and rest area, all near Newark. He made a few shots as the plane circled an interchange adjacent to the Cecil County Airport just over the border in Maryland.

Carmella shared views of sites recognized including the University of Delaware stadium and campus, just off the interstate. Norman was too busy making pictures to enter the girl's conversation. John kept himself occupied flying the plane at a low but save altitude while look-

Call Me Maggie

ing for other aircraft and a landing site should the plane have an emergency. Three four lane highways and two grassy areas in city parks were his choices.

"This is not what I expected. Everything is small from up here," Maggie observed.

"That's Delaware Park horse racing track." Carmella said.

On the northbound leg, Norman photographed other identifiable points on the interstate's route not be easily shown in ground level photographs. Sometimes the city skyline appeared in the background. They continued on to the Pennsylvania line and reversed their flight.

"Let's go around again," Norman ask John so he could photograph the tower and right of way bisecting the city.

A moment later they flew over Minquadale yard where heavy equipment was stored. Normally the equipment was kept moving about twenty-three hours each day and the yard was empty except during driver changes and maintenance.

"That where Kevin and Ernest work," Norman said, as the pace of his picture taking slowed.

The equipment yard sat along an access road off the interstate leading to the Delaware Memorial Bridge and into New Jersey. Norman's shots included the connecting the interstate to the bridge which would be paved into four lanes. When Norman felt confident that he had his interstate shots, he directed John to follow U.S.13 south. In the rural areas south of the city, farmers were cutting hay or planting late spring crops. John kept a special watch for agricultural aircraft spraying the fields. An oil refinery east of the highway was his next shot.

At the bridge just north of Odessa they circled while Norman made shots of it. A wide angle showed the highway, bridge, and little town of Odessa in the background. A twenty acre horse farm separated the town and bridge on the west side of the highway. A line of trees stood between the farm and creek on two sides from the highway on back. Norman made a shot of the farm for his personal file.

"I wouldn't mind owning that little farm. But I'll have to shoot a lot more film first," Norman advised the others.

All during the flight Maggie was busy feeding cameras and lenses to Norman. She had no trouble reloading the cameras even when the closely spaced shots of the interstate were being made.

South of Odessa the plane's path followed the river until a point just east and north of Dover and flew even lower than before. Startled birds joined the plane in the air from their terrestrial or aquatic resting places. Deer and cattle fled from the passing plane. As they flew over the Capital city, Norman's camera kept clicking away. Just south of the city he made shots of the intersection crossing his picture editor had requested. Four-lane U.S.13 ran northeast to southwest across the north and south two lane U.S.113. East of the intersection lay Dover Air Force Base and its fleet of C-133 Globemaster cargo planes.

"Usually there more planes on the ground, but some of them are on trips to Germany or the Far East. They carry mostly cargo. No stewardess on cargo planes, and if they do they are called stewards and are all male servicemen."

"They are so big," Maggie exclaimed.

"Not too much bigger than the ones you'll be flying on."

From Dover they flew on toward Milford and another intersection on the list. John gave an "AgCat" spraying peas plenty of air space. Just north of the little town, highway U.S. 113 split and U.S. 113-A led travelers to the ocean resorts while 113 traversed down the center of the peninsula. After he finished in Milford, Norman requested they fly out to river again. He photographed a red and white light house stood at the mouth of the stream John followed out of Milford, made shots of ocean going oil tankers too large to continue upstream unloading their oil to be barged northward. Just south of the tankers, Cape Henlopen jutted out like a large finger where the bay emptied into the Atlantic Ocean. The bay was on the west side of the cape and the ocean on the right. One lone fisherman standing on the fingertip of land was included in one of Norman's photographs. He made another shot of two hikers on a long lonely stretch of beach south of the cape.

"That place is so beautiful," Maggie exclaimed again.

"You should see it up close and on the ground."

They flew southward as Norman made pictures of Rehoboth Beach and some of the changes made since the last vacation season. A few early season sunbathers were on the beach. After the flight down the beach, Norman announced he had finished his list. The final flight leg brought back old memories to John. Before entering the Police Academy, John had spent two summers towing signs behind a small plane flying over the water in front of the resort town. A few minutes later, John put the plane down on Rehoboth Beach's grassy runway, just as he done with the tow plane many times before.

"Thank you for my first flight. And John thank you especially for not letting the airplane turn upside down."

Call Me Maggie

"We're not home yet, Maggie. Maybe it will on the way back," John kidded her.

"I'm ready for lunch," the tired and hungry photographer said. "Is anyone else ready to eat?"

Norman rented his car and the four drove into the resort. As they ate, all agreed to meet at the bath house where John and Carmella planned to change into beachwear.

"See you at six o'clock. Meanwhile I have to find some working college students," he said as lunch ended.

Maggie stayed close to Norman while he searched for resort workers. Within two hours he had interviewed and photographed more than a dozen summertime "beachies."

"We have three hours until dinner. Would you like to swim?" Norman asked Maggie. "We can get you changed in the bath house."

"I didn't bring a swimsuit, but I would like to walk up where we saw the man fishing on the cape."

Soon prolonged gasps filled Maggie with salt laden fragrances of beach plum and wild flowers as Norman led her down a sand-fenced corridor to the cape's bay side beach. A gentle wind pushed an even gentler mist from the rippling bay across the surf and onto the shore. Millions of yellow, orange and red candle-like sparkles flickered on wave tops that rolled over Maggie's bare toes in the damp sand. Small white eddies swirled under lifted heals. Waves lapped her skirt. Water and wind played their duet for her. Unseen delight boiled within her. Pleasure effervesced from her every pore. Waterside stimulants inundated each of her senses. The pupae within her metamorphosed. The butterfly emerged. She swirled and spun, danced and pranced, leaped and laughed, as strawberry tresses masked and unmasked her face in the wind. She wrapped herself in her own arms and danced gently with surf. The skirt and her hair hesitated in midair as her dancing legs leaped for Norman's camera. She puckered as her own wind blew sand from sea shells to be more thoroughly inspected by her eyes. Her ears sought sounds reverberating from long evacuated conch. Norman's camera followed her as artifacts came under her inspection. Smooth pebbles the color of turquoise, amber, ruby, tan, black, white or clear were collected for future examination. A feather rubbed her chin. Textured driftwood, scalloped fans, and numerous spiral shells succumbed to the touch. The camera and film captured all the scenes she played out before a panorama of sea, sand and surf. Unconsciously impassioned with discovery, Maggie rambled up the shore line, drawn toward the cape, seeking and savoring even greater pleasures on the appendage of sand. An increasing line of footprints followed them northward to the cape's tip. She had known only one other pleasure that awaken her senses more, a pleasure she longed to share with Norman. Would she share it today?

"I have never felt so good. Thank you for inviting me and sharing this with me. I had no idea a place like this existed. I have only seen the beaches at Atlantic City and Wildwood. This is nothing like those beaches. No noise and no crowds kicking and in my face. Just you, me, the sand, surf, and birds."

"Sometimes I come here alone. Thank you for coming with me today. I'm glad you are here."

Without waiting for Norman's acknowledgment, she removed her clothes, hung them on dune plum bush and returned to the water. Thousands of droplets surrounded her as waves broke upon her back. Lowering herself to the waist, Maggie posed, and reposed. Lowering more, floating hair surrounded the island that was her head. Wet hair draped her swollen breasts. She spun the hair around her head. Hair lashed her face as she froze herself facing the camera and for her own intense pleasure. She rolled and twisted into ever changing positions in the surf, and on the dry sand of a small dune. Silica clung to her. She became an animated sand sculpture, striking one pose, then another.

Maggie ran to the water, dove under the waves, and returned. Miniature river-ettes cascaded from her hair down into the valley of her chest. She moved damp strawberry blonde tresses behind her shoulders exposing uncountable droplets clinging to her breasts. Norman's camera clicked, capturing the facets that changed and then changed again until the luster dulled and a sheepish pride enveloped both. Both knew the other was enjoying their stroll on the cape's beach.

"Let's make love here. You don't have to seduce me. The cape already has," she stated, then locked him in an embrace beneath an orange sun over the western horizon.

"It has the same effect on me, sunrise or sunset, winter or summer, but I can't. I didn't bring you here to seduce you."

Maggie stepped into her briefs and skirt. Her arms reached into blouse arms that soaked moisture from her water covered torso leaving her upper womanly attributes covered but still visible.

For the past all too short hours Maggie and Norman had a piece of the world all to themselves to observe, explore, savor, and enjoy. As evening neared, a pair of footprint trails in the sand would attest

Call Me Maggie

to their presence until the moon rose and the tide came in and washed all away except their memories and the pictures in Norman's camera.

The high tide of Saturday's lunch crowd had ebbed in the Reed's Submarine Shop. Linda dialed 999-1999 on the shop telephone. Loraine's husband took the call and went to the garage where Kevin, Ernest and Ernest's girlfriend busied themselves with the racer. Both planned to drive that afternoon, but it would not be jockeying a dirt pan.

"Kevin, Linda wants you on the phone," he said as he and his can of beer joined his sons near the dogwood tree.

Kevin cleaned his hands en-route to the telephone. In a few moments he returned.

"Linda wants to come with us. That's if one of us will go and get her," he announced after the telephone conversation.

"Good, I'll have someone to sit with me. I'll go get her." Ernest's girlfriend replied.

"Let's hook this baby to the tow bar. I'm anxious to see how she runs." Ernest said.

"Better load the tools first," Kevin advised the two.

The second and third Kennedy brothers closed their father's Craftsman chest, carried it to the family station wagon and slid it in the space a third seat usually occupied. Ernest's girlfriend drove into the city while the brothers linked the racecar to the station wagon; two pushed, Ernest steered.

The brothers came out of the garage with clean jeans and black tee shirts as the two girls arrived.

"Anybody forget anything?" Ernest asked.

"Not me," his girlfriend said.

"Me neither," Linda replied.

"Nope," Kevin said after reviewing his mental checklist.

"We're off to the races," Ernest concluded as his girlfriend took the hump and waited for him to tak the driver's seat of the station wagon next to her while Kevin and Linda rode in back. The rear hump divided them from the vacant other half.

Cecil County Dragway was opening eits season. The brothers did not want to miss the day. If they worked on Saturday, they would race in Atco, New Jersey on Sunday. If they finished well, they might race both days.

"Anybody got any gum?" Ernest asked as his tension mounted.

"I have Juicy Fruit," his girlfriend answered.

"Mine's Spearmint," Linda added.

City Girl, Farm Boy

"I'll have a stick of yours, Linda. Juicy Fruit is too sweet for me," Ernest said.

They discussed the plans and strategies during the 20 mile drive. Their plan was that each would take turns in the practice sessions and the one with the best time would compete in the races. The girls offered their suggestions too.

"You ran a good time on River Road," his hump rider said patting him on the leg.

Neither of the four had raced on a track, but all had tested the car on a long and straight flat road near Newark or at night-time along River Road prior to submarine races off New Castle.

The foursome arrived at the drag way, checked in, and each made practice runs. The girls kept notes for the brothers. Little tweaks were performed between runs. Ernest had good times, but Kevin had the best times with a good third and a better final run. They had not considered this outcome. A coin was flipped and Ernest became the competition driver.

"We had better go to the bleachers," the girlfriend suggested.

"Not me, I staying here to be with Kevin." Linda stated.

The boys stayed with the car and the girlfriend sat alone in the station wagon rather than in the bleachers.

Kevin didn't need to perform any more tweaking on the engine. Instead both rubbed and cleaned the Ford while nervously waiting.

"Ernest and I are getting engaged tomorrow. But don't tell anybody until after he gives me the ring," the girlfriend announced.

"I won't tell," Linda promised.

Ernest was called up and his practice time gave him lane choice. His competitor lost lane choice and the race. Between races, Kevin checked hoses, wires, fluids, belts and bolts. Ernest did more cleaning and polishing.

"The car is running fine. If there is anything we can do, I don't know what it could be. But let me know if you find anything on the next run," Kevin advised his brother.

This routine continued until quarter finals when Ernest missed a gear and lost. Newer cars and larger racing budgets had won out over the Ernest's seven year old backyard special. But he had come within two cars of winning his class. Kevin did better when he raced the car, winning his class. Ernest had plans for the little purse that was not to be taken home that night. As they hooked up the tow bar, a father and son approached owner-driver Ernest and crewman Kevin. The brothers chins dropped when the father said, "We would like to buy your car. Would you consider two grand be a fair offer?"

"I'd consider four grand fairer," Ernest answered with dulled enthusiasm and sharp economics.

"It's old. It's not worth four thousand," the son said.

"Yes, it's old, but we've put new parts in it worth five thousand dollars," Kevin said, attempting to help his brother.

"Twenty-five! That's my final offer," the father said.

"I'll keep it till I get four, maybe five when it starts winning," Ernest replied.

"If you change your mind, let me know. I'll give you my name and telephone number," the father said, still hoping.

"My mind won't change," Ernest said while Kevin finished attaching the racer back to the station wagon.

"You wouldn't sell it, would you? We have worked so hard getting it ready for this racing season," Kevin asked.

"I'd sell it for three thousand right now. I need the money. Becky and I want to get married. Don't say anything until tomorrow."

All four now knew why winning was so important to Ernest.

The girls joined Ernest and Kevin. The foursome joined the snail-paced line leaving the raceway. Each was deep in his or her own thoughts during the drive home. This time Kevin drove. Ernest and his girlfriend sat behind whispering, kissing, and snuggling.

"I really wanted to do better tonight. If I had, that guy would have given me four thousand, maybe even five," Ernest stated.

Linda was happy for her friends. In the back seat, Ernest and his girlfriend quietly discussed plans for their engagement and marriage. As Kevin drove, he worked on a plan to make buying the car happen. When parked the two cars across the street from their home, he was ready to reveal his plan.

"I'll put it away in the morning. Let's take the tow bar off the station wagon now, so I can take Linda home," Kevin said when he met his brother between the cars and added, "I'll give you three thousand for the racer."

"You don't have that much money," Ernest replied.

"No, but I will by the end of next month," Kevin said while detaching the tow bar from the racer

"Okay, if you are sure you can come up with the money."

Ernest went to his work truck where Linda was speaking to his girlfriend through a window. Kevin followed in silence. Ernest climbed behind the wheel of the truck Becky and he spent the morning together washing.

"Kevin wants to buy the drag racer," Ernest announced.

"Alright!" his girlfriend shouted as she hugged Ernest.

Linda hugged Kevin and said less loudly, "I thought you were saving for Dodge."

"I was. With the prize money I win, I'll have the Dodge sooner," he replied.

"You really believe in that car, don't you?" Ernest asked his younger brother.

"With all my heart and soul. I know it through and through. As well as I know myself. It won't let me down," Kevin stated.

Ernest and his girlfriend left for her home. Linda and Kevin slid into the station wagon. He started the car to take her home. She turned it off.

"Could we talk for a little while, please?" Linda asked.

"About what?" Kevin asked.

"A couple of things. Well, some of the things that happened this week. Would you go with me to the funeral tomorrow for the kids who were killed in the accident, Friday? I really don't want to go alone. I would feel better if you came with me."

"Yes, I'll drive you."

"That could have been us. We were there in the same place on Monday night. I saw the left turn you made."

"I remember that stupid move."

"I saw the firemen pull them all out of their car. It gives me nightmares. They were my classmates. I knew all of them, but in the dreams, we are them."

Linda put her hand on his chest and began rubbing. She realized it was the first time they had touched other than dancing or sharing a booth at the Charcoal pit. She hesitated for a moment and continued. Kevin sat silent, recapping his Monday night driving maneuver and questioning what her hand on his chest meant. She pulled him closer, wrapped both arms around him, and asked, "What are you going to do with the racer?"

"Race it, win some money. Buy the Dodge."

"You really believe it can win?"

"Yep, but I'm not going to drive it."

"Who's gonna drive it for you? And why not you?"

Call Me Maggie

"I'll get somebody. Maybe Ernest. If his girlfriend will let him. I'm better at fixing cars than racing them."

"Let me drive it, Kevin. Please let me race it."

Kevin thought for a moment. He had already convinced himself that he could not be a good mechanic and a good driver too.

"We'll have to get you a driver's permit."

"I don't need a license to race. But I will go to Motor Vehicle Monday after I enroll at Goldey-Beacom College."

"Goldey-Beacom?" Kevin was taken off guard by Linda's request as much as some of her other surprises.

"Yes, I'm enrolling, if it's not too late."

"When did you decide that?"

"Last night after the party. Maggie's in stewardess school, why not me in college? I'm taking the business management courses, not the secretarial stuff."

"I wish now that I hadn't quit. I could have gone to school. I ended up working nights anyway."

Kevin laid his head on the driver's window. Linda climbed into the station wagon's middle seat and leaned hers on the passenger side center window. He stared at silvery leaves on the dogwood canopy in the moonlight until she said, "Come back here with me, I have one more thing I want to talk about."

Kevin hesitated, then climbed back as Linda made room, then moved close to him and asked, "What else do you want to talk about?"

Linda was now the one who hesitated instead of Kevin. She wanted to say what was on her mind and say it so it would be heard as she meant for it to be heard.

"Maggie and I have been talking about Bandstand and the trouble we had with Vinnie. It put a scare in me so bad that I don't want to go back. I don't even want to watch it on TV anymore. Maggie said Vinnie sent Dominic over to me to line me up as one of his whores. I didn't think much of it when he asked me if I would put-out, but it made me mad, really mad. And on the street, they called me a dike. That made me even madder. All of that scared me real bad. Kevin, I'm no whore and I'm not a dike. I'm just a girl who has been spoiled by my parents and by my friends, especially you. I have always gotten what I asked for. Even the stuff in the street with those creeps. I asked for that by leading the creep on the way I did. I like to tease. I like to get guys worked up. I like to get worked up too, but I don't let it go too far. As they said in health class, this the age we explore our bodies. The most

94

exploring I ever did was to let a few guys grab a quick feel. And that was always through my clothes, like this," she said, putting his hands on her breasts.

Kevin let his hands remain where she placed them.

"You are the first guy to ever hold them like this. I was lying about putting out with guys. I mean I would if he was the right guy, but then I was mad and said what I would do, not what I have done. I'm sorry I said that and made you think I have been all the way. I have not. I've been trying to get a moment alone with Maggie to find out what to do when the time came. I'm still not sure if I can do it right. Forgive my lie. Please forgive me."

Kevin knew he had always had difficult personal interaction with anyone, especially a girl, even Linda. They had been pals for a long time, but he had never been so close to her as he was tonight. Not when they began studying together five years earlier. Not when they shared a booth at the Charcoal Pit. Not when they danced at the Armory or when she rode places with him. A new element had come into their relationship. He wanted her as his girlfriend now. He was sure. She was his best friend, dancing teacher, cruising companion and more meaningful things he could not bring to mind or speak out loud. He began his difficult response anyway. If they were really friends, she would understand, he hoped.

"I have wanted to be more than just friends with you for a long time, but I never could get up the nerve to come on to you and be sure you would let me hold you the way I'm holding you now."

"I would have let you hold me long ago, but you never did anything to indicate that you were interested in me as your girlfriend," Linda stated.

"I was, but I didn't know how to tell you or show you. Maybe I could use some advice too."

Linda reached behind her back and undid three hooks, then took Kevin's hand and slipped it up under her blouse until it rested on a rounded mound of bare flesh, and then said "I'm glad I came down this afternoon."

They lay together touching and exploring each other's tolerance. Sensations neither had ever known raced through each. Linda began kissing him, modestly at first with gentle touches to his cheeks. Once confidence that he was receptive, she became more aggressive with lip contact which soon became more assertive until their tongues met and entwined. Kevin asked himself if he should this new experience let it continue, or stop. Linda provides his answer in ways he had only imagined as he thought of her when he was far from her; she raised her skirt, removed her panties, unzipped his fly, pulled his pants down, lay back, spread her legs and pulled him on top of herself.

Neither spoke for several moments after the station wagon stopped bouncing.

"I would have done this with you a long time ago if I knew it was going to be this good," Linda said once she caught her breath. "The priest will probably give me a million rosaries when I go to confession, but it was worth it. I'm not ashamed we did it, are you?"

"Are you sure?"

"Yes, I'm sure."

"I'm no ashamed either." he murmured as she embraced and kissed him again.

"I hope thing are working out for Maggie. She is an interesting and fascinating girl. I hope she and Norman get together like you and I."

"Is Norman's seeing her?"

"I'm not sure. He came by her apartment the night you left me with her."

"I saw a picture he had taken of her when we were at her apartment the other night."

"I saw it too. She had taped it on the refrigerator."

"I saw one I was in a book and she had no clothes on."

"Do you think they have done it with each other yet?"

"They may have. If they have, I don't think it's something they would tell us about. I know I don't want them knowing that we went all the way and did it tonight."

"She didn't say anything after you left, but she had a glow all over her face when Norman arrived and she sat close to him while they drove me home."

"I had it bad for her. With what I know now, I don't think I could be with her as I am with you right now. Since we helped her set up her apartment, I've done some thinking. No more Bandstand crushes for me. She is in my past. No more Bandstand for any of us unless we want to tangle with Vinnie and his gang," Kevin said to the girl in the station wagon with him.

"They could be doing it now."

"Yup, they have apartments and don't have to do it in a car."

"I don't mind the car. It's better than not doing it at all or getting caught by our parents doing it on the couch."

City Girl, Farm Boy

Soon each felt the urge to repeat their satisfaction again before he drove her home.

Hundreds of moving red and white dots connected Milford with Dover, Dover with Smyrna, Smyrna with Odessa, Odessa with the Wilmington skyline blanket lights in the night further north. A few pair moved southward. Others raced the Cessna carrying Norman, Maggie, John and Carmella.

"Nice, slow and easy. Move to the rhythm of a waltz, not rock and roll, when you're up here," were Maggie's first flight instructions from John.

Maggie sat with feet light on the pedals and her hands gently grasping the yoke as he continued instructing her. Gently, her hands pulled the yoke delicately toward her chest and the plane rose. Rotating the yoke, it rolled in the direction she twisted. Subtle joy of discovery filled her subconscious overflowed into her self esteem. An unheard voice told of an elevated joy. Her memory told her it was a sensation she had never known. A joy similar to one on the beach, she could savor forever. Maggie craved more of her new found fascination as the plane turned, rose, and descended, each bank, climb and dive complying with her delicate touches on the pedals and yoke. It was a ballet in the dark night sky. The girl who danced beneath American Bandstand floodlights had a new partner as she danced across the night sky. Maggie was the choreographer, ballet mistress, director and conductor. Creeping headlights, moving in synchronized pairs, snaked across the dark chasm below and passed beneath her. Farmhouses, barns and houses clustered in little neighborhoods under streetlights creped stage-front from stage-rear beneath Maggie. She remembered that a small farm laid just south as they moved beneath Maggie. The refinery they passed in daylight now stood as towers and globes basking in thousands of lights interrupting the blackness. Soon a half oval topping two long strands of gleaming pearls grew larger on the horizon. The pearly strands passed in ascending frequency until they were again only lights outlining the Memorial Bridge she had seen from the New Castle Wharf.

John returned to piloting and Maggie assumed her passenger role. Her unspoken enchantment told John, Norman and Carmella she would be as much at home in the air as on the dance floor when stewardess school ended in September and she would have wings of her own.

A little after midnight Maggie opened the door to her apartment and said, "Thank you for taking me to the beach, Norman. I hope the pictures captured some of the joy I felt out there away from everyone but you. Would you like some scotch?"

"Yes, please. Just a little. Then I'll go."

"I wish you didn't have to go."

"Maggie, thank you again for the pictures on the beach. I know some of them will be great. I will process them tomorrow with the aerials and whatever assignments I get. I'm sure I'll have some sort of Mother's Day assignment. We usually have to get something special for special days. Last year I shot a mom and her new triplets in the hospital. That was an unusual assignment," Norman said and sipped.

"What are you doing for your mother."

"Maybe between assignments I can find time to take her some flowers."

"That's nice. I think I will call mine. Let her know I am okay. But not tell her where I am. Vinnie might force her to tell him where I am."

"She should like that."

"If she is sober, she might."

Norman thought it might be best to change the subject before Maggie go quiet and withdrew.

"How did you like your plane ride?"

"Oh, that was great. I was uneasy for a few minutes believing that it might really turn upside down. After that it was fun. Flying at night was great, too, but the cape was best. I felt so good out there. The wind, the water, the waves, they brought me back to life."

"The cape always does that for me. What did you do for fun in Chester?" Norman said, returning to the unwanted subject.

"When I was little, we went to the farm a lot. Then when we got older and didn't have to be watched all the time we went to Hershey Park, the zoo, and sometimes the Poconos. We usually went with another family. Mother never had the money to take us. May I lay on your shoulder?" she asked and had moved closer before he could answer. "What did you do on special days when you were young?"

"The biggest on was always the third weekend in June. It was Father's day, but it was the Sunday around my grandfather Kennedy's birthday. All his kids and all their kids would come to his home for a combination birthday, Father's Day, Mother's Day, family reunion. Most of his children left farm life for jobs in the city during World War II. Everybody brought food. You would not believe the food they would put out. We ate, we played, and we took hay rides. He always left a little hay on one of the wagons. It went on late into the Sunday night. Of course there were other days too, cotton planting day, syrup making day, and hog killing day. Hog killing was always on Friday after Thanksgiving Day and the day after. My father would kill two or even four hogs toward the end. We would cut them up and prepare them for storage. Everybody had a job. Mine was scraping hair and later grinding sausage. Grinding was lots of work, if we had just slaughtered four large hogs. Then there was cotton ginning day and cotton market day. That's the day we got new clothes and shoes when we went in to town. I saw Hank Williams in town on one market day."

"Sounds like a good life. You sound like you miss it as much as Kevin. Do they really have to pipe in sunshine?"

"Of course they do. Moonlight too. But there are too many rocks in the river to race submarines. It was good, but it was hard on all of us. There was never enough time to get the work done and there was never enough money to have many new things. But our neighbors and our aunts had children. They gave us their children's outgrown clothes. We raised all our food except for sugar, salt, flour and a few other things. Yes, it was a good life.

"Do you miss the farm life now? I heard you mention that one today. Do you think you will ever have one?" Maggie asked.

"Yes I miss it. So does my father. Maybe someday I'll have one. A little one with a few animals and lots of flowers. I take after my father; I like roses and fruit trees. Aside from all the labor it takes to run and maintain a large piece of property, it takes a special kind of person to live out in the country on a farm away from people. It requires someone, who is happy with themselves and doesn't need a lot of company. Maybe just a wife and a couple of kids to share the farm life with. With my work schedule, I can't take on too much because I'm gone a lot."

"Are you that kind of person? Could you live away from people? Don't you need people for company?" Maggie continued her questions.

"When I'm working, there are lots of people I meet who are interesting and I enjoy meeting them. But at the end of the day, I wish I could turn that part of me off like turning off a radio. I guess that I am talking about a sanctuary. A farm would be a sanctuary. On the other hand there are still many pictures I want to take. I may be able to make both fit, someday."

Call Me Maggie

"You will find a way to make them both fit," Maggie said as she gave him a reassuring hug, then, held him in a firm embrace drawing her chest tight against his.

"Tell me about you, Maggie what do you want besides being a glamorous stewardess and going to faraway places?"

"Pretty much the same things you said. Have a little place of my own so I can come and go as I need to. With the airlines, turning it off comes with the end of the flight. Four days off would be nicer than two. But that's four days to fill. I can't go shopping like some girls. And I am not going to do the night club bit. My sister was under age and look what it has done to her already. It would be nice to come home to a husband, or a good boyfriend, but no kids when I flying overnight or international flights. If not that, maybe an understanding boyfriend, a couple of horses or a dog that will be glad to see me return."

"Keep your dream alive, Maggie. Keep your dream alive. Right now I should be going I have lots to do tomorrow."

"Do you have to? You could stay here with me. If you would like me to freshen your glass, I have more scotch. I'm still excited from the beach seducing me and from the plane ride home. I ready for bed, but not ready for sleep. I wouldn't resist if you wanted to start a new type of partnership with me tonight."

"What I said this afternoon still holds. I don't expect you just to allow me that liberty just because we were enjoying an afternoon on the beach or because we are alone together now. I would like to but I have inhibitions that won't let me take advantage of you that way."

"You are not taking advantage of me when I suggest that we make love. You can still stay her without having a physical union. You don't have to stay if you think that's all I want. I love being near you and one of the reason's is not having you groping, grabbing or enticing me into sexual intercourse. You could tell me another of your stories and I would be happy lying beside you and listening," Maggie said as she lowered the foldaway bed complete with covers.

"Son of a gun. I thought that was an armoire, or a closet."

Maggie took both his hands and led him to the bed.

"You'll have to sleep nude, just like I did the first night at your house." she said as she locked the door, turned off the lights, and began unbuttoning his shirt. In a moment she climbed in bed beside Norman and said, "Tell me about your life on the farm."

"When I was a little boy, maybe eight years old, cotton seed planting day arrived. Before going to the barn, Dad went to the cupboard and brought out a gallon jug of moonshine. 'You boys want a swig?' he asked Ernest and me. Ernest said, 'yep.' I said 'nope.' Dad took swig and let out an 'awe we.' Ernest took a swig and he said 'awe we.' But when dad left the house for the barn I got the jar out and filled a juice glass. I took a swig and gave out a big 'awe we.' I left the glass and jug on the counter and went to help hitch the mules. Dad came back in for another snort before we went to the field. In a little while I was having a lot of trouble carrying seed and fertilizer bags to the planter. Stumbled all over the place and I saw two mules and two images of my father coming across the field instead of one. Pretty soon I saw four of both. Dad made another round, stopped the mule and came over to me. I was standing over a bag of cotton seed cover with my breakfast all over it. Dad turned me around, gave me a little push, and said 'Butter ga'wn back to du house, boy.' He and Ernest worked the whole day without me while I was hanging my head off the porch wishing I had never seen that jar of moonshine," Norman said.

"Didn't he punish you later?" she asked.

"Dad never mentioned my drunkenness, ever."

 "I wish I could remember my dad."

"You still have your mother," Norman reminded her.

"Yes, I still have her even if she hasn't been a real mother for years; not since my father died." Maggie said as she snuggled up to Norman seeking a new sanctuary.

Norman's internal clock failed to wake him early enough to find flowers and drop in on his mother and father before work. He went to the newspaper photo lab and began processing. He made a run developing the aerial photos another run of the pictures he had made of Maggie on the cape, and then printed two sets of proofs of each. One set of aerials he placed in the photo editor's office. The other he kept on his desk. He placed one of set Maggie pictures in an envelope and wrote an "M" on the front. The other he marked with an "N". Both sets went into his camera bag. The news room was coming alive when he finished. One of the deskmen had filled in for the photo editor and asked if there were any pictures from the flight that could be used in Monday's paper. Norman found the frames on the contact sheets, drew rectangles around the fisherman on the cape, the hikers on the beach, of the deer running, and made his suggestion. His Mother's Day assignment was to photograph a mother in Ogletown with thirteen children.

Norman prepared for the assignment, went to the home made the photograph, stopped at church fund raiser found a white azalea for

Call Me Maggie

his mother, and drove to his parent's home. He made a politely short visit and returned to the newspaper office. While his film was drying he printed nine Greenbank Mill photographs. He made prints of his Mother's Day plus one of the interstate and turned them in to the deskman with caption information. The editor suggest he go home and stay by the phone, but Norman stayed in the lab, gathered negatives and proofs of the bathroom group he had shot plus the ones from the beach, matched negative numbers to red rectangles on the proof sheet, placed the first strip of film in a carrier and focused the image on an 11x14 printing easel. He removed a sheet of photographic printing paper for a yellow box and placed it in the easel. For ten seconds he studied the image projected on the paper. He restarted the enlarger timer and held his hand over the paper allowing areas he wished to make darker to illuminate the paper. When satisfied with his darkening technique, he placed the paper in the developer tray for ninety seconds, moved it to stop bath tray briefly and then to a third tray of "fixer" chemicals. Waiting a few seconds, he turned on a light above the third tray and studied an image of Maggie on the paper floating in the fixing bath.

A second enlarger was loaded with a negative and focused. Norman reloaded the first enlarger, made his exposure; moved back to the second enlarger made an exposure of its image and developed two prints at the same time. He continued his two exposure technique until all images with rectangles had been printed. The fixed prints were then placed in a barrel that tumbled the prints in water rinsing away the processing chemicals. The washed photographs were laid on a linen belt that carried them around a four foot drum to dry. Dried prints dropped in an out-feed tray. While other prints dried he dialed "MARYANN" on the lab phone. Maggie answered sobbing. A fat brown envelope nestled against his side as he used his key to open her apartment door ten minutes later.

She sat with the old teddy bear against her chest at the kitchenette table, her back to the window. She was still sobbing. Six wilting white roses lay on the table.

"This afternoon I drove to see my mother. It was the same thing all over again."

"Tell me about it," Norman pressured her.

"She was on the floor half dressed. Bottles and vomit lay beside her. The place was a wreck. I tried of wake her but she wouldn't wake up. She was too drunk like hundreds of times before. I could not

102

make myself wait until it wore off, so I came home," Maggie said between sobbing and sniffling.

"Maggie, I'm sorry it turned out that way for you. I wish there were something I could do. If there is, tell me," he said.

"Norman, is that what I will be like in twenty years? Lord knows, I don't want to end up that way." Maggie sobbed.

Norman knelt beside her and held her.

"Maggie, you won't let it happen, you have come too far and you are too smart for that. Look at the progress you have made this week. New job, a nice new home and some good new friends. When classes start you will make more friends. You're too strong and you have too much courage to end up like that," Norman said.

"I am scared, scared to the bone. I didn't see my sister. She could have been just as bad."

"Maggie, they did it to themselves. It probably would not have made any difference, if you had been there. Don't do this to yourself. Put it out of your mind," Norman pleaded.

He stroked her disarranged hair as he held Maggie. After a few moments he began lightly kissing her brow. After a few more minutes, Maggie placed a light kiss on Norman's cheek, leaving moist deposits upon his temple. He led her to the sofa and the two embraced until daylight.

Linda and a lone policeman were in the sandwich shop the next evening as Kevin entered. Linda was cleaning the grill. The policeman was finishing a foot-long 'hoagie' sandwich. One of the newly introduced twelve ounce Coca Cola bottle sat half empty next the sandwich. The shop's television was tuned to "The Ed Sullivan Show."

"Hi Linda, Hi Ralph. Things quiet tonight?" Kevin greeted.

"How about a sandwich?" Linda asked Kevin.

"Just a Coke," he answered.

"Real quiet or I wouldn't have time for Linda's sandwich," the policeman replied.

"Don't rush. I have time. Gave Mom the day off. Dad too. He's taking her to see "Sound of Music." Mother's Day you know," Linda told the officer and Kevin.

"You boys still plan on racing that Ford?" the policeman asked.

"Yep! Ernest made quarter finals with it last night." Kevin answered.

"I'm gonna drive it next Saturday," Linda added.

"Not too many girls can drive a drag racer," Ralph noted.

Call Me Maggie

"This girl can," Kevin said.

"I do pretty well on River Road. Oops!"

Ralph let the confession and oops go by, but he policeman in him made a mental note of her slip.

"Going in for my learner's permit tomorrow morning. I graduated Friday. Applying to Goldey-Beacom after the permit."

"Good luck. I guess I won't be seeing much of the little girl in her Saint Thomas's uniform anymore, like when I was a crossing guard. You kids grow up fast," Ralph said.

"That was more than six years ago," Linda said.

"Been that long, huh. Gotta go now. They open Cecil County Wednesday nights for practice. Do your racing on the track, or else," Ralph said, as he tapped his ticket book.

"She will," Kevin answered.

"Good night, Ralph. Thanks for the tip on practice night. I'll do off track practice in the Motor Vehicles training area." Linda said, smiling sheepishly.

Linda passed her hand over Kevin's shoulder rolled an index finger to him as she went toward the light switches. Kevin patted her thigh as he followed her to through the darkened shop into the back room. Linda turned out more lights leaving the room lit only by a large wall clock, came to Kevin, pushed him onto some boxes entwined themselves and kissed him over and over.

"Last night was wonderful." Linda said.

"Yep. And I'm not driving tonight," Kevin added.

Monday morning sun coming through the window spotlighted six wilted roses and a manila envelope lying on Maggie's little dinette table. The sun had wilted them even more turning them more brown than white. Maggie wore no clothes as she went the avacoda dresser, removed what she would wear after a shower, and headed for the bathroom, only to stop short passing the table a second time. She lifted the envelope, slid the contents outward and sat with her back in the morning light.

Norman awoke, sat up, and saw Maggie slowly examining the photographs he had printed the previous day, raised his Leica, focused the lens, The viewfinder image showed the front of her outline in shadows, except for a halo outline of her hair, arms and shoulders beneath the window. He pressed the shutter button, put on his pants and then sat quietly as the Maggie slowly examined each print.

City Girl, Farm Boy

"Norman, you have outdone yourself again. These are more beautiful than any others you have taken," Maggie said while continuing her examination.

Norman went to the table, moved a chair and sat to her right. Each time she looked at him the sunlight brightened one side of her face and the hair surrounding that side of her face. His Leica recorded this image too.

"Would you pour us some juice, please?" Maggie asked.

Norman returned with two glasses to the table where Maggie sat viewing the photographs. He removed the black album from the coffee table and sat again beside Maggie. As she finished with each print, he slid them into the album. Clothed views were placed in the front; nude views near the back. He slid the last print into the album and looked to see Maggie rubbing the glass across her lips. She made no effort to hide raised nipples pushed through strawberry blonde hair draping her chest.

"I am speechless. Norman, they are so beautiful."

"Does that mean you like them?"

"I love them. I was never photographed the way you photograph me. Yes, I like them very much, especially the beach ones. You're a terrific photographer."

Maggie sat her glass beside the roses, stood up and wrapped both arms around Norman's neck, pushing her breasts into his face. Norman made no effort to push her away and allowed the embrace to continue until she pulled back to place a short kiss on his lips.

"Take a shower with me. We would be close to each other and we could do more than we could have on the beach."

"It would be too tempting to take a chance. I would be taking advantage of you. I might offend you if I did something you didn't like."

"Take a chance and find out. I don't offend easily and you would not be taking advantage of me."

"In my mind I would be."

Maggie lifted her clothes and went to the shower leaving the wooden door open. Norman finished inserting the pictures.

"What assignment do you have today?" she asked from behind pebbled glass shower enclosure he had photographed her behind a week earlier.

"Don't know yet. I do have to print the aerials, if the proofs have been edited. What are you going to do?"

Call Me Maggie

"Going to check out school and maybe see Linda this afternoon," she said, after the water sounds died off.

"I thought the school was all in order."

"I'm going to check anyway."

"You did okay on the physical, didn't you?"

"Yes, everything was okay," she was brushing her hair.

"Well, good luck, anyway."

"Thank you," she said, standing by him in only a towel.

Norman's eyes travel down from her eyes to her toes and up again to the freshly brushed hair. His eyes lowered and met with hers and remained frozen for a long moment.

"You wouldn't be taking advantage of me this morning any more than you would have when we returned from the beach. If you think you would be, you would not. It would be exactly what I want," she stated and kissed him with more passion than before.

"I have to go back to my place and shower too," he said.

"Wanna stop back for dinner? I owe you one," she said giving him a short hug.

"We'll see. I'll call you between nine-thirty and ten."

As he unlocked the door he turned and saw Maggie's entire figure outline in the halo of sunlight. He instinctively raised his camera and made a photograph. Maggie blew a kiss to Norman from across the room.

During the drive to his apartment, Norman whistled a few tunes to himself. At a red light he lowered the top but left the tunneau unsnapped. He took the long way home, cruising. He drove up Market Street to Eleventh Street instead of turning west on Second Street until a travel agency sign caught his photographers eye. He pulled to the curb under a red on white sign reading "NO PARKING 8 a.m. to 6 p.m., pulled a medium telephoto lens from his bag, and clicked off three frames as two waiting for a bus and holding hands under a sign reading, "Virginia is for Lovers." He got their names for the caption and continued up Market Street and turned left at Eleventh Street headed toward home. Eleventh Street soon became Delaware Avenue at intersection at Washington Street. He met a street washing truck that gave him and his open convertible an unwanted shower. He turned south on Adams street and parked again. He them exposed a dozen or more frame of the city's skyscrapers reflected in a pothole of water left by the street washer. When he parked near his apartment building, he noticed a bulldozer pushing debris off the block diagonally across the intersection from his building. A clamshell earth moving machine was lifting the debris into a large truck. Norman went to the roof of his building and photographed the equipment. They had uncovered a sheet of stone covering the entire city block. He was not scheduled to start working for another four hours yet he had taken three publishable photos already.

Maggie dressed as soon as Norman left and drove to Chester High School. Ten minutes later she was southbound on U.S. 13 for the second time in fifteen hours. At Claymont, she took the scenic river route of "13-A" southward until it became New Castle Avenue and parked at William Penn High school in New Castle. Thirty minutes later she leaped on the steps outside the school door. Her hands held a Chester school transcript and William Penn admission papers.

The school was less than a mile from New Castle's Battery Park submarine race viewing wharf and within two miles of Maggie's apartment and the airport. If her little car died, she could walk from her apartment to the airport or to William Penn for night school classes, Maggie told herself. The thirteen year old car was not dead yet. She headed for Linda's parents shop, hoping Linda was there helping with the lunch crowd.

Closing the door, Maggie yelled. "I'm back in high school for my diploma."

Linda ran around the counter, raised Maggie off the floor and the two began spinning amidst a crowd of lunch time customers.

"When do you start?"

"Tuesday after Memorial Day."

Linda's parents and a few older customers applauded. Maggie acknowledged them with a little curtsy.

"If you can stick around, we'll go to Goldey-Beacom together. I'm going in to enroll," Linda said. "Have a sandwich. I've got a Maggie Special waiting to be made."

Maggie took an empty seat closest to Linda.

"Kevin bought Ernest racer and I'm going to drive it for him. He says I a better driver than he is. It must be something to do with my dance co-ordination."

"It could be," Maggie gave her agreement.

"I got my learner's permit to drive this morning."

Linda's parents frowned at each other. Her father raised his palms upward, cocked his head and shrugged his shoulders.

"Why don't you girls go on when she finishes her food? Your dad and I can take it from now," Linda's mother said.

107

Call Me Maggie

Maggie and Linda parked near the business school and found the admissions office. Linda presented her high school transcript and an application she had picked up and filled out earlier in the day. She also filled in a blank check her parents sent with her. The admissions person chastised Linda for waiting so long to apply. However she did have two cancellations and Linda could fill one of those.

Maggie grabbed herself a few pamphlets plus an application while Linda was being processed and told herself, "Just in case."

Once Linda finished, she suggested they drop in on Kevin and the racecar. Maggie agreed. Both wanted to celebrate.

"Linda is even happier and more cheerful than on Friday when she graduated. She behaves like she's in love. I hope it's with Kevin. It will take his mind of his interest in me," Maggie said to herself, as they walked the drive to the Kennedy garage.

Only two lawn chairs were near the dogwood tree instead of the dozen or more that had been around it Friday evening. No sign of the hastily made tables was visible.

The two brothers had finished mounting two oversized tires Lionel had taken off a Coupe Deville Sunday afternoon. The treads were below the height of the ring around a penny, no longer legal, but ideal for the racer. Kevin was applying tire black as Lionel wiped dust off the car. Kevin rose and gave Linda a long kiss, while Lionel gazed downward. Two dark greasy hand prints remained on Linda's buttocks when the huddle disbanded.

"She is in love with him, and it looks like he feels the same way about her." Maggie said to herself.

Lionel put his hands over Linda's eyes and led her to the side of the car. When he removed his hands Linda saw letters above the door reading "Linda Reed." Another sign on the hood read: "Owner/Mechanic, Kevin Kennedy.

"I just lettered them this morning," Lionel said.

The four embraced each other leaving another handprint on Linda's rump and one on Maggie's shoulder.

"Looks like Kevin's learned she's not one of the guys anymore. Maybe Norman will learn I can be more than his model," Maggie sighed.

Norman's father soon arrived with his mother. He had showered and changed at his shop, but his mother wore a denim shirt and slacks soiled with multiple colors of stain. Obviously not all the stain was put on the leather she colored, Maggie observed silently then left the young people and went into the house after an invitation for iced tea from Mom Mom Kennedy. Pop Pop stayed with the boys. When they returned Kevin and Lionel were inside providing their father and Linda with measurements which Linda was writing on a sketch for a roll bar Pop Pop would bend into shape and welded mount plates at his workplace.

"The Kennedys do look out for each other!" Maggie silently observed again.

"Come into the greenhouse with me while I water my plants," the elder Kennedy suggested.

Maggie couldn't refuse.

Hundreds of small plants stood above black soil in wooden flats along the windows of the greenhouse. Pop Pop identified each as he gave them a gentle shower.

"What do you do with all these seedlings?"

"Sell some, plant, harvest, freeze or can some, and enjoy them fresh when they're mature. I always raise enough for my in-laws, too. There are six of them to feed and seven of us plus two of the boy's girlfriends a couple times a week. Come outside and I'll show you ones that will be ready in a week or two," he suggested again.

Maggie followed his lead again. She had noticed the garden, but didn't venture near it without an invitation. Pop Pop pulled spinach, green onions, lettuce and snow peas for her to taste, insisting that she taste them, pod and all.

"I have never tasted peas so tasty. What's your secret?"

"Good soil, a little extra lime and lots of care."

Maggie saw that each plant was tied to a wire fence so the pods could not touch the dark soil. Traces of white lime could be seen around each plant. Soon Mrs. Kennedy called Kevin and Lionel to help their father set up for eating on the lawn. She insisted Linda and Maggie join them. The girls volunteered to go inside for food and dishes.

"Do you come from a large family, Maggie?" Mrs. Kennedy asked.

"Just my mother, she's been widowed since the Korean War, and a twin sister. My father parents are no longer living and I never knew my mother's. They live somewhere in England."

"Large families are nice. If you're a friend my kids, you're always welcome at the Kennedy home. Of course you might have to take part in the chores. I see you've already been introduced to the garden by Pop Pop," Mom Mom said.

Call Me Maggie

"Chores, gardens and I are no strangers. I used to spend summers on my grandparents farm in Pennsylvania. They even had a few cows, some pigs and one horse. My first chore was gathering eggs. I helped with feeding and stable cleaning after I got old enough. The happiest day of my childhood were spent on their farm," Maggie said.

"Then you'll be right at home here, and welcomed too. 'Course we haven't had animals since we moved off the farm."

Maggie knew the invitation was genuine. And she would look forward to visiting Pop Pop's garden again. Linda said she had been like another daughter there nearly six years. Maggie told herself if they accepted her half as much as the accepted Linda, she would be grateful.

"These people are more like family to me than new friends," she concluded.

At dusk, the dogwood tree canopy transformed into a warm golden hemisphere against and equally golden sky and lanterns were lighted as the stars came out. They remained on the lawn near the dogwood tree well after dinner was finished.

Pop Pop made his evening stroll around the garden. Maggie followed and helped him pull a cloche over the bean plants reminding of the times she tucked children under covers when she babysat.

Kevin went to work saying goodbye everyone in the yard and a longer goodbye to Linda in the drag racer. He drove it to work for the first time, leaving the station wagon parked.

"Thank you for insisting I come tonight, Linda. It was the first time I been close to a real family in a long time," Maggie said at the end of the evening.

Norman spent the first two hours at the lab finishing the Virginia lover's picture, the reflection and the debris loading shots. He placed them in the photo editor's office. He had also printed three shots made of Maggie in front of the window and slid them into an envelope. He drew a couple of assignments for Monday afternoon. One was the demolition of the old Wilmington High School building. Since the school site was closest, Norman went there first. The three floor building's front side had not changed since it was built sixty years earlier. A sister brick building had been erected in 1932. Linda was in the third class to graduate in the new building at the western edge of the city. Norman went to the rear looking for signs of demolition. The entire shop class section of the building had been razed leaving tumbled bricks, broken timbers and shattered glass. Sitting on the rubble was a single bent-back chair.

City Girl, Farm Boy

Norman made a few exposures of the chair and placed it in his car when he left.

His second assignment was a new ambulance being put in service by the Five Points Volunteer Fire Company in Richardson Park. The 4:30 appointment left him more than an hour to kill. He made a few shots of young teen-agers playing in a stream below a massive bolder called Indian rock. The afternoon sun filtered through the trees casting strong highlights on the rock, water and wet youngsters. Eight or ten years earlier, Norman might have been one of the youngsters frolicking away summer afternoons in the stream. Norman remembered those teenage visits. He had visited the stream and rock often, sometimes with girlfriends before he began working at the newspaper. It was similar to one on the family farm back in Alabama. Norman smiled and sighed before reluctantly left for the fire house.

Two ambulances were parked in front. One was an old traditional Cadillac manufactured as ambulance and hearse. The other was a large metal box mounted on a six-wheel truck chassis. The newer model carried greater amounts of first aid and rescue equipment. He made shots of the interiors and exteriors of the two showing their differences, then drove back to the office, processed the film and delivered prints.

Before dinner he dialed the Philadelphia student nurse's number. The student answering the phone informed Norman that Diane did not want to speak with him. Norman shouldered the Leica, walked one block, ordered a Coke at the Woolworth's lunch counter and sat alone and spent the evening photographing rehearsals in the Arden Playhouse.

Remembering Maggie's dinner invitation, he called her on the theater's telephone. In a second call, the photo editor told him to finish the assignment and retire for the night. Norman offered no argument. He was carrying the bent back chair and an envelope when Maggie answered her door an hour later.

"A little addition to your apartment." Norman said, setting the chair inside the door. The envelope and Leica, he placed on her coffee table as before.

Maggie wore a long burgundy satin dress with one leg revealed in a slit running up almost to her hip. White pearls and her cleavage were revealed at the top between the lapels of a short jacket. He took her hand, spun her twice, and admired her dress. She pushed his jacket off, placed it on the oval chair back, loosened his tie, and slowly pulled it around his shoulders before the tie joined the jacket. She locked her hands behind his neck, rose on her bare feet, and kissed his cheek before whispering, "Let's have dinner."

Her table was set and lighted by candles standing in a flower pot saucer of sand. Filled salad plates sat with a teapot and two white cups. Violet blossoms lay in each plate.

"This is nicer than prom night in the Gold Ballroom. And not nearly so many people," he said softly.

"So, Norman Kennedy, how was your day?"

"Good and bad. Not real bad," he answered.

"Would you share it with me? I'll share mine with you. I think you would approve of what I did."

Maggie listened as Norman listed highlights of his workday, but omitted telling her about the first phone call he made. By the time he finished his recap of events Maggie had served quartered red beets, half long corn on the cob and broiled flounder filets.

"This is very beautiful," Norman complimented again.

"I went in to see Linda this afternoon and discovered Sansone's Market. The rest is history."

"I graduated with one of their daughters," Norman added.

Dinner went quietly. She suggested tea be drunk on the sofa. Maggie had saved her news until the tea. The two took their usual position; knees toward each other. Maggie's dress revealed more leg than Norman had seen on previous nights except when he was nude. His eyes often drifted downward to her neckline and the leg showing through the dress's slit. Once settled on the sofa, Maggie gave her news.

"I enrolled in night school at William Penn High School today. I will have my diploma before the end of summer," she announced, smiled and waited.

Norman sat upright and said, "Maggie that's great. Absolutely great!"

He sat his tea cup on the brass legged table next to hers and gave her a tight embrace over their touching knees. Maggie finished giving details.

"I won't have much time for pictures during the summer with classes in two schools."

"We'll fit them around your classes somehow."

"Linda got in to Goldey-Beacom today, too. Kevin bought Ernest's car. She is going to drive it for him. Lionel painted the names on it this morning. And she is going to make some practice runs Wednesday night. They invited me to go down with them. I want to go. And to the race on Saturday too. How about coming with us?" Maggie said.

"Saturday, yes. Wednesday, no."

"That's too bad. They will miss you as Linda practices. Tell me more about the kids in the stream."

"It was nothing special other than I got there when the sun was right for good light on the rocks, leaves, and kids in the water. The kids swimming were so shinny they looked like they had been swimming in shellac. It reminded me of a stream near our home back in Alabama."

"Tell me that farm story, too," Maggie requested as she moved so her back was against his chest pulled his hands up onto her breasts.

He moved them back down and began his story.

"When I was a little boy, five or six years old, Dad came out of the barn carrying a length pipe, a shove, and some tools in a peach basket. 'Come on boys, we're going to the branch,' he said to Ernest and me. After about a ten minute walk on the dirt road we went up the side of the branch for about a hundred feet. Two rocks the size of a car laid in the stream close enough to each other to form a little waterfall about as high as I was tall. Dad rolled himself a Prince Albert from a can he carried in the pocket in his bib overalls and studied the waterfall as Ernest and I floated leaf boats in a pool. Dad removed his shoes and socks and waded in over his knees. He put the pipe between the two big rocks and weighted the upper end down with a lot of smaller rocks. Water shot through the pipe. He had made us a place to bathe other than the big washtubs we always used in the kitchen. Dad took off his overalls and showered himself. Ernest and I did the same. All three of us stayed there skinny dipping until almost dark. The mountain water was really cold, even in August, but we washed away all the red clay dust that covered us. Dad was a genius at turning his poverty and curiosity in to a little luxury for us. They may not have been the best or the most beautiful, but they were his solution to our needs," Norman said.

"Mister Kennedy must be someone very special."

"He is. Ernest, Kevin and Lionel are a lot like him. I'm more like Mom."

"What do you mean?" Maggie asked with a wrinkled brow.

"I have never been big and strong like them. I have always been weaker and very thin. Being sick when I was little may have caused it. I may never know. Plus I don't eat very well. I'm always on the go taking pictures here and there."

113

Call Me Maggie

Again she placed his hands on her chest and guided his hands across her body.

"That was a lovely dinner you. Thank you," Norman stated to change the subject, kissed the top of her head then moved to the other end of the sofa when he realized she could feel his arousal against her back.

"Maggie, I am not ready for fondling you yet. I want it to be right and beautiful when we start petting or going all the way. It's my old fashioned ways. It's not you. It's my hang-up. I'm not a queer. Or a momma's boy, either."

She wondered for a moment if Norman might be like the "pretty boys" she had danced with. Her attempts at picking pretty boys or pretty men always failed. Those boys usually danced with girls who matched their dancing ability. Pretty boys always went home with other pretty boys, not girls. Vinnie called them queers or faggots.

"When you want me, I'll be here," she said.

"I'm off tomorrow. And I'm all yours for the day. What would you like to do?" Norman asked.

"I loved you stream story. Could we go to my grandmother's old farm? I would love that and I am sure you would too."

"We can do that," Norman said, reaching for the envelope he brought with him.

"These are nice," Maggie said still laying with her back on Norman's chest as she viewed the pictures three or more times. She passed them to Norman and he slid them into the book with other photographs of her nude.

"I would like to photograph you in that dress. Would you mind if I did it now?"

"I would not mind. I would like model this dress. Get your lights while I brush my hair."

Norman set up three lights near the avocado dresser. Maggie brushed her hair and wrinkles from the dress.

"What made you sign up for night school."

"It's just something I've gotta do. This was the dress I wore to the junior prom when I was sixteen. Bought it with money I earned babysitting. I never made it to the senior prom. By then I was hooked up with Vinnie and he wouldn't let me go. He said it was not masculine for him to stand around in tuxedo looking like a faggot."

Maggie assumed catalog looking poses. Norman made a few shots. She moved to the chair and the model in her began to erupt. She posed standing, sitting, and with the leg showing through the slit and others. Later, she removed the dress and he photographed her posing without it on.

"What time should I come for you in the morning?"

"I would like to stay here with me now."

"You may not want me to after I tell you I called Michele this evening. She refused to take my call. I guess she is still peeved at me for standing her up last week. Two days with her mother probably convinced her more so. Her mother once said Michele should find someone in her own area; a doctor I suppose."

The statement had come without warning. Maggie slipped into Norman's jacket, lay her head on his lap, decided to listen and let Norman continue.

"I meant what I said earlier. I'm not ready for an affair. I always enjoy being with you. It's not just the picture taking either. I enjoy the conversations we have. I'm glad you chose me over the safe house last week. You have made a big change in my life, Maggie, a big change. I am confused. Just a week ago we met. My whole world has changed since then. And I want you in that world. Not just as a model, but as a friend, a companion, a partner, and a lover."

"I wore this dress hoping you would want me as much as I want you."

"Oh, I want you too, Maggie. I do want you. To be honest, I wanted you tonight as much as on the beach. Moving away from you tonight was harder than not making love with you on the beach."

Maggie raised and kissed him.

"May I talk about Diane again?" Norman asked, paused and then added, "If it makes you uneasy, I won't."

Maggie sat erect and said, "I wish you would if it will put you at ease."

"When I first met her I was blown away. She was similar to me in many, many ways. She's tall, almost six feet tall. She's thin like me with hardly any shape. But she is so studious. I guess I am too. You saw my book shelf. She is dedicated to nursing. I'm dedicated to photography. I have been for seven years now. She studies medical books while I study art or photography books and go to every seminar or workshop that I can. She is learning her profession formally, I am not."

"You could. You could go to night school too."

"I have known for a long time I could not go to college. It was not in the family budget. And it's not in my budget now. Every extra

115

Call Me Maggie

dollar I have is tied up in Photography equipment. I've been lucky to have some good stimulating coaches push me along. There was a distance between Diane and me. It's as if I not really wanted, just tolerated. I've given it lots of thought since I talked to her Wednesday. I do not want to be tolerated. I want as much coming back to me as I put forth. Maggie, you seem to give me much more than I give you. I'm not accustomed to a relationship like you offer. And the last thing I want to do is blow it."

"You are not blowing it," she whispered as she kissed him on the check.

Maggie pulled him closer, lifted the pictures he had brought and studied them much more thoroughly than she had earlier.

"You are dedicated to your photography."

For many moments they studied the photographs. Maggie was discovering that she could be a good model, and Norman was rediscovering and reliving the afternoon he made the pictures of her. Maggie hung his jacket back on the chair back, killed the lights and they lay together on the bed.

"Tell me about the chair. Did you use it in school?"

"I might have, but the coat looks better on you than the chair or me. I love seeing you in my clothes. You're more desirable in them than when you're naked."

"I'll consider the chair a good luck omen and study in it every night or hang your clothes on it when I not wearing them. Tell me another story before we go to sleep."

First Real Date

Shortly after 9:30, Norman guided the Chevy past a hand carved sign hanging from a mailbox attached to a stone pillar onto a gravel driveway and parked next to an all glass building near Booths Corner, Pennsylvania. A sold banner had been added to Realtor's sign mounted to identical pillar on the opposite side of the driveway. Five minutes later, he was snapping pictures of Maggie smelling blossoms in a garden overgrown with weeds. He tugged her into an all glass building behind a stone farmhouse when the drizzle that had lasted throughout the night became a downpour. Dark black soil filled hundreds of red clay pots sitting on shelves running along the walls of the greenhouse's length. Hundreds more were stacked upside down on the structure's center table, their soil dry and their planted wilted from neglect.

Placing soil in one, Maggie said softly, "Madeline and I often spent the day with grandmother filling these, putting three seeds in each pot and watering them."

When the deluge subsided, they went to a porch spanning the width of a house where she peered through each of its windows. When she reached the door, she pressed her face against its glass. It creaked and swung inward. Maggie stepped inside. Norman followed. He found she had lifted a sepia toned photograph of a youthful man in a uniform, a young woman looking amazingly like Maggie, a man in soiled overalls, an older woman in an apron from a foyer table and held it against her chest, then began exploring the rest of the house.

Old sheets covered a sofa and two chairs facing a stone fireplace in the first room off the hallway. Unburned logs and an inch of ashes lay in the fireplace. Pictures of two toothless girls sat on a dusty mantle. Soon she wandered down the hall into room containing a pair of beds with matching covers. Photographs of older girls in braids hung over each bed. A Raggedy Anne Doll lay on each. Maggie lifted one of the dolls and held it against her chest with the three-person photograph. Norman raised the camera and fired once as she sat motionless in a rocking chair.

After a few long minutes Maggie announced softly, "Two little girls were very happy here long ago," then strolled into room where colorless flowers drooped from a green Mason canning jar in the center of a table set for two. Norman made more exposures as Maggie replaced the lid back on an old cracker tin, rubbed dust from dishes, and lifted an enamel coffee pot sitting on a cast iron stove. Across the room a galvanized laundry tub sitting near the fireplace and a large black pot hanging above the fire grate reminded him of the evening baths he and his family took when they lived on a farm in Alabama where he spent his younger years. As he made pictures of them, Maggie moved to the door and gazed through a screen filled with water droplets. Norman made three more shots before Maggie opened the door and headed toward a weather-faded barn. When she came out a horse bridle had joined the photograph and Raggedy Anne doll. After placing them in the car, she returned to the garden and pinched flowers until her arms were filled. She joined Norman in the Chevy and he was was about to drive out onto the paved road when Maggie yelled, "I have to go back inside."

She jumped from the moving car and raced back into the house. Norman, turned the engine off, set the parking brake, and ran after her. Following rustling sounds and found Maggie on the floor of what he assumed was her grandparent's bedroom. He could only see her hips and legs as she asked if he had a flashlight in the car. He returned to find her sitting on the bed shuffling through envelopes from a dusty Saltine cracker tin. She laid some envelopes on the bed, others she kept in her lap. Each had feminine handwriting on its front. One read, "Mary Anne Johnson." The second had the same delicate handwriting "Madeline Anne Johnson" written on it. Another had the letterhead of a West Chester attorney and a fourth had the logo of State Farm Insurance. She opened the attorney's envelope and started reading the two sets of papers inside to herself. The first was a deed to the farm with a notary seal embossed in the lower corner. "Mortgage Satisfied" had been rubber stamped at the top. She took the flashlight and went under the bed again. Another cracker tin was removed and placed on the bed. On her third trip Maggie placed her head into the floor's void searching for other hidden items, but came out with only dust on her face and down the front of her dress. She attempted to brush the dust away but it only spread as it turned to mud. Norman ran to the car and returned with a clean white shirt.

"I saw Grandmother put these here once. I wonder if she knew I saw her? I didn't know what they were but I knew they were important. Thank goodness I remembered them today," Maggie said and began reading the second set of papers out loud. "The Last Will and Testament of Elizabeth Anne Johnson. Upon my death, the estate of Elizabeth Anne Johnson shall be sold by the executor, Michael D. Copeland, Attorney at Law. Proceeds from the sale will be used to satisfy all claims against the estate and the remainder divided equally my granddaughters, Mary Anne and Madeline Anne Johnson upon their eighteenth birthday." The document was signed "Elizabeth Anne Johnson." in the same grandiose penmanship,

"I'm now sure Grandmother wanted me to know these tins were under the floor," Maggie said with a wavering voice.

Wanting to get Maggie away from her memories, Norman led her outside, removed the nameplate from beneath the mailbox on his way the car, placed it in the trunk. Again her eyes flooded as she examined the documents while he drove. She wiped them on the shirt sleeves several times before returning the papers to the tins and asking, "Would you drive me to West Chester before we go back to Wilmington?" as they neared U.S. 222.

Within half an hour, Maggie removed the envelope with the attorney's letterhead from the cracker tins she held in her lap and passed it across a desk to Michael Copeland.

"Miss Johnson, I have been attempting to locate you and your sister for almost three years. My last address for you was in Talleyville," the attorney said.

"Today was the first time I've been to the farm since grandmother died. We've moved us several times since then," Maggie replied.

"Your grandparents were friends before they were clients. My parents tended an adjacent farm. It was sold two years ago. The Montgomery farm was sold March first, last year. Both are now owned by the same investors who plan to build a housing project on both farms. I have satisfied all encumbrances against the estate. A considerable sum remains. I was required by the Commonwealth to wait one year before disbursing the surplus funds. That waiting period is over. Your grandmother was most specific in her bequest to you and your sister. You now meet your grandmother's age stipulation. Checks will be mailed to you and your sister. Is this current address for you and Madeline?" he asked, looking at her driver's license.

"No, but it is the correct one for Madeline," she replied and requested he not mention her visit in correspondence with her sister or mother.

"May I have a current address for you?" he asked again.

Maggie provided her Wilmington Manor address and said, "I have former acquaintances in Philadelphia who would do me great harm if they learned my location. Don't even let my sister or mother know where I now live. In three months, I will not be reachable due to travel. Please make any contact with me by mail."

"I'll honor your requests, Miss Johnson. Your grandmother was a grand lady. I will give her granddaughters the same service I afforded her."

Maggie and Norman left the attorney's office. She began sorting the remainder of the tin's contents as he drove. Suddenly she held up a fan of $100.00 bills and shouted, "Grandmother was grand indeed. This is too much money for me to carry around. Let's stop at the first bank we see in Delaware."

Later that afternoon Maggie placed the flowers she had gathered into two pottery crocks. One she sat on her little table, the other she placed near her bed. She added the sign Norman had taken from the mailbox reading "Mr. and Mrs. Montgomery P. Johnson, Sr," and the bridle to her wall ensemble. The framed photograph of the soldier was placed on the dresser with the other photographs Norman had taken of her. The "Raggedy Ann" doll joined her Amish toy collection.

"You now have a nest-egg thanks to your grandmother."

"Nothing is going to change until after my stewardesses training is finished. Let's keep today's events to ourselves."

"If you wish," Norman replied.

"I wish we had brought the rocking chair."

"We can go back and get it."

Maggie thought for a moment, went to the kitchen phone, held one of the lawyers letterheads in her left hand with the receiver, dialed eleven numbers with her right, and said into the mouthpiece, "Mr. Copeland, contact the new owners of Grandmother's farm and arrange for me to purchase some of the furniture in the farmhouse, please."

A few minutes later the attorney called back. Norman fired off one exposure while Maggie listened showing deep concern on her face. The expression became less intense as the call went on.

First Real Date

"I can have all of it. I just have to move it out within two weeks. I guess I'll store most of it for the time being. This place is much too small to bring it here," she said to Norman.

"My brothers and I will move it for you," he quickly volunteered. "How about this Saturday? I'm free."

Maggie offered no resistance or argument to Norman's offer, smiled, said "Yes," and embraced him.

"Someday I'll get a little farm out in the country and grow flowers like Grandmother did. I might even get a horse," she said as she joined Norman on the sofa.

Linda had worked lunch hour that morning and the dinner hour the night before. Her father agreed to close the shop Tuesday evening and give Linda all of Wednesday evening free. She gave Kevin a call and was standing under the Park Theatre marquee between Third and Fourth Streets when Kevin pulled the station wagon to the curb.

"Sorry I'm late," he said.

"Just got here myself," Linda said.

The two locked themselves in a long kiss.

"I'm so glad we now doing it," Linda said.

"Me, too! But we gotta work on shifting the gears smother tonight. You will be practicing dragging tomorrow evening," Kevin said.

Linda continued to remain close for the trip to his father's garage. The Ford dragster had been pushed into the garage, backwards. Kevin drove the station wagon up to the Ford. They kissed for another five minutes as rain pelted the station wagon roof, the windows fogged, and he began trying to remove Linda's clothes.

"Save it for later. If I have to practice shifting. Let me get that done and we'll make out afterwards," Linda said, leaving the station wagon and up going to the dragster.

"I rigged these lights to help your take off," Kevin said.

Four yellow, one green, and one red bug light bulbs were connected to a rotary TV channel selector switch. As the switch clicked to a channel number, one light came on. When he rotated the dial the came on and went off in rapid sequence. If she started shifting too soon, he turned on the red light. Kevin sat the light on the hood and from the shotgun seat demonstrated to Linda. Kevin had hooked a voltage meter to four "D" cell batteries wired and duct taped them together. As each battery was added to the line, the needle jumped higher. From a board in his lap, he operated both switches and offered advice as Linda pumped the clutch and moved the shift lever.

Call Me Maggie

"Shift as close to 8,000 as you can. Above that you are losing torque," he said.

"I'm aiming for 7800 to keep the low end up," Linda said.

Linda watched the needle and shifted the transmission for more than an hour.

"Look, I have gotten blisters on my hand from this shifting. I've got to ease off. I can't make sandwiches with the skin on my hands rubbed off."

Linda got out, switched the garage lights off, and returned to the shotgun seat, pushed him against the passenger door and removed his shirt. After a few kisses she removed her sweater, skirt, and underwear. Soon water beads were running down the inside of the Ford drag racers steamy windows as their hips ground against each other.

About 1:30 the next afternoon Norman closed the door at the sandwich shop, gave Linda an eyeglass case, and said, "For your race driving."

"Can you come with us while I practice?" she asked, opening the case.

"Not tonight, but I'll be rooting for you."

As Linda put on a pair of aviator glasses with yellow lenses, Norman gave her a second larger box from which she removed a pilot's flight helmet.

"Gotta go now, lots to do today. Maggie will be by to pick you up later. Good Luck."

"Thank you for the glasses and helmet," Linda replied.

Norman was early as he entered the newspaper office. He immediately sat himself at a typewriter mounted on a rolling stand that the photographers shared and typed a header across the page reading "Picture Stories." Then he began listing his ideas. The list read: 1) Offloading oil operation in Delaware Bay; 2) Linda Reed, female drag racer; 3) Amish farmers and craftsmen in Lancaster county; 4) Pictorial study of old buildings in Wyeth country. 5) Hot swim suits for '62; 6) Stewardess School at Wilmington Airport, then scribbled Norman Kennedy at the bottom and took it to the picture editor's office.

"I like your ideas. I'll have the news editor put some writers on them. Jackie will have to approve the swimsuits. I saw her and a new model together yesterday. The girl has shining dark hair down to her calves. I'm sure Jackie could set you up with her, unless you have someone else in mind," the editor said.

First Real Date

"The girl should be interesting. You know my fascination with long haired models. Ask Jackie to set it up for the girl's convenience. Unless you want send us to Cape Henlopen, we can shoot it at Lum's Pond Beach or in the studio." Norman said.

He would have preferred to photograph his new discovery, if the Philadelphia incident were not so recent. Vinnie might be looking in Talleyville and see a newspaper.

"Henlopen is out. Shoot studio shots," the editor said.

"About the stewardess school, it will last about three months and when it's finished the girls will be on charter flights taking passengers to England, Rome, Egypt, and countless resorts in the Caribbean. I would like to make it an ongoing story, dropping in every few days and photograph what they are learning as they go. If you would break the ice for me, I will shoot it during the mornings whenever I can, otherwise I will mix it in with my other assignments, and I will write the story to go with the pictures, it that would help." Norman wanted the editor's approval and offered every extra he could.

"I'll break the ice. On the oil tanker story, hold on to that until something happens. We have a governor's office candidate running on an environmental platform. I don't want to be accused of supporting his issues. I'm using one of your aerials of tankers in the bay with a feature on him."

"The Reed girl is driving my brother's car. I will play him down and concentrate on her."

"Yes, play him down. You know the rule on family members used in newspaper pictures. Do your best on the Amish story. They don't like being photographed. Get me some Wyeth country shots and go ahead on the drag racing girl. No go on the tanker idea and I'll get back on swimsuits," the editor said.

Norman was about to leave when the editor handed him three jobs for the day. He read the assignment sheets and said, "I can't do anything interesting with three damned headshots!"

Norman decided to stop in the camera shop and pick up some supplies for his home darkroom when he discovered he had an hour to kill before his first assignment. When he arrived, the shop operator was demonstrating a new ultra wide-angle lens nicknamed "The Fisheye." Norman asked to borrow the lens for the afternoon and promised to publish a picture taken with the lens plus a brief review. The shop operator agreed. Half an hour later, he was leading the mayor out to the staircase rising from the first to third floor, the raced back to the first floor. Norman raced down to the first floor, laid on his back in the center of the spiral and shot a few frames with the lens. Winding stair rails started near the mayor and wound in an oval before ending at the ground floor. The picture appeared to have been shot from inside of a giant corkscrew.

Later he made a photo of the school coach through his office door. Newly applied lettering read: "Coach Abe Goldman."

Maggie had little more than a week before school started. She wished Norman could be with her that evening while Linda practiced racing. She wanted to prepare herself mentally for the summer in two schools. Primarily she wanted to put re-occurring thoughts of her mother, sister and two years with Vinnie out of her mind. Having Linda as a friend helped. Spending time with Norman helped more. She was still unsure of Kevin's acceptance of her. An evening with Linda and him might provide clues.

Maggie's relationship with Norman was different. She enjoyed modeling for him. She felt at ease with him, although she avoided any discussion of the past year as one of Vinnie's women with him or anyone else, not even Linda. Norman had made many pictures of her and never once made her feel inadequate, cheap, or dirty, whether she was nude or clothed. He always included 'please' in his directions to her when she was modeling, even though his coaching was less now. He never made lewd shots of her as her previous photographers had attempted. In the frames he or they selected enlarge; her pubic area was never seen, even though he enlarged many shot of her naked chest and body. In most of the prints, her long hair partially hid her breasts. Norman photographed her as a model in a situation, not as a suggestive sex object. The candid pictures of her on the beach, at the farm or even in her rain soaked blouse were photographs any woman would be proud to have even if more flesh was visible than seen in snapshots or studio portraits. They had warmth about them that made her proud to be the model she told herself as she folded her dried laundry and added the album on top of Norman's jeans and shirt. Her stomach told her Linda was in the peak of lunch hour traffic at the sandwich shop. There was still time before she would meet Linda. Another trip to the "Second Chance" thrift store would fit into her drive.

Ninety minutes later, she took a stool in front Linda cleaning the sandwich making station. Before they left the shop, Linda promised her parents nothing would harm her during the practice sessions that evening. Her father gave his helpless shrug. The two young women were off to start Linda's drag racing career.

First Real Date

"Maggie how did you avoid getting knocked up when you were. . . were with Vinnie," Linda asked shortly into the drive to met Kevin.

Knowing no delicate response, Maggie answered, "Condoms!"

"Kevin and I started doing it Saturday night. And a couple of time each night since," Linda confided.

"Get yourself some condoms. Put a few anywhere you think you might get the desire. Be even more diligent keeping a few in your purse than you are with tampons. When the urge hits you, you won't want to make a trip to the drugstore."

"But I'm Catholic. The priest will have me saying rosaries all week if he knew we were using rubber and getting it on."

"How many pregnant priests do you know? Rhythm doesn't work. Diaphragms can cause irritations so bad you can't do it. Abstinence or condoms are most reliable."

"I won't be able to abstain! I like it too much to stop doing it. I'm sure Kevin won't either now that he knows how good it feels," Linda confided again.

"Linda, I can't tell you what you should do, I can only tell you what will avoid pregnancy. It's a decision you and Kevin must make," Maggie concluded.

"Stop at the Elsmere Pharmacy long enough for me to get some rubbers."

Linda returned to the little Nash with two dozen condoms. Maggie offered instructions on wearing them while they drove to the Kennedy home. As they walked toward the garage, Maggie noticed the dogwood tree's leaves were shaded under a sky of cotton white clouds.

Lionel continued with the car as Linda and Kevin embraced. Again, Linda's slacks held oily hand prints on the buttocks when they separated.

"Still think she's one of the guys?" Maggie asked aloud.

"Nope!" Kevin answered, adding a third handprint.

"We're burning daylight," Lionel announced.

"You're not going," Kevin said curtly.

Not to be left at home, Lionel came back, "Why not, I have the night off too."

"Let's get going." Linda announced from the front hump.

Lionel sat shyly close to the door in the he shared with Maggie. Linda slid closer to Kevin as soon as they were under way. In earlier phone call, Kevin's dispatcher had informed him that the rain had left the soil too wet to be moved. He would not have to rush back and work that evening. Ernest and his girlfriend were waiting at the drag way. His dirt moving had been canceled as well for the evening, but he had volunteered to work the day shift Saturday and earn extra wedding money. Maggie and Ernest's girlfriend sat on Ernest's pickup roof while Lionel and Ernest assisted their brother, the car new owner and crew chief. Linda placed the amber sunglasses over nose, strapped the helmet on and made two dozen or so runs down the track. Sometimes she raced other cars; sometimes she raced only the clock. Each time she finished with the confidence of a veteran driver and when she won a pass over another driver she acted like winner who had run the quarter mile hundreds of times.

After the track closed, they visited an Elkton Dairy Queen and drove home re-capping each of Linda's runs. Back at the garage, they moved the car fully inside. Lionel and Kevin had stored much of the garage's contents overhead that morning.

Maggie left shortly after they arrived quietly wondering if her advice would be taken by Linda or Kevin.

Kevin sprayed painted the garage door windows and climbed in beside Linda sitting reading a user information sheet from one of the condom boxes.

"I'm not wearing one of those," Kevin announced.

"No rubber, no nookie. I want to do it as much as you, but I don't want to get knocked up. We took a terrible chance doing it without one. If you want to do it again, you will have to use one each time," Linda said.

"I'll use one, but I won't like it."

"I won't either, but I will feel better if we use one."

Norman processed and delivered his pictures, made a final check with his editors, packed his camera bag and headed home. He planned to print the pictures taken that morning and the night before in his home darkroom. Outside the building, Norman found Maggie's car parked next to his. Maggie jumped out and hugged him and asked, "Would you like to go for a walk or maybe a soda?"

"I would like both. Leave your car here."

Maggie and he cruised to a little drive-in on the west end of the city with curb service and intercom order taking similar to ones at drive-in theatres. Soon they were in Brandywine River Park walking beside water swirling over rocks. Neither spoke much until Maggie tried to break the ice when his chill became intolerable.

First Real Date

"Linda did really well at practice."

"Good, I have permission to do a picture layout on her as she races," he replied.

"It will be a good story. She's a natural."

"I also have permission to do one on the stewardess school, but I can't center it on you. The Philly gang might see it.

"That's probably best. If they find me, they might find Linda and Kevin, too. It wouldn't be pretty if they do."

"I don't want them to find you and Linda. Kevin can take care of himself pretty well," Norman said from behind a frown.

"What else are you thinking about? You've been quiet tonight. Was it me meeting you tonight without calling?"

"Oh no. I was glad to see you. But there is something I want to talk over with you," he answered.

"Then let's talk about it."

"Let's talk at my place"

About 10:30 they picked up Maggie's car and she followed him to his apartment. The brief drive alone gave her a chance to ponder what might be causing his silence. The drive also gave Norman time to organize his thoughts.

"Maggie, the pictures we have made of you are great. You know that. They are the makings of a book. As I see it the first half will be the nudes and figure studies. The second half would be the candids of you smelling flowers, dancing, crying and anything else we come up with, even your flight school and the trips you take after you begin flying," he said as soon as the door closed.

"So what's the problem?"

"You're Philadelphia friends might see them. You'll in danger. I worry about that as much as I worry about taking pictures of you that show to much of your body."

"Those people aren't going to look at an art book. Don't worry about it, they won't see it. Art books and newspapers are not the type books they look at."

"I do worry about it. I don't want them beating up on you again. I promised you those pictures were for you and me and the book we will publish someday when this all dies down."

"Are we partners in this deal? Let me have my input. Besides, we have many, many more pictures to shoot. How long will it take to print a book?"

"A year, maybe a year and a half."

Call Me Maggie

"Okay. At the rate we are going we are going to be shooting through the winter. Add your year and a half and we won't have it out for maybe three years. Remember we aren't going to be shooting as many when school starts or when I'm flying. School will come first. But, I will make myself available whenever I can. We just have to plan our shots in advance. I want to show you a new dress. We can start tonight, if I may use your bathroom to change. I don't believe you want to see me and my contortions getting in and out of my clothes or yours. It's not very ladylike."

Maggie took the large bags from the thrift into the bathroom, and came out a few moments later wearing an oversized hat, and closing buttons on a tight bodiced Victorian gown. With no shoes on, the long full-length skirt dragged the floor until she lifted the gown's skirt and revealed an immense multilayered underskirt. A large sash was tied in the middle of her back and the ends dropped down over her hips. The hat fell plummeted to the floor as she leaned forward in an exaggerated bow toward Norman.

Fearing an unflattering picture would result if her breasts came out of the low-cut bodice, he lowered the camera without making an exposure.

"Maggie you are stunning. I can't believe it is you. Where did you get that beautiful dress? And that great hat? You didn't spend any of your grandmother's money, did you?"

"No. I stopped in the thrift store again this afternoon. Now about that tree covered lane, Mister Kennedy." she asked as she adjusted the huge hat ribbon on her head.

"Can we shoot it tomorrow morning?"

"Try and get out of it. I have two more I will show you," she said entering the bathroom again.

The second dress did not have a skirt as full as the first. Its bodice was lace over an almost clear backcloth. The neckline's deep "V" that displayed all her cleavage and most of the lower hemisphere of her breasts.

Norman fired off a dozen shots and lowered the camera.

"I have more to show you," she said before going into the bathroom again.

Maggie returned pulling an oversized white cardigan sweater closed over her chest, and posed again. Norman shot a few with the sweater closed, a few with it open, and a few more when the sweater dropped to the floor.

First Real Date

"I will leave this here so I don't have to wear your clothes," she said and went to change again. She returned bare legged in a see-through blouse and stated, "I wasn't so sure about this one."

"I'm sure I can't photograph you wearing it in public," he stated and began shooting with Maggie standing behind the urn of flowers. After a few exposures he shot more of her standing seductively in front of the picture covering the door to his studio. The top she wore and the one in the picture were almost identical. Norman shot the remainder of the roll but kept the face on the door out of the picture, then opened the door, led her to a sheet of backdrop paper hanging from the ceiling and asked her to repeat the poses.

"If I knew you would be modeling so many outfits, I would have brought you in here earlier."

"If I had known a studio was in here, I would have insisted that you did, but I thought it was a closet."

Maggie posed for another hour in her thrift store finds.

Thursday they rose early, drove through the countryside around Chadds Ford, and were at the tree lined lane leading to an old stone house as the morning sun filtered through the haze. Maggie hurriedly removed her Banlon and pedal pushers, and then slipped into the Victorian dress. Norman clicked away as she posed in the hat and dress. He made some with a telephoto lens compressing the lane, some with a wide angle which exaggerated the lane's length, and he made other shots of old homes set in what could have been hundred year-old Currier and Ives Lithographs. At one location he was shooting with a faded old farmhouse on a hill as the background when Maggie unexpectedly lay on the grass in front to him. She removed her clothes and posed for him to shoot again. Later they stopped for a hike along the upper Brandywine. Maggie provided Norman with several shot of her bathing in the river, drying herself and nearly a hundred posing on huge boulders. By lunch time they were back at Norman's apartment where he prepared for work. He invited her to meet him there later that evening and they would print the shots they had made that morning. She went back to her place and he went to work. Maggie put on her business suit, stopped at the stewardess school making sure her enrollment was in good order, and spent a few hours with Linda at the shop.

Linda signaled Maggie into the storage room when the last customer left and said, "No rubber, no nookie. We did it with a condom. At first he was against it but he finally put one on before we jumped each other's bones."

129

Call Me Maggie

"If you are going to do it, use a condom every time. It doesn't protect you in your purse, dresser or glove box."

"The first few times we did not use one, but thanks to your advice, we have used one every time since I got them."

Maggie felt that Linda confided in her as she would a close friend. She remembered asking one of the Vinnie's other girls similar questions two years earlier. Linda and Kevin are doing it out of passion. Will they always take an extra moment to use a condom and avoid pregnancy, Maggie ask herself.

"Do you see a lot of Norman?"

"We see each other every day. We take a lot of pictures together. He's working on two big stories and has taken me along. I like watching him work. He's going to do a story on your racing this summer. Oops! I should have let him tell you." Maggie said.

"I'll pretend to be surprised." Linda promised, "Have you tasted his sweet wine yet?"

"No."

"Would you do it with him?"

"Maybe, but that's not a question to ask a young lady?"

"You've got that glow. Something must be going on."

"Not really. We spend most of our time taking pictures."

"Nothing more?"

"Nothing more."

Linda and Maggie talked on and off between customer orders. She had not spent an evening of girl talk for a long while. She found herself enjoying Linda's girl talk. Linda was even spunky, but in a happy way, as she gave her helper pointers until Kevin came in to have an hour with Linda before his dirt-pan rendezvous.

"What time are we meeting Saturday?" Maggie asked.

"Four at the car," Kevin answered with his usual omission of un-needed words.

Maggie stayed a few minutes longer until Linda turned out the shop lights, then drove to Norman house and waited. Watching night workers on the interstate being built across from Norman's apartment, she wondered if Kevin would get to work on time and hoping he would use the condoms Linda had bought for them. As the time lagged on she wondered if Norman would agree to using condoms when they became as intimate as Linda and Kevin. And she wondered when that time would come. The questions still had no answer when he parked in front of her car.

130

First Real Date

"I have this fashion layout tomorrow and I would like to do some tests shots tonight of you if you are up to it?"

"I'm up to it," Maggie answered, giving Norman a waist-locking hug.

He embraced her for a short moment and began to unload his camera bag, light case and a large electric fan.

"The girl I'm photographing tomorrow is supposed to have very long hair and I want to make a few test shots with the fan blowing your hair."

"Let's do it. You seem to be excited about the idea. I like it too. And I know you like to photograph my hair."

Norman sat up lights and the fan and then hung a black sheet on one wall with push pins.

"Maggie you could fit into any office in the city wearing those slacks and the vest with that blouse. If your stewardess uniform is as attractive, I'll ask you to model it often."

"I hope you do. Give me instructions on what to do so you will get more pictures for our book."

Norman placed the fan in front of the back drop and a stool in front of the fan. Maggie stood behind the stool, placed both hand on the seat and leaned forward. Her hair flew uncontrolled about her head once the fan started blowing. Strobe lights froze her hair in tentacles around her face and head. Norman made a dozen shots, stopped and stared at Maggie.

"Is the outfit alright?" she asked, while brushing her blown hair back into order.

"Alright, but not the best."

"May I have your sunglasses?"

"I wish all models were as easy to photograph as you are, Maggie. You are the best I have worked with."

"I have a good teacher and great inspiration." she said, then put on the sunglasses and posed until the film ran out.

As Norman reloaded Maggie removed the vest, blouse and her underwear, and then put the vest back on again, but leaving it unbuttoned. He had made only a dozen more shots when she removed the vest, brushed her hair again, and presented herself for more exposures. He shot two more rolls before turning the fan off.

In each shot, it was Maggie's face, sunglasses, and backlit strawberry hair that he recorded. In some frames, her hair froze about her head, in some it blurred about her.

Call Me Maggie

"That was our best session," he complimented her.

"Thank you, Mister Kennedy. I thought so too. A few times I remembered our first night shooting. You were wound up real tight that night. I was too. Tonight it was just right."

"I should thank you. Without you I'd be looking at a book and wishing I could shoot pictures like these."

She gave him a long hug and an even longer, soft kiss.

"If you are up to printing, I could set up the equipment."

"I would prefer to wait until tomorrow morning."

"That will be fine."

"Let's wait until then, okay? Norman, we have spent the last ten nights together. Some of those nights I needed your tenderness and support. Tonight I just want to share that happiness with you. I loved being with you this morning and I want to be with you tonight." Maggie said.

"I like that too. How about some warm wine? I did a story on this old Italian winemaker today and he would not let me leave without one of his bottles."

"I would love that too."

Norman took a bottle from his camera bag, took a corkscrew from a drawer, two glasses from the cabinet, and asked Maggie to pour while he put his lights away. She poured, then asked for a coat hanger, removed her slacks, hung them, her blouse, bra and vest on the hanger, but put the vest back on.

"This was a great night. They'll be good pictures." he said as he joined her on the sofa with their knees touching as they toasted and talked over two warm glasses of desert wine.

Soon Maggie's hand moved over Norman's pants leg. He move his up and down her bare calf until each asked in unison, "More wine?"

Norman stared at her face draped in long light red hair that reached almost to her knees as she leaned over the glasses. Maggie poured teasingly slow, sensing his pleasure. She had brushed it again as he packed his gear. The strands began at her centerline part, fell outside her eyes, and joined at the lower ends forming a long oval around her face.

"You're beautiful, Maggie, really beautiful." "Being told I am beautiful is nice to hear. Feeling that I am beautiful is even better. All my life I have heard: 'Look at the beautiful little girl. Or look at those beautiful twins.' Being an identical twin is hard on a person. I saw all of my flaws in her and hers in me. Other people only see theirs in a mirror. Being a twin, the flaws are seen whenever we are near each other. And they're doubled. When we got into puberty, it got worse. She became free with herself early. Guys thought I was too. They wanted me to be loose and free like she was. Her guys wanted me in some buy one, get one free, deal. I can't tell you how many guys wanted a threesome. I guess she had the same problems. I know she went her way and I went mine. We have not been real sisters since."

Norman wanted to interrupt and end her painful discourse, but she continued. "Being beautiful means I meet most people's idea of beautiful; a pretty face, and a good body. I learned to say what they wanted to hear. I learned that guys want my body, but women were put off by my face and cannot be friends with me. A pretty face get the guys. I quit wearing make-up to play down my face. Beauty comes from inside a person, not from the make-up they put on or the clothes they wear. I want to be a beautiful person, not just a pretty face and a good body for some stud to show off."

Maggie played her lips across the glass for a moment and continued, "When you photograph me, I feel like you need me for the picture, not just a pretty face, or a naked body you want to seduce. With you, I don't have to worry about a bulge in your breeches. I don't have to worry about being felt-up or squeezed. Feeling that way makes it easy for me to model for you. I feel needed. Feeling needed is feeling beautiful, too. You have taken me to see your brothers, your parents, plus John and Carmella, but I wasn't shown off like some new sports coat or flashy jewelry. I felt accepted and that felt beautiful. Keep on needing me in your pictures and at night sitting on the sofa. When you need me in your bed, I want to be there too. Keep showing me that you need me and that you think I am beautiful. Tell me with your kind words, your gentle touches, your warm smiles, and the soft little kisses you place on my cheeks. Show me with the beautiful pictures you make that have me in them. That's when I will really feel truly beautiful. And you will have been the one who has made me feel beautiful."

Maggie tipped her head, grinned, and smiled fully. She placed the glass behind his neck and pulled him forward. They looked in each other's eyes, only inches apart. Their foreheads touched. She lightly kissed his eyes, and then kissed his lips feverously. They embraced even longer with his hands slowly traveling up and down her back. When the wine was gone they sat in silence, touching and caressing each other until Maggie rose, removed the vest, took his hand, led him to the bed, and began slowly removing his clothes. She slipped her back against his chest, took his hand and held his hands over her breasts,

Call Me Maggie

"I feel so feminine. So wanted. Take me. Make love to me. We can take more pictures and make love again," Maggie whispered as she guided his hand across her silky pelvis and the hardened projections atop swollen mounds on her chest.

Norman stopped caressing her. His hands no longer held her breasts or rubbed her stomach. He backed away, spun around, tried to conceal his swollen appendage and said, "Maggie, I photograph you because you're a good subject, not just a beautiful person. I spend each morning and night with you because I want to be with you and take pictures of you, not to get you excited, or to make it easier for me to cop a feel or to have sex with you."

"I said the wrong thing and I am deeply sorry. Please forgive me. I have hurt you, Norman. You don't deserve to be hurt after you have done for me. Offering to repay that way is no way for a girl of my past to use. I want to make that hurt go away. I have never known anyone as gentle, tender, kind or as thoughtful toward me as you are. This may be the end of our relationship. But if it is, I'm not leaving until I make my mistake right again. What can I say to make things good again between us? What can I do?" Maggie asked.

"Just let me photograph you," he replied as pulled on his pants. "I'm sorry I am so sensitive. It's my hang-up, not something you said or did. You don't need someone who gets worked up seeing you looking beautiful and desirable as you were after we finished taking those pictures. You were more desirable then than when I was photographing you. When we finish shooting a great picture, I have great excitement in me so great I can't explain it," he said.

"I can tell when you are excited. I am just as excited? I want that excitement to last. If it leads to having you hold me in an intimate way or making love with you, I want that too, and I want you to want me for more than my modeling."

"Forgive me for over reacting. I should have known what you meant. It's my fault, not yours."

"Can we put this misunderstanding behind us? Can we still be photographer and model? Friends and partners?"

"Yes, if we can remember friends and partners don't have to repay each other, they share what they have. I just can't share you in a sexual way yet," he answered.

Maggie put the vest on again, went to the bathroom, came out a short time later wearing the white sweater, and carrying the clothes she had modeled and the suit she worn on hangers. After suspending them

134

on the clothes rack she joined Norman on the sofa again and poured the remaining wine into their glasses, passed one to him and lay with her back against his, but made no other affectionate advances.

A little before four, Maggie awoke alone. Norman was not in his bed, the kitchen or the bathroom. On her way to check the studio she heard water running in the darkroom, tapped on the darkroom door and waited for him to open it. Two minutes later he took her to the fixing tray and held her business clothes picture. Then he held up a shot of her in the vest that showed only her face and blowing hair against the black sheet. In a third picture Maggie was blowing a kiss to the camera.

"Now that you are awake, let's take a break for some coffee." Norman suggested as he grabbed a grease pencil and the proofs sheets and went to the kitchen table and said, "Choose a frame you want to print."

 Maggie choose the shot of her back on the textured rock taken in the in the river.

"Put it in the carrier shiny side up. Focus on the white paper in the easel. Close the lens down. Hit the timer and wait. Hit the timer again to "burn in" the areas to me make darker. Develop it for three minutes, fifteen seconds in the stop bath, fifteen in the fixer and we can turn on the white lights," Norman instructed her through printing steps.

Four minutes later a fourth print lay in the fixing tray.

"That's amazing," she said under her breath.

"You do the next one, and learn how to print, but don't become so expert at it that you put me out of a job." he said.

Maggie chose a shot of herself bathing in the river. She talked herself through the steps Norman went through earlier.

"I'm not sure what to burn-in or how much."

"Burn anything that would distract for the main subject in the picture, In this case, trees around the outer edges and strong highlights on the water are too strong. Burn them," he instructed.

Soon Maggie had developed her first print. She studied the photograph for a moment and was ready to print another one. They chose the shot of her drying in the sun.

"I see me in this picture, but yet it's not me. It's similar to what I felt when you were shooting. I was there but I wasn't there. I could just as well be a tree or a rock. At the time, all I wanted was to be part of a good picture. It's if I have something no one else can contribute. Here I see a girl drying her body, but it is not me. Does that make any sense?"

Call Me Maggie

"It makes sense. When we're shooting, you move into the role of a model. Your mood becomes serious. You don't exude the personality I see at other times. You become model M. A. Montgomery. She is different from Maggie Johnson, yet both of you are both the same person. On some jobs and some of the situations with you I can't believe that it is you in the picture. I look at the prints and ask myself, was that really Maggie?"

She printed the one of her in the meadow.

"That's Christina's World with a nude you created!"

"It's your creation. I was shooting the house and you put yourself in the picture. I'm glad you did. I would not have asked you to, but you did without me asking."

She stared at the picture longer than the others before they printed the one of her wearing the Victorian dress posing in the tree-covered lane.

"Let's print two of these, one for my wall."

"Let's print three so you can tape another one to my refrigerator," Maggie said.

They printed the shots of her cross-legged on the sofa, through the spindle back chair, with sunglasses and others from their session the night before.

"I'll let these wash in the sink and dry them this evening on my dinner hour. Right now I have to go to work and shot that girl with hair down to her knees."

Maggie had been shuffling and reviewing the prints as he spoke with one arm around his waist.

"Let me help. I can't believe you set this up without waking me," Maggie said.

"I wanted to get set up so you could see the prints before I have to go to work."

"Norman, don't let me infringe on your photography. I'll model. You shoot. Let me be that tree that you photograph over and over again. When I go overboard, put me back in my place, whether is in photography or my invitations for love making."

He took some fresh clothes into the bath and got ready for work. Maggie put back on her business clothes from the night before. He went to work. She visited Linda again.

Maggie sat near the sandwich station as Linda worked. Soon Linda motioned her in to the storage room and said, "You have got that look. What's happening with you and Norman?"

136

First Real Date

"What on earth do you mean?"

"For one thing you are wearing the clothes you wore last night. And you have a glow in your face. Tell me what you did last night."

"Shot some pictures. Had some wine."

"There has got to be more than that."

"Learned to print the pictures we shot," Maggie answered, smiling broadly.

"No hankey pankey took place?"

"None," Maggie stated with a straight face, and went to the shop's front.

"I've got some stops to make and you're getting busy. I'll see you tomorrow for the races," Maggie said, leaving.

Maggie made a stop at the Army-Navy store. Her second stop was at the thrift store where choose two peasant dresses, a knit shawl and another wide brimmed hat. She carried the items with her as she checked her mailbox. Inside, she sat at the table and opened a letter from the West Chester attorney, removed a folded check and a short note, then made two phone calls, showered, dressed, went to the bank and made two other stops. Afterwards, she climbed the observation deck at the airport and walked its length.

"Norman is going to see what a great partner I can be with a little more education. I will be the best model he will ever find, too. I just wish he would be more than just a friend. He's already the best friend I ever found. Linda tries so hard to be my friend. I wish she did not try so hard to have the experiences I have had. Having them and being glad to have had them are not the same. I hope she doesn't discover that for herself anytime soon," Maggie told herself during her walk.

By four o'clock, she was back in her apartment hanging her clothes when the phone rang and Norman asked if he could pick her up at five o'clock. By half past five when she wasn't examining the old homes that lined a quarter mile cobble stone bordered lawn called "The Green," she was watching Norman photograph the Old State House, in New Castle, Delaware's capital in Revolutionary days. In the peasant dress, shawl and hat Maggie wore, she could have easily been a tour guide for the old town. Norman included her in some of the panorama shots he made of The Green and Old State House and gardens of the two hundred year old homes.

By seven, they were being seated in a restaurant lighted only by candles with a service staff in revolutionary period attire. The hostess complimented Maggie's costume.

137

Call Me Maggie

The building was originally an arsenal during colonial days. The menu informed Maggie it was converted to a restaurant, the name "Arsenal on the Green" was retained. Maggie ordered blackberry tea. Norman ordered the same as he made shot of her receiving compliments from the porter surrounded by the lighted candles.

"How did your session with the long haired girl go?"

"She brought her mother. They got her in the first outfit. Her mother brushed her hair constantly, even as I was shooting. I turned on the fan and her hair was too heavy to blow. I had to give up on that idea or get a heavier fan. The copy boy went to Woolworths and got the largest one they had. She also kept covering the bathing suit top. I would tell the girl what I wanted; the mother would change it over and over. Finally, I offered the camera to the mother, told her I had had enough of her interruptions and if she could do better, shoot the pictures herself. Jackie, the women's editors, agreed to chaperon, handle the suits, and hair draping, then told her to wait in the women's department office. All during the session, the girl kept tugging her halters and trying to cover herself. Later I saw that she had more hair in her cleavage than I have on my chest. I did get one tall thin shot of her hair coming off her shoulder and down below her knees. The fan shot never worked," Norman said.

"Too bad your idea didn't turn out the way you hoped."

"The one of you did. You have another print for your refrigerator. It was not one of my better days."

"The mother and the girl knew it was swimsuits. They should have waited for something to come along where she could pose without showing the hair on her chest, shouldn't they?"

"They should've," Norman said. "It was her first modeling job. I guess wanting to have her picture put in the paper overcame their good sense."

"Enjoy your tea. Do you always dine in such exquisite places?" Maggie asked as she sampled the tea made with fresh blackberries.

"Only when I dine at your place, Miss Johnson."

Norman blushed.

"Did I tell you Linda and I had dinner with your parents and brothers last night. We sat on the lawn enjoying the sunset until the stars came out. I'm glad you're eating with me tonight. I don't like eating alone. Norman, we have seen each and slept in each other's arms for the last twelve nights, but this is our first real date," Maggie said, placed her hat in an unused chair and moved to the chair next to Norman.

"I've done all the talking. How was your day?" he asked.

First Real Date

"This morning I learned to print photographs. This afternoon I visited Linda, stopped at the Army-Navy store and my favorite thrift store for this outfit. Tonight I came to dinner with a darling man on our first official date. And I found this letter in my mailbox," she said, handing him the envelope.

He read the contents, remained stunned for a moment, and then read them again.

"This is surprising and quick." he finally said.

"I rented a storage space and reserved a truck to move the items I want. Mr. Goldman, the second hand store owner will take away what's left."

"When do you want to go get it?" Norman asked.

"Early tomorrow. I would like you to go with me. I don't want movers to go up there. You saw how I went to pieces before," Maggie requested.

"I'll call Kevin, Ernest and Lionel," he announced and left the table.

Maggie had placed rose petals in their tea when he got back.

"Kevin is lining up Lionel on his way to see Linda. He'll line up Ernest when he gets to work. We will pick them up after we get the truck." Norman explained his plan.

"Thank you Norman." she said. "I wish I were part of a large family and could get with just a phone call."

"We are just some country folks relocated to the suburbs. We are still farm people at heart enjoying simple things found on the edge of a city."

"You're proud of your country roots, aren't you?"

"Yes, I am now. At first, it was difficult for all of us. We suffered through a lot of ridicule when we first moved here. Our accents gave us away. And, we wore bib overalls for a while, but when we started wearing chinos and jeans, things got better. I found that when I exhibited pride in being a southerner, I got less ridicule, and I used to mimic voices on the radio trying to talk like a Yankee. It helped the way I felt about myself. You can judge whether it helped my speech," Norman told Maggie.

"You have a lovely voice and speech pattern, Norman."

"Kevin still has a lot of his and so does my sister. Of course Kevin never says more than he has to, but you can tell he still has lots of the southern characteristics in him and in his speech when finally has something to say."

Call Me Maggie

After dinner, they strolled up the promenade to the rhythm of horseshoes striking stone as a carriage moved up the cobblestone street. Soon she and Norman wandered into the courtyard of a flood-lit old church on the corner, and Maggie wandered the cemetery reading two hundred years old headstones. Later they walked back down The Green lined with amber gas lamps while candles stood in windows of each old home, Maggie held her arm around his waist and the large hat in a hand on his hip, while his hand rested on her shoulder. A few times their laughter broke the silence of the evening, strolling and talking, and alone in the street. Across from the Old State House they window shopped little store fronts with candles, candy, crafts and quilts.

"My mother used to do a lot of quilting in the winter. She would sit late into the night sewing patterns together. She made baby quilts while waiting for us five kids to be born. She doesn't do that anymore, not even for her grandsons."

"Why not," Maggie asked.

"In the summer she and Dad prepare can or freeze the vegetables they grow. All of us kids get in on that and help. They always send some home with Ernest and me. It helps 'em stay close to their roots, I guess. They enjoy it and they haven't slowed down since we got off the farm."

After studying items in the gift shops they wandered two blocks east where a harmonic sonata of water striking granite in the darkness replaced clogging hoofs on cobblestones. Maggie informed Norman he would be held to another date on the June when submarines would be racing in the brightness of a full moon. On their casual return stroll back to The Green they passed storefronts displaying assorted antiquities, newly woven wool wear, and crafts of every sort, they discovered a handcrafted cage containing several parakeets.

"When I was a little boy back on the farm we sometimes visited a widow woman who had a parakeet in her sitting room. I would talk and whistle with the bird while Ernest and Kevin played with her grandchildren. During supper, I asked Dad if I could get one the next cotton market day. He said he would help me build a trap to capture farm parrots instead, preferably a female. Farm parrots were the name I gave cardinals after coloring several with my crayons. They were almost as colorful as a parakeet and I would not have to wait until the cotton was taken to market. Sunday morning after breakfast, he taught me to assemble several slivers split from shake shingles into a pyramid not quite as large as the harvest baskets he had made during the winter. At same time I was assembling my trap, he was carving the trigger mechanism. In no time at all, the trap was done, the trigger loaded with a corn cob, and crushed corn sprinkled in a line leading to the trigger. Dad went to the kitchen, poured himself a cup of coffee and took a seat next to me at the window anticipating my bounty. I would capture a red male to share the cage with the multicolored momma bird, they would have baby farm parents and I would have a farm parrot family. They would have more babies and I could market them like Dad market the cotton. At least that was my dream while I waited. In no time, a female began picking up the loose corn, working her way into my trap. She was beautiful. Her colors were magnificent. She was the most perfect parrot in the whole county. I would be the envy of everyone who saw her. Waiting for the trap to fall was the longest time in my life. She would pick up a few kernels, fly back to the fence, and look for one of the cats before swooping back to the line of grain; a caution she practiced many times as I waited. Finally she pecked at the cob on the trigger and the trap fell. I rushed to the trap, ever-so-slowly slipped my hand inside, screamed, and jerked my hand back. She flew away, leaving me with a few feathers and a bleeding finger. I still have the scar today where she nipped me," Norman said, holding his finger up in the dark. "The next morning, a female with missing feathers fed from the feeder pan while keeping a sharp eye on me. Wanting something beautiful and having it are not the same. I have never asked good-looking girls for a date or got in a friendly relationship with a beautiful one. I figured they will always be trying to leave or there will be someone more colorful come along that they would rather be with than me," Norman concluded.

"When we deny a creature from its own choices, we can never be certain we were meant to have it. If we set it free and it returns, it wants us to have it. I know this from having been locked up by Vinnie." Maggie said, as tears formed in her eyes. "You set me free from him. If you want me, I will comeback as your cardinal did. If you had caged that bird on the farm, she would not have been able to fly away and return to you as she did that morning. When I get my wings, fly away, and return to you, you can be certain that with you is where I want to be."

"And with you is where I want to be. Especially tonight. I don't want my first date with you to end." Norman said.

"It can last until we pick up the truck I rented for tomorrow. You have tomorrow night off, we could have another date then and another Tuesday," Maggie suggested. "Tonight has been our real first date and it is one I won't forget."

Call Me Maggie

Early the next morning she several signed rental forms while Norman signed an insurance form. She co-piloted as Norman maneuvered the truck out of the rental yard while his convertible stayed parked. They stopped at his parents' house, passed-out coffee and sweet rolls, then led Kevin and the station wagon away with Lionel riding shotgun.

"Are you sure your father doesn't mind you using his station wagon to move me?" she asked.

"He never had a car or truck back on the farm. He always had to ask someone to drive him some place, if it was too far to take the mules. When he did get the station wagon in 1955, he promised that we could use it as long as it kept running if we would help him buy it. I worked in a laundry, Ernest delivered newspapers, Loraine baby-sat, Mom worked and Kevin carried shopper's groceries home from the A&P. Lionel was too young then but he works now. That was eight years ago and the station wagon's still running. Dad has a Chevy truck he prefers to drive. Dad says if it can be fixed, we should keep it. We have kept both. Kevin keeps them running," Norman said.

"I wish I had a caring family like yours."

"Maybe that cardinal inside you will bring you back to their house after you finish school and after your flights. A few more visits and you'll be almost family like Linda is."

"Your mother and father have baited the trap. Now they'll have to fence me out to keep me from coming back."

"To put Linda in a race car he has spent so much time building, Kevin must be getting serious with Linda. I would think he'd drive it himself," Norman said.

"He'll be spending more time with Linda than with the car, unless she is in the car with him. Does your family know about my past?"

"Only Kevin, Linda, and I know."

"Linda could just as well be another sister for me, and she may be a real part of your family soon."

"Is there something going on I have missed?"

"Let's say Kevin doesn't see her as one of the guys any longer," Maggie answered with an alluring grin.

"It took him long enough. How serious is it?"

"Serious serious!"

"That serious, huh? So you thin I may be having another sister-in-law soon."

"Could be."

First Real Date

As they pulled in Grandmother Johnson's farm driveway, Maggie said tearfully,"I may lean on you and your brothers too much while we load. Especially you Norman,"

"Consider yourself family. Lean as much as you need."

"You and your brothers make that easy."

Kevin and Lionel unloaded boxes within boxes and put them on the porch as they had a week earlier in Chester. Maggie walked through the house and met with the three brothers in the kitchen.

"We won't be taking everything. I would like the woodstove, rocking chair, and a dresser in my apartment. Load them last. The rest can be boxed or taken to the storage facility. I can sort those things later. My grandparents did not have many things, and like your parents they cared for what they did have. I intend to do the same. I appreciate you guys coming out when you could be sleeping late on a Saturday morning. The sooner we get it moved the better for you guys," Maggie said, fighting to hold back more tears.

The three brothers embraced Maggie for a moment and began packing and loading small items in station wagon and larger one in the truck. When they finished the house, the barn and greenhouse came next with Maggie making dozens of difficult choices of what would go where and what would be left for Mr. Goldman. When those buildings were depleted, she suggested Lionel ride with she and Norman while Kevin picked up lunch form Linda's shop, gave him a hug and sent him on his way. By one o'clock they were lunching under the dogwood.

A little after three, Linda arrived to show off her graduation, a pink and white 1955 Ford Crown Victoria, Kevin immediately nicknamed the Double Nickel Vic.

"Got it this morning. Passed the test yesterday in the party wagon."

Kevin smiled as he looked over the Vic, a sister to his racer, but with tiara and an automatic transmission. After a quick inspection, he asked to be awakened in an hour and folded himself in the station wagon's middle seat for the first sleep had in thirty hours.

Back in her apartment, Maggie admired her stove and farm table complete with fresh flowers as she sat rocking the Raggedy Anne and the old plush bear in the chair that once sat by her bed at Grandmother's Johnson's Farmhouse. Norman shot a few pictures.

"I must get ready for Linda's race, and then we must get you cleaned up. I have a shirt and jeans of yours that I borrowed and wore to Chester. You can shower her or I can grab a few things and shower at your place, if that's alright with you," she stated after a brief respite in the rocker while Norman made another picture of her.

As three o'clock approached, Norman said, "Jeans aren't quite what I wanted to wear tonight. Something a little less James Dean-ish might be better. I'll have to run back to my place and change."

"Give me a minute and I'll come with you."

Maggie grabbed fresh slacks, blouse and underwear, opened the buttons on the old denim shirt she wore, tossed it in a hamper, and unsnapped her bra, stopped, then held it over her chest, and said, "I'm sorry, I still have some old habits to break."

As she showered, Norman lifted the album he had assembled for her viewed the pictures and said, "These are good pictures of you. This is the first time I have seen them all together. You take a good picture, Miss Montgomery."

Maggie rushed to him still drying herself and stated, "You take good pictures, Mister Kennedy, and I'm just a tree that moves her limbs for your camera."

As she dressed and packed, he studied the album again, but too no pictures.

"When we at your apartment, my clothes are here; when we are here, your clothes are there. I'll take some of mine there when we go, if you don't mind mine sharing the rack with yours, bring some of yours here when we come back," she suggested.

"Saves driving back and forth."

As they drove into the city, Maggie sat close to him, closer than she had in the truck. Norman felt her leg against his and her chest against his arm. At his apartment, she hung the clothes to be left there on the clothes rack while he removed ones he would wear to the races and hurried to the shower. Before the water became hot, she joined him under the spray and asked, "Are you thinking what I'm thinking?"

"I'm thinking that if we do what you're thinking, we will be late," he replied. "You had better let me shower alone before this leads to something that will make us late for Linda's race."

"Linda already thinks we're doing what you think I am thinking. No matter what I said when I told her we weren't, she didn't seem to believe me, so I let her keep thinking we are.

Maggie asked to stop at the Army-Navy Store en-route. Ernest and his girlfriend were at the Kennedy home when Norman parked. They would tow the racer. Kevin got his first ride in the Crowe Vic as Linda drove back into town for her parents. They were not about to miss

First Real Date

her first race, nor would Pop Pop and Mom Mom. Lionel had invited a fifteen-year-old girl from around the corner. Linda had her fan club ready for the road.

At the track, their parents found seats while Norman photographed Linda and Kevin filling out registration forms. Ernest and Lionel prepared the racer while Lionel's guest and Maggie waited for an opportunity to present the Army-Navy store bag to Linda.   Linda pulled a blue Air Force flight suits from the bag with a pair of golden wings over the breast area, and the words Linda Reed embroidered on the other side. Kevin received a matching one. Norman made pictures as they dressed between vehicles. Linda left hers zipped low, showing a pink "push-up" and abundant cleavage. As soon as Kevin adjusted her helmet and sunglasses, Linda strapped her belt and was ready for her first race.

She drove to the starting line, made a long burn-out before Kevin positioned her for the start. The Christmas tree blinked. Two cars screamed, smoked, and lurched forward. Linda missed second gear. Her opponent missed second and third. She returned to the others and leaped wildly onto Kevin, hugging him as Ernest squeezed some grease on the shift linkage and Lionel tweaked the carburetor. Norman made a picture of Kevin and briefing Linda reflected in the racers mirror. Maggie sat between the fifteen year-old and Pop Pop Kennedy. She learned the girl's name; Madeline Whiteside, and she was in Lionel's homeroom at school. Maggie remembered another Madeline of time past when she and her sister were also fifteen years old and were beginning to date.

Linda savored her victories and craved more. Her last competitor was another '55 Ford, identical except its colors were red and white. She put her Ford ahead in the first 100 feet and held the advantage all the way to the finish line.

Maggie had rejoined the Kennedy brothers when Linda returned to the pit area. Linda, climbed onto the car's roof, and began waving. When she collected a small trophy and a $100 check, she unzipped her jump suit lower shouted loudly. The open jump suit and pink bra revealed that she was not just one of the boys.

Maggie hugged Linda swinging her round and round. They grabbed Kevin and became a celebrating trio. The others came down from the bleachers to join the victory merriment that lasted until the track lights went dark, and celebrated again at the Elkton Dairy Queen.

As they drove home, Maggie remembered a Pennsylvania Mountain hayride and twin girls sitting close to a couple of boys and slid over close to Norman. At his apartment, she asked him to open the convertible's trunk. She removed a suitcase and another Army-Navy bag. Once inside, Maggie presented the bag to Norman.

"Thank you for this morning, yesterday and all the yesterday's since we met," she said, removing a jacket with countless pockets.

"Thank you, Maggie. I never have enough pockets."

"Let me try it on. You said seeing me wearing your clothes turned you on."

"Did I say that?"

"You said that or something close to it. I'll let you in on a secret; it arouses me too. We could do something about our stimulation when you get the pictures you want," she answered as he made a photograph of her modeling a safari jacket he assumed she would wear more than he would.

"I enjoyed talking with your father tonight at the races. He invited me to come by tomorrow for some of his roses. I will take him up on his offer while you are working, if that's okay with you, Norman?" Maggie said, placing candles on her table.

"Visit them as often as you like, but be careful. They have a way of growing on you. You will learn to love them, and be like another daughter to them in no time. And you will probably learn a lot about gardening from Dad and motherhood from Mom if you are planning a large family in the future."

"I already have," Maggie said while tears filled her eyes.

Norman noticed the tears and said, "I apologize, Maggie. I forgot that you did not have your father as you grew up."

"We missed out on so much not having him as I grew up and Mother was unable to take care of us. Getting to know your parents made me realize how much."

They embraced and snuggled and forgot about sipping scotch.

"I start night school Monday evening. But, it's only two hours a night, Monday, Wednesday and Thursday. I'll have to get used to homework again."

"What kind of student were you before?"

"Good, but not great. School was easy for me. I did not have to work hard at it and I got mostly A's. I will be cracking the books more this time. If I hadn't started going to Bandstand and got hung up with Vinnie and his crowd, I would have graduated this month like Linda," Maggie said as her eyes moistening again.

146

First Real Date

"If you were good before, you'll be good now. I won't take up much of your time. But I'll miss stopping by after work, finding flowers on my food and in my drinks. But most of all, I'll miss taking pictures of you."

"I'll miss those too. And, I'll miss Linda, Kevin and your parents almost as much as I'll miss you. You don't work on Tuesdays and I don't have night school."

"You're seeing Dad tomorrow. Let's take both of them to brunch. I only gave Mom that azalea for Mother's Day. We could go out with them and I would still get to work on time. Say you will get up early and go with us."

"If you are sure, I would like to go,"

"I'm sure. It's a date."

"Another date? Are you trying to spoil me? If you are, it's working." Maggie stated as she laid her head on his shoulder.

"I'm trying real, real hard. But, it was you who gave me the safari jacket. You're spoiling me!"

"And now, look who is wearing it, me, not you."

Maggie wore a bib dress when Norman pulled in front of the white fence and went directly into the house. Mom Mom was washing canning jars. Norman gave her a hug and began pouring a coffee in a mug he took from a rack above the coffee pot.

"Ya picked a busy time to stop in fer coffee. Pop Pop is in the garden pick'n beans. The rest are still sleeping. Kevin got is real late last night. He'll be in bed 'till noon," she said, before she gave Maggie a hug and returned to the yellow porcelain sink and her jars.

"We came to take you to breakfast or brunch."

"Have to wait till I wash my jars," his mother answered.

"We knew you would be up, but I didn't know you would be canning so early. Let me help and we can get to the restaurant before the church crowd," Maggie said.

"When di beans are in, we're work'n early. Cooler den."

"I used to help my grandmother can before she died. I don't remember much other than snapping beans on her porch and smelling vinegar as she cooked them," Maggie said, drying jars as Mom Mom washed them.

"Der's nuthin' like fresh beans and white pork for supper. Can ya stay?"

"I'd like that," Maggie answered.

"Morning, Pop," Norman said, walking into the garden.

147

Call Me Maggie

"Morning, boy," Pop Pop answered.

His father rarely addressed him as Norman, always said "Boy."

"Garden is looking good this year. Should be plenty to put away for winter," Norman complimented his father.

"Been getting 'nough rain to raise catfish," Pop Pop said.

"I can help you dig a pond," Norman jokingly offered.

"I got three days off next weekend. We could get started then," Pop Pop said.

Norman should have known his dad could come up with a plan as quickly as his boy could and said, "I'll be working Sunday and Monday, but I'll have my mornings free. We could start Saturday morning," Norman said.

"Be cooler in the morn'ns," Pop Pop said.

"Maggie and I would like to have brunch with you and Mom. I have to be at work by noon. How about the Farmhouse?"

"Better check with your mother. Any place is fine with me," the father said. "But I gotta pick my beans first,"

Norman had been straddling a row, and pulling yellow wax bean since he entered the garden. His father had only glanced up briefly when Norman arrived. Soon both men's pants were damp with dew and two bushel baskets were filled. The elder Kennedy would repeat the task at daylight the next morning before leaving for work. Norman carried the beans to the edge of the dogwood tree canopy. His father brought a washtub from the garage. Norman ran water and began filling a wash tub. His father brought gallon bottles of ice from the freezer and added the beans. The beans would sit in the ice water bath until after brunch. With his Barlow pocket knife, Pop Pop cut two buds from his rose garden, lifted two Coca Cola bottles from a case, filled them water, and presented one to Maggie and one to Norman's mother. Mom placed hers on a window sill behind the kitchen table before they left for brunch. Maggie placed hers there while Mrs. Kennedy changed into a dress and retied her apron. Mr. Kennedy remained in his denim overalls.

The Farmhouse was a large Georgian brick structure sitting on a large lawn across from the airport. A tree-lined lane and large columns welcome them as they turned from U.S 13. A few diners mistook Norman's parents and Maggie for The Farmhouse staff when they arrive. Suburban sprawl had not take The Farmhouse and the quarter-mile long wooden warehouse just behind it with the appearance a military barracks of the World War II era. It now housed booths where vendors marketed their wares each Friday, Saturday and Sunday under the generic name of

First Real Date

"The Farmer's Market." Almost any item imaginable could be found in the booths from fresh vegetables brought by Amish and Mennonite farmers to retired antiques farm implements to Japanese tools and toys.

During brunch Mom and Pop invited Maggie to spend the afternoon snapping and canning beans and "sitting' by the dogwood.

Sirens interrupted their post brunch coffee. Through windows across the room, they could see flames rising from The Farmer Market building. Norman took a hand full of change from his pockets, passed it to Maggie and asked she call the newspaper, inform them he would be late and report the fire as big one out of control, then bolted outside, fired a few shots with the Lexica, sprinted to his car, added a large bag to his shoulder, and raced toward the market. For more than two hours he photographed firemen from all over the area fighting the blaze. Pop Pop helped pull fire hoses. Maggie and Mom Mom Kennedy carried drinks from The Farmhouse to the firefighters.

Soot and ash soon covered Maggie's face, clothes and hair. The strawberry blonde color soon changed to salt and pepper gray much like Mrs. Kennedy's, but with reddish highlight. Black smudges crisscrossed her face contrasting her white teeth, which she flashed to each fire fighter. Fatigue evaded Maggie as she raced to resupply the firefighters. Satisfaction from helping them filled her veins.

Firemen and volunteers were still hosing embers as the sunset.

A wood burning canning kitchen was set up at the barbecue pit near the dogwood tree. Pop Pop explained the history of the tree to Maggie. Two had been dug from their farm in Alabama, pampered on the trip to Delaware. He planted one in their yard, and one at Mom Mom's father's home. Pop Pop taught her to snap beans, about gardening, plus raising cotton, corn, and sugar cane for syrup. Mom Mom gave her canning tips, kitchen aids, quilting stitches, and her formula for canning. Maggie learned that Mrs. Kennedy and her sister had been raised by their father during the Depression era after their mother passed away after an unknown illness. The sister had peen handicapped since a fever when she was a toddler. The sister still shared a home with her father and two children and but without a husband. Mr. and Mrs. Kennedy had always and still did plant a garden large enough to share with her sister, her father and the children, as well as Norman, Ernest and Loraine. Linda came by to take Kevin away from the racer to spend the late afternoon at the Sand Pit swimming. Lionel and Madeline walked about the neighborhood holding hands.

Call Me Maggie

Norman returned around seven o'clock for grilled pork chops, mashed potatoes and fresh beans flavored with okra and white pork. He did not return to the office, but made a night shot of the Farmer's Market remains before he and Maggie returned to her apartment. She still wore her bibbed jumper heavily stained with ash, soot, coffee, tea, bean and tomato stalk sap deposited during the lesson in "sucker removal" from Pop Pop. Norman had made a picture of her and her stained jumper at the fire scene. He added a print of her serving drinks to the firemen to her album as she showered.

"Your parents treated me like one of their own today," Maggie said, placing her jumper in the bathtub to soak.

"Looks like they kept you busy too."

"I could have stayed all night gardening, canning, pruning, and talking with them. They seemed to have enjoyed me sharing their chores and spending time with them. I enjoyed it."

"I'm sure they did, too. Since we kids got older, we're not around as much as they would like. They have each other and share almost everything with each other as well as friends, visitors or even strangers."

Maggie remembered Sunday's with her grandmother. There had been chores that her grandmother did, but there was time for sitting, talking, visiting, and sipping iced tea.

"Your mother shared a sketch book with me this afternoon after I mentioned that I have modeled for you. It contained figure study sketches you did in school. Now I understand why you make such beautiful pictures. You are more than just a photographer; you are an artist as well," Maggie said.

"I thought she threw it out long ago," he said, wearing a strong red blush.

"She did not throw it out. She put it away in the attic. I think she is proud of it and the scrapbook of your photographs she has kept," Maggie informed Norman.

"I remember it embarrassed her when I showed them to her. She was a bit prudish at the time, I thought."

"She can't be too much of a prude. She had six babies and raised five of you. She could have been like my mother. No modesty at all. Always naked and sharing her bed with strange men was second nature to my mother."

Norman remembered Maggie had told him she too was naked half the time until she reached puberty.

First Real Date

"Borrow the book, and shoot some pictures based on the sketches you made."

Normal and Maggie spent four hours shooting figure studies after Maggie's night school class. They discussed her first night's classes as she posed and Norman changed and re-changed his lighting setups then volunteered to print with him the next morning. Her schedule would change after Memorial Day weekend. She wanted to get as many photographs finished as possible. Her album now contained nearly a hundred prints. Maggie stayed close to Norman as he photographed a parade in the city, an armed Forces show at the airport and shared coffee until midnight.

Saturday morning they dug a fish pond in Pop Pop and Mom Mom's yard. Sunday morning they placed stones over a rubber pool liner and filled the pond with water before Norman went to the newspaper office.

Call Me Maggie

5

Buying the Farm

Norman stayed with Maggie through the night and left as she entered the Nash dressed in a navy blue jacket and skirt.

"You look like a stewardess already," Norman said before he kissed her for luck.

June first, Maggie joined eighty other young women at Intercontinental Airways' stewardess school. Two night classes the week before eased her nervousness.

"If you last name begins with A through J, sit on the left. Those with K through Z, you'll find your name on the right side," an instructor said from the font of the room.

Maggie found her name on a packet in the last row to the left. "It's just the first day and already I'm at the back of the class," Maggie told herself.

"But I won't be for long!" she added.

Paperwork was first on the agenda. Even the Avery stick-on rectangles were paper. "Mary Anne Johnson" had been neatly printed in blue block characters and clipped to a folder containing a greeting letter, enrollment forms and a manual Zeroed from another airline with long winged eagle logo.

Two women in blue uniforms stepped before the class. Each had a pair of gold strips on the cuffs of their blazers. One said, "Good morning, ladies. Are we ready to become airline stewardesses?"

Eighty voices answered, "Yes."

"Again, louder!"

The voices repeated louder with the same answer.

"I am Bonnie Barton. I am your chief instructor. Call me Bonnie. Call me Miss Barton, or call me Bee Bee, but call me when you have a problem. If I can't fix it, Miss Hartmann can. She is the school superintendent."

153

Call Me Maggie

"Hello ladies. Our job is to make sure everyone of you women will be qualified to fly our aircraft in three months. Other airlines take six. We'll cut some corners, and cut some extraneous instruction. We'll work harder and be finished by August thirty first. Won't we ladies? Give me a loud yes if you agree." Miss Hartmann said.

"Yes," the young ladies yelled.

"How many of you have flown in a large plane before?" Bee Bee asked.

About half of the class raised their hands.

"We are a contract carrier. We were a charter service. We make vacation hops, drop our passengers off and come home. Our passengers pay your salary the same as diners pay the waitresses in your favorite restaurant. Your job will be to serve the passengers, re-assure them, feed them and make their flight as comfortable as possible. It not as easy as it looks. Study hard, learn well and good flying," the superintendent said.

"We have fifteen aircraft. Some are Stratocruisers modeled after the bomber that ended World War Two. Some are Constellations and some are Super Constellations. The supers are the same but longer and carry more passengers. The Air Force calls them C-121's. We call them Connies. Let's go to the apron and meet Connie," Bee Bee said.

A huge four-engine plane sat just beyond the classroom. Three vertical fins rose above the horizontal stabilizer. Her black tipped nose was equally high and drooped slightly, but her wing tips pointed skyward. Her metal skin glistened even though it was more than ten years old. She had recently been polished and accent paint freshened. She had been retired from another airline that had moved into the age of jets. Like workhorses before her, Connie had taken a rest, been refurbished, and brought out of retirement to proudly fly again and to fill the aircraft shortage. Planes could not be built fast enough to meet the public and military need in the early '60's.

Long rollaway stairs lead to a left side door in front of two huge engines. Inside Maggie looked down a long tube lined with two rows of upholstered spats beneath tiny windows. A wall of cabinets lined a narrow short hallway was at the far end.

Bee Bee took a microphone from the wall. "Please be seated, ladies. Welcome to Intercontinental Airways. This is your aircraft. Get to know it better than you know your boyfriend. She demands good stewardess's and we are going to train you to be that; a good stewardess or flight attendant as we are sometimes called," Bee Bee began and continued until a lunch break.

Buying the Farm

"I would ask that an attendant serve lunch, but you are our attendants, so lunch--airline style--will be in classroom A. At one o'clock we will meet in classroom B. Join me for lunch, and let's get to know each other over ham sandwiches," Bee Bee kept her upbeat patter going. During lunch, she moved among the tables putting faces with name tags and keeping moral up.

"Where are you from? I love Salisbury! Havre de Grace, nice town. West Chester! Pennsylvania or New York? Both are pretty towns. You should see the other one two. Yes, we'll supply uniforms. Yes, we have overnight lodging for you. Yes, you can fly with us after you get married. Of course, you can fly after you have your baby. You look great today, don't change a thing," Bee Bee went on and on.

"It's one o'clock ladies. Let's move across the hall. Put your refuse in the barrel. It's part of a stewardess's job, too," Another two stripped said.

Maggie moved toward the door and barrel with Donna Carol Clark. They met during a coffee break with a "Call me Maggie, Call me D.C." exchange. D.C. said she was a University of Delaware student who signed up for the school rather than work or attend summer classes. She would make the decision to fly as career after the school ended and just before the university's fall semester began.

The afternoon class began with a second two striper began the introducing herself as Clara Potter, a former stewardess. She began saying, "Call me Clara. Forget the Mrs. Potter stuff. Yes I am pregnant," and concluded, "It's 5 P.M. Let's call it a day. If you know any nurses that don't get air sick, ask them to come see us. We still need nurses who want to become airline stewardesses. Tell the ones that get air sickness, too."

"Come with us to Steve's Tavern," D. C. asked Maggie. "The auto plant workers hanging out there will buy our drinks all evening."

"Thanks, but no thanks. I have night school."   Maggie drove the one mile to her apartment, opened a can of Chef Boyardee Beefaroni, tore some lettuce, chopped a small tomato, poured a glass of milk and reviewed her night school textbook while eating. By ten of seven, she was in her classroom, reviewing again. A little after nine Maggie pulled into parking space 101. A pink and white Crown Vic pulled into space 102 followed by Kevin's black racer. An electronic organ playing "Telstar" played in both cars. High above a man-made satellite with the same name coasted through space relaying messages around the world.

155

Call Me Maggie

"How was your first day?" Linda asked before getting out.

"Long! And great." Maggie said. "I'll give you a Reader's Digest version."

"Kevin has to leave soon, but I don't. Tell us about it before he goes," Linda said.

"The instructors are upbeat. The planes are big. The manual is fat. The paperwork will choke a horse. The hours are seven to five until August thirty-first. Start flying after Labor Day. And I'm gonna love it." Maggie condensed her school day.

"Anything else?" Linda asked as she passed out Seven Ups.

"A lot of lectures and demonstrations. I did get invited out for drinks, but turned it down. Just a few of the students going out to a place called Steve's to milk the bar flies from a car assembly plant," Maggie continued.

"You wanna stay away from there!" Kevin advised.

"I intend to," Maggie stated.

Kevin began looking through the book of photographs that lay on the coffee table while Maggie stepped around Linda to get to her stewardess school packet of papers.

"You put in a whole day at the airport plus night school. I only have four hours a day at Goldey-Beacom. That's gotta be tough on you"

"It will be tough, but only for three months. Then this chick is going to fly. We take charter flight of vacationers to faraway resorts. I can volunteer for those and visit exotic places. I would love that. But the book work has to be finished first."

Maggie sighed as she ran her fingers through her hair, and then commenced to arrange the papers into two stacks: Those to be filled out in one pile and a pile to be read, across the table where Linda had sat.

After taking a seat with Kevin and the picture album, Linda said. "I thought you were putting me on. You really have been making some pictures. These are fantastic, really fantastic,"

"Linda!" Maggie's temper had been aroused. She started to yell, but composed herself, and started again. "Linda, I have lots of studying to do. You are sharper than I am. You grasp thing a lot quicker than I do and don't have to study as hard as I do. I have to work at it. Please excuse me tonight and let's get together Saturday. I'll come to the races with you and keep records for you. We can talk before and after you race."

"Works for me. I'll scat and see you Saturday."

"No hard feelings, Linda?"

Buying the Farm

"No hard feelings! Those are fantastic pictures."

"Ready to go, Linda, I've gotta get to the yard and move some dirt if you want to race the Ford Saturday night," Kevin said rising and then waiting at the door as Linda hugged Maggie.

Maggie felt her privacy had been violated by Linda looking the album, yet after Linda and Kevin left, Maggie was sorry for being firm with Linda and regretted leaving the book on the table. She removed her suit, folded it and placed in a bag of laundry, washed her face, slipped on a bulky sweater, and returned to her paperwork. Half way through filling out the papers, Norman's key opened her door.

"I'll wait 'till you're finished," he said, going to the sofa and placed more prints in the picture album while Maggie filled in blacks on a dozen or more forms.

She came to the sofa, lay her hips next to his and her back against his chest, twisted a section of her hair, but said nothing until Norman said

"Something's bothering you. Want to tell me about it?"

"Linda saw the picture book."

"So that's what's bothering you. Not something at school. You had me worried for a moment wondering if some hitch had come up."

"I wasn't ready for anyone but you to see them. You are so clinical, so professional, other people might not be, especially Linda or any of your family."

"Did Linda say anything off color?"

'She just said they were fantastic. I didn't give her a chance to say anything else. I cut her off before she said anything bawdy. I had a long hard day and felt overwhelmed by everything."

"Unless we keep them put away, everyone will see them sooner or later. It is better that she was first instead of Kevin or Lionel. I think Kevin is too shy to have said anything off color," Norman said, slowly rubbing her arms.

"I'll get over it, but I'll put the book away till I am ready to have anyone but you to see our work."

"Now, tell me about stewardess classes?"

"The instructors are cheerful, upbeat, and super encouraging. They don't just lecture and ask questions, they explain and interact with us. The other students are all about my age. I think I made friends with two girls. One asked me to go out for a drink with her, but my bar hopping, pick-up days are over." Maggie spun herself enough to face

Call Me Maggie

Norman and added, "The bad thing is I won't have enough time to lay close like this with you. I am going to miss that a lot."

"I can come by after I get off work, but I am not going to interfere with your studies. We still have Saturday's and Sunday mornings. Our schedules don't conflict then unless you are overloaded with studies. And besides it's only for three months."

"If that book and those papers on the table are any indication of what's ahead of me, it's going to be a long three months," Maggie said as she pushed her hair out of her face.

"Shouldn't you be getting back to them?"

"I should, but I have a craving for some pizza. Let me slip on some slacks and we can run down of Piccotti's"

"Let me run out and get one while you crack the books and shuffle papers. We'll celebrate your first day of school when I get back."

"Sausage, onions, and peppers, but easy on the onions if you are staying here tonight."

"Easy on the onions, it is!"

Just after sunrise, Norman kissed Maggie goodbye in the parking lot. She wanted to get to the airport and familiarize herself more with Connie before class started. And she had promised herself she would get a seat near the front of the classroom.

Maggie had to show driver's license her papers and manual to a security guard before going onto the apron where the plane remained. She made a slow walk around tenderly touching the propellers and tires.

"We are going to become good friends before too long, ole girl. You are going to take me to wonderful new places far away from where I have been till now and see things a working girl from Chester, Pennsylvania could never expect to see" she whispered.

Slowly she climbed the stairs, pushed a large lever, and walked inside. The cabin was even more cavernous without people. She slowly walked to the rear, rubbing seat backs until he reached the stewardess work area. She pulled a few doors and drawers that resisted until she found their latches, examined their contents, and closed them again. Within fifteen minutes, she was in front row seat in classroom B. Soon a petite, demure brunette sat beside Maggie.

"Hi! I'm Midge McGinnis from Georgetown," the brunette said.

"I'm Mary Anne Johnson, but call me Maggie."

"I signed for this to get away from the farm. My dad is a pea farmer, but there is no future in that for a girl, except to marry another pea farmer. I tried Wesley College for two years. Figured there will always be a need for teachers even though it was not what I really wanted. One day I saw the airline's ad, so I drove up and signed up. Now I'm going to be a stewardess and see more of the world that a pea field."

"Did you ever wait tables?" a voice behind them asked.

"Only at church socials," Midge said in an affedtedly shy tone.

"Put them together, ad safety, rescue, taking care of frightened passengers plus others who drink too much, try to grab your ass and you have an airline stewardess. Except the pay is better, the hours longer and chances are you won't land a doctor or lawyer. But you might land a pilot or traveling business man," the voiced said.

"That's why I am here, to find a husband who can keep me the way I would like to be kept," another voice said.

"I intend to keep myself the way I want to be kept. I have since I was fourteen," Maggie answered the girl she later learned was named D. C. Clark.

"Me to," Midge agreed.

"On most airlines, when you marry a pilot, you lose your job. When you get pregnant or overweight you have to stop flying. But your husband or boyfriend keeps on flying. With me, it was double jeopardy. We kept our marriage a secret, but I couldn't keep this hidden," Clara said, rubbing her stomach.

"But you are a stewardess," Midge said.

"No, I'm an instructor. I only fly to evaluate other stewardesses' performance. You girls will have to stick together after you graduate or your careers could be a short one like mine. File some lawsuits, foam a union, refuse to work, organize a sick-out, walk a picket line, write lots of letters and do whatever it takes to get yourselves some security. Airlines are growing, planes are getting bigger, more stewardesses are needed, and we can't find enough women to fill the slots. Men will be in our ranks soon, just as they are in nursing. Our first stewardesses were nurses, but that has changed and it will change again when men, married women, or anyone who believes fairness and equality get themselves heard," Clara told the young women.

"The man that pays the fiddler picks the tune," D.C. said.

"Only if we keep letting them. Let's learn our jobs and learn them so well the airlines can't get along without us," Clara said.

During the conversation, Maggie realized that she had done things the way she wanted for the past two years. Someone paid and she picked the tune or fulfilled the act they paid for.

Call Me Maggie

"Sorry to start your morning on such a serious note, but it is serious. Let's get started on today's instructions. Half of you will remain here with me for morning classes and half will go to the other classroom. After lunch, the instructors will switch classrooms and give room B the same lesson. You will learn more in smaller groups," Clara told the students.

Maggie sat through a morning of lectures on evacuating the aircraft and first aid that she would be expected to know by the end of the summer. In the afternoon, she and the other applicants were taught how they were expected to greet passengers, serve food and drinks, and how to handle choking situations should a passenger have a problem swallowing their airline food with a new technique called the Heimlich maneuver.

"All our flights will carry food, milk, and soft drinks for our passengers. Only the vacation charter flights will carry liquor, beer or wine. The first cocktail or wine will be free to any passenger who wants it. The second one will cost the passenger two dollars as long as the supply lasts. Third servings will be denied. We are not a flying cocktail lounge, even though some of the passengers think it might be, particularly when comes to the 'tail' part. Some of you are too young to have had contact with that type of passenger. We will pass on pointers that will help you to spot and handle passengers who expect or want more than a good stewardess should provide. Pair off and let's get started," Clara told the young ladies.

Maggie agreed as Midge selected her with hand signals.

"I don't have much experience dealing with unwanted advances from drunken men. Do you?" Midge asked.

"More than a few," Maggie answered.

Midge saw a stupor come over Maggie and chose another subject.

"I have never flown before," Midge started again.

"I hadn't either until a couple of weeks ago when I went flying with three friends. The pilot let me handle the controls. It was an enormous sensation of satisfaction. That's when I knew applying for this school was a good idea," Maggie said.

"How did you learn about the school?" Midge asked.

"A friend told me about it. I was waiting until I turned twenty-one and apply to one of the big airlines. Looking forward to a summer serving pizza or pulling taffy in Rehoboth for the summer was not a bright prospect. How about you?" Maggie asked.

Buying the Farm

"Each morning and afternoon I drove past the big planes at Dover Air Force Base on my way to college. One day I saw a notice on the bulletin board at Wesley College, drove up here and applied instead of going to class. Now here I am studying to be stewardess, instead of elementary education. Not bad for a country girl, I guess," Midge said.

Mid-morning Norman stopped in photographed a mummified Maggie that Midge had bandaged and returned twice a week for other pictures. He called Maggie often before leaving the newspaper office, but came to her apartment only on Tuesday nights. Saturday nights he photographed Linda racing.

Each morning Maggie and her classmates returned to the classroom. Each afternoon they traded classrooms with another forty students. She counted the days until her classes ended. Five o'clock Friday arrived in no time at all. Four Fridays went by equally fast. The Fourth of July weekend arrived. Most of the girls made plans to go home or to the beach for the long weekend. Maggie wanted to relax and catch up on her relationships with Norman, his parents, brothers and with Linda. She began Friday evening asking Linda, "How is your racing career?"

"Four wins at Atco, three at Cecil County. I'll be promoting Fords at the dealership with the car Saturday morning before the race. Got a thousand dollars from them to put their name on side of the car for the season. Norman has been making plenty of pictures of me, Kevin and Lionel. He says he has a story. At any rate, I've got a nice scrapbook. Not as nice as yours though. Still Friends," Linda said.

"More like sisters. I'm sorry I was short with you that night you wanted to share my first class and look at my pictures. I sure you didn't see anything you haven't seen in a locker room." Maggie said. "I hear angels ringing the midnight chimes every night. Weekends too."

"You look worn out. Are you and Norman getting it on yet?" Linda asked. "He doesn't seem to be the same old Norman. Seem to be tired when he drops in, and more tired on Saturday. "

"No, we are not getting it on. I only see him on Tuesday evenings and that looking across a book. We have rarely made any pictures in the past month, except a few with my face in a book,"

"Kevin and I are. We use a box of condoms every week."

"I don't need the details, but I'm glad you are using condoms. Keep winning. I hope I can have dinner with Norman tonight. I'll see you at the track tomorrow night if I get my studies done."

Call Me Maggie

A tall young woman wearing a dark pants suit entered the newsroom at 6:30 and asked to see Norman Kennedy, then followed a copy girl to the photo editor's office. The editor spotted the strawberry blonde and invited her into his office. Norman turned and asked, "Is anything wrong Maggie?"

"Only if I have to eat dinner alone."

"Give me a few minutes and I'll join you."

"I have all night."

"Chief, this is Mary Anne Johnson.

"Hello Chief, call me Maggie," she requested.

"Hi Maggie. I'm Hershel Phillips. Are you the cadet he's using in his police academy layout? If you are, fill my daughter in on what to expect," he said as they shook hands.

"No. I'm just a friend."

"Norman, I'll have one of the guys print these. You cover the Reed girl tomorrow, get me some holiday stuff for Monday, the fireworks show Sunday night, Maggie a tour of the newsroom and take her to dinner. I'll see you Sunday afternoon, Norma. Nice to meet you, Maggie," his editor said.

"You're getting soft, Chief," Norman said.

They toured the newsroom, starting in the teletype room.

"I started here tearing copy from these machines and taking to the editors. They bring us national, international, sports and business news stores. We have a college girl doing that now. She's the first female copyboy in the paper's eighty-two year history. They didn't have female writers or editors until World War II. Now we have two women reporters and one editor."

He took Maggie upstairs to the noisy composing room and to the basement where a two-story press waited silently for workers to prepare the Saturday morning newspaper.

"Let's go to your place for coffee. I haven't been there for a month. Mine is cluttered with books, papers and unwashed laundry. Got an old shirt and jeans I can wear when we get there. I hope you missed seeing me in your clothes as much as I have missed wearing them," Maggie suggested after dinner.

"Nothing has changed. I did get a larger table. Use it more as a desk or for editing my pictures."

"Norman's been busy," she told herself, seeing stacks of prints on the table.

"Tell me about school."

162

Buying the Farm

"Made some friends, read the manual every night, stay up late, get up early, study again, go to class and start over. Still go to night school Mondays, Wednesdays and Thursdays. And I missed you and my evening with you a lot."

"And I missed you, too. I would much rather cuddle with you than my cameras, pictures or even a good book," Norman said as he led her to the sofa.

"Those few Tuesday nights were not enough for me, so I had to come over tonight," she said, and then lay her head on his shoulder.

"Ditto. I'm glad you are here. It has been much lonelier now that it was before I met you."

"Norman, I am going to make it. In two months, I will have my wings. The other girls have their reasons for getting into the school. Some to escape small towns, some for the glamour and adventure, but it is also a good career. That's what keeps me going. Every morning I tell myself I am going to be the best stewardess they have. Some of the stewardesses already flying teach special classes and give us different insights. I know I made the right decision. I will have a much better life than the one I had when we met. Thank you for giving me the incentive to sign up," Maggie said, then yawned. "And the time to study"

"I am happy for you, Maggie. Very happy for you,"

Saturday morning they went to the Ford dealership with Linda and Kevin. Saturday night they went to see her race. And Sunday afternoon, too. Sunday morning Norman got one of his holiday pictures as they helped an old man raise a flag in his yard and another at Delaware Veterans Memorial Cemetery. Sunday night they attended a fireworks show at Rodney Square. Norman placed pictures taken at and between his assignment in the album at Maggie's apartment while she made tea with rose petals and hen cuddled with him on the sofa.

He remembered her remark about flowers and tea, and said, "The color isn't showing yet, my hair is still white."

"It takes time to show up like the submarines races."

Before Norman could answer, the windows rattled, the building shook, and their tea spilled. Norman called the county Emergency Communications Center.

"Two ships have just collided in the river off New Castle Wharf. If it as bad as the noise we heard, it's a big story. I have got to get over there," Norman said.

"I am going with you," Maggie blurted out.

In a moment, they were their way.

Call Me Maggie

"We have been interrupted to run out on a story in everything from dinner to snuggling and everything in between," Maggie said as Norman drove.

"It comes with my job and with me," he replied.

"I was making an observation, not complaining. I like going with you on your assignments. Don't stop taking me along."

Norman dropped in behind a passing fire truck for the drive to an orange glow filling the eastern sky, parked on The Green behind the Old State House, and then they ran two blocks to the wharf and the catastrophe on the river. Maggie soon learned this was not a stroll to look for submarines. Two huge infernos more spectacular than the fireworks show earlier rose from burning remains of a ship and barge. More flames rose from oil spread over an area that would engulfed a small town the size of Pennsville, now seen as clearly as it had been in daylight.

"I'm too far away. I have to get closer," Norman stated, after taking a few shots.

"Get going!" She had not seen this passion in him before.

The boat Norman hitched a ride on went out, but could not get close to either craft. Spectators on both shores saw silhouettes of rescue boats and pleasure craft circling the inferno searching for seamen that might have survived the collision. Others searched downstream and along both shorelines. All were helpless as a ship's cargo and an oil laden barge burned in the night.

The reporter Judith Rawlings and Robert Walker, another photographer arrived within the hour. Judith interviewed fire fighters and residents drawn to the firestorm while. Robert photographed those she questioned while Maggie passed out coffee and cold drinksfrom a Salvation Army disaster relief vehicle.

When dawn arrived six hours later, Norman's boat returned while two flaming columns continued to rise over the river. The burning barged drifted downstream before for grounding in front of Pennsville's riverfront beach. The ship sat in shallows off New Castle's Battery Park.

Robert took Norman's film back to process and put out on the wire photo network. Maggie and Norman drove five miles to the airport where tops of the flames could be seen above the landscape. He found the Dutch Pantry telephone and called the plane rental operator at home. After the sun rose, a small plane headed for the river with Norman, his cameras and Maggie to reload film. By 8 A.M., he was delivering proofs

Buying the Farm

while writers were preparing what would become three news stories in the afternoon and morning papers.

Robert brought Norman copies of wire photos transmitted to publications around the globe along with a large coffee and two donuts that remained un-eaten until Maggie washed and dried the prints and Norma delivered more than a dozen pictures for the afternoon's paper to Hershel and the other editors waiting in the newsroom.

A little after ten, Maggie pulled pants off a sleeping Norman who lay on her bed. A story that would have lasting world-wide impact had just begun with the two ships collision twenty-four hours earlier and five miles from where Maggie now lay with Norman. She had been with him on many of his self-imposed assignments and some smaller news stories. She had seen him transform from the easy-to-like young man she admired into an all absorbed photographer that ignored food, rest, and her until his mission was finished or his body had succumbed to exhaustion. She admired both sides of the man she lay with.

Three hours later, he rose and went back for more shooting. Maggie went with him again and would not return to her books or cluttered apartment until late that evening then told herself, the clutter could wait, but the paperwork and books could not, then lifted a manual.

"You're wasting daylight. There's a classroom waiting for your beautiful face to brighten," Norman said, after bring her coffee and kissing her forehead as the sun came through her cluttered apartment's window Tuesday morning.

Both went to the airport, she to the classroom while he took a short flight over the ships again before heading southward where all metal tanks, chimneys, and pipes filled the his viewfinder. Two smoke columns rose from blacken hulks up river. He continued southward until he found a tanker off loading onto another barge in the bay.

Maggie grabbed a second coffee from a vending machine and took a seat at the front of the room. Midge and D.C. soon joined her and D.C commented, "You two look a little worn down, Midge. Heavy date this weekend? I had a great one."

"No. There's not a datable guy in all of Sussex County, if you ask me. The good ones are taken or married. The others are off in the service. Chances are slim that I'll find on down there. Even the pea pickers running past my bedroom on the last night started to look good. Maybe I should start looking for one up here," Midge replied.

"I can show you a few good places to start," D.C. said.

Maggie and Midge shook their heads, no.

Call Me Maggie

Bee opened the class with upbeat patter.

"Bring some grubbiest tomorrow ladies. We are going to Georgetown Airport for fire training. It will be a lot of smoke, soot, sweat and you will get filthy," Bee Bee said.

"I just drove up from Georgetown this morning," Midge said.

"And I saw a horrible fire last night on the river. An oil tanker and a barge collided," Maggie reported.

"I started one five or six times this weekend," D.C. stated.

"I'm sure that was not the kind of fire you wanted to get out of. The one tomorrow will be a little hotter. . . and very dirty. Remember the grubbies. If you're late we'll go without you," Bee Bee added.

"The Georgetown fire will burn you. D.C.'s fire will leave you looking like me," Clara interjected.

"Class A will go over burn treatment here with Clara. Class B will practice emergency escapes from Connie," Bee Bee said.

After his flight, Norman stopped by the train station newsstand before returning to the newspaper office. While his film dried, he clipped stories from out of town newspapers until the phone rang.

"Good Morning, Kennedy speaking," he answered.

"Hello Norman. This is Al Alsop of American Geographic in New York calling. I have you shots of the river accident before me. Do you have anything on the tankers off loading in the Delaware Bay?" the caller asked.

"Just a few aerials," Norman answered.

"I want you to document the whole operation for us. Tankers coming into the bay. Barges being filled and towed upriver. Off loading the refineries along the river. Can you take a couple of days and shoot us a layout on the whole operation. Get everything you can get. They say they are practicing all the safety measures, but we want to be sure. Include lots of shots of the refinery at Delaware City, too," Alsop said.

"I am familiar with the refinery. It new and state of the art. I have had a few assignments down there," Norman replied.

"We pay five hundred a day plus expenses, film, car, plane, boat rental, or anything you need to get the story," Alsop said.

Quick mathematics told Norman that was more than he made in a week.

"When do you need the prints?" Norman asked.

"August fifteenth, at the latest. August first would be better. Can take the assignment?" Alsop continued.

"Yes," Norman said.

Buying the Farm

"A writer will team-up with you. When you finish, come up. We'll do lunch," the New Yorker said.

"Lunch will be great. May I show you some other projects too?" Norman asked.

"Call me when you have the pictures. I'll look at your projects, too," Alsop said.

"This gives me something to do while Maggie is in school. The money is good too. I already know where to spend it," Norman said to himself after finishing the call.

The next morning, Norman and John Choma were flying south again. Norman made shots of everything he could find at the refinery, small tankers unloading at the dock, and two larger ones off loading onto barges just inside the bay's mouth, plus a supertanker coming into the bay just off Cape Henlopen. On the return, trip Norman photographed everything he thought would be impacted by the collision and spilled oil from the cape to the refineries at Marcus Hook.

Thursday, he made more shots of the Delaware City refinery from land. His newspaper ID helped get him into the safe areas of the refinery. A public relations representative answered most of his questions and made sure he took no flash shots.

Friday night he told Maggie of his assignment. Saturday and Sunday she studied in the open Chevy as Norman made shots of bay fishing boats, watermen and their homes in villages along the bay from Big Stone Roach to the shallows south of New Castle where the burned out barge rested as a new sightseeing attraction.

Tuesday Norman and a Geographic writer chartered a boat to reach the offloading operation close-up and remained on the tanker until the charter returned Wednesday morning. For the next three weeks he made shots each morning of other aspects of oil transport, refining and consumption he thought relevant, plus shots of the stewardess schooling, photographed every auction sale up and down the state and assembled them for a presentation to Alsop.

Early on the last Tuesday in July, he boarded a train to New York City. As Norman dined with Al Alsop, Maggie finished her two classes of the day, gobbled down a salad, a Sloppy Joe, a glass of milk, and went to the high school for another two hours of study. Each night an instructor stepped before the class, lectured for forty-five minutes, and gave a ten-minute multiple-choice test. The second hour went the same with a different instructor and subject. The third hour followed a similar format.

Call Me Maggie

Norman was waiting when Maggie finally got home. She ran to the steps, dropped her books, and sat on the step beside him and asked, "Well, are you going to tell me if they bought your pictures?"

"We are not going to be interrupted tonight. The assignment is done. I'm all yours till the next one comes up," he replied.

They met each Tuesday at the same time and on Saturdays for the next month. On the last Friday of August, fifty-four young women who began the class with Maggie were issued uniforms, hats, ID badges, passports and certificates in a ceremony next to a Super Constellation renamed "State of Delaware. The new stewardesses congratulated each other wildly and returned to their families and friends. Maggie's mother and sister had not been informed of the ceremony.

Norman made the final pictures for his airline stewardess school assignment as she celebrated with members of the family that had accepted her three months earlier and had supported her since. A picture layout and story on the school filled half of the local news page and a full page inside Saturday's morning paper. Maggie's face appeared in none of the close ups. Her name was listed midway down the list of graduates.

"You have four days off. By some lucky break, so do I. Would you let me spend them congratulating you in any manner you wish?"

Dark circles below her eyes lightened as she found strength to smile, hold him close and respond yes.

He had anticipated her answer and prepared a celebration far from the classroom, and the newspaper office. Three hours later Maggie raced toward swells of the sea breaking upon the shore. Endless blue ripples danced beneath diamonds before her eyes. Waves rose over her feet. Salty vapors filled her nose. Wind teased her hair. Tender arms encased her. Soft words said, "I'm proud of you and what you have achieved, Maggie."

"Your faith in me carried me through. You chose the perfect place to celebrate. I came to you scared and hurt. My future was bleak. You brightened it. You soothed my pain, and gave me courage. Why, I'll never know, but I'm glad you did."

"I could not let you leave to bear an ugly past with no future in sight. You had no friends or family to support comfort and support you, I had to do something. And you are a great photographic subject."

"The past is gone and my future has never been brighter, a future I want to share with you," Maggie said, holding him tighter.

Buying the Farm

Norman took no action nor made no actions that indicated he was ready to fulfill her dream of total communion and partake of her sweltering feminine attributes.

Again, watery tracks marked Maggie's path to an unheard and unseen summons. Norman followed her, sharing the countless joys she found as she rounded the cape and marched toward a divided horizon, ocean on the left, dunes on the right, sand below and sky above. Heavy surf rolled onto the shore. Mist and vapors rose around her healing each wound, each scratch, and each scar. Remnants of her past pains rode out to sea on cleansing ocean surf that erased the footprints behind them.

Total commemoration would not come until Maggie liberated the inhibitions in the one who instigated the events that had filled the days and nights of her life during the summer of 1962, a task that until now seemed as insurmountable as the one hundred and ten foot silica summit before her now. Onward and onward, upward and upward, she journeyed, searching for a way to neutralize the restraints that prevented Norman from treating her as a total woman. Her silhouette summoned him from atop the dune's apex. He submitted, and climbed hand over hand, foot by foot, up and up, until their forms joined and embraced on the pinnacle of sand high above Cape Henlopen.

Maggie took his hands, put them over her chest, and said, "Release the lover inside you. Take the woman you are holding and become her love partner as you have become her partner in so many other ways.

"I am ready to be yours. I am not very experienced. I may not meet your expectations. I have never made love this deeply. I am not much of a ladies' man. Too tall and too thin. An egghead with a snowcap. Always have been. I was never a dancer or a jock that attracted girls. I don't have any pick-up lines that work. I was born a hundred years too late. My values are idealistic, Victorian, and very out dated. Years ago I would have been called a gentleman. Today I am labeled a nerd. I am not much of a Casanova, but I want to be your lover now and forever. Part of me wanted to make love since the first night in your bed. The Victorian part of me would not allow me overcome my inhibitions. I could not take advantage of you as others have," Norman whispered.

"You are not a nerd. You are a gentleman is the best of ways. And I would not have been moved by a pick-up line, if you had used a thousand. Your gentle touch, your soft kisses, your kind words; those attracted me more than any line or suggestion. I craved you from the first night. I offered myself and you hesitated. You could have had me many times, but you did not. I gave you opportunities for pictures and opportunities to make love. You choose pictures and avoided lovemaking, a covet I had never known. You did not want me for your bed."

"I had to be sure you weren't offering yourself to repay me for a debt you did not owe."

I'm glad you want me now and I want you too," Maggie stated.

As the descending golden sun pulled a star-filled blanket over them and their pinnacle, Maggie remembered others who had mixed forcefully taken or purchased sexual union with lovemaking while believing one was the other. They had bought her lovemaking, but not her. In those encounters, she had satisfied their fogged cravings in fulfillment of her need to survive. She was now the survivor of the most demanding period of her life. She had left an abusive pimp. She had abandoned a dysfunctional home. She had begun a career for herself. She had found her inspiration in moments of despair and her strength in the gentlest man she had ever met. He had earned her love with no barter or imbursement. For months she had wanted to share herself with the man possessing the most compassionate virility she had ever known. And at last, he wanted her. Maggie moved his hands under her blouse and onto swollen mounds on her chest.

Norman allowed them to remain and his passion build. The culmination of their celibacy ended in a moment of ecstasy on a summit above a river emptying it's self into depths of an ocean. The ocean flooded the shore again, and again in a torrential serenade Norman and Maggie heard and felt, but did not see. Both hoped the river would never empty, the ocean would never fill, and the culminating satisfaction they shared together would never end.

Others cape celebrants came for sun, sand, and surf in the last holiday of summer. Maggie and Norman sought celebrations elsewhere. They spent much of their short walks in pine forests, canoeing inland lakes, watching farmers harvest their crops and sharing loving interludes with each other. Labor Day had arrived. Maggie had earned her wings and would leave on her first flight Tuesday morning.

As they drove back to the city Monday afternoon, Maggie spied an auction sale sign on a small farm with a modest house, stable and two fenced pastures bordered the highway on the edge of a town called Odessa barely ten miles from the airport.

"Let's take a look," Maggie suggested.

After an hour tour, he concluded, "This would be perfect. I would like to buy it."

"Let me be your partner in this little farm too."

Buying the Farm

"Let's go over to Elkton and get married tonight."

"I would like to say yes, but I must say no. It would be unfair to you. There are still a few issues I must settle. We have been together six months and I know I want to stay with you forever. We are truly sole mates. We are partners in the pictures you shoot of me and in everything else we do. I have everything now that I need; you, a home, and a career. We can live together until they are resolved," Maggie said, then came to Norman, embraced him, and added, "I am the cardinal who will always come back to you, but I can't marry you yet."

Just after sunrise on Saturday morning six weeks later Norman lowered the top and snapped the tunneau in place on the Chevy convertible as Maggie pulled the rubber band from her hair and shook her hair vigorously until it lay over her shoulders and chest. They pulled onto the inside southbound lane of U.S. 13 and remained there. They drove under the Basin Road interchange, past the Dutch Pantry until a traffic light stopped them at the Frenchtown Road corner of the airport. A Super Constellation with Maggie's airline colors flew overhead spinning the weather vane on The Farmhouse Restaurant. Behind the restaurant, bulldozers were loading debris from The Farmer's Market remains. A new concrete block building would rise on the footprint of the old wooden warehouse. A mile further south Norman steered left in a "Y" intersection and continued south on U.S. 13. After passing under the New Castle and Frenchtown Rail Road, they entered the farmland of northern Delaware. Flat land had replaced rolling hills. On both sides of the highway, golden corn and soybeans could be seen. From the canal northward, mostly grains grew on the farmland. South of the canal, vegetables and winter wheat were the staple crops. Crossing the canal was leaving one climate region and geographical zone to enter another. Demographics of the residents changed as well. Younger people commuted to jobs in Wilmington, older residents tried to hold on to their farming lifestyle in a time of high cost feed, seed, fertilizer, fuel, and equipment.

Norman and Maggie would only be going to Odessa this October morning, a twenty minute drive from the airport or ten more into downtown Wilmington. He turned right just below the Appaquinimink Creek between two brick gateposts bearing a sign at reading, "Auction Saturday October 15, 8 A.m. 40 acres and improvements," and parked in a pasture of dusty trucks, cars and a few Amish buggies. Sections of wooden fence had been removed allowing vehicles to park in the pastures. Other fences lined two pasture areas on either side of the farm lane, the highway, and south side of the farmette. Trees lined the north and west sides that bordered the creek. Herons stalked the creeks edges for their breakfast. Muskrat lodges could be seen in the marsh along the creek. A small brick house, a red wooden barn and shed stood at the end of the dirt lane centered in the farmette. Several hundred people milled about examining furniture that had been place on the lawn. Others strolled amidst horse and farm implements outside the barn and shed. Both Maggie and Norman knew the property layout well from a photograph he had taken on Maggie's first airplane flight, their Labor Day Weekend stop, and several times since that Monday afternoon when she wasn't flying.

"We'll know soon," she said as he raised the car's top.

Maggie had called the West Chester lawyer, who briefed her on legal details, and Norman's father had given her pointers on how to bid.

Bidding started promptly at eight.

Maggie greeted the thrift store operator, Mrs. Levitz, the thrift store owner, and Mr. Goldman, the used furniture and junk dealer as she bid against them on some objects. Maggie purchased a lacy white gown, a wooden wheelbarrow, plus a few pottery crocks including a butter churn. Mrs. Levitz purchased all the kitchen ware and most of the small furniture. Mr. Goldman bought about half the larger furniture, and several pieces from the barnyard lot. Norman purchased the kitchen stove, a dusty carriage in the barn, farm implements, flower pots and garden tools plus an old faded photograph of the farm taken some forty years earlier.

"Mr. Goldman, That sofa belongs by the fireplace inside. Please forgive me for outbidding you. We plan to purchase the farm. I will call you Monday to let you know if we outbid everyone else. I'll call you also, if we don't," Maggie said.

Norman and Maggie helped him load their purchases into an old dairy delivery van, then drank more coffee and ate donuts purchased at an Odessa Volunteer Fire Department tent as the farm implement sales wound down.

"Sit here with me, please, Maggie. Wearing your shoes out is not going to make the sale go any faster," Norman said even though he was equally as nervous.

At 12:15, sale of the buildings and land began. At 12:35, Maggie Johnson and Norman Kennedy each presented cashier's checks to the auctioneer's clerk and became partner-owners of the farmette.

"Thank you, Norman."

"Thank you for being my partner," he answered.

Buying the Farm

Norman, Mr. Goldman, and a pair of strong Amish boys moved the stove back into the kitchen. Maggie brought her treasures inside.

The president and chief of the volunteer fire department congratulated them, and invited each to join. A few other neighbors introduced themselves and pointed out their homes just a half mile away. A lady who introduced herself as Mrs. Thomas F. DuPont-Bayard, III, president of the Odessa Historical Society, insisted she should be addressed as "Muffy" by her new friend that she had outbid on several pieces during the auction.

Odessa was a town of twelve hundred living in a collection of homes dating back to colonial times lined the east-west main street of the town. Some were brick, most were clapboard painted white, yellow and a few were light blue. Each was covered by weathered cedar shingles. Brick sidewalks lined both sides of the wide street with spaces left for two-foot thick trees at the curb. The street could have easily been in New Castle, Old Dover, or Alexander, Fredericksburg, or Williamsburg, Virginia.

By 2 p.m. most of the crowd was gone. Maggie and Norman strolled through the house planning what would be placed where. Three bedrooms and a bathroom were on the first floor as well as an eat-in kitchen, and a parlor room with brick fireplace was entered through the front door. A flagstone patio lay outside the kitchen door.

Grandmother Montgomery's sofa and the one she bought by out-bidding Mr. Goldman would form a conversation area in front of the fireplace, a photo lab would be installed in an east-facing bedroom sharing a wall with the bath. Another smaller east bedroom would become an office and the third with French doors opening to the west and the patio would be kept as a bedroom for guests. The second floor would become a large bedroom as both had known in their apartments minus the kitchen and dinette areas, Maggie suggested.

The house had been built in the mid 1920's for a family of four. The owner's daughter had died as a youngster and their son was buried in a stone marked field in France, Maggie learned from Muffy. Norman and Maggie knew from the plot map that three grave markers stood in the northwest corner of the property beneath a cluster of dogwood and redbud trees. One was a child's grave. The other held the remains of the child's father. His wife now resided in a Wilmington senior care center. She would be interred there someday as stated in the sales contract. After the sale, Maggie and Norman paid their respects at the markers during a walk around the farm's perimeter.

173

Call Me Maggie

"Both my grandparents are buried on a little hill behind their farmhouse," Maggie said. "I wish we could have gotten their farm instead of this one. I loved that place so much."

"If we had, it would always be Grandmother Johnson's home and farm. This one will be Maggie and Norman's farmette. You will learn to love it as much as theirs and probably more in years to come. I know I will."

"I think Grandmother Johnson would approve of how her money was spent," she said as she stood for a moment gazing.

"I'm sure she would," Norman assured her.

By 3 p.m. the auctioneer's clerk began locking the house, but gave Maggie and Norman a copy of the keys. The house would not be officially theirs until paper work was filed at the county offices the next week. Maggie wandered through the house again touching the oak doors and window trim, the oak mantle and the white porcelain sinks. A white cast iron stove with porcelain doors converted to burn propane gas stood its original spot in the kitchen. It had been. Maggie planned to add a second stove, one used by her grandmother that burned wood on chilly mornings to heat and cook her kitchen.

Norman followed her up the oak stairway to the large attic and as she moved about the attic room. The attic was one long room almost as large as Norman's studio and equally bright and airy by means of four dormers, two facing east, two facing   west, plus two double windows on each end. A large lion claw bath tub sat between windows on the end facing the creek to the north. Matching windows at the other end revealed an open field between the farmhouse and the homes of Odessa further south.

"Someday that field will be filled with flowers," Maggie said before she turned from the window offering him a soft smile after hearing the shutter click.

He made a second exposure and held her in his arms. The embrace continued until interrupted by the firehouse siren. From the windows they saw black smoke at the east end of the town's skyline where the old homes ended at creek bank.

"I know you have got to go, but I'm going with you."

Norman made his first shot showing the closeness of one home to the burning pilings where a waterman's shed stood at the edge of the creek. While he made other pictures, Maggie treated the injured waterman.

"Where did you learn first aid?" the fire chief asked.

Buying the Farm

"I am a flight attendant," Maggie answered.

"Are you a nurse too? My mother had to be a nurse before a stewardess," he stated.

"No, I'm just a stewardess fresh out of school."

Norman expressed pleasure that Maggie made friends with the fire chief as they drove back to her apartment, something he had forgotten to do at the fire scene.

"I will miss this little place when we get to the farm." Maggie said as they ate.

"I will miss mine too. A garden and a real darkroom will be a treat."

"Especially a garden! And a horse or two."

"Do you remember the mare we saw at the sale a few months ago? I found her doing my Amish story. Would you like to take a ride and see her tomorrow?" Norman asked.

"Would I? Oh yes!"

"I would like to take Dad along if you don't mind. Dad would enjoy meeting the farmer and seeing his farm," he said. "And he knows a little about horses and equine breeding. I'll call him now rather than drop in tomorrow."

"Say no more. I'm convinced, but waiting until morning will be hard to do. Let's go tell them now."

Fifteen minutes later Norman announced, "We have some news to share with you. We were highest bidders on the farm today."

"By the end of the week, it will be ours. You have to come and see it and a horse I want to buy," Maggie said as Norman poured coffee into mugs in his parent's kitchen.

"Take them down tomorrow afternoon while I'm working. You will be gone Tuesday when I am off. We have a key."

"I would love to drive him down, but let's leave early so you can go with us," Maggie said.

At 7 a.m. Pop Pop said, "Take your coffee with you and let's go look at the horse you called about last night. The boy has to work this afternoon so he can buy horse feed."

He got no argument from Norman or Maggie and half an hour later he was getting a tour of their farmette. Within another half an hour and a few miles drive west of Cheswold, Pop Pop had counted fourteen mailboxes marked Yoder since leaving U.S. 13. Norman made a left turn into a lane beside a mailbox marked Jacob Yoder where a white horse and half a dozen cows grazed in a pasture beside the lane.

Call Me Maggie

Maggie asked if it was the same horse she kissed and called Storm four months earlier. Norman confirmed her reservations saying, "Yes, I'm sure. I kept my notes, just in case you wanted to find her."

Mr. Yoder carried two milk pails from the barn as they parked. Four young boys followed him. A half dozen barn cats followed the boys. The visit was a surprise to all the Yoders, but he recognized Norman's car and it's not so plain continental kit.

"Come and sit thee on yonder porch," Mr. Yoder invited.

"Thank You," Maggie, Norman, and Pop Pop said.

"For what brings you back to the farm?"

All three noticed Mr. Yoder wince when Norman said, "We wish to discuss the horse with you, Mr. Yoder,"

"Doeth thou wish to buy the horse? I cannot speak of it with thee on the Sabbath. Thee may address me as Jacob."

"Maggie and I bought a little farm yesterday. She saw your horse at the sale. She wants to start a small herd of her own. We drove down from Wilmington to see it again. Maggie is going overseas tomorrow morning and she cannot come back for more than a week," Norman explained.

"We will not discuss sale on your Sabbath, Brother Jacob. In general discussion of horses, may we talk with you?" Pop Pop asked.

"We can speak of horses with you. Speak of sale, I cannot. Momma, bring our guests some tea and come sit with our English lady guest," Mr. Yoder called into the house.

"Thank you, Mr. Yoder. Or should I call you as Brother Jacob?" Maggie asked.

"Whichever pleases thee. I have English neighbors. I respond to either."

"What do you call the mare, Brother Jacob?" she asked.

"The misses and children call her Eve. I call her mother mare. She has the promise of many foals. The horse is now with the first," Yoder said.

He was more comfortable with English formalities than Maggie, Norman, or Pop Pop were with his customs. The English visitors rose as Mrs. Yoder brought five cups of tea onto the porch. She rendered them a slight bow.

"Momma you must greet Brother Norman Kennedy who will tell the English man and the miss's name to you."

"This is my father. Pop Pop Kennedy to his friends. And the lady is Mary Anne Johnson. Her family is from Booth's Corner."

Buying the Farm

"Call me Maggie. My friends do," she said shaking hands with both.

"Your hostess is Rebecca, wife of Jacob Yoder," the farm-lady said as she pulled a chair beside Jacob, lifted a basket of quilt patches, and began sewing.

"The hath a farm now, eh Brother Norman? And thee wish horses?" Jacob asked.

"We have the farm, Norman and I are partners. I'm the one who want to have horses," Maggie interjected.

"Are thee ready to give it care one would give one's children? Hath thee birthed a breached foal on a cold winter night by a coal oil lamp?" Jacob asked.

Maggie shook her head indicating no.

"I birth many foals and many calves before moving to the city and several pup litters since then," Pop Pop injected.

"Thee hath tilled the land, eh, Poppa Kennedy?" Jacob surmised as he offered Norman and his father a corncob pipe.

"And picked the cotton, wormed and cropped tobacco, raised sugar cane and sorghum for syrup and the horses, just as you and the Amish. In winter, I cut timber. Norman was just twelve when we left. He went to the barn, fields, and forest for the last four years. What we can't handle, a veterinarian can."

"The hath tilled the land? Eh, Norman?" Jacob asked.

"Only as a boy," Norman answered.

Maggie listened but watched Rebecca hands sewing.

"Let us come and walk to yonder horse, Brothers Kennedy and Sister Maggie. Momma, thee will walk with Miss Maggie," Yoder said.

The five walked down the lane toward the horse and cows.

"If thee were to speak of the horse's sale. I must have my purchase price, feed, and stud fees, if you ask. I promised the sons of mine, they would get new cycles and scooters with the foal's sale profits," Jacob said.

"If we were to speak of a sale, not that you compromise yourself, or your Sabbath Laws, have you a price in mind?" Norman asked.

"Aye, thee can be sure of that. But thee must see the animal first," Jacob said, pushing down one wire down and lifted one for the others to cross the fence. Rebecca and Maggie passed last. Pop Pop was first to the mare, rubbing her neck and then stomach. He examined each of her feet, felt her legs and chest before looking at her teeth and pronouncing his findings "A sound mare. Eight months along I'd say."

177

Call Me Maggie

"Yonder Brother Ely provided the mare's stud, a fifteen hand white," Jacob said.

Maggie rubbed the mare's face with one hand, snuggled her muzzle with the other, and said, "I'm Glad Norman found you. He and I want to give you a new home."

"If you have a price, would you share it with us so we don't have to make a second trip, or someone else makes another offer?" Norman asked.

"Fifteen hundred, in American paper notes. But let's keep the Sabbath enterprise free, Brother Norman," Jacob added.

"Fifteen hundred is agreeable, Brother Jacob, I will see you at milking time tomorrow. We can finish our discussion of the horse then. Now I must leave to help publish tomorrow's morning's newspaper," Norman said.

"You will stay for Rebecca's breakfast the morrow. I married her for her cooking and the fine boys we are raising."

"Perhaps," Norman said.

Maggie promised herself a return visit to the Amish farm wife and quilter.

The bank opened at nine Monday, mid-day by Rebecca and Jacob's schedule. Norman returned to the Yoder farm too late for Rebecca's breakfast, but not too late for her seven item lunch. He gave Jacob thirty $50.00 bills for the horse and asked that Jacob to keep the horse until Tuesday evening.

Tuesday evening Norman's father towed a horse trailer up Jacob's lane. A pair of black metal two-wheeled scooters and a pair of bicycles were unloaded before the horse entered the trailer. As they prepared to leave, Jacob invited Norman and his father to a barn raising November 25th. Norman asked if he could take pictures. Jacob promised to speak with the elders about bringing a camera.

"Englishmen would watch football before feasting on turkey while the Amish would raised a barn prior to their feast," Jacob joked.

"Do all you can to get their approval to photograph the barn raisin'. It's a dying craft," his father said.

As Norman and his father left, two of Jacob's sons rode new bicycles on the farm lane along with two smaller brothers racing alongside one foot hitting the lane, the other resting on the scooters. For a moment, Pop Pop saw Lionel and Kevin running after Norman and Ernest on an Alabama farm lane ten years earlier.

Buying the Farm

A week later, Norman heard Maggie's car in the lane and was on the patio as she parked. Carrying a pale of apples and carrots, he led her to the barn and stood back as she greeted and caressed the mare between morsels. Norman remembered a day in Alabama when his father presented his mother with a mare and the joy they had shared.

"I know I can't ride until after your baby comes, but I can love you and the men who brought us together," Maggie whispered to the mare.

Norman tried to imagine Maggie as a little girl discovering life's pleasures on her grandparent's farm as he had more than ten years earlier on a farm nine years and many miles away.

Saturday morning before Thanksgiving, the Kennedy brothers moved Maggie's apartment furnishings, her Grandmother's stored items, and some of Norman's larger items to the farm. Norman and the station wagon had carried small items down U.S. 13 each morning during the week while the convertible stayed parked. Monday before the holiday, Norman met with Amish elders. Judith Rawlings came along. She had seen Amish in Indiana and wanted to learn more for a story s he would write, if they agreed.

"Judith and I record today's news events that become history to generations coming after us and you. It's a record forever and for everyone. If you did not save seeds from your labors in the autumn, none could be planted in the spring and the lineage of that plant is lost. If ancient scholars had not written and recorded the events of their time, we would have no Bible today. If I do not make photographs and Judith does not write, our witness to life as we have seen it is lost. I can make pictures of your work and make certain no pictures of your faces are recorded. I do those kinds of pictures often in my work. If my camera is forbidden at the barn raising the history of your life, your skills and the heritage you leave for your descendants will be lost, except for the structure you will build Thursday. We three Englishmen wish to attend your barn raising and assist you. Judith, my father, and I will honor your wishes and customs, including not making photographs, if that is the decision of the elders," Norman told the Amish elders.

Following an hour of cloistered discussion, Norman got permission he wanted.

By Thanksgiving, the farmhouse was painted inside and ready for Maggie's first attempt at roasting turkey for the Kennedy clan Thursday. Her flight kept her away until Wednesday evening, so subsequently Mom Mom and Linda were recruited to help.

179

Call Me Maggie

Judith returned Thanksgiving mornings and two mornings after with Norman and his father for the barn raising. Maggie's dinner was served late in Thanksgiving Day's evening.

Maggie flew as often as she could and always seem to draw shorter tourist charter flights, right up until one on Christmas Eve. It was short; only from Baltimore to the Bahama Islands and back empty while more senior stewardesses took the good paying runs. She busied herself serving refreshments up and down the aisle. As she leaned over pouring coffee, a passenger squeezed the tightly drawn slacks on her buttocks. A moment later another passenger did the same. She rose, spun around, and began pour the pitcher's remainder on the vacation bound student and said, "I'm terribly sorry sir. I was never a good cocktail server."

"What are you going to do with all the money you're earning, buy a farm with Midge and live like old maids?" one stewardess asked on the return flight.

Maggie entered the candle lit farmhouse a little before midnight carrying an arm full of packages. Norman brought steaming tea from the kitchen on an old serving tray. A white poinsettia separated the cups. Beside it lay a red, white, and blue Cracker Jack box with a peppermint candy cane beneath a red bow. A large box recycled from the washing machine sat before the fireplace between the sofa from Mr. Goldman and opposite the one from Grandmother Johnson's farm. Gold paper and a wide red ribbon covered the labels. A large white rose lay at the ribbon's intersection.

"I have to go back to my car," Maggie said as she dropped her parcels at the attic stairs, then went back to her car, and returned with a box half the size of the one near the fireplace, and sat it on the coffee table. Before the tea cups were half empty, church bells ran twelve times in the steeples across the pasture.

Chirping sounds came from the white paper wrapped box.

"Must be a clock for the mantel," Norman deducted.

"Lift the sides and see," Maggie said.

Norman lifted the sides. The chirps grew louder. Two white parakeets were perched in the cage before him. After a moment with the birds, he turned to Maggie.

"They're great. Thank you. Now open yours."

She lifted the bottomless gold box. A saddle the color of Maggie's hair remained on the floor.

"We can exchange it, but it's the one you seemed to like best," Norman said.

Buying the Farm

"It won't be exchanged," Maggie assured him.

Norman handed Maggie the Cracker Jack box. Maggie pulled the tab and flap open. Several red and white scarves followed. One had a knot in the center holding a ring of thatch-woven gold.

"This isn't new. It was new in Paris thirty four years ago."

"Have you ever seen me wanting anything new?"

Norman raised her right hand and slipped the ring on the third finger. Neither engagement nor marriage was mentioned. He knew she would let him know when the ring would be moved as she lifted their four hands, kissed the ring and them Norman.

The smell of new leather and a cherry wood filled their home through the night and throughout Christmas Day.

"Merry Christmas, Mom. Merry Christmas, Pop. Merry Christmas little brother, Linda, Kevin, Loraine, Ernest," rolled off Norman and Maggie's tongues.

"Merry Christmas, son. Merry Christmas Big Brother, Merry Christmas Maggie," the greetings continued.

"Coffee is in the kitchen. Hazelnut for Christmas day with Mrs. Serpe's rolls. We'll do the presents in the dining room. Bring your coffee," Norman's mother said.

Handwritten place markers stood atop wrapped package at twelve spots around the table. Each box had a red and white peppermint cane on top held by a thin ribbon. Lorraine, her brothers, and their girlfriends added more packages to each location.

"Maggie, you are the newest member of the family, open yours first," Mom Mom suggested.

A cartoon of home canned vegetables and fruit was revealed when she removed the ribbon and wrapping paper.

Mrs. Kennedy excused herself early. Lionel helped her upstairs.

Norman excused himself at one o'clock for an assignment at two o'clock in a retirement home. Maggie went along to pass out a few dozen candy canes his mother sent for the residents.

As they were leaving, an elderly woman approached and introduced herself, "Miss Johnson, Mr. Kennedy? I'm Rose Gusewic. I'm glad young people bought the farm. When the mister and I got older, there were lots we couldn't do to keep it up. I hope your years there will be as good as ours were," Rose said.

"You did fine. We are very happy there," Maggie replied as she gave Rose a cane.

Call Me Maggie

"We would like to have you down to the place and have you tell us all you can about it and share any pictures you have of it with us," Norman said.

"I can tell you lots. The mind still works just as well as when the mister and I built them buildings, but the legs do not," Rose said.

The next morning's paper carried a photograph of Rose and an unidentified hand.

Before Spring Rose's mind would follow her legs and they would see her check the mailbox before hobbling up the lane to the house as a Greyhound bus pulled away.

Early in the next morning Maggie was a member of the flight crew making a red eye run to pick up the passengers they took to the Bahamas a week earlier. The passenger who had touched her on the earlier kept his hands to himself during the entire flight. The one who had squeezed her offered scouring looks each time she walked past.

After the flight she braved an hour ride in six inches of snow instead of the usual twenty minute drive without snow, she noticed the barn lights on and Pop Pop's truck parked near the barn. Going inside, she found Pop Pop and Norman with Storm about to give birth. A few minutes later the dried the foal, caressed him an old blanket, and gave him the name, Snowball.

For the rest of the winter Maggie made as many flights as she could, filling in on short flights and two-day ones that fit in between her overseas flight schedule. Her statement of "earn now, spend later" was not spoken in jest. In six short months, flying had become her life. Vacation hops were akin to being a driver's aid on a school bus load of energetic schoolchildren. Military flights to Europe were only a notch above those jaunts. She told herself often that she could handle that type of flight better than anyone else her stewardess sisterhood. They often told her she was best in those roles too. Yet she still avoided lengthy details of events with Norman. Her time at home with him was limited. She preferred to spend it sharing herself with him, not her stewardess career. On days when Maggie was home, Norman would wait until 1:15 to leave for the newspaper. On other days, he would he fed the animals, finished projects around the farm or their office and leave as soon as he could. On days when both were out of town Norman's father would drive down, feed their animals and relive his farming days.

This morning was special to Norman. He wished she did not have a flight to make and did not look forward to his workday. They had met on this date a year earlier, an occasion he marked with an anniversary card carried upstairs with her coffee and a white rose. A single flower usually accompanied rarely missed morning coffee when both were home. They shared their moments together whenever they could find time between her flights and his photography. Both made efforts to serve the needs of the other. Her modeling was less frequent, but she never declined a request to pose for him when he wanted to capture a picture idea. Their home life was fine, what little of it there was. They shared everything. Their partnership had matured.

Snowball the foal matured well too. He now followed the mare as Maggie rode about the farm or led them along the creek. Norman had made many pictures trying to capture the repoire Maggie had with her horses. Following them with his camera, he sought to capture the essence and beauty of the mare, her foal, and Maggie in the morning mist or the light of a setting sun.

Kevin and Linda sometimes came down on Tuesday evenings for a few hours before going to work on the Interstate now received its roadway. Kevin's new duty was to bring loads of topsoil to the built-up as shoulders alongside the concrete road surface.

Mother's Day arrived again. Maggie joined the Kennedy clan. It would be Kevin and Linda's last weekend free until November. After dinner, Linda took Maggie outside.

"Maggie, I'm pregnant," Linda stated.

Both young women cried as they embraced in shadows by the dogwood.

"In a way I'm glad. But it creates problems for Kevin and me. I don't want to ruin Kevin's life with a baby. We're not even twenty-one yet. I could have an abortion, but I won't. I'm not a very good Catholic, but I am Catholic. I could go to an unwed mother's home and my baby would be adopted. I won't do that either," Linda said.

"I can't tell you what you should do. You must decide what you want to do for yourself," Maggie said.

"I want to marry Kevin and have his baby."

"Does Kevin know you're pregnant?"

"Not yet. Nor my parents. Just you and me."

"He should be told."

"I know, but he may not want a baby yet."

"You know Kevin better than anyone. He's not the kind of guy to get you pregnant and run away. If I know Kevin, he will support you in whatever you decide. Tell him. Tell your parents. They are going to

Call Me Maggie

find out as you get bigger. Don't surprise them or Kevin," Maggie advised her friend.

"I was looking forward to racing again this year. The season's been open a month already. If I quit to have the baby, Kevin will have to train another driver who can read his "yeps" and "nopes.""

"You ran still race. At least part of the season."

Norman and Kevin, Lionel and his girlfriend from around the corner joined Linda and Maggie.

"Happy Mother's Day, Kevin. You are going to be a father in about six months," Linda burst the news.

"I thought so. The signs are showing already. If you want a dusty road builder and greasy mechanic as a husband, let's get married," Kevin said.

"Of course I do, if you want a smart mouthed big bellied driver driving your racecar. I want to drive it as long as I can. I'm not letting you sell it or get another driver," Linda said as her arms locked around his neck and her stomach pressed against his.

A little before midnight Maggie and Norman stood witness while an Elkton, Maryland magistrate married Linda and Kevin.

"Have you thought about having children, Maggie?" Norman asked.

"I can't think about having one until I'm sure of a few other things," she replied.

On the weekdays Maggie was not flying or Linda not in school, Maggie and Linda shopped thrift stores for baby furniture, items for Linda and Kevin's apartment, maternity and baby clothes or old dresses for Maggie. On Saturday nights when Maggie was flying Norman photographed Linda's growing race career. Linda had become a celebrity at both tracks where she raced and at college. She would have her diploma before next spring. Kevin and Lionel changed the car from street set-up to race condition each Saturday afternoon and Sunday morning at the track and changed it back after each competition. Kevin drove it to work each week day for his now sixty or seventy hour work week. Kevin, Linda and Lionel worked late into the weeknights, but not race weekends. Lionel earned his driver's license in the spring and began driving the old station wagon. Loraine moved her husband and two sons into a small house in New Jersey. Ernest his wife awaited their second child in a contest with Kevin and Linda for the first Kennedy boy. Norman saw a four lane wide trench blasted from blue granite across the street from his former apartment finally paved and become a super highway through the

Buying the Farm

city. Houses lined only one side of Adams and Jackson Streets as the interstate neared completion and would be opened in mid November. He also kept up with construction elsewhere on the highway almost weekly.

On morning when Maggie left for a trip she and Norman usually said their goodbyes well before daylight. Maggie would drive up the dark highway to the airport. Norman would finish his coffee and walked through the garden, still damp with dew, went to the barn to feed and visit their animals, poured a coffee can of birdseed in the feeder and returned to the house to printed pictures he had taken while Maggie was away.

Norman often wondered whether she had a burden larger than her capacity. Stewardess's are suppose to be carefree, beautiful flight companions serving snacks and drinks much the way lovers serve each other while watching late night TV movies. One serves the other and gets served in return. At least that was how stewardesses were portrayed in movies. He searched for something or some way he could get inside the new fortress of silence that encased Maggie. What it could be? What he could do escaped Norman.

At 1 p.m. on the last day of August in 1963, Norman dressed in clean shirt, but no tie, and prepared his safari jacket for work as he did other days. The jacket held anything he might need. He returned to their farm late Saturday evening in October after watching Linda race to the winner's circle again. The phone was ringing as he opened the door. Maggie was home and took the brief call saying only, "Hello, Okay, and, be there in an hour."

"Norman, I've got to go. I can't tell you where and I don't know when I'll be back. I probably won't be able to call either. Don't worry, I'll be fine. The dispatcher only said to pack all my uniforms and report to the airport as soon as I can. You might want to call your office. He said not to discuss this with anyone, but the television news might give us some hints," Maggie said as she packed uniforms jackets, pants, blouses and underwear in her satchel. When the satchel overflowed, she crammed leftovers in an old overnight bag. Within thirty minutes, she on her way to the airport, driving as fast as the little Nash would go.

Norman turned on the TV and sat on the edge of the bed to watch the 1 A.M. repeat of the night's eleven o'clock news, a practice he did often when Maggie was flying.

Photographs of Russian missiles in Cuba capable of reaching anywhere east of Dallas and Wichita or south of Chicago and Boston changed frequently on the little screen. Television commentators noted

185

Call Me Maggie

that if launched, they would destroy one third of the country and most of its industrial capability.

Norman followed Maggie up U.S. 13 from their farm haven. For three weeks Maggie ferried troops to Georgia, Alabama, Louisiana and especially Florida. Norman photographed ships leaving navy bases in Philadelphia, Brooklyn and Norfolk plus Dover Air Force planes coming and going. By now Norman knew Maggie, her airline and all available planes had been ferrying troops in a build-up near Cuba and so threatening to a new World War that nuclear bombs were loaded in bombers, put into the air with detonators armed and ready to be dropped. When the build-up eased, Maggie brought troops westward out of Turkey as Russian troops were sent eastward from Cuba. Cargo planes began removing American missiles from Turkey. Russian ships removed theirs from Cuba. Maggie called him at the newspaper office and at home a few times during the longest 21 days Norman had known since he met her. She made flights across the Atlantic constantly, resting only on the return leg of each trip.

For the past three weeks a line under her name on a gold rectangle read: "Chief Stewardess." She supervised loading of food and beverages, blankets and pillows and other items the flight attendants would need for the flight, and the pay was better.

Maggie frequently stopped to visit with Linda before going home when Norman was working. Their friendship and big sister, little sister relationship grew. Linda emulated what she perceived to be Maggie and Maggie copied the things unique to Linda, except her swelling stomach. Linda always kept Maggie up to date on the developing baby, he college classes, and her less frequent romps with Kevin.

"There have been three turning points in my life," Linda said one evening. "One was the day I met you at Bandstand. Kevin and I finally discovered each other and ourselves that day. Another was racing the car. When I got pregnant last February we learned how close we really were. Attending Goldey Beacon helps, too. Someday I'll be more that smart mouthed horny broad. Things change so quickly I can't keep up with them. I'm a wife, a storekeeper, a race drive and soon to be a mother. I'm not the same girl anymore. Have you felt that way since you met Norman and started flying?

"Every day! There is so much I missed as I grew up. Getting rid of Vinnie and finding Norman changed me. I feel more fulfilled. He and his parents have tried hard to help me discover new things. Many I discover on my own, but it's better when Norman and I are together. He

Buying the Farm

can't be there as I fly, but he makes up for it when I get back home. I'm as comfortable with him as I am in an old pair of shoes, and I love the feeling. He always has something interesting planned for us to do or see. He has fresh flowers waiting when I get back each time," Maggie said.

"Things will really change when Kevin finishes the interstate. He has been asked to move down south for more road building. Western Maryland, Virginia or West Virginia interstate construction is moving more slowly. They have to cut the roadway out of stone mountains. It would be three or four more years of good work," Linda said.

"You don't have to leave. Both your families are here. It would be a shame for you to leave them. I would have no one for girl talk and maternity lessons," Maggie said.

"Want to hear Junior's heartbeat?" Linda asked, the pulled off her sweater leaving herself topless before Maggie could reply. "I need some larger bras. My old ones don't fit any more, but Kevin like my larger boobs."

Norman opened Linda's door, saw Maggie holding her ear to Linda's stomach, and instinctively made a picture of the two sharing the unborn child's heartbeats.

"Come and listen, Norman. You can hear Junior's heartbeat and feel him kick," Linda said undaunted by his arrival or seeing her bare body.

"I'll wait until you're dressed," Norman said.

"Come on. You have seen Maggie's boobs. Get used to seeing mine. I'm gonna breast feed him as long as these monsters have milk," Linda said as she pulled him down bringing him and Maggie eye to eye, then held both tight against her stomach.

"Isn't that something, Norman?" Maggie asked.

"You guys are our choice as Junior's godparents," Linda stated.

The days Maggie welcomed sixty Camp Jejune Marines onto a Connie renamed Freedom for a flight to Guantanamo Bay Cuba. John Glenn had just ridden a space capsule with the same name around the earth three times and became the first American in space although the Russians had sent a cosmonaut a few months earlier.

Maggie celebrated her twenty first birthday amidst flights carrying nervous nineteen year-olds to Europe. Russia had encircled West Berliners preventing them from uniting with anyone in West Berlin even their immediate families. Those attempting to cross barbed wire barricades were shot by Russian soldiers, and left in the wire. Erection of a solid wall to replace the wire Eastern in and Westerners out was begun.

Call Me Maggie

In everyone's mind, questions were raised whether a new war would break out in Berlin, or Cuba. An invasion at Cuba's Bay of Pigs by a group of Cuban exiles had failed and every liberating invader was killed, or captured.

"You'll never guess what happened on this flight," Maggie said after one flight.

"No, but you're about to tell me, aren't you," Linda replied.

"I helped give birth on the plane. A woman began screaming and pointing to her stomach. We couldn't tell what she wanted until a little girl's head popped out. We cleaned it and lay it on her chest. A moment later a second baby girl was born. I hope yours comes as easily as hers," Maggie said.

"Easy or not, I hope Junior comes soon. I haven't seen my legs in weeks and sleeping with Kevin is not as fulfilling as it used to be. We have made love in more than a month," Linda stated.

"Junior will arrive when he's ready and you will want Kevin to be making a little Linda in no time at all," Maggie said.

"I already do. But we going to use condoms again."

On the weekdays Maggie was not flying or Linda not in school, Maggie and Linda shopped thrift stores for baby furniture, items for the apartment, maternity and baby clothes On Saturday nights when Maggie was flying Norman photographed Linda's growing race career and stomach. Linda had become a celebrity at both tracks where she raced and at college. She would have her diploma before next spring.

Kevin and Lionel changed the car from street set-up to race condition each Saturday afternoon and Sunday morning at the track and changed it back after each competition. Kevin drove it to work each weekday for his now sixty or seventy hour work week. Lionel earned his driver's license in the spring and began driving the old station wagon. Loraine moved her husband and two sons into a small house in New Jersey. Ernest his wife awaited their child in a contest with Kevin and Linda for the first Kennedy boy.

Houses line on one side of Adams and Jacksons Streets. Norman saw a four lane wide trench blasted from blue granite across the street from his former apartment finally be paved, and become a super highway through the city as he photograph the interstates construction on an almost weekly basis constantly looking for a unique or unusual picture. He prepared an exhibit of the pictures for an exhibit at the Rest Center as the interstate neared completion and would be opened to traffic in mid November.

Buying the Farm

November fourteenth arrived as a windy, chilly day, much chillier than most workmen on Interstate 95 would have liked. The two night shifts had been busy grading the right-of-way Wednesday night. The day shift had stopped at 11 a.m. to attend the dedication set for 4 p.m. Sunset was a little after five. There were still two or three more weeks of work to be done. By noon, tailgate parties had sprung up in fields on either side of the Mason-Dixon Line, which separated Maryland from Delaware. Many of the partygoers wore commemorative white helmets with the numbers "95" on a red, white, and blue shield. They had sweated and froze for more than two years building the highway. Now it was their day to celebrate as they surrounded a large "H" painted on grassy area lined with snow fencing.

Tollbooths were installed but not opened and motorist would have a free ride for a month. The toll plaza had been built closest to the Maryland state line. Cross state drivers would have to pay twenty five cents to use the shortest toll road in the country, but local motorists could drive from the Route 896 south of Newark to Pennsylvania and not pay a toll. Wilmington workers soon learned using the Delaware Turnpike could save themselves $2.50 a week and as much as an hour going into and out of the city, whether they lived north, or south. Office complex centers remained in or close to Wilmington, chemical capitol of the world, but industrial sites were being built along the highway.

A little after 5 a.m., a silver and blue Lockheed Super Constellation touched the runway at Andrews Air Force east of Washington, D. C. It began flying more than two days earlier at Saigon, Vietnam with fueling stops at Wake Island, Honolulu, and Oakland, California. Maggie Johnson had made the trip every twelve days for the past month. She was accompanied five other young women, two of them nurses, two medical corpsmen four pilots, and two flight engineers. The airline now employed nearly 150 stewardesses. The newer ones had tested their wings on the flights during the Cuban crisis. Russia had removed it missiles from striking range of the United States, but tensions remained in Europe, and worsened in Southeast Asia. Now the newer stewardess accompanied GIs to potential battlegrounds in European nations surrounding the columnist countries under Moscow's influence. Maggie went back to Asia, after her a role the most dangerous times since World War II.

At Andrews, they unloaded twenty-nine stretcher-bound passengers into ambulances and buses bound for Walter Reed Army Hospital and Bethesda Naval Hospital. After the plane climaxed its trip

Call Me Maggie

at the Wilmington Airport three black bags were taken from the plane's cargo hole and driven to Dover Air Force Base. The plane would be serviced, checked, and rechecked for a departure again Monday morning. The routine was almost always the same, only the sites for pickup and discharge changed. It was nearly 3 P.M. when Maggie finished her stewardess duties, checked herself out, went to the thirteen year-old Nash Metropolitan, she had owned for nearly four years. She sighed and sat for a moment before starting the car.

Maggie should have bought a new car before she began flying or moved to the farm, but the Nash had served her needs so far. Surely it would last a little longer.

She cranked the little Metropolitan's engine and headed toward Newark on Frenchtown road. Her friends who had helped build Interstate 95 would be at the road's dedication this afternoon. Maggie saw the crowd gathering as her plane approached its final stop and wanted to be with them.

Norman and the other five photographers of Wilmington's two newspapers sat on tables in the newspaper library as their picture editor laid out assignments for the day. Norman's assignment was to get photographs of the main dedication guest shaking hands with regional and local officials. His secondary task was to get tight portraits for use in the coming months whenever a headshot of the president was needed for a story and to stay late in case the workers celebration got rowdy.

"Remember fellas, travel in three cars, separate yourselves so you don't get crowd bound if something happens, and bring back great photographs," Hershel concluded.

The six photographers grabbed their camera bags and headed toward Newark on secondary roads. They planned to return on the new interstate highway

An hour later, three gleaming olive drab and white helicopters flew northward along the interstate, circled and landed near the "H" behind the dedication platform. Washington press corps and security people left the first two flying machines and hastened themselves to the platform area. A few minutes later President John F. Kennedy's hair rubbed the top of his helicopter's door as he stepped before hundreds of waving helmets and applause more deafening than the helicopter engines.

Norman and a hundred other photographers snapped away as the president made his way through the crowd of the workmen on his way to the platform as Ernest, his wife, Kevin, Linda, Lionel, Madeline

190

Buying the Farm

and Maggie watched. After reaching the platform, the president shook hands with several state governors and celebrity guests then took his seat and brushed his hair with his fingers. Norman was standing less than forty feet from the president for the third time in three years. Through his telephoto lens he could see a driver's license size image of the president. He clicked off a half dozen frames with people blocking most of the president except his brow and hair. The president looked toward Norman and made a mental note of his behavior. Norman continued making close ups during and after his dedication address when the president cut five woven ribbons stretched across the northbound lane of the interstate. Red, yellow and black represented Maryland state colors, blue and gold represented Delaware's colors. Following the ribbon cutting the president again made his way along the snow fence again. Norman stayed in front of him clicking away until the president asked, "Why were you snapping when people blocked your view?"

"To get your trademark eyes, brow, and hair, Mister President. That's the way cartoonist and most of the public see you, sir. Brow, eyes and hair," Norman answered.

"Especially the cartoonists. I would like to see your results," the president said.

"It would be an honor, Mister President!" Norman replied.

At the helicopter door the president waved, and pointed an imaginary camera at Norman, then stepped through the helicopters door and headed for New York City.

"I shook his hand, again," Kevin shouted after Norman made his way to his brothers and friends.

"I put his hand on my big belly," Linda said.

"I'm gonna wait for the rush to get over, but I have time for a coke. Then I'll have to head back to the office," Norman said, and for a half an hour he partied around the station wagon tailgate. After dark, Norman photographed a huge bonfire built using timber from the platform, and left.

The other photographers had processed and proofed their film. Norman made an extra set of his rolls. Soon the picture editor returned to the lab with about fifteen red rectangles on as many contact sheets. Norman's shot of eyes, brow and hair was not selected, but he made two prints anyway. After the mayhem of printing Friday newspaper pictures was over, Norman made 16x20 prints from two tight shots of the president's heavy eye lids, hair and brow. He printed the picture of Linda holding the president's hand to her stomach and pulled out an old file, and printed one of Kevin and the president taken three years earlier. He dried them and called Maggie. They would have only a few hours together before Maggie would be flying out again.

"We have lots to catching up to do," he said, handing a cup of hot tea along with two photographs of her with the president after he reached their farmhouse.

"Lots and lots," she replied.

Norman heard the exhaustion in his voice as he kicked off his penny loafers and sat on the sofa, one foot on the floor, the other against the sofa back. She moved close to him, snuggled her hips between his legs, laid her head on his chest, and moved his hands through a slit in robe to her stomach, then she opened the envelope.

"You were pretty busy at the interstate today," Maggie said. "And you got to speak to the president."

"It wasn't so bad. I managed to get one outstanding picture of him. Take a look; a copy is in with your pictures. How was your flight this time?" Norman asked.

"About the same. We carry a load of scared boys to some military outpost who wonder if they will come home in one piece, in a body bag or be blown into the sky by some nuclear blast. Something has got to be done soon to put an end to this insanity before nothing is left to fight over," she said.

"You could apply to one of the domestic airlines. You have enough experience for one of them to take you on," he said.

"And have war contractors and bomb salesmen slap me on the ass. No thanks. The boys going over need to see a friendly face that gives them assurance the will be coming back. I've got the kind of compassionate face they need to see." she replied.

"Make that a beautiful compassionate face, Maggie, beautiful."

"Norman, beauty is only a mask I put on when I need it. If I were a not a girl, I could be one of the boys going over. I have to have my best mask on. They don't need some unfeeling stewardess feeding them cute night club remarks. If one of them wants to slap my ass, I'll put old glory on my butt. I can assure you, most would prefer a smile to copping a feel. And I am going to give them that smile as long as I can, and leave the breast grabbing, butt slapping flights to the vacation tending stewardesses," she said.

Maggie was silent for a moment hoping she had said the right things to Norman, especially about butt slapping and breast pinching. She want to be sure there was none of that taking place on her flights.

Buying the Farm

"Norman, you have seen the best and worst of me for the last year and a half. I take off my clothes and put that beauty mask on for your camera. When it's just you and me, I don't need the mask. I feel truly beautiful then. It's the opposite with flying and modeling. The mask is part of my uniform or outfit I wear for pictures. I have to wear it for those soldiers. I'm just as scared as they are. I don't need to hide behind it with you when I'm not modeling. But thank for saying I am beautiful," Maggie concluded.

Norman sat his cup down next to a chrysanthemum blossom on his saucer.

"More tea?" she asked.

"I have something in mind better than tea," he said

Maggie snuggled closer and said, "I'll be here until 3 A.M."

They had four hours to make up for eight days they had been separated. But they were in no hurry.

"Kevin is still working with Ernest on the early evening shift. Graveyard shifts were canceled. They should have quality time now that Linda is due any day," she stated.

"She looked good today, even with the big belly she's lugging around," he replied.

"Looking good and being well are not the same. She and Kevin are worried about what he will do when the interstate is finished. Having the baby due any day only makes their worries worse. When I get back I'll go see if there's anything I can do," Maggie said

"She would like that. Back on the farm when I was a little boy, it was one chilly April morning in 1945. Ernest and I got up and went to the already burning fireplace. We moved close to warm ourselves, and our shoes. I was five and Ernest was three and a half. Dad brought a blanket and placed it in my arms. He opened the folded flap and revealed a tiny baby with red hair just like his. It was his third son and my second brother. Sometime during the night he had been born. Neither Ernest nor I can remember any activity during the childbirth. She would give birth to Loraine sixteen months after that morning and to Lionel after fifteen more months. During the summer after that, we would climb in to the wagon and ride bumpy dirt road to show off our new baby. Mostly we took only Sunday trips, Dad spent his spare time shoeing horses, weaving baskets or making chairs. He had five mouths to feed now. Soon the red haired baby was strong enough to scurry about on the floor. He did not crawl, but pushed himself backwards. Sometimes he scurried into the yard if the dog didn't block him. He loved to

Call Me Maggie

ride on my shoulders. He and I were inseparable until I started working. I hope I get the chance to be as close to Junior as I was to Kevin," Norman said.

"I loved your story," Maggie said, snuggling closer.

"On another occasion Kevin developed a high fever. Mom sent Ernest and I up to a blueberry patch to get roots for tea. Since she did not request berries, we ate the berries off the plants pulled up. We had blue lips until Kevin pulled through, but the next year there were no bushes or blueberries."

"We can plant some blueberries for Kevin Junior next spring."

"Okay. Do you ever think about us having babies?"

"Sometimes, but with our jobs, we could never fit one in. Babies take lots of time and work. I want to do a better than my mother did with my sister and me. We practically raised ourselves," she said.

The conversation had hit a tender spot within Maggie. She went upstairs and run a bath. Norman closed the fireplace, locked the doors, turned off the lights, and carried two cups of tea to their bedroom. He could not be sure if she had gotten over the memories that brought on her withdrawal when she slid up to him after the bath.

Maggie rose at 3 a.m., with only an hour of sleep. Norman served her re-warmed Danish rolls while she prepared for her next departure. The flight was thirteen hours out of Philadelphia with a stop in St. Louis for fuel and more soft drinks for sixty kids and chaperons, then on to Los Angles with noisy youngsters running up and down the aisles, back to St Louis, and finally home. The good news was the plane would come home empty and Maggie could sleep most of the ten hour return flight while the kids romped at Disney World. They would pick up the youngsters three days later for the west to east flight. The phone rang as Norman made more tea.

"It's your dispatcher," Norman yelled from the kitchen.

"If you are sure you can't find anyone else, I will take the flight. Call me back if another stewardess shows up, otherwise, I'll see you at five," Maggie said replacing the phone in its cradle.

"What's happening now?" Norman asked.

"Three attendants have not checked in. There is a flight to Viet Nam tomorrow and they are short handed," Maggie said.

"You could have said no. You only got back yesterday."

Maggie did not make the trip to California. Instead she headed back to Vietnam carrying frightened boys over and bring home wounded young men and coffins.

194

Buying the Farm

The following week was quiet in Wilmington until 11 A.M. Friday.

Norman's barber was putting the finishing trim on his hair. The barber commented his hair her of a picture she had seen in the newspaper a week earlier of John Kennedy's, except that Norman's was white. Norman said he had made the picture especially to show the president's hair, eyes and forehead and then told of his fascination with hair and in particular Maggie's. When he held his hands in front of her to show its length, he brushed her breasts. Norman was still blushing when he paid, tipped, and thanked the barber for the compliment. Two minutes later, he dashed back into the shop. Chimes on the door rang loudly startling the barber and taking her breath away.

"I need to use your phone. The radio said President Kennedy was been shot. He died a few minutes ago in a Dallas hospital."

Within twenty minutes, six photographers sat around the newspaper's library table with their picture editor.

"Robert, you go with the political reporter for the governor's reaction. Jim, you get pictures of people watching TV at store windows, in taverns, in offices, and anywhere you find a crowd. Charles, get some flags being lowered to half-staff. Norman, take Judith, get interviews and pictures of people who may not know yet, in factories, construction sites, even movie theaters. Harry, I want you on standby, printing shots from the dedication last week. We have the front page, second news front and four open pages to fill in a special early edition we want on the street by five o'clock. I need prints by four. This could be war starting. Stay sharp. Be alert to anything unusual. Castro may be getting his revenge for the Bay of Pigs incident or the Missile Crisis. If this was the work of the Russians, we may not be here to publish tomorrow's paper," their editor advised.

Norman and Judith teamed up for another story going first to the Warner Theater. Reaction of people exiting the theater ranged from tearful outbursts to one lady swinging her purse at them for bearing such a fabricated unbelievable story. They found disbelief everywhere they visited. All schools and most factories closed at 1 P.M. Flags were lowered. Restaurants shut their doors. Streets soon emptied traffic. A quiet mayhem set in as word spread.

An intercom buzzed as Maggie's plane flew eastbound near Hawaii with a cabin full of Marines en-route home and civilian life.

"Put that Honolulu station on the P.A. system," the pilot called to stewardesses.

Call Me Maggie

"President John Fitzgerald Kennedy died of gunshot wounds just a few minutes ago in Dallas, Texas," a voice on the radio announced.

Maggie put a hand over her open mouth for a long moment pondering what she had just heard before pushing the corners of her lips upward and going forward to comfort and put her passengers at ease.

"Have the Russians finally begun war?" one marine asked.

"Probably just some nut trying to get him a place in the history books like the one who started World War I or the one who shot President Lincoln," Maggie answered.

Most of the Marines wept with heads bowed. Others prayed quietly. All had survived a combat tour in the mountains and jungles of a Southeast Asia war, yet their Commander in Chief had been shot while riding in an open convertible back home on a sunny on Friday morning.

By little after seven that evening, the photographers had delivered their prints and the special edition was being set into type and picture halftones were being made when Norman answered the darkroom telephone and raced to his picture editor's office.

"Chief, I need to go out for a while. If anything else comes up, I will be in room 322 at Saint Francis Hospital," Norman said, and raced away without waiting for a reply.

Hershel never looked up from his editing duties, but answered "Okay," into the empty doorway.

Norman instinctively clicked off a few frames as Kevin leaned over Linda's bed with arms and elbows on the sheets watching Linda nurse a red haired baby. Some included Linda's parents and Kevin. Others were taken of Linda and her baby alone. Norman let his camera hang from his shoulder, knelled at Linda's side mirroring Kevin's position and stared at the baby with red hair not quite as dark as Kevin's.

"Hello Junior, I'm Uncle Norman," he greeted the baby.

"She's not junior anymore. She is Deanna," Linda said.

"Hello Deanna. Uncle Norman is going to teach you to take pictures of your Daddy and your Mommy, Aunt Maggie and her horses, and both your Mom Moms and Pop Pops," he said to his new niece.

He called the newspaper and told the picture editor, "Chief, I have pictures of a little girl just born. The president's face is in on the TV in the background.

A few moments later Norman made a statement Deanna's parents and grandparents had heard him use many times; "I have to get back to the lab and process." The next day's newspaper carried Nor-

Buying the Farm

man's pictures of the woman swinging her purse at Judith, school children passing under a half staffed flag, one showing the eyes, brow and hair of President Kennedy that did not get printed the week before, and one of new parents and a just born baby girl.

Norman stayed in the darkroom until past midnight printing pictures of his family and the president taken a week earlier. He made display enlargements of Linda holding the president's hand on her large stomach and one of her and the baby. He printed another of Kevin and the president taken three years earlier during a campaign stop at Wilmington, and then typed a brief note and slid it and several photographs into a brown envelope addressed to Mrs. Jacqueline Kennedy, 1600 Pennsylvania Avenue, Washington, and D. C. The noted read: "The president asked to see these pictures when he dedicated the Maryland and Delaware Turnpike last week. My regrets that the pictures are arriving late."

"If you are free Tuesday, I would you like to drive with me to Washington while I keep my promise and pay my respects on behalf soldiers I brought back," Maggie asked after her flight.

Tuesday morning as they waited in commuter traffic at the Chesapeake Bay Bridge, Maggie watched a white swan swimming alone in a pond beside the causeway. For several hours Maggie and Norman stood in a slow moving line of mourners until she got her chance to lay eleven Purple Heart medals among thousands of flowers and other mementos near a small flame burning in the night on a hillside in Arlington, Virginia.

"There was no reason for his life to end this way. Why can't people accept others as they are, even if their ideology, politics, life styles, religions, and skin colors are different? All the man wanted was to fulfill everyone's dreams of a great and better society. I hope those dreams weren't buried with him," Maggie said as they left.

"A dream for some is a threat to others," Norman said.

"He was leading us against the threats in Europe, Vietnam, Cuba and the ones here at home. We may never know why he had to die for his dreams, but in our lifetime, we will know if his dreams will come true of if they died with him," Maggie said.

Four weeks later Maggie's plane left for San Diego with minimal cargo except for flight crew and crew supplies. No passengers had been loaded and none would be loaded in San Diego. Even the Pentagon officials lack the brass or courage to ship out replacements three days before Christmas.

Call Me Maggie

Rather than cross the Pacific empty, they would load the plane's belly with small arms ammunition and strap need supplies to the Connie's cabin stretchers. It would be a dangerous flight by any measure. One lucky shot to the cargo hole over enemy territory and the Connie would explode in a fireball.

Eight stewardesses had been asked to volunteer for the flight. Maggie, Midge and two others were left when four others declined then only accepted the flight when told they would be needed to care for wounded on trip back to the states. Maggie apologized to the flight's timing and for not being home for Christmas She did not mention her west bound cargo. As they left on the leg to Honolulu, Manila and Saigon tension was at an all time high. Little conversation was exchanged as they huddled in the rearmost seats until the plane landed in Vietnam then they exploded with relief.

At the end of 1961, nine hundred Americans were serving as advisors to the Vietnamese military. By the end of the 1962, there were 11,326 serving as advisors and in combat as well. Thirty two died in action and hundreds more were injured, many by booby traps, in ambushes, or mortar attacks. In the coming year those numbers would rise higher. Maggie would be home for New Years Eve and celebrate Christmas with Norman a week late. The return flight was like others, caring for wounded passengers.

January first, Maggie and Norman welcomed more than a hundred guests to the little farmette. The crowd almost equaled the one during the day they bought it. Townspeople of Odessa joined residents from the nursing home where Rose Gaelic spent her last two years as Rose was buried near her husband and daughter in the earthen rise at the corner. Maggie returned to the rise that night and placed a lighted candle on the freshly disturbed soil where the white snowy pasture met the bare gray trees.

6

Baby Boomers

The summer of 1963 came and went all too quickly for Maggie and Norman.

Several of the old Connies had been grounded for overhaul and the number of injured needing stateside medical attention was overflowing facilities in Vietnam. Simple walks wandering around abandoned farms filled some summer mornings. He looked for photographs or sought out abandoned relics as she collected flowers and seeds. She stepped in or out of his photographs and her clothes as easily or as eagerly actress stepped on stage. Maggie increased her long dress collection by sending those from her grandmother's closet to the cleaners with her uniforms, and taught herself to use a typewriter in the evenings when home. On Saturday mornings that Maggie was not flying were always spent with Norman and his parents harvesting or canning or freezing produce from Pop Pop's garden.

Maggie made flights overseas, plus jaunts with in the country ferrying soldiers from one post to another over taking tourist to resorts. When given a choice, she chose overseas military flights.

"Do you spend all your after work hour this way when I'm away? What are you, some kind of a hardcore workaholic?" Maggie asked, after finding him still in the darkroom just before daybreak when she returned from a flight one night.

"I suppose you're not. When you're gone I'd rather be here working than sitting in an afterhours club bragging about the things I did that day," Norman replied emphatically.

"You don't brag about your pictures, Norman. You don't have to. They speak for themselves. Let's spend the morning shooting more. I found some new old dresses to wear in them."

Call Me Maggie

The dew had not yet evaporated as Maggie sat on the rocky perimeter of a spring fed fountain in Valley Garden Park. Three dozen buttons on her bodice sparkled as she looked skyward basking in the sunlight that flooded and warmed her. After Norman had made several exposures, she undid the buttons and allowed her unencumbered chest to be photographed. When a few more exposures were made, she walked down a path meandering through an acre-sized field of brilliantly blooming flowers. Sunlight pierced the skirt and silhouetted her legs. Soon she kicked off her shoes, lifted the hem of her long skirt nearly to her hips, and left the path to stroll through the blossoms. Norman's camera clicked in unison with his rapid breathing.

"Another good one," Norman said, and continued shooting when she removed the dress and struck a few poses nude.

She changed positions a few times, returned to the yellow field, strolling through the flowers and striking several poses, then lay among the blossoms and finally posed in the spring feed stream before slipping the dress over her wet body. Norman made a final shot of the dress clinging to her damp skin as she re-buttoned the bodice. Her album had grown thicker by another dozen pictures when the prints were added.

After lunch was served the next day, Maggie made several trips up and down the cabin checking and rechecking. On one trip back a soldier followed her, grabbed her buttocks and squeezed tightly while she poured coffee into cups on a service cart. Maggie suppressed a scream, but dropped the pot as she turned to her assailant.

"Long time no see. How about a feel for old time sake?"

"Vinnie!"

He squeezed the breast beneath the tag. Her mind flashed back to a drunken vacationer months earlier and to a time more distant when Vinnie squeezed her before forcing himself upon her or if he just felt like being mean.

Vinnie folded forward when Maggie's knee crushed into his crotch. A young officer was on his feet before Vinnie hit the floor. The officer pushed him the rest of the way and held down.

"Sorry about that Ma'am. Are you okay?" he asked.

"Yes. Just some spilled coffee." she replied as grimaces formed on her face.

"You know this soldier, Miss?"

"I use to!"

Maggie rubbed her body in several places as memories of other abuses and beating from Vinnie returned.

Baby Boomers

"I'll make sure he doesn't do anything like that again, maam," the officer stated.

He lifted Vinnie and seated him by the window in the rear most seats, then took the aisle seat. For the rest of the flight on to Hawaii, Maggie and Vinnie exchanged glances as she made trips up and down the cabin. During the refueling stop in Hawaii, he escorted Vinnie to the second plane in the flight.

The officer was large young man with red hair over his massive arms and shoulders. Maggie imagined she saw Kevin in the uniform. During her break, she sat with the officer and said, "I want to thank you for what you did. The incident might not have ended as it did without you help."

"I have a sister about your age and I would not want her to put up with that kind of crap. We get a lot of common soldiers in the draft," the lieutenant stated in a slow drawl.

"I thought you might be a southern gentleman. My adopted family is from Alabama. My boyfriend is a southern gentle man too. He says it's so hilly there, they don't get sunshine till after ten o'clock," Maggie said.

"That's northern Alabama. Is he a miner or a timber man?"

"He a photographer, but his parents used to farm in Alabama until the 1950's."

"My dad said early on, 'Its Auburn or the University of Alabama, farming is not for my children. I chose Virginia Military Institute."

"How many brothers and sisters do you have?"

"Just four brothers and a baby sister. Farm families are big, you know. Lots of work, farming."

"Did you ever lie in a cotton listening rain on a tin roof?"

"Yes." the lieutenant answered. His eyes filled with tears.

"Norman and I did one afternoon on Uncle J. W.'s farm. I loved it."

"Excuse me Ma'am. Soldiers are supposed to cry. Especially in front of a lady," the officer stated.

"You'd be surprised at how many do."

She passed him a small pack of tissues, and introduced herself. "I'm Mary Anne Johnson, call me Maggie,"

"I'm Army Lieutenant Robert J. Montgomery. Bobby Joe to my friends." he said, shaking her hand.

Call Me Maggie

"My dad's first name was Montgomery. And my boyfriend has cousins whose last name is Montgomery. I met some of them in Alabama a couple weeks ago, near a little town called Wadley. Good friendly people."

"It wasn't J. W. Montgomery, was it?"

"Why, yes it was."

"Lives a few miles north of a town in a house on stilts on top of a hill called Bald Rock?"

"Yes."

"Is your friend Norman Kennedy? Cousin Norm is a photographer'"

"Yes."

"Hello Cousin," he said shaking hands again.

"Hello yourself, Cousin. I wish we had more time to know each other. I don't get to know many of my passengers."

Maggie interrupted the conversation with Bobby Joe only when stewardess duties called her away or when he napped. Before leaving the plane in Vietnam, they exchanged hugs while another soldier snapped a picture. As he waved from the terminal, Vinnie Gambini limped past Maggie's newly discovered cousin. She waited until Bobby Joe disappeared in the terminal, turned, and began helping the other flight crew ready the plane for stretcher patients they would carry home.

Three days later, Maggie walked into the photo department of the newspaper.

"He's in back printing," Robert said, after greeting her.

Maggie walked through the light trap and into room lit only by dim yellow safelights. She waited until he placed the negative carrier into the enlarger and then asked. "Do you have plans for dinner, Mister Kennedy?"

"I do now." Norman answered as her arms wrapped around his waist.

"Watching the image appear still amazes me," she said, then added, "I met your cousin, Bobby Joe, on the flight over,"

"Bobby Joe Montgomery? I haven't seen him since '58. Went to his Thanksgiving Day football game before dinner," Norman remembered.

"He's a first lieutenant in the army now, not a football player. He's on his second tour over there."

"Good for you. How did you meet him?" Norman asked as the print fixed.

Baby Boomers

"I had an incident with one of my boys and he helped take care of it," she replied, maintaining her habit of not discussing details of incidents happing on her flights.

Norman washed his prints, typed some captions while the prints dried and delivered the prints to the picture editor.

"Get me a shot of the new bank building in Middletown before you come in tomorrow. Take Maggie out for a quiet dinner and don't come back tonight," Hershel said.

"Thanks, Chief," Norman answered.

"Don't call me chief!" the editor said, tossed a pencil toward Norman and laughed.

"Okay. Good night Chief," Norman yelled as he dashed away.

His ragtop followed Maggie's Nash until she parked at the Dutch Pantry on U.S 13 at the airport under the "Friendly Skies of United" billboard. The two chose a corner table they had used since Maggie entered the restaurant with Kevin after moving out of Maggie's mother's house.

"Fill me in on Bobby Joe and the others."

"Bobby Joe is on his second tour in Vietnam. Uncle Marion still raises cotton. Aunt Wilma is now a county commissioner. Howard is a dentist. Michael is an extension agent. Hoyt teaches agricultural technology at Auburn. Sister Bess is in pre-med. Hap's son, Doug is at West Point. The three older boys are all married and have given Uncle Marion and Aunt Wilma eleven grandchildren. When Hoyt's next baby arrives, they'll have a dozen, and I missed you terribly."

"Sounds like you and Bobby Joe hit it off well."

"I gave you the Reader's Digest version. Uncle Marion only plants eighty acres of cotton. The market is kaput! Synthetics are replacing cotton. He put beef cattle on a hundred and twenty and a hundred in grain."

"Didn't you and Bobby Joe talk about anything besides family, farming and the market?" Norman asked.

"My boys usually talk about home and their families on the way over, and even more on the way back, if they talk at all. They regard us as counselors, girlfriends, or sometimes as mothers. They never talk about the war or the events taking place over there. I had one fellow who couldn't wait to get back to Harlem and spent all night riding his wheel chair through Times Square. Another plans to attend a protest march in California next month even if his artificial legs are not ready."

203

Call Me Maggie

Norman would allow Maggie to cleanse her mind of the flight as he had after each trip she made during the past six months. He would listen, wanting to know more about uncles, aunts, cousins and the incident she had mentioned, but asking only about the relatives. He allowed her to choose or not choose to discuss the event.

More stewardesses were added to the airline; Maggie's flights were back to three or four a month. Her career became bearable again. She had time to spend with Linda and Norman's parents. When with Linda, she spent most of her time with the little red haired baby while chit-chatting. If she stopped to see his parents she could count on a late night dinner and be back at the farm when he got home. Early evenings were spent freezing or canning vegetables and filling pots with soil for Pop Pop's rose bush cuttings. Once the garden plants were mature, he began propagating roses in little pots that soon filled the greenhouse. One Tuesday morning Maggie asked what Norman would think if they had a greenhouse of their own. By evening a 12x18 foot assemble it yourself was being built near the barn. With help from Pop Pop it stood completely assembled.

Soon her flights were back to one every four days, but all flights were to simmering Southeast Asia.

Maggie tried to sleep on thin damp foam mattress, but unmercifully did not manage to get more than a few abbreviated naps between helicopter flights over her barracks throughout much of the night. Some flew so low she could feel the building tremble and wind from their rotors blowing through open windows. Flights over the barracks to and from the nearby hospital were commonplace, but more frequent this night making sleep impossible.

The luminous dial on her Timex read 2:45. Maggie remembered a Pocono Mountain resort dormitory years earlier after she sat up to orient herself. A sweaty T-shirt clung to Maggie's skin. Damp hair lay tight against her shoulders. She was not in an air conditioned resort dormitory tonight. Rows of two level bunks divided by lockers lined both long walls of the building. Toilets were placed in one corner; shower stalls opposite toilets and washbasins. It was sleeping quarters for nurses, female employees of contractors, advisors who shunned price gouging hotels and airline stewardesses waiting for their planes to be serviced for flights back home. Interior wallboards had been omitted. Light could be seen through cracks in exterior planking. The roof did not leak and the women could wash away tropical sweat and mosquito spray two or three times each day during their layovers.

Baby Boomers

"Maggie, are you awake?" a voice whispered from the bunk above.

"Yes," Maggie whispered back.

"Is it always like this," the voice asked.

"Not always. Sometimes it is worse when lots more chopper are coming in than came in tonight. They are bringing your passengers for the flight home."

Maggie carried a hanging garment bag and a satchel toward the lighted doorway of the toilet. The woman in the bunk above followed.

"I don't think I got an hour's sleep all night. I'll be in poor shape for the flight back, thanks to those helicopters," the voice in toilet stall stated.

"Sometimes it's this way. Take a long shower and freshen up. Forget your makeup, it'll only makes you sweat more," Maggie advised the new stewardess.

Maggie left the stall headed to the shower. Leanne McPherson followed and copied Maggie. Leanne was on her first flight that took her halfway around the world from Farmville, Virginia.

Maggie removed her wet clothes, put them in a plastic bag, and handed another one to Leanne McPherson who copied Maggie again.

"How long have you been coming over here?"

"Since early in '62. This is my twenty-ninth trip. I've made lots more stateside and to Europe." Maggie answered.

"How do you like being a stewardess?"

"Some flights are better than others. The real measure is the flight home. On this one we will be caring for a lot of wounded, judging from the choppers traffic tonight. Brace yourself for a lot of pain and suffering," Maggie advised again.

"Will it be that bad? In school we spent only a week in trauma training. I hope I'm ready for it thanks to nursing school," Leanne said.

"This is real. The wounds are real. It's hard on everyone. We can't do enough for them," Maggie said.

Both dried as best they could. Maggie brushed her long hair and pulled it through a rubber band into a pony tail. Leanne brushed her short bob until it lay in place. Both slipped on blue slacks and buttoned white blouses, omitting their little uniform neckties. Maggie removed a pistol from her purse and placed it in her satchel bag with bagged clothes. Both carried a shoulder purse across their chest, a satchel in one hand and a garment bag in the other as they passed a sign reading "Mess." Inside two dozen GI's were drinking coffee and killing time.

Call Me Maggie

They too couldn't sleep because of the heat, the chopper noise, or from exhaustion unloading and servicing the aerial ambulances.

Maggie carried a tray down the chow line containing scrambled eggs, bacon, toast and orange juice.

"Eat up. The food on the way back was no better than it was coming over. Besides that, if those choppers were any indication, you won't have time to eat on the way back." Maggie said, noticing Leanne's tray held only coffee.

After eating Maggie rested her elbows on the table and crossed her arms. Her hands covered a pair of gold stripes on each shoulder.

"Leanne, let me say to you something woman to woman, not as your chief stewardess. For your own sake, don't make any attachments to the men we bring over here. On your next flight back you might be nursing the same man in bandages or putting him in a black bag. When we lose one that we remember, it can tear you apart. We lose more than one third of the stewardesses' who sign on. Even the nurses who are supposed to handle their injuries we deal with don't all stay with us. When you get home, find something good to get your mind off the flights. Teach day care, raise a garden, babysit neighbor's kids or lay on the beach. Stay out of bars and away from a bottle. Many of our attendants stay stoned or drunk in their off time trying to forget the torn up men we carry home. If you have a boyfriend, love him with all your heart, but don't dump this stuff on him. It maybe party time and grab ass sometimes on the way over, but it's totally different going home. Protect yourself from the pitfalls of this job," Maggie said.

"Is that why you carry a gun, to ward off the guys who want to play grab ass?"

"I carry the gun for protection on the ground. I'll put up with a little grab ass on the plane coming over, but I have never had a problem going home. I don't want to be raped in some alley. I've been raped, and beaten in the streets of Philadelphia the city of brotherly love. It will never happen to me again."

"I was too, the night I graduated. I couldn't get away from the small town sneers and tittle-tattle, so I went to college. That was no better, so when I got my nursing certification I went to flight school. I'll see if this is better than being the center of gossip," Leanne said.

"I'm sorry. I did not know. Let's check in and do something positive to get our minds off our past."

Baby Boomers

Other attendants began passing down the serving line with sleepy eyes and wet hair as Maggie and Leanne took their bags and walked to the building housing their airline offices.

"Bad news. We've had a busy night. The commies started a large offensive. Make room for all you can carry," the dispatcher said.

Maggie got home just before daylight, saw Norman sleeping, quietly lay down her bags, and went directly to the barn. She brushed both horses until they shined. Norman had told Maggie the young mare was ready in a phone call the night before and made arrangement to take her to her stud today.

Soon Norman arrived with two coffee mugs. They exchanged greetings amidst their usual embraces. He helped her saddle Storm and watched as they rode in the morning sun. He smiled as he saw Storm's mane and Maggie's hair blowing behind their heads; one chalk white, the other strawberry blonde, both easy on his eyes. Their second cup of coffee was savored on the deck where they could greet the birds and watch the horses frolicking in the pasture.

"Had a new stewardess on the flight this trip. She's a lot like Linda and me. I think you would like her. Her home is down in central Virginia, too far away for commuting. Would you mind if I invited her down here on layovers sometime?"

"No. You don't have many friends besides Linda."

"Maybe after the next trip. Those to Europe were a snap compared to this one. The dispatcher had to call in extra planes. The Communists have begun a new offensive. We thought our hands were full with the Berlin situation. But these trips to Vietnam are worse. One more and we will be over swamped."

"Take a long hot bath; I'll bring you some tea."

Although they could not foresee it, the Berlin crisis and Cold War would last for another twenty-five years and involve Norman's baby brother, Lionel. The "hot war" in southeastern Asia was obviously escalating, if the number of flights Maggie made were examined. Rumors overheard during return flights told of American servicemen assigned to outposts in Laos, Cambodia and Thailand.

Some of Maggie's returning passengers told of crude booby traps being set by Viet Cong while others told of injuries they received from misdirected friendly fire and uncharted mine fields planted by American soldiers. Newer aircraft began replacing leftovers from the Korean War and their updated replacements as well.

207

Call Me Maggie

Vietnamese medical facilities were overloaded. Vietnamese natives began appearing on Maggie's eastbound flight. Some flights included Viet women and children needing treatment not found in their homeland. One included a young girl running away from her village that had been burned who became a poster child for anti-war activists.

Six weeks later Maggie's plane was left for San Diego with minimal cargo except for flight crew and crew supplies. No passengers had been loaded and none would be loaded in San Diego. Even the Pentagon officials lacked the brass or courage to ship replacements out three days before Christmas.

Rather than cross the Pacific empty, they would load the plane's belly with small arms ammunition and strap needed supplies to the Connie's cabin stretchers. It would be a dangerous flight by any measure. One lucky shot to the cargo hole over enemy territory and the Connie would explode in a fireball.

Stewardesses had been asked to volunteer for the flight. Maggie and Leanne took the flight when all others declined. They accepted the flight only when told they would be needed to care for wounded on trip back to the states. Maggie apologized to Norman for the flight's timing and for not being home for Christmas, but did not mention her west bound cargo. As they left on their leg to Honolulu, Manila and Saigon tension was at an all time high. Little conversation was exchanged as they huddled in the rearmost seats until the plane landed in Vietnam, then they burst into a strong and noisy release of tension. She would be home for New Years Eve and celebrate Christmas with Norman a week late. The return flight was like many others, caring for her wounded passengers.

One winter morning Norman slowly guided his Chevy behind a snow plow making its second pass westbound on Pennsylvania Highway 41. Branches of fir trees on either side of the road bent to the ground under their load of clinging snow. Ahead lay a wide white valley and a long low mountain so distant their trees blended into a gray blur. The valley was dotted with farmhouses, barns, and little hamlets every few miles. Gray smoke rose from chimneys on each of the farmhouses and met the gray line of trees in the living mural before him. He had his answer. The snow was a bonus.

Norman made a left turn on to Strasburg-Gap Road, drove up a small rise, and began looking for a break in the trees beside the road running along the top of a hill on the east side of the valley. Silently he asked himself if the trip would be productive. Soon Norman stopped the car, removed three cameras from a large camera bag in the passenger foot-well stood on the door jam and began clicking each of his three cameras. Panorama, telephoto and normal lenses diversified his shots of the valley to the west of him from his elevated vantage spot. Fence lines and hedge rows broke the valley land into neat rectangles. The hillsides were divided into curved plots following the contour of the hills. None of the plots could be larger than a city block. To the east a horse pulled manure spreader deposited a line of steaming brown feces on the fresh snow. A young boy guided the team below the sun rising behind him. Norman got of shots of the scene. Morning had come to the Pennsylvania Dutch country and Norman was photographing the awakening.

The dial on the Gap Town Clock read 7:45 as Norman crept down the hill past the shingled clock tower. He pulled into the unplowed parking lot below the clock leaving deep tracks in the snow. Heavy wet snow clung to the tops of farm equipment placed in front of an antique shop next to the tower. He could leave no tracks near the equipment. In a moment he was taking pictures of the snow covered implements and their shadow patterns on the white blanket. The township of Gap and its clock sat at the bottom of the hilled eastern boundary to the Pequaua Valley, heart of the Amish Country. A low area in the hill gave the township its name, Gap. It was the gateway of commerce and tourism in and out of the valley from the east. Less than a quarter mile ahead, Gap-Newport Pike dead-ended at U.S. 30. To the road started at the New Castle Wharf, nearly fifty miles east. Before the Christiana River was bridged, the road ended in Newport providing the road its name. In Delaware it was the Newport-Gap Pike, in Pennsylvania the name was Gap-Newport Road Railroads lines and boxcars had almost replaced the pike at the beginning of the twentieth century. Midway through the century trucks on the pike were replacing the railroads. Electric engine passenger trains could still be ridden into Philadelphia or westward to Harrisburg or even Pittsburg and Chicago. He had crossed the rail line a few miles east of the little town.

Norman returned to the warmth of his car and a Thermos of coffee. He turned left on U.S. 30 for about a mile and then right on the unplowed Route 772 at an arrow shaped sign reading "Intercourse, 8 Miles." His tracks were the only ones on the road.

At the first farmhouse a sign roadside marker read "Belvedere, circa 1680." He left the car in the road and photographed the barn and tree encircled house with the town of Gap in the background. After another three minute drive he pulled into the yard between an Amish

Call Me Maggie

house and a barn. Two greenhouses stood with one end next to the road. A larger greenhouse lined the back edge of the yard. Smoke rose from stove pipes at near each end of the larger glass walled and roofed building. The smell of burning oak filled the air Norman and his parents had visited the nursery farm many time each spring for seedlings and potted plants. Inside an Amish man with straw hat and black coat was watering the plants. His wife, two sons and a daughter were placing seeds into plastic trays with three quarter inch soil filled squares. Norman greeted each as brother, sister and their given name while he made a few pictures of their hands working above the trays with fifty four spaces, placing one seed per square, excluding their faces. The oldest boy was Kevin's age and worked alongside his parents each day. The youngest boy and his younger sister would normally have been walking to Gap Amish School at this hour, but the snow had blessed their parents with four extra hands for planting seeds. The boys were clones of their father except for his beard. Each wore black pocket less pants with buttons on the fly area and a vest under a blue shirt pinned down the front. Each wore a beige straw hat. The girl and her mother wore pinned burgundy blouses under black aprons and black skirts. They wore white bonnets. None wore shoes even though four inches of wet snow covered their nursery farm. Black coats were hung on pegs near the door.

By May the seedlings would be three inches tall and transplanted in four inch pots ready for sale to tourists and gardeners alike who wanted Pennsylvania Dutch grown seedling and plants. Norman knew he could look forward to three or more trips back with his father and perhaps Maggie if she wasn't flying. If she was, he and Pop Pop would make choices for her in both volume and variety.

Norman spent nearly an hour with his Amish friends before driving on toward Intercourse. He found buggy tracks on the road and soon found the buggy. Three Amish children looked at him from the open rear window of the buggy. Norman made a few shots as they lead him toward the little town. To his left steam rose from the backs of Black Angus steers leaving a large barn. Norman stopped to photograph the scene including steam rising from the barn's silo. The sun was now about thirty degrees above the horizon providing additional brilliance to the steam. The nearby metal windmill did not turn. Its skeletonal structure was duplicated in a long shadow on the snow. Norman made a picture of the rising sun through its blades. To Norman's right a buggy was cresting a hill on The Old Philadelphia Pike. White clouds contrasted the deep blue sky. He made a few panoramic shots of that scene

210

which included a farmhouse, barn, silo and another windmill. Though little motorized traffic had disturbed the snow, buggy tracks and smoke indicated that the valley was awake and disciplined Amish customs were already being repeated on family farms, in small shops producing wooden articles, iron tools or food products. Tourists would be seen everywhere once springtime arrived six weeks later. The tourists were gluttons for Amish artifacts, crafts quilts and food. Like them, Norman loaded a few cases of food, and a quilt into the snow topped convertible, made a dozen or more photographic studies of the stores, in shops and shot post card-type pictures of old homes in the town of Intercourse. He climbed the banks up to the tracks of the Pennsylvania Railroad and made shots of the railroad bed; two dark lines in the snow leading into infinity. The Strasburg Depot and Pennsylvania Railroad Museum became subjects for calendar pages. Later he shot a buggy passing an airplane at the Smoketown Airport. Up Hartman Station Road Norman found more scenes. He crossed Highway 23 and found a covered bridge across the Conestoga River. Norman left a trail of his footprints around the bridge as he circled it making photographs from every angle. He found three other bridges nearby and repeated his snowy trek. His thoughts often turned to Maggie wishing she were with him and sharing the beauty and serenity of the valley, it's sights and the people he was drawn to. Several times during the day Norman crossed the valley between Lancaster to Morgantown taking pictures of the valley under snow. He spent nearly an hour at the quarry at Terre Hill before he returned to the Smoketown airport, rented a plane and spent another hour flying up and down the valley making aerial photographs. He spent the evening processing his film and printing proofs in his home darkroom.

Kevin did not drive his dirt pan any longer. Instead he drove a large dump truck on the Chesapeake and Delaware Canal. The canal was being widened, straightened. A bad curve was being taken out after a few near misses occurred between meeting ships using the waterway rather that steaming around the entire Delmarva Peninsula. With the large amounts of sleet and snow, his days driving were sporadic, but he could deposit a check each week; often small, but nonetheless a check.

About 6 p.m. Linda, he and Deanna closed the shop, due to the snowfall, went home and unwrapped presents with their daughter, then exchanged presents by the fireplace. Kevin received a burgundy robe. Linda got red pajamas and a fire resistant jump suit. Both were worn briefly and soon discarded to the carpet of the living room floor. It was Valentine's Day.

Call Me Maggie

In an old Constellation over the Pacific, Maggie slowly ambled to the rear of the plane checking her passengers for whom the war had ended violently. Some slept peacefully with their seats reclined, others mumbled in low voices while a few tussled about restlessly while. She placed a finger under the ear of those lying motionless on stretchers hanging along the cabin walls, adjusted belts and straps on a small number while Midge followed few feet behind pushing a cart with coffee, juice and soft drinks. With few takers for her refreshments Midge, tucked blankets around those that needed to be recovered offered a smile to those still awake. When their walk finished, Maggie took a seat in the rear with a cup of Midge's coffee in her right hand and a pen in her left, she slowly began paperwork to be turned in at the end of the flight the next night. It was not a job she enjoyed, but it was a part of her duties and had to be completed before the flight ended while details were still fresh in her mind. Following its completion and a brief nap, she walked forward again but got only to the third stretcher where the uncovered occupant thrashed his freed arms about violently. Vivid red stains obscured the camouflage shirt on his chest. Open wounds on his torso and upper legs that were covered with bandages when she last checked the young man oozed more red liquid. From his mid thigh downward no knees, thighs or feet remained.

Maggie pushed the overhead call button and pushed her thumb between her index and second finger once Leanne awoke and looked forward. A moment later Leanne injected a hypodermic tip into the man's inner elbow, pressed the plunger forward and wrapped a blood pressure reading strap over the man's bicep once his thrashing ceased.

"We had better notify Guam to have an ambulance and type O blood waiting. If he makes it that far he will be lucky. He needs more blood than we have in the cooler," Leanne announced as she pumped the sphygmomanometer ball again.

"Stay with him. I'll call ahead." Maggie stated.

Ninety seconds later she returned with a box of bandages, three rolls of tape, and two bags of blood.

"If it weren't for that damned paperwork and me falling asleep, he wouldn't have regressed this far," she said with wrapping paper from the bandages gripped between her teeth.

"Don't blame yourself. Midge and I fell asleep to too," Leanne said as she injected the soldier's other arm. "What we need are more nurses and corpsmen on these flights. We send them out to get shot and blasted away, but we don't take in to account what happens out there."

Baby Boomers

Norman received Maggie around midnight the following night with his rose and hot chocolate served before their warm welcoming fireplace. After catching up on events at home, she joined him to view Amish country snow pictures lying on the kitchen table next to the album containing her pictures with wet red hair clinging to her neck and the top of a white terry cloth robe. Nothing was mentioned of the emergency she Midge and Leanne met on the plane.

"Why are you so dedicated to the Amish?"

"The Amish have managed to preserve a way of life I knew on the farm. It will be gone someday. I want to make a record of their life before it is lost. Even they have to practice other trades to survive on their little farms. The tourists don't see the real Amish up before daylight or late into the night. Sometimes they see non Amish who pass themselves off adapting Amish clothes and manners to hook tourist and reel them in to purchase non Amish goods. The Pennsylvania Dutch could easily be my father and mother, or my uncles or grandparents making a living off the land with the help of a few cottage industry enterprises to make ends meet. Dad did black smithery, basket and chair weaving to make it on the farm. Uncle Jay has to cut timber and pulpwood. Grandpa spent the winters cutting logs on the hillsides and the rest of the year trying to till the clay and stones. The Amish still practice their two hundred year old traditions for cultural and religious reasons. My family did it out of poverty. Even now, a lot of the Amish leave the sect. I want to make sure it is documented before they're all gone. It's my way of showing respect for their dedication, for my own roots and the ones who came before me. My parents came to the city and worked as a millwright and a leather tanner to support their family, but their hearts are still in the soil. They still plant seeds, chop the weeds, preserve food for the winter and live as they did on the farm." Norman said.

A few weeks later Norman finished shots of the Wilmington and Western Railroad volunteers restoring an old Baldwin locomotive and cars they would begin operating on excursion runs to Hockessin in the spring. They leased track from Marshallton to Hockessin for their five piece train, a much smaller version of the one in Strasburg, Pennsylvania, but with spectacular scenery along the Red Clay Creek valley. He would have to return for pictures of the riders on a weekend. After a few minutes with his mother, Norman headed for town. A new connector across Canby Park's north end became his next subject. The new road eliminated two blocks of one lane traffic and two sharp turns for drivers going into the city. It also eliminated one of the area's best snow sledding hills. Norman shivered this spring morning remembering the evenings he had spent sledding the hill.

Three blocks north sparks erupted from one of the little garages below Lancaster Avenue. Norman instinctively investigated. A helmeted man was cutting the roof off a 1949 Lincoln sedan with a gas torch. Soon the sparks subsided and the helmet was lifted.

"Joseph Jobbe, I thought you were in the Marine Corps. You left right after we graduated, didn't you?" Norman asked as he remembered dating Joe's sister before becoming consumed by photography.

"I did and spent two years fighting in Nam plus one in Lebanon. I ain't gonna fight no more, unless it with this here baby. It was getting rough over there when I left," Joe answered through dark glasses.

"You came home in one piece, didn't you?" Norman said shaking hands with the former high school acquaintance.

"I came home with extra pieces in some places and missing parts in others; five toes on one foot, two on thee other. Shrapnel in legs and a hole in my shoulder, compliments of the Cong," Joe replied.

"Sorry to hear that, Joe," Norman said, feeling guilty for his flippant remark.

"Marines don't complain, they carry on."

"That's a sharp car you have. The continental kit is an add-on isn't it. Chevy didn't market that as stock that year nor did Ford or Lincoln. I'd like to put one on this old girl's," Joe changed the subject.

"Kevin and Lionel should get the credit," Norman followed.

Visions of a school yard bully ending up second best to Kevin in a fight came to Norman.

"Tell me about your Lincoln," Norman tried again.

"Gonna rebuild this baby and get some dreams fulfilled before joining my ole man in his body shop. Gonna chop her six inches on top, lower her six in the back, four in the front, blend the bumpers, strip the chrome and hit her a dozen times with candy apple red. She'll look like this when I'm done," Joe said, and then pulled a copy of Hot Rod Magazine from inside the car.

Norman snapped a few shots as Joe held the magazine facing the camera showing a red chopped Lincoln was on the magazine's cover.

"Want a beer before you go?"

"No thanks. She'll be a beauty. Mind if I drop in and do pictures as you go along. The newspaper might print a feature on you and her. I know a writer who is familiar with automobiles. Either way you'll

214

get progress pictures to show at the drive-ins or car club rallies," Norman said.

"Shoot away. I'll be here with her till she's done. Just me, her, and my ole Bud." Bud and I have been great friends since I arrived in that hell hole over yonder," Joe said.

"You cut and I'll shoot," Norman answered.

The Beach Boys roared "Little Deuce Coupe" from Joe's radio and visions of a drunken high school athlete came into his mind as Norman left. Back at the office he gave Judith a lead on the custom car story. Judith's brother was a car buff and her father was an Indianapolis timer. She knew cars as well as most male car enthusiasts and better than the staff writers. He felt certain Joe and his Lincoln would get in depth coverage from Judith.

"We may have a drinking problem to deal with to get the story," Norman added.

She tipped Norman on another story. "You meet the nicest people on a Honda is more than an advertising phrase. It's become a cultural phenomenal," Judith told him over a dinner of Belly Bombers. Hershel liked both ideas and Norman began collecting pictures of motorcycle and moped riders shared parking spaces with car cruisers at both Greenhill Drive-Ins before the evening became morning.

Norman dropped by Joe Jobbe's garage every few days for updates pictures of the Lincoln. Judith dropped in to record the chopping on paper and share a beer. He also made pictures as Lionel and Madeline souped-up a 1957 Chevy Nomad. It seemed like Kevin and Linda all over again as they tinkered in front of the garage until Kevin went to the service station and Madeline walked up to the new Price's Corner MacDonald's each afternoon to cook hamburgers and French fries.

Madeline and Lionel even appeared on Bandstand a few times during the summer. They kept a picture less television with only one volume setting; blaring, unless Linda dropped in for a visit with Mom Mom or Maggie stopped by to learn rose bush propagation or seedling cultivation from Pop Pop.

Al Alsop called just after Norman got to the office and said, "Norman, I have three other assignments I want you to take. One will require a couple of weeks. One will take a lot of mornings. And the other will be split into one day a week for ten or twelve weeks. I'll speak to your publisher and arrange for a vacation for you for the first one.

"I have vacation time built up. That won't be necessary; I'll take care of it. What are the assignments?" Norman asked.

Call Me Maggie

"We liked your job on the girls bringing wounded back. We want to show the other side of the story. I want you to go to Vietnam and get all you can get on the medi-vac chopper guys and the mobile hospital staffs. They are the ones saving our boys over there. Return with one of the crews like you did before, but focus on one or two of the nurses, corpsmen, and enlisted personnel, as well as Maggie's crew with angels of mercy tie-in. The job for the mornings will be rehab at Walter Reed Army Hospital. Get in close as their bodies and lives are rebuilt. Get me lots of tear-jerking stuff. And then we will have you and our writer, Lindsay Brown check out medical training in one or two of the advanced courses the Marines and Army give their boys. That one you can do flying down once a week as they progress. Are you up for it?" Alsop asked.

I'm up for it."

"We'll have Lindsay Brown contact you and work out the details. Come up and get any equipment you may need from our supply room. If we don't have it, there are plenty of shops nearby. Pick up a couple cases of film while you are here too."

"I'll be there Tuesday morning. Have the writers Xerox any leads they have and rush them to me. I can be on a plane with a day's notice,"

Tuesday morning Norman watched the sun rise over the Manhattan skyline as he and his Chevy waited in New York traffic near the Newark airport before he met with Alsop, copy writers and editors all morning, shared a sandwich with the supply room clerk, spent the afternoon in New York camera shops, packing his Chevy's trunk and was back with the Also and the writer for his final two hours in the city, then watched the sun set over the Newark Airport as he headed home.

The radio played a John Denver song recorded by Peter, Paul and Mary. "I'm leaving on a jet plane. Don't know when I'll be back again." was sung over and over as Norman counted down mile markers on the New Jersey Turnpike.

Two hours later he sat around the kitchen table with his parents telling them of his impending assignment and trip. Madeline joined them at 10:15 and announced she should be called "Maddy." The name appeared with a pair of golden arches appeared on the name tag over her heart. Lionel joined them a moment later in his Esso uniform.

"Lionel, will you drive me to the airport Friday night and take care of the ragtop for me while I'm gone?"

Lionel smiled and Maddy's hands covered a scream.

Baby Boomers

Norman promised to be back Friday night for dinner and good-byes. His mother promised a good diner. He spent the rest of Tuesday night and Wednesday morning fitting new Nikkor lenses to four Nikon "F" cameras and dry shooting almost everything in his with and without motor drives mounted on two of the cameras. Thursday night he typed a four page letter until he dozed over the dinette table. Friday morning he finished the letter. He packed his shoulder bag with chino pants, Banlon shirts and Fruit of the Loom briefs plus an extra safari jacket. He planned to travel light. Friday he repacked his camera bags, the trunk of his car and drove to his office.

Turning onto Delaware Avenue from the interstate, now named The John F. Kennedy Memorial Highway, he stopped and photographed a complete rainbow hemisphere encasing the city skyline. To his right a clam shell crane dropped remains of his old high school into a dump truck. Only a few classrooms remained. The red brick front had been ripped away. Two Honda mopeds passed him and he made a couple more shots of the wet riders with his shouldered Leica. Norman processed the film, typed captions and met with his editor and photo editor. The photo editor wished him well, shook his hand and sent him home at six, four hours earlier than normal.

Norman made a stop at the florist shop on the corner and drove south toward his parents' home. He let himself in and placed the flowers in a ceramic crock sitting on the letter he finished that morning, and then went directly to the grill area. Smoke rose from the grill by the dogwood tree as he parked next to the picket fence. Pop Pop stoked the grill with split hickory logs cut from a tree next door.

His father wished him luck, passed a large Swiss Army knife to Norman and said, "It does a lot more than my Barlow. It was awarded for safety two years ago and it has kept me safe every since. It will keep you safe, too.

Norman slipped knife into his jacket and embraced his father.

His mother placed a tray of hamburger patties on the twelve foot picnic table. Maddy brought rolls and condiments. Lionel placed a large bowl of Cole slaw and another of baked beans on the table. Linda and Kevin arrived with two cases of "Tastee Kake" pies. Ernest placed twenty four soft drinks in a tub of ice. His wife pushed Grand paw Wood's wheel chair near the dogwood tree. Aunt Mary, cousins Janet, and Bobby followed. Loraine arrived with her husband, two sons and a large sheet cake. Norman's picture editor dropped off a case of Miller's High Life and left quickly. More than a dozen neighbors came, wished

217

Call Me Maggie

Norman well, and left. His mother had been bragging again. Maggie was the only one missing the send-off that lasted till midnight.

"I'll only be there two weeks," Norman kept telling them.

Norman's mother stood at the edge of the porch as he waited for Kevin seated Madeline in the hump seat of the car. Norman returned to the porch and the arms of his crying mother holding the letter intended to be opened if Norman did not return. His father left his rocking chair and joined them.

"I said goodbye to young men going to World War II and to Korea. I hope this is the last time." she told Norman.

"I'm just going for pictures and a story on medics. They won't let me or the writer anywhere near the fighting."

She stared and cried as Norman left.

Lionel and Madeline each carried a case of film into the Philadelphia Airport. Norman carried a large camera bag and his clothes bag. The met Lindsay Brown, the Geographic writer at the Pan Am check-in counter. Lionel and Maddy said their goodbyes and went to a window overlooking a silver and blue "707." Norman waved from the steps. Norman clicked off a shot with his Leica of the Wilmington skyline and one of the Price's Corner Shopping Center. Lanterns still burned at the house he left an hour earlier.

"The Defense Department hopes this trip shows how well the war is going over there, otherwise they would not be so cooperative. They are expecting it to be a recruitment piece for enlisting more men and women. They are only going to show us what makes them look good and the VC look bad. We are going to do a little behind the facade investigations while we are there. They will be very helpful at first. We'll gain their confidence and do our own research in the bars, R&R areas, and any place we can find soldiers and Marines away from their officers. I've done research that show things are getting worse, and getting worse fast," Lindsay said, briefing Norman early into the flight.

Norman took her advice, but spent much of his time with his new cameras.

The plane stopped in Anchorage and Tokyo for fuel and finished the flight at Saigon where an Army lieutenant with a car was waiting.

"Maggie," was Norman's greeting to the woman when he approached a strawberry blonde.

"I'm Madeline but I have a sister, Maggie. I can be your escort while you're here. Five hundred a day buys my car and me around the clock. If I don't have or can't get it, it ain't available. I'm sure I have better connections than your government issued driver," Madeline said, handing him a business card.

"No thanks. I have a car and a driver," Norman said, examining the card reading "Madeline Johnson, Civilian Personal Services" printed in French on one side and English on the other. A yellow happy face appeared on both sides.

"Looks like you have yourself a girl, too," Madeline said. "If I can do anything for you while you're here, look me up. I can be found her in the afternoons and in the Hard Luck Grill in the evenings. Ask any cab driver is you need to find it or me."

Norman blushed, and then re-joined the Lindsay and lieutenant.

The lieutenant drove him and Lindsay to an indoctrination building in a shining new green station wagon with an eight track playing "American Pie." Norman clicked off pictures of moped riders and outdated American cars on streets on the way.

"Women can't go into the battlefield. It's against Defense Department policy." an indoctrination official told Lindsay.

"I have all your paperwork that says I'm going."

"We assumed Lindsay Brown was a man," he added.

After several phone calls and a lot of loud words Lindsay recorded but could not print, the issue was still unresolved. With each argument Lindsay shook her fist in the officer's face. Leaving she shouted, "I am going to the battlefield, if I have to walk."

Norman signed a lot of papers and joined Lindsay at the station wagon. As the lieutenant took them to a hotel, he bragged on his deferments to finish law school.

"Drop off your bags and come to my room."

Norman dropped his bags and knock three times before entering the door she had left cracked. Lindsay stood by a mirrored dresser wearing only black panties and a Playtex girdle covering her breasts while having a loud conversation with someone at the other end of the phone. Norman shot a few pictures of her pulling the girdle down and a stretchy from her ponytail, then a close-up, as she shook her head until the black hair framed her face.

"The Geographic staff is going to love this," he said when she when she finished the phone call.

"I don't give a damn. Cut my hair till I look like a man," she demanded, handing him a pair of scissors.

Call Me Maggie

Lindsay turned, faced the mirror, and collected her hair as Norman cut. He made a few more pictures as Lindsey glued and shaped a moustache and heavy eyebrows, then took Lindsay to dinner that evening and photographed every, airman, soldier, Marine and Naval serviceman Lindsay interviewed before and after dinner.

"This worked tonight. It better work tomorrow!" Lindsay said over 2 A.M eggs as Norman fumbled with a happy faced card.

The next morning she carried a bottle of Carter's cement and another of lemon juice in her backpack when the left. A fifty dollar bill bought the driver silence at least until a Bell Jet Ranger left for the field hospital.

Mid afternoon they hitched another chopper ride. Norman photographed two gunners, pilots, and four nervous replacements fresh from the states on a "Huey" to a mountain outpost. Norman made pictures of one vomiting his helmet. Lindsay made more notes. On the way Norman leaned out the door to get pictures of two other Hueys marked with large red crosses on a white squares headed toward the hospital. One gunner sprayed the trees with an automatic rifle several times around the outpost before they landed while another fired rocket grenades into the perimeter.

A twenty year-old, three stripped sergeant assigned Lindsay and Norman to the same tent. Lindsay sipped lemon juice from a green bottle as she made notes on her ninth notepad. Norman dictated into his recorder. By evening they congratulated each other.

"Alsop likes your work, Norman. Ever think about coming on board the Geographic?" Lindsay asked in the darkness.

"He hinted at a staff job a few times," Norman answered. "But I would be lost in a big city job. I'm just cameraman shooting hometown news, sports and feature pictures. This trip is something out of the ordinary for me."

Lindsay explained that root and early roots were in local news writing before she moved to New York and the big time.

"You should give it a try. The money is great. The nightlife never ends. I could show you around," she said lighting a Marlboro.

Norman turned and saw large nipples rose from brown rings that topped her breasts as lay on her bunk wearing only black briefs.

"We both can fit on this bunk, if we're friendly."

Norman said nothing.

Lindsay finished the cigarette and moved onto Norman's bunk. Again he did respond even when lay her chest across his.

220

"Are you afraid of something?"

"Yes!"

"Who was the red headed hooker at the airport?"

"The sister of a friend."

"You can have me tonight and her again when you get back to Saigon. I'd bet she is good a good roll in the hay."

"I wouldn't know."

"Are you going to romp with me or not?"

"I'm not."

"Got a young wife waiting for you?"

"No, I'm not married."

"Then let's get it on."

"We're not going to get it on unless it's on the assignment we came to do."

"You sure know how to spoil a girl's evening in the mountains."

Lindsay returned to her bunk, lit another Marlboro and sat quietly. Norman watched as she held the Bic lighter as though it were a candle until the cigarette was only a stub then lit another.

"I'm right here if you change your mind," Lindsay said as the flame above her hand died.

Booms, cracks, and rapid splat, splat, splats kept them awake as gunfire punctuated the night.

"I noticed something ironic today, Lindsay."

"What did you notice?"

"Almost everyone here was born during World Two of just after in the baby boomer years,"

"I'll bet you were too."

"If I get through tonight, I'll be twenty six tomorrow," she said, and then asked, "When were your born, Norman?"

"One year to the day before Pearl Harbor."

Norman's Timex read 1 a.m. "It is tomorrow. Happy birthday, Lindsay."

A cold morning fog covered the mountain as Norman exited the tent. Lindsay was still sleeping as he returned with two cups of coffee. He sat on her bunk blowing coffee vapors and calling her name softly, then louder. She rolled over, sat up pulled him to her, and held him against her bare chest.

"I'm not giving up on you yet. That I promise."

Call Me Maggie

"We're fogged in. The choppers will be late. Get dressed and meet me in the mess tent. It's full of wounded from last night's firefight. We'll get better stuff than we did yesterday. Bring an extra notebook," Norman said passing her a coffee cup.

Lindsay said thanks, sighed, sat up, sipped the black coffee, and wrote a note in her reporters pad. Norman grabbed the straps of his camera bag, raised it over one shoulder onto his back and left the tent. He was less than fifty feet away when a mortar shell exploded in the tent where he left Lindsay. Fragments penetrated the bag, peppered his back and knocked him to the ground. Screams came from shredded tents on either side of a crater where his tent had stood.

Someone dragged Norman to a sandbagged pit. A soldier pulled off his Banlon shirt and wiped blood from several holes above his hips. Another cut the legs off his pants. Norman's clicked away with his Leica as best he could while laying on his stomach as medics bandaged our GI's lay on tables wearing only bloody olive drab boxer shorts. Two others sat shirtless as their wounds were dressed while two younger soldiers carried a blanket covered stretcher away. A sergeant took Norman's camera and photographed his legs and buttocks being bandaged. Two more mortar shells exploded. Everyone kept working, taking time only to blink and subdue their reflexes

"You're a damned lucky man, but your buddy wasn't so lucky," the soldier returning Norman's camera stated.

Soon Norman walked outside, watched, and photographed as two soldiers placed pieces of flesh into a black bag. A PFC brought Norman the remains of his camera bag and Lindsay's backpack, then helped Norman duct tape the bags into usable shape. Two cameras and most of the lenses were still usable. Half the film was ruined. Two Nikons were left with his shredded clothes on the mountain. One held up black panties briefly, then threw them toward the bag. Norman joined them collecting Lindsay's notebooks. A laminated ID card similar to Norman's was duct taped to the black bag.

Norman knew he was in shock and experience told him only one way to work off the dread he felt. He resumed shooting with the Leica, telling himself this was just another bad car wreck or fire back home. A burning sensation in his back and legs told him it was not.

The enemy's threat eased by late morning as the fog lifted and his recorder picked up machine gun fire and rockets whistling down on the enemy from a "Skyraider" roaring overhead. Helicopters began to come and go. Norman used the Leica to photograph chopper crewmen treating their passengers as he rode out with the last helicopter carrying four stretchers.

The next morning Norton boarded another helicopter. A safe area in the Mekong Delta was their destination. Shortly after landing he learned "safe" was a variable assessment. A band of guerrillas encircled the "LZ" just after he jumped from the hovering chopper. He headed for a stream feeding rice paddies, and belly flopped into the yellow water between two replacement soldiers who flew in with him. He raised the camera above the ditch and clicked a frame every once in a while, but kept his head near the water. The three water rats spent the next hour pinned down by rifle and machine gun fire until the guerrillas stopped firing and left when a "birddog" began circling the paddies and another Skyraider arrived. Norman shared the ride back and photographed a crying Vietnamese woman and two stolid children. All three wore bloody pajamas. He spent the afternoon photographing field hospital personnel patching up native women and children.

Back in Saigon, the law school graduate, station wagon driver was waiting to drive Norman to a de-briefing that Norman sized up as more lawyers trying to enforce Pentagon doctrine. The driver swore only a man with a moustache boarded the chopper with Norman the day before. A three hour re-indoctrination with several higher ranking officers refreshed Norman's suspicion a cover up was coming.

"Females are not allowed near hostilities," was repeated dozens of times by each.

"Here is the story. Lindsay Brown, a writer with American Geographic Magazine died yesterday morning in a mortar attack by overwhelming enemy forces. There will be no mention she was a female who went into hostile territory impersonating a male," the major said.

Norman grimaced as the major finished reading the note.

"We want your film too," a captain said.

Norman refused his request.

"We will process it, inspect it and return it," he promised.

Norman refused again.

"This is a war of words as well as bullets and bombs."

"And a war of pictures," Norman added and remained steadfast.

Micro cassettes, film, and notebooks carried in his jacket were full of observations he had recorded in the three days in Viet Nam. Once the meeting finished, he went to Intercontinental Airlines offices and passed a box addressed to Maggie Johnson, White Horse Farm, Odessa,

Call Me Maggie

Delaware containing his film and cassettes to Midge McGinnis. Midge promised to deliver the box on her drive down US.13 going home.

Norman had wanted another day or two of shooting pictures before going home on a "Connie," but the major lifted his field pass. He headed for the airport to find the girl who gave him the happy face card, hired her for the remaining two days using all of his money and some he had put in Lindsay's satchel.

"I can provide any kind of dope you want, women, or you can have me. A girl has to make any way she can over here," Madeline stated.

"I don't want anything like that. I want you to take me where the soldiers go when they're off duty and want to get away from the war. Do you know any of those places?"

"Now I see what you want."

"I don't think you do. I've got lots of important things to do the next two days and I really need someone who knows their way around. Would you help me please?" Norman asked, almost begging.

On second evening a Red Cross canteen worker spotted the Kennedy strip on his chest and delivered a letter that brought tears to Norman's eyes, and then offered to arrange a night flight home, but Norman declined. He slipped out of the hotel and spent the night at the base hospital making pictures. On the third morning he said goodbye to Madeline at the airport gate, carried his camera bag and Lindsay's satchel up the long steps against the nose of the "Connie," turned, and snapped off a single frame as Madeline waved. To his left a forklift raised stretchers and black bags to the plane's rear door. To his right a spotless young soldier wearing sunglasses leaned on the hood of a station wagon with his hands in his pockets.

"Do you want Maggie's present back?" Midge asked.

Norman asked her to wait until after they were airborne and made his way through Connie's cabin taking pictures.

"Watch where the hell you're going. This man is bleeding!" a voice in nurses uniform yelled.

"Michele?" Norman asked as she turned to face him.

"Yes, now get the hell out of my way."

Norman stored his bags and began photographing her tending patients.

"Put the camera away," Michele yelled.

"He's doing his job, you do yours," said a voice behind Norman.

Baby Boomers

"Maggie!" Norman exclaimed and continued shooting.

"What's a nice guy like you doing here?"

"Taking pictures," he answered from behind the camera.

A couple hours after takeoff, Maggie lead Norman to the rear seats, sat beside him, grasped his hands, leaned close and asked, "Have you seen any Red Cross people yet? They told me about your writer getting blown up, too,"

"Yes," Norman answered as his eyes filled again.

"I took the first flight back hoping to find you. Saigon dispatch said you would be on this flight," she said to him.

"I'm glad you're here. Thank you, Maggie."

Maggie summoned to Michele.

"Bring him something to help him sleep, please."

"He's a civilian. He's not a casualty," Michele snapped.

"The hell he's not." Maggie pointed to the blood stains on his shirt and then raised two fingers to a pair of gold strips on her shoulders and waved the index finger of the other hand.

Michele's shoulders carried only one strip on each. Norman listened to her starched skirt crackle as she raced away.

"That's Michele from the psycho ward, isn't it?"

Norman nodded.

"It's her first flight. Probably her last. She hasn't got the right stuff. He may have great nursing skills but she has none when she works with these scared boys," Maggie said, then gave Norman a pair of pills and details of his mother's death until he fell asleep.

Michele avoided Maggie and Norman for much of the flight home.

Sunday morning and he entered the side door of the newspaper building with Maggie. In an hour he and Maggie slipped film into storage sleeves. He exposed paper while she developed proofs. Two hours later he packaged three sets. Placing the negatives in with the proofs Norman said, "Now I have to make prints. Let's do them at home."

They printed, washed and dried photographs until late Monday night. Tuesday morning before daylight he dropped a box of prints outside Hershel's office. When daylight broke over southern New Jersey, Maggie was guiding the convertible up the New Jersey Turnpike while Norman wrote notes on the back of prints by light from the glove box.

"Al, please have someone transcribe these tapes while I bring you up to date. They have some conversations I'm sure you'll find inter-

225

esting. It's too bad Lindsay couldn't finish the story," he said, passing her notebooks and his tapes to Alsop.

"We got a late telegram Thursday," Alsop said.

Norman recapped his trip to Alsop, a stenographer with a tape recorder, and the magazine's publisher, a man named Samuel Brown.

"You really cut off Lindsay's hair?" the publisher asked.

"Yes. She insisted, sir," Norman answered, showing the publisher prints from his box.

Alsop and the publisher reviewed the prints of Lindsay Brown, Norman and Maggie had enlarged. The publisher called in another writer to interview Maggie. Questions lasted most of the afternoon.

"This girl with the mustache was our best investigator. I think she would be pleased the way you turned her research into a first rate story. We'll transcribe the tapes and prepare the story. Would you mind sharing a byline with Lindsay?" Brown asked.

"It was her story. I was just a photographer on a story with her," Norman replied.

Samuel Brown rose from the meeting holding a picture of short haired Lindsay and said, "I want to talk to you again Norman. I'm sure her mother would too. Can you make a trip to the Poconos Saturday? Maggie will you join us?"

Both answered "Yes."

"Pick up a map from my secretary," Samuel said as he left the meeting.

"You didn't know Lindsay was his daughter, did you?" Alsop asked.

"No." Norman answered gasping. "If I had, I would not have shown prints of her I took just before I cut her hair to him."

"Let's do lunch when you're back in the city. You know you have a job here anytime you want it. You've earned it. Take care of your back," Alsop said.

"Working in New York is a decision both Maggie and I will make," Norman said.

After dropping Maggie at the airport, Norman entered the newsroom from the side street entrance walking with a slight limp. Several reporters and both copy editors rose and applauded. Judith was the first reach him. She started to embrace Norman, but grasped his biceps instead and said, "It good to see you, Norman. Really good."

"Same here," he said as hands held her at the elbows.

Baby Boomers

Other coworkers greeted Norman. The picture editor raced in from the hallway to the photo lab.

"I'm back, Chief."

"My office now. Close the door behind you." Hershel ordered.

Norman dropped his duct taped camera bag outside the door, entered, and pushed the door closed.

"You ask for some personal time off to photograph medics and helicopter crews and end up on a mountain in a battlefield. Got your butt shot and don't even mention it in a note or phone call. This is you getting patched up isn't it? Did you get some kind of brain damage too? Or forget how to use the telephone or write?" Hershel began.

"No brain damage, just dog tired and a little pepper shot," Norman answered.

"I've got the pictures you dropped off. Judith has the transcript. You've got some blanks to fill in," his picture said, shaking the folder of pictures.

"I will, Chief."

"Why didn't you say something when you called me at home Sunday or when you delivered the prints and transcripts last night. The staff has been in the dark and worried since we saw you getting patched up when we went through your pictures," Hershel said.

"The job wasn't finished Sunday. Everyone was gone this morning. Besides it's just a little discomfort. I can deal with it. Lotta guys on the plane came home lots worse."

"Spend the afternoon with Judith. Fill in the gaps. See me again when Judith is done with you. She'll produce copy for your three part story to run next weekend."

"You got it Chief."

"Drop the Chief crap. And get a new camera bag before you come back Monday. Bill the paper," Hershel ordered.

"How about a couple of new Nikons?" Norman asked. "I left mine on the mountain after the shell hit me."

"Don't push me. You already use three times as much film as my other photographers. And don't show your face in here until Monday. Sleep, vacation, take a ride, go fishing, but get lost for the rest of the week and keep your butt out of here and off mountains."

"Okay, Chief."

"Do you ever hear what I say?" the picture editor asked.

Call Me Maggie

"Have dinner with Judith. Bill you. Pick up a new cameras bag. Buy two new Nikons. Shoot more film. Take a vacation and see you next week."

"Nice work, Norman. I was very worried about you until I saw your butt in the newsroom," the editor said.

"Thanks, Hershel. And thanks for the time off."

"What are you going to till Monday?"

"Spend some time with Dad. Help him cope with the loss of Mom. Visit the parents of the writer who took the motor shell and take a long ride or two. That's when I relax best."

Norman lifted the taped bag, left, and sat it near Judith's desk.

"Hershel says you have some gaps for me to fill in. How about four o'clock?" she asked.

"Works for me. I'll drop off my bag."

"Give me another minute to find a few new notebooks."

Norman left Judith and went to the photo lab. A large print of him being bandaged on the hill in Vietnam was taped to the wall above the communal desk. Beneath it a lay box and a five word note: "Norman. Good job. Thanks, Chief."

The box contained a motorized Nikon F camera and three lenses.

"Thank you, Hershel," Norman whispered.

Judith led Norman to the Woolworth lunch counter and recorded their conversation on a tape recorder identical to his, but made numerous notes as well.

A little after four he met Maggie in the farm's driveway.

"I'm flying out at 1 A.M. Stateside flights moving recruits to basic. Basics to advanced. Saint Louis to San Diego tomorrow. Los Angles to North Carolina the next day and back here Friday night. What's your schedule?" Maggie asked.

"See Dad for a while. See you off and take a long ride tomorrow. My head is full of cobwebs," Norman answered as he hung her clean laundry on the rack.

"I'd like to go with you when you go to see Pop Pop, unless you want to be alone with him. When were you planning to see him, tonight or tomorrow?"

"I would like to go now. I thought about going before coming home, but figured you might want to be with me. Please come. I know he would appreciate it."

Baby Boomers

Kevin and Pop Pop sat in rockers on the porch when Maggie and Norman arrived. Neither seemed to be talking. Pop Pop rose to hug Norman and Maggie. After a moment Kevin joined them/

"I was about to leave. Weather's good. Pulling sixteen hours tonight, tomorrow and Friday. Linda's racing Saturday. Can you come?" Kevin said leaving the embrace.

"Sorry, I can't make it. Maggie and I have an appointment in Pennsylvania,"

"Kevin took good care of the arrangements. He could have used some help though," Norman's father as returned to the rocker.

"I'm sorry I was not here, but I couldn't get back in time," Norman said.

"It's a two or three day flight to get back here from Viet Nam, Pop," Maggie said.

"Well you're back now. And Maggie, too," Pop Pop said.

Norman pulled the Swiss Army knife from his pocket and stated, "It was a lucky charm. Thank you for letting me borrow it," but made no mention of his close call on the mountain.

"I didn't loan it to you, I gave it to you," his dad stated.

"Pop, Maggie and I are going to see Mom's grave. Would you like to ride over with us?"

"Yes, I would."

Maggie stood near a crypt in Silverbrook Cemetery as Norman placed a white rose and a small box on the fresh yellow dirt, then joined his father knelling as chimes inside the box played "Music Box Dancer."

After a few minutes Maggie said, "I was part of her family too," and joined them.

An hour later, she, Norman, and his father strolled about the garden until the sun dropped below the horizon and then settled in the kitchen waiting for coffee to percolate.

"I have two days for myself. Maggie's leaving tonight. Let's you and I spend them together, Pop,"

"Please say yes, Pop Pop. It will be good for both of you," Maggie spoke out.

"Alright. I got some kinks to work out."

Back at the farm a little after 9 p.m., Norman reached his arms around Maggie's waist until they grasp her stomach from behind, and then held her tightly.

"Give me a moment,"

Call Me Maggie

She gave him a soft kiss and went to bathtub returned, removed his jacket, and lifted his shirt as she kissed him again. A moment later both inched their way under a mountain of bubbles rising under a spray of water. Maggie took her usual position, her back to his chest. He reached around her and said, "I saw your sister in Saigon."

Norman felt Maggie tense her body.

"What was she doing in Saigon?"

"Escort service for visitors."

Norman dried his hands and reached for his wallet in the pants by the tub and placed a card with happy faces into Maggie's wet hands.

"Escort as in tour guide or as in prostitute?"

"From the back I thought she was you for a moment. Based on what I saw and heard, tour guide maybe. She propositioned me in the airport, be we spent our time doing interviews with people she introduced me to."

"Was she alright? Did she seem to be happy? Did she mention mother or ask about me?"

"I never told her I knew you and she did not mention your mother, but she seems to be happy and healthy," he said before going to the darkroom.

When he returned he held out a picture taken at the Saigon Airport. "Maybe I should not have mentioned it?"

"Yes, you should have. I may bump into her sooner or later, and now I'll know what to expect if I do."

Norman could not see her face, but whimpers told him she was crying. He removed the happy face card from the hand she held over her heart and blotted it on a towel.

The next morning Norman returned to his father's house and asked, "Where would you like to go, Pop?"

"Makes no difference to me, just drive."

Norman drove west to Avondale on the Lancaster Pike, stopped at a produce farm where the owner offered a pint of blueberries, a dozen apples and a half gallon of cider for Mrs. Kennedy. Norman explained that his mother was buried a week earlier and that he thought visiting the farm would be good for his father. The farmer agreed saying her visits would be missed. The elder Kennedy stared at the orchard where he and his wife once picked their own apples, peaches, and pears.

"Let's go someplace where nobody will ask about your mother," Pop Pop said as they left the orchard.

Baby Boomers

Norman drove on toward Lancaster passing the Amish nursery and other farms familiar to his father. Pop Pop counted forty one horse or mule teams working alongside U.S. 30. Later he counted the semi trailers they met. Soon they crossed the Susquehanna River. Norman stopped at York for lunch and a walk through a large antique sales yard with his father. The elder Kennedy described many of the item's usage on his farm and those of Norman's grandparents. Norman found himself immersed in his father's archaeology lessons and photographing their finds. Later they followed signs to Gettysburg National Military Park. Both found maps and restrooms in the visitor's center. Pop Pop suggested that they tour the park. Norman found the statues of the park compelling camera subjects. One by one he photographed them, sometimes in panorama, but many in close ups of the bronze and marble faces looking out to visitors or enemies of long ago. The light and Norman's camera angles gave almost living qualities to the statues. Norman studied and photographed the statues and faces again and again. Pop Pop studied the plaques and markers. Both wanted and found distraction from the previous week.

After sunset Norman's father held strobe lights as Norman made night-time exposures against a black sky. The statues had even more life at night, Norman felt. Pop Pop agreed with his photographer son. Both returned the next morning for more photographs. As the afternoon approached they neared Antietam. Norman made pictures of the bridge with and without his father.

Norman drove aimlessly again for nearly three hours. Their next stop was Manassas and Bull Run, a buggy ride west of the union capital, Washington, D.C. A hundred miles and a two day march southward of Washington or Bull Run lay Richmond, the confederate capital. Norman felt drawn to these now peaceful battlefields and compelled to photograph them. Pop Pop wanted to walk the ground his grandfather fought a hundred years earlier. With the help of the maps, he and his son found a marker listing the Georgia infantry company of their ancestor. Norman began making photos of his dad wandering the park and recalling memories of his grandfather.

"Grandpaw met a nurse in a Culpeper hospital twenty miles to the south after he was injured here. He found her after the war and took her back home. His father and mother didn't want a camp follower in the family, but he ran off with her anyway. Nurses didn't have a healthy reputation back then. We use to sit by the fireplace as he told me of the battle. By then he was too old to farm. Grandmother sat by his side

Call Me Maggie

rocking and quilting. She used to brag about birthing over two hundred babies as a mid wife after the war while five girls of her own and my father. She even birthed me and your mother. Grandpaw made a good choice." Pop Pop said.

"You made a good choice too, Pop. Mom gave you four sons and a daughter to remind you of her."

Norman's father suggested they get a motel for a second night, rather than drive the 150 miles home at night. Norman agreed and with half an hour he headed toward the motel bathroom stripped to his briefs.

"What's with all the Band Aids? They nearly cover your back. What about your leg? Is that why you're limping and why you didn't come to your mother's burial?" his father asked.

"I picked up some souvenirs in Viet Nam. Just mortar fragments. Maggie redressed them last night. They're a lot better now. Her whole life centers round caretaking her boys and me."

Friday evening a Connie passed overhead as they waited for a red light at the airport. Prop wash bathed the topless convertible removing their cobweb and kinks. Their healing process had begun.

The next morning, Norman, Maggie and Pop Pop turned off a Pennsylvania highway on to a narrow dirt road marked "Brown Mountain Drive" and began a mile and half climb. Pop Pop remembered other dirt roads like it in Alabama. Norman's back reminded him of a mountain halfway around the globe while Maggie recalled her youthful Poconos visits. Samuel Brown was found hanging another sign reading, "Lindsay Lane." His wife sat on another horse nearby.

He introduced himself to Norman's father from horseback insisting he be called Samuel and his wife be addressed as Jesse by their guests. Norman and Pop Pop offered a similar request. Jesse reached down from her mount and greeted them, "Welcome to Brown Mountain, Mr. Kennedy, Norman, Miss Johnson,"

"Unless you call me Maggie, I can't you Jessie," Maggie said.

"My family never named this road. We decided Lindsay Lane was a cut above 'The Little Road' or 'The Lane," Samuel explained.

"Drive on up to the house and you can saddle up for a picnic at the stream. English or western?" Jesse asked.

Pop Pop answered western, Maggie answered English and Norman said either and drove up Lindsay Lane behind the two horseback riders. Horses were brought by a stableman. Jesse led the way with Maggie on trails circling the mountain top granite retreat, guesthouse, barn, and carriage house. Hardwood trees replace lawn as they rode

Baby Boomers

downward. Norman's father trailed them. Samuel held Norman back a football field's length.

"I found a note from my daughter." Samuel said. "It was the last page written in a pad describing the night fight."

Norman stiffened in his saddle.

"The note said, 'Kennedy is tough, Keep after him.' And that's what I intend to do. Come on board the Geo with me. I think Lindsay wanted that," Samuel Brown said.

Vivid images of Lindsay came to Norman. Her question, "Are you going to romp with me?" rang loudly in his head. Her statement, "I'm not giving up on you yet," burned painfully inside Norman. Tidal conflicts raged in him. Should he take Samuel's offer or should he tell Lindsay's father what Lindsay's note really meant?

"Name your job and your price. I'll meet any reasonable request plus a generous benefit package."

"I can't accept your offer right now. I have some things yet to do. Maybe in a year or two. Thank you, but no thank you."

"I have Brown and Brown publishing, the Geographic, and three metro papers. Lindsay didn't want to get on the ladder above her head. She started in Philadelphia as a writer. Any of the Brown publications can offer a larger audience and liberal salary. We're at the forefront in publishing, salary, readership, and advertising. Answer yes. Write your own ticket; photographer, editor, or publisher of one of the metros. Get your feet wet on metros and move up to the Geo in a few years or now as a photographer." Samuel Brown continued.

"I don't have the education for management, just an eye for pictures. There are still lots of things I want to photograph and a few books I'm working on. But I do need a book publisher for a few things I have been shooting," Norman said.

"Show me your pictures. If there close to what you brought back Tuesday, your ticket is already written. I have seen the oil refinery and beach study. Expand the beach job to include the whole east coast and you've got a Geo series and a book. Tell me your other ideas, son."

"I work at the newspaper from two till ten. I use my mornings to research and shoot pictures important to me. My job pays the bills. In the evenings I print and write a little. Maggie is gone all but eight days a month. Our social life is around books and pictures. One is the Amish in Lancaster County, Pennsylvania and Kent County, Delaware. They're nineteenth century farming holdouts as my father did until 1950. Some left the farm for craft trades; others just simply left the order seeking

Call Me Maggie

twentieth century temptations and luxuries. Another is classic Pennsylvania architecture. There is lots of it near home. It should not be replaced with plywood box tract houses and strip shopping centers. I would like to do one on the loss of farm land in Alabama and the southeast to corporation timber growers. I'm even doing one on the two sides of Maggie. We shoot art book situations of her and the ordinary things about her that make up the "new woman" she exemplifies. I wanted to do one on a couple growing old together, but my mother died the same day as your daughter. I need a new pair of subjects now. Dad and I spent the last two days photographing Gettysburg instead of grieving. I was planning to send that one to Al Alsop for a one hundredth anniversary piece on the battle. I shoot pictures when I'm happy and even more when I'm sad and troubled." Norman realized he was possibly boring his host.

"Young fellow you just convinced me you're the man I want. Accept my offer and send me your pictures. Write your own ticket. You could step into my shoes in a few years. Lindsay spotted a good man in you," Brown said.

"Thank you sir. But for now I must stay in Wilmington and finish a few things there. I will show you what I've done next Tuesday in New York or when we get back to my car."

"When we get back to the retreat will be fine."

"Thank you, sir," Norman answered.

"I am going to take Lindsay's second piece of advice; I'm going to keep after you until I hire you. Jesse and I are indebted to you for saving Lindsay's possessions and a large bonus for the story you two did. Let's catch up to the others. And stop calling me sir," Brown said before he galloped ahead.

Jesse, Maggie and Pop Pop were dismounting at a heavily stoned stream as Norman and Samuel Brown caught up to them.

"Your business all settled, Samuel?" Jessie asked.

"Yes dear. There all yours now," Samuel answered.

Jessie removed two wine bottles and five glasses from one saddle bag. A table cloth and six cheese bricks were removed from the other. She and Samuel covered a large flat rock and invited their guests to sit and picnic.

"Norman, Maggie. Samuel and I appreciate you bringing Lindsay's personal effects home. How can we thank you for your thoughtfulness?" Jessie asked.

"Samuel already has," Norman answered.

Baby Boomers

"Norman and I will need another hour before dinner, dear. I want to view some pictures he brought with him."

"I'll entertain Maggie and Pop Pop. Shall we dress for dinner or dine on the lawn?"

"The lawn would be ideal," Maggie said.

"Dad and Mom used to draw quite a crowd dining on the lawn," Norman said.

"The lawn it shall be. For now, let's picnic," Jesse said.

"Mr. Kennedy lost his wife the day we lost Lindsay," Samuel informed his wife.

"Our regrets to you, Mr. Kennedy," Jessie said.

All four entered a few period of silence whether intentional or not. The silence ended when Samuel asked, "What's the assessment of our young visitors and Mr. Kennedy on the Vietnam problem?"

"It's a public relations mess being run by politicians, desk jockeys, and industrial puppets in Washington. They're handing out inflated contracts and bribes in the name of democracy for the South Vietnamese. We are fed propaganda like babies are fed Gerber's. In ten years we will be run out and in thirty we will be friends again. In the meantime it's high body counts for the VC and falsified losses for our side. The infantry, Calvary and Marines go out with two day old intelligence reports that have to be cleared by some bureaucrat in the Pentagon who has never seen the battlefield. And then it's a big game of cover up or buck passing. It's a war of words backed up by bullets and bombs. Each week my plane brings a load of shattered lives or black bags holding our young men. And young women too! I see only a small portion of ours and none of the Viet Cong or ones from the north. If we believe a small fraction of what we are told it's far too many. I would cut my hair and flatten my chest in a minute, if it would stop the maiming, mutilation, and killing of my boys," Maggie said.

"Thank you, Maggie," Jessie said, applauding.

"Here, here!" Samuel said.

"This is the Baby Boomers' war. The term baby boomers has come a generation of youngsters throwing grenade, firing cannons, and pilots dropping bombs on women and babies the warriors in Washington tells are a threat. Mr. Brown, you have the power and resources to make a difference. Don't let your daughter's death be in vain. I see sixty casualties each week and my other attendants bring back more. That's fifteen thousand in a good year. The number will be more next year and the year after. I was only three years old when my father died in Korea.

235

Call Me Maggie

All I can remember about him is from a few photographs and some dim memories. Don't let today's little girls grow up like I did. Do something in memory of Lindsay. I and the other baby boomers like me will join you and follow when we're given the truth," Maggie said.

Maggie's eyes filled. Samuel and Norman held her hands. Jessie rubbed her hair.

"Lindsay suspected there were more secrets and cover-ups in Vietnam and in Washington that need to be revealed. She planned to return for more research after the medieval airlift story. She was also cultivating contacts in Washington that can unlock some of those secrets and the ones behind the cover ups. I will do something, Maggie. I will uncover the truth for you baby boomers in memory of Lindsay's sacrifice. She was a good newswoman first, and the publisher's daughter second," Samuel said.

"Again, thank you for your thoughtfulness, Norman. We are glad you came to Brown Mountain and joining us today. Continue taking good care of our boys, Lindsay. Please pardon me. I should have said Maggie. I'm sure her memory will be held in high esteem by you and Norman. I must beg forgiveness for my premature departure and retire," Jesse said as she held Maggie for a long moment before leaving.

"Thank you again, Norman. I'll see you Tuesday when you meet with Al. Your picture books have a publisher."

Norman had driven nearly an hour when his father said, "Pull over. I need to trade seats with Maggie. I'm about to doze off." They switched seats, but Maggie moved over the hump to be closer to Norman. The trio had said little since leaving Brown Mountain.

"I was surprised to see you handle and ride the horse so well back there, Pop. What's it been fifteen years since you were on horseback," Norman asked.

"As they say, like riding a bicycle, but I never rode a bicycle. Riding that horse brought back lots of memories. I rode one courting your mother. She sat in the saddle and I rode his hips behind her. I told her the second horse went lame, but she knew better. We rode close to each other like you and Maggie are riding now. And we had picnics along the creek in the hills like we did this afternoon. But, we didn't have wine on the rocks," Pop Pop said.

"My horseback ride was enjoyable. It would have been better if I had a western saddle. Anyway, I'm glad we rode," Maggie added.

"Me too. Samuel wants me to join the Geo staff or one of his newspapers," Norman informed his partner and father.

236

Baby Boomers

"That's great news, Boy," his father said.

"Real great news, Norman," Maggie added.

Both hoped Norman would fill in the blanks quickly. But Norman continued driving southward following the broken lines and looking for the right words.

"What kind of job did he offer you, Son?"

Pop Pop couldn't wait.

"Photographer or editor, whichever I want."

"Would you have to move to New York City?" his father asked.

"If I saddle a desk, yes, if I stay with photography, no. Either way I would not be in Wilmington much of the time. As a photographer I would be flying all over the world. I wouldn't be around much to help you and Maggie garden or raise horses. As an editor I would be in New York all week and home on the weekends. Maggie's weekends don't always fall on Saturday and Sunday. We would miss a lot of time together unless she spent her time off in New York or moved there. We would not like that. We both have plans centered on Delaware and the family. That is most important. She has her flying. I have photography. We both have dreams for the little farm."

"Sounds like you two have some sort of partnership plans in the works," Pop Pop observed.

"We sure do," Maggie answered as she placed a hand on Norman's leg and laid her head on his shoulder. The wind blew her hair around his neck.

"Would the new job change that?" Pop Pop asked.

"Taking Samuel's job would take her out of the picture and out of the partnership equation. I would not like that. Maggie doesn't deserve it. She deserves better than to be cast off just because Samuel Brown wants to hire me and my cameras."

"Thank you, Norman. Don't pass up Samuel's offer because of me. Your future may be in New York. If it is, we'll find it together. We have made things work so far. We'll make'm work if you take his job. I can commute down when I fly out and commute up when I get back from a trip."

"That would be unfair to you Maggie."

"Take me out of the equation."

"I can't and I won't."

"We can find a little farm up north. Commuting would only be a train ride down and a taxi ride to the airport for me."

237

Call Me Maggie

"Living that far away would take the family out of the equation. Besides we could not afford it. We can wait a few years. You may get an offer from a major airline. We'll add what I make from the trip last week and some more I plan to shoot. Maybe then. Samuel and I haven't finished yet. I have to see him again Tuesday with the pictures Dad and I took at Gettysburg. He'll make another offer and I will refuse again. I do have high hopes for him publishing more of my pictures and some books."

"Be sure that's what you really want."

"Relocating would not be the best for either of us. We're country folks, not urbanites or even suburbanites. We have simple wants and tastes. You like to shop thrift stores and the Army-Navy store, not Macy's. I like auction sales, old houses and anything country. You and I prefer to stroll on the beaches to Broadway and a moonlight submarine race over a big city rat race. Almost everything I photograph is within two hours of the newspaper office. With the new interstates I can drive anywhere east of the Mississippi in a day or fly there in a few hours. Your airline is half an hour from the farm, your horses and the gardens. You can have a garden as big as you want or as many horses as you want down here."

The trio rode in silence again. Pop Pop did not doze off. Norman was driving and thinking. A highway sign reading "Welcome to Delaware, The Diamond State" greeted them as the neared home. Maggie smiled and slowly rubbed his leg.

"I got dibs on Delaware. I found a diamond here a few years ago," Maggie said.

"So did I!"

"You sure did, Boy," his father added.

7

If They Were Family

By 1965 the U. S stepped up its campaign and by December had more than half a million American servicemen in South Viet Nam. More and more of them were being killed in combat and even more were coming home injured.

Rumors had been circulating among the airline personnel that they would be getting new Boeing 747's and carry four times the load of the aging Connies. Economic factors proved the rumors to be just that; rumors. The airline managers bought a few used 707 jets from major airlines, overhauled them, and put them in service to aid in getting more troops to Southeast Asia. Now they could cut flight time in half, carry twice the passengers, and avoid some of the costs of new jets. The Connies were saved for shorter stateside hops and trips to Europe. President Johnson had stepped up Air Force and Navy bombing runs to include Hanoi and Haiphong vowing to bomb North Viet Nam back to the Stone Age after an attack on an American ship of the North Vietnamese coast.

The stewardesses went to their plane at 5 a.m. to help ground crewmen remove seats and hang stretchers in the rear section of the aircraft. The seats would be flown stateside in the aircraft's cargo hold. Enough were left in the plane for thirty six ambulatory passengers. Four more remained for attendants.

Around 5:30 Maggie went forward to board passengers. Leanne secured stretcher patients in the aft area. At 6:37 a.m. the plane took off and headed east.

Leanne assisted another flight nurse on stretcher bound passengers. They adjusted splints, changed bandages and held straws as they sipped their drinks. Leanne had modified one of her instructors greeting

Call Me Maggie

techniques. By engaging them in conversation, she could appraise their condition better observing them than reading their charts; "Where are you from? Chicago. That's my kind of town. Cub's fan, I bet. Got your season's ticket yet? Maine, huh? Know any good lobster houses or vacation rentals? The Bronx? Gat a date lined up for New Years Eve? Texas, is that so? Are you a rancher or oilman?"

Leanne used her stewardess school examples and nursing school skills to their maximum.

Midge used a different approach. She played the news woman role informing and updating them on things back home; the weather, who was in the ball game finals, which new cars were the fastest or most economical or what new movie had just been released, and she joined them in devotions if they wanted to pray.

Maggie used similar techniques when she served drinks, snacks, magazines, or medications and always managed to tend her charges with an interested smile, a practice held over from her Bandstand days, although she didn't realize it was. She was only trying to do her best. If her boys needed a big sister, they got it. If they needed conversation, she provided it. Bandstand had been gone from her mind since the incident with Vinnie and she had had no other incidents to remind of that encounter.

"When I was a candy stripper it was never like this. Some have bleeding wounds. Most still have post trauma symptoms. The worse ones remain in shock and don't know they are on their way home or that some parts of them are still in Vietnam," Leanne said later when she and Maggie were together.

"It couldn't get worse unless they were family."

As they approached Hawaii, Leanne joined Maggie in the stewardess seating area. Both hoped for a few minutes rest. Leanne laid her head back but could not sleep. Maggie managed a short nap until one of the new male attendants woke her saying, "We got a problem with an injured officer."

"Are we losing him?".

"Not yet. He keeps asking for Mary Anne Johnson."

Maggie raced to the middle of the plane and joined two nurses attending a soldier wearing bandages from his nose up belted to a stretcher. Both arms and his chest had red bandages. One nurse injected a hypodermic into his strapped leg. The other held a hand to the side of his face. She could see one arm was severed below the elbow; the other was severed near the shoulder.

If They Were Family

"How can I help?" Maggie asked.

"He's been calling for you since he came to. Do you know him?" one nurse asked.

Maggie lifted his dog tag, read the raised letters, then said, "Bobby Joe. This is Maggie Johnson. What can I do for you, Cousin?"

"I heard your voice, but couldn't place it until just now. At first I thought my little sister was here," Bobby Joe Montgomery answered.

Maggie searched her mind to find a distraction.

"I have cotton plants glowing in a wash tub from your seeds. They're doing fine. Just like you," she as strained to force the waiver from her voice.

"Uncover my eyes. I'm a bit short-handed."

Maggie pushed the bandage upward and lifted gauze. One eye remained closed. The other blinked rapidly.

"Hello Cousin. You are a site to see. Lovely as before."

"You are the beautiful one; still a southern gentleman," Maggie replied as she kissed his forehead.

"I guess that booby trap has put this ole war horse out to pasture."

"I have three horses now. Norman gave me a white mare and she gave me a philly soon after and another last winter. We named them Lucky and Storm. Norman will be glad to see you."

"I guess you two have gotten married and have a couple of kids by now."

"No. Not yet. We don't have time for that. Norman stays busy with his photography and I am flying most of the time. When we do, I will count on you to give me away."

"I'll be there. I'll be patched up in no time."

Maggie stayed with Bobby Joe until they reached Hawaii, then slumped in one of the rear seats as they prepared to land. Leanne brought two cups of coffee. The two sat in silence until Maggie rose, and began walking the aisle comforting her passengers, spending extra time at Bobby Joe's stretcher. As the plane refueled in Seattle, the two sat again.

"Captain Montgomery is special, isn't he?" Leanne asked.

"He's family. Norman's cousin. I met him going over."

"This has gotta be hard for you to handle."

"He's the first and only one I have gotten close to. He gave up a good farm life for an army career to become the next Robert E. Lee. Now he's lost his hands and can't have either."

Call Me Maggie

"Maggie, you warned me about forming attachments to our passengers. Please take your own advice. Let me spend more time with him instead of you. You don't want him to see you like this, do you?"

"No, I don't but he's family. I have to do something to show him he still has a life worth living.

A moment later Leanne said. "Bobby Joe, I'm Leanne McPherson. I'm helping Maggie take of you. Where did you did you get your commission?"

"Virginia Military Institute."

"Really, I'm from Farmville. Ever been there or date any of the girls from Longwood College? Really! I dated a few VMI cadets before flying. Don't date anyone now. I'll bet you've been to a few Randolph Macon sorority parties and hiked lots of the Blue Ridge Mountains trails," she began.

Leanne did give Captain Montgomery special care and a lot of her time. She held cups as he drank, fed him, read to him, kept cold cloths on his feverish face while the two talked sharing common interests; schools came first. Leanne had spent two years at Randolph Macon and Bobby Joe attended Virginia Military Institute. Appomattox Court House and the mountains of Virginia tied for second place. Farm life rate third; her grandparents were farmers, so were his parents. Soon a repoire developed. After leaving the plane, Leanne asked Maggie to drop her off at the Wilmington train station. Two hours later she was by Bobby Joe's side in Walter Reed Army Hospital.

Maggie and Norman left the farm at 4 a.m. the next morning and joined them. Seeing Bobby Joe in good hands with Leanne, Maggie asked, "Would it make you late if we went by the Capital for a few minutes? It shouldn't take more than fifteen minutes. I want to see our senators and give them a piece of my mind."

"My press card should open some doors."

The senior senator was in a committee meeting but they caught the junior lawmaker in the hall.

"Pardon me Gov. . , I mean Senator. May we have ten minutes with you?" Norman asked.

"Norman, my friend, what brings you to Washington? It must have something to do with my environmental bill. Your pictures gave my Wetlands Act great support. Tell me how can I help you today?" the former Delaware governor said.

"Get the U. S. out of Vietnam. One of our cousins checked in to Walter Reed last night, but both his arms and one eye are still in the

If They Were Family

Vietnam jungle. He can't even feed himself. How is he going to make a living or support a wife and family?" Maggie interrupted.

"And who is this young lady?"

"Mary Anne Johnson, one of the flight attendant who brought him and forty others home who will never have a normal life. I sent twelve more to the Dover morgue. Senator, you can do something to stop this waste of our young men's lives. You have to do something."

"I am only one vote of two hundred. Come into the office. I will need help from you."

On the way in he said. "Bring me a copy of the Roster, Mrs. Harvey. These young people are going to need it."

"Please be seated. Norman I understand you bought the Gusewic farm outside Odessa," the senator said.

"We bought the farm," Maggie said, emphasizing ''we.''

"Congratulations. My son was second highest bidder."

"Please stop by for coffee when you're in Odessa."

"I'll be there for Colonial Homes Open House weekend. Lots of influential people will be there. You two, also, I hope. Now let's get back to your demand of me."

"It wasn't a demand, Senator," Norman said.

"Yes it was!" Maggie declared.

The senator passed a copy of the roster to Maggie.

"Mary Anne, your opinion is as important as my vote. Write lots and lots of letters to the Senators in this book; especially ones on the Armed Services, Veteran's Affairs, Finance, and Foreign Affairs Committees. Send some to the White House and the Secretaries of Defense and State. Talk your friends and families into writing also. And don't forget the fellas like the one you brought home yesterday. Have someone write letters for them. We pay as much attention to our mail as we do to the opinion polls we conduct. My daddy use to say, 'If you want something done, do it yourself, or get very good help.' I'll get something done down here, but I'll need your help, Mary Anne."

"I'm sorry I came on to you angry and misbehaven."

"As my mother use told my sisters, Well-behaved women rarely make it into the history books."

"We know you are busy, Senator. Stop by for coffee when you are passing through Odessa," Norman said, trying to conclude the conversation.

Call Me Maggie

"I would love to have coffee with you and see your white mare and two foals. My daughter is a horsewoman and just as demanding as Mary Anne." Good Luck, Miss Johnson."

"Call me Maggie. When you stop by, I'll be happy to serve coffee and show you my horses. Thanks for your time."

Walking to the car Norman said "You only used nine minutes, door to door, Mary Anne," and placed his arm around her.

Maggie wanted to sleep as Norman drove home, but could not. She was close to napping when echoes in Baltimore's Harbor tunnel roared through her ears.

"Norman, every day you photograph news stories that become history. How do you keep yourself out of the limelight and the history books? I don't want to be a Dolly Madison and save the White House or Martha Washington who stays home and runs the farm. I want to keep flying, but I want to stop hauling young men off to their death and bringing home ones who are nearly dead. The war over there is a civil war. It's their war, not our war. We're trying to do what the French could not do. I meet some GI's who aren't shot up but they are the ones running the mill that runs the war. They do a good job doing the cover up, get awarded a promotion after their stint, work in the Pentagon and send more boys into the jungle to face an enemy that really no threat to themselves or their family. We put officials in office over there and they become Asian millionaires skimming off the top or refusing to let us bring in supplies until we bribe them, I'm just a girl from Odessa, Delaware, USA. What should I do? Should I take part in the anti-war protests and peace rallies? I can't turn away and forget young men like Bobby Joe who have their dreams ruined. What would you do?"

"I take pictures and do a little writing, stand back and see if I did the right thing. I don't always see my results immediately. It takes weeks or months until I know how well I did my job. I don't march in a protest, or carry a sign, but I make sure those that do are seen and heard. They say the pen is mightier than the sword. I say the camera is, too," Norman stated.

"You and the senator are correct. I didn't see it till now. I can make myself heard. I can write. I can speak. I can even take pictures of the injuries these young men received in the war that is not theirs. I can give my input. Recommend a camera that a klutz can use and drop me at the stationary store. Maggie has got some homework to do. And if you want more of my input, Bobby Joe's rehabilitation would be a good series for you to shoot, maybe even a book of it. Invite Judith to visit

If They Were Family

Bobby Joe the next time you go see him. She might want to do the story, unless you want to write it yourself. Both of you can spend mornings at the hospital and be at the newspaper within two hours."

"Good idea, Maggie. I'll discuss it with Judith, my editors, and Samuel Brown, if they don't buy it, I do it anyway."

They continued northward with Maggie's head lying on his lap. At the library, Maggie made a list of names and addresses she would use for her letters as she added a new responsibility in her crowed life while trying hard to maintain her relationship with Norman; to convince others to help end the conflict that took the arms of her adopted cousin.

Judith, Hershel and Alsop liked Maggie's idea on Bobby Joe's rehabilitation. Samuel Brown agreed to finance their expenses.

Frequently, whenever Leanne had a layover too short for a trip home or see Bobby Joe in Washington, she used the farmhouse guest room; her friendship with Maggie grew stronger. They shared many common bonds, particularly the special passenger they had brought back whose dream of a lifetime military career had ended in a Vietnamese jungle minefield. They had never mentioned another incident that bonded them; each having endured rape. Both lived for the future. Bobby Joe's rehabilitation and the desire to care for others like him.

One evening as they chatted, Leanne picked up Maggie's black album. Maggie joined her as she neared the back. Both studied the pictures from back to front again.

"These are something you must be very proud of Maggie. They are so natural in the way the womanhood, the professional flight attendant and your life beyond flying are shown. I have seen you wearing this same face when we fly, now I see it in pictures. Your dignity is displayed. The one in back are far better than magazine pictures I see soldiers carry on the plane or the ones I see on newsstands. These aren't trashy or perverted. A girl could show these to her parents."

"They're certainly different from the ones made of me before I met Norman. Those were cheap and trashy. Norman doesn't shot that kind. I was going to be a model before becoming a stewardess. Modeling has helped me forget about the damaged bodies I see coming home. I come home and make pictures with a sensitive man who shares my desire to see a whole beautiful body. It could be you or Midge. Even if it were a man, the pictures would still be great. Yes, I'm proud of them and I love the way he treats me when we are making them. It never leads to anything except a good feeling and great pictures. We hope to publish a book someday showing both facets of a woman. You're the first to see them all. Linda saw a few when we first started."

"I would like a signed copy when the book is published."

They finished the album together. Maggie returned to a picture showing Leanne, Bobby Joe and herself in the hospital, removed the photograph and presented it to Leanne.

"We can replace the picture, but I can't replace my friends," Maggie said, as they stared at the photograph.

"I can't replace Bobby Joe's arms, his eye, or his career, but I can help him adapt and help him find a new career. We'll be a team like you and Norman."

"Norman knows about my childhood, and my first career. He accepted me as I was then, and as I am now. He accepts my past and the time I can't be with him while there are others who need my help getting themselves back home, patched up and on the way to a better life. We share our dreams. We share each other's lives. We accept each other's careers and share them, even though there are times when more time would be nice to have and enjoy what we have found in each other."

"Bobby Joe knows about my past and why I became an airline stewardess. It doesn't seem to affect our relationship. I wonder if there are more men out there like Bobby Joe and Norman?"

"I wonder if there are more women like you or I, and if they will find something or someone to help them forget their past?"

Norman came in poured himself a glass of juice and joined Maggie and Leanne.

"What time are you leaving tomorrow, ladies?"

"Take off at 3 p.m. Go to Ohio, and fly all night."

"I am on standby for the same flight," Leanne answered.

"I'll be going to photograph Bobby Joe in the morning. I can have you at the airport by one or one-thirty. If you'd like to ride along, be ready by six."

"I want to write some letters and get the plane ready. Maybe Leanne would like to go. The other attendants and I can fill in for her, if she does," Maggie said.

"I wouldn't miss it. Every morning with Bobby Joe is a good morning. Right now, I'll tuck myself in and give you two a little time to catch up," Leanne answered.

"Coffee's at 5:30," Norman said.

If They Were Family

By 11 a.m. he had his pictures and Leanne had had another visit with Bobby Joe. She was also becoming like a sister to Maggie and to him as well.

Families were discouraged from living on military posts, even if housing was available. It usually wasn't. Commissaries and PX's cut their hours and merchandise selection. On-post service stations closed in late afternoon. If one did not get to the PX, commissary, or service station before closing off post shopping was necessary. Someone got the idea that small stores similar to mom and pop grocery stores could meet the needs of the mobile military, if it sold gas. Small buildings were erected near military post gates with minimal inventories. Coffee makers, pastry cases, hot dog grills, coolers for milk, soft drinks and beer shared space with shelves of bread, cereal and baby food, A drive up customer could pick up six Budweiser's, a jar of Gerber's, a box of Kellogg's Corn Flakes, hangover medicine and a pack of Marlboros before reaching their living quarters or the speed limit. If they forgot something they could drive back; the store would be open late, some all night. A variety of these generic convenience stores one-stop-wonders popped up with names like Fast-Mart, Shop & Go or Highway Pit Stop. One group used it hours as its name, Seven-Eleven, kept the name when 24-hour service began. Larger retailers copied the convenience stores and poured six acre asphalt parking lots around two acre stores offering anything from aspirin to lawn mowers to prescription drugs to zebra skin rugs, Downtown Woolworths became suburbs Woolco. Kresgees became Kmart only to be replaced by Super Kmarts. A Ben Franklin employee quit his job and built hundreds .across the south, then hundreds more in little towns across America with dreams of opening thousands more around the globe before the century would end. He named them after himself, Wal-Mart. High school students, and dropout's alike, found employment in the marts with retirees escaping golden year's boredom, or mothers who had raised their child to school age.

And these marts, convenience stores, and big box discount outlets accepted a new kind of money, plastic. Credit cards offered anytime interest free loans to cardholders if payment was made within ten days after billing. American Express, Visa, and MasterCard signs hung next to another reading: "No cash accepted after dark; credit cards only." Banks soon adopted these magnetic cards and began dispensing cash, accepting deposits or bill payments any time of day or night. Machine banking machines called ATMs began appearing everywhere from Wal-Mart's to MacDonald's to dry cleaners and truck stops.

Call Me Maggie

In the 1960's small restaurants began to pop up on street corners and shopping centers food franchises offering food ready to eat-in or takeout. Their owners would buy a franchise, have a small cookie cutter building constructed identical to ones in hundreds of other towns, and offering customers hamburgers, roast beef, pizza and fried chicken developed in test kitchens that meant food customers bought in Boston was identical what a customer in Boise ordered. These matchbox food vendors thawed their entrees and had it ready in less than a minute and got America's baby-boomer generation in the habit to eat, lick their fingers, drink paper cup beverages, drive two ton, overpowered, chromed covered dream machine at 65 MPH on interstate highways and beltways, while listening to AM, FM or eight track tape stereo quadraphonic music, and calling citizen band radio good buddies at the same time.

Their vehicles were available in a dozen designer colors with matching colored leather, magnesium wheels, radial tires, electric sunroofs, electric windows, electric windshield defrosters, electric seat warmers, and three year warranties.

Maggie often noted the cost of a tank of gas for her little car had risen greatly since she left Chester. In seven years, the cost had doubled. Repair costs to keep it running had risen too. The car was often parked while parts were found to repair it. The car's maker had been absorbed by another manufacturer and ceased making Metropolitans years before. Most of the little cars had been crushed into basket sized blocks, re-melted, and made into everything from barn buckets to Tonka Toys. Lionel could not find salvage parts in auto graveyards any longer, as Kevin once did. Frequently she had to ask Norman to drive her to or from the airport. Sometimes Midge would drop Maggie at the farm on her way to Georgetown or to the young minister with a church in Harrington. She finally agreed with Norman and Lionel: The little car was not reliable any longer. It was more than twenty years old. She needed a new one.

Maggie wanted the openness of Norman's convertible and the hauling ability of Pop Pop's truck. She and Norman had avoided the car craze that almost everyone else feel victim to. Attending Linda's races provided both with examples of autophile's conspicuous consumption. Walking to her plane one day, the answer nearly ran Maggie down.

The next morning Maggie asked Norman for a ride to town. She drove the Nash's replacement home from a used car lot. It was small. It was economical. It wasn't fast, but it was strong. It could take her anywhere, anytime, in any weather. It wasn't beautiful. It wasn't

If They Were Family

sleek. It didn't even have a radio, cassette player or drink cup holders. It was a Jeep, the mule of automobiles. And it did not carry a single piece of chrome, but it could haul half a dozen bags of horse feed or fertilizer while wind blew through her hair on sunny days with the top removed. "Chrome doesn't get me there any quicker," she told herself.

Within a week, a red Jeep station wagon shared space with her white Jeep soft top. Norman had the capacity he needed; she had wind in her hair that she wanted. The twelve year old convertible and the Metropolitan were retired to the barn.

The cold war in Europe went on, a few short fighting ones between Israel and Arabs neighbors flared up, while the one in Viet Nam that began after World War II continued to escalate. More and more young men flew west to halt the spread of Communism in Southeast Asia. Others flew east to quell uprisings in the Middle East and a few African nations.

More and more came home in bandages and black bags.

Maggie finished a morning ride on each of the horses, bathed them, brushed them until they shined and released them in the pasture. She came in, made tea, showered and invited Norman to make rounds of the second hand shops and thrift stores with her. She sweetened her invitation with lunch at the Farmhouse Restaurant with Linda and Kevin, if Kevin wasn't working his extra job. Kevin was, but suggested bringing Linda and Deanna down for crabs in the late afternoon. Deanna had begged him to take her to see the horses while Norman steamed blue claw crabs caught in the farm creek. After Deanna wore herself out on the horses, filled herself with crabs, and dozed off, Linda loaded her in the car and left.

"I drew an assignment for next week you might like to go on, the Democratic National Convention in Chicago. There's going to be lots of satellite rallies and alternate conventions with people touting the anti-war and peace platforms. President Johnson has withdrawn from the race and we have ticket seekers on both sides of the fence. Can you adjust your schedule and go?"

"I'll be taking a load of sailors from Norfolk to The Great Lakes Navel Center on Wednesday. I'll meet you in the city, if I can ride home with you," Maggie answered.

"Good!"

Political activism became a way of live for many. Pete Seeger, Bob Dillon, Woody Guthrie and Joan Baez song became as big a rage as Johnny Cash's plain country poetic recordings. Seeger, Tom and Dick

Call Me Maggie

Smothers were banned from appearing on television shows. Jane Fonda got in hot water for her statements on the war and for a trip to Hanoi forbidden by the U.S. State Department. In Europe and the Middle East, political activist had a different strategy to change leadership. Fanatical terrorists hijacked airplanes, then made demands that political leaders step down and jailed opponents be freed or they would explode bombs and destroy the planes, the passengers and themselves.

Norman made pictures of the selection process and antics of delegates who would select a candidate to replace Lyndon Johnson when he refused to accept a nomination for a second term in the summer of 1968.

Hubert Humphrey was the front runner after Robert Kennedy was assassinated while campaigning in Los Angles. His campaign was popular with young people, especially peaceniks. His promises included getting the U.S. out of Viet Nam and the U.N. Unfortunately for Humphrey, Richard Nixon and a gang called The Plumbers bugged his Watergate Hotel campaign headquarters and knew the Democrat strategies before they were enacted. The junior senator from Delaware and his wife were among Norman's subjects.

"Maggie darling, we love the horse. She's quite a show off in the ring. You must come to Fair Hill next week and watch our girls perform," his wife said.

"Copies of your letters cross my desk often. Your penmanship has gained you quite a reputation and it is causing some in Washington to have doubts. The candidate we're putting on the ticket shares your wishes. Keep writing your letters." the senator said.

"I'm not doing it to gain a reputation. I doing it for the young men I have take over and bring back," Maggie stated.

Norman took her as he went to cover a rally in nearby Grant Park and left her alone as he used a high window for an overall shot. Maggie wandered into the park. A full-fledged riot developed between demonstrators and police who had been sent to disperse the crowd. He saw and photographed a Chicago policeman beat her to the ground and kick her in the back after she was down. She received three broken ribs and a concussion before he carried her out of the park to safety and medical attention. Within two weeks she was flying again after spending her time off with Pop Pop planting young rose bushes in the west field.

Maggie invited Midge and Leanne to stay at the farm where they dozed while she waited for Norman. She soon followed them and dozed off after he arrived. At 3 a.m. the three attendants left on a twenty

minute ride up the dark highway. As they crossed the canal, each transformed back into skyward bound nurses, big sisters and faith givers; a
metamorphose each experienced as they approached the airport.

Fresh squeezed grape juice awaited Norman on a bedside table
as well as flowers. Others were on the kitchen table, coffee table and
patio. Uncountable jewels sparked from the grass as he viewed the farmette and a glistening silver diamond overhead as it moved westward
over the pasture. Norman took a coffee can of grain and apples to Maggie's horses, then ended a conversation between cardinal on the feeder
and parakeets in the cage when he brought the cage inside fearing it
might rain before he returned. The scene was repeated the next four
mornings before his father came down to the farm and each grabbed a
hoe and weeded the roses.

In Saigon, the diamond Norman saw redeployed on a pre-
holiday junket home for nearly two hundred soldiers. They would be
home for the last holiday of summer and home cooked food rather than
cans or freeze dried packets of un-palatable concoctions. Celebrating
began on the plane. Rice liquor was passed around. The cabin soon
filled with odors of beer and marijuana. A few pipes with a burning sub-
stance in marble sized bowls of were being passed between the rowdy
passengers.

Midge returned to the attendant's station crying, unbuttoned her
blouse and inspected five red marks on her chest.

"One of the passengers slipped up behind me, grabbed me, and
squeezed me so hard, I had to come back see if the skin was broken and
I might be bleeding," she said.

Leanne ran back, grabbed a box of bandages and said, "The
guy who grabbed Midge has been stabbed. I'll need help."

Maggie led the way forward. Leanne followed Maggie. Midge
followed both. Blood covered the uniform of the soldier and was flow-
ing onto the floor where a knife lay.

"He's the one who pinched me. Let him die," Midge said

"Yea, let the SOB die. He was bragging about the women he
had raped, beaten and wasted after he got rough with the stewardess,"
one of the other passengers yelled. "The bastard deserves what he got
and more."

Leanne rolled the young man onto his back, pulled scissors
from her apron, cut the buttons from his shirt, and spread his shirt open
as she remembered him grabbing her buttocks a few moments before he
squeezed Midge. The memory would have been forgotten like the other

incidents times when a passenger when one of the passengers slapped or grabbed her backside, but he was now her patient.

Maggie screamed "Vinnie," picked up the knife, stuck it under his chin and said, "I let you get away with it when you hurt me. Now you've hurt one of my friends. I can't let you get away with it this time."

"Don't, Maggie!" Leanne shrieked out.

Maggie paused, stared at her and Midge for an instant as she remembered Vinnie grabbing her breasts on another flight and tried to suppress memories of him beating and raping her. "Take her. I don't want the whore anymore," burned in her mind. She fought to forget the pain she felt afterward and the shame she still felt.

"Maggie, drop the knife," Leanne shouted.

Maggie fought to suppress memories of a teen-age boy on American Bandstand and her first dance with him. The song was "Twilight Time." Even now the smell of his English Leather remained vivid. She turned back to Vinnie, and then shouted, "Damn it Vinnie, don't die. Don't you dare die on me!" as she sliced his undershirt to the waist and spread it. Gurgles accompanied bubbles oozing from his chest.

"Midge, help us," Leanne shouted out as she packed gauze pads around the holes.

"I can't. Let him die." Midge replied.

"Do it Midge. I've gotta help him breathe," Maggie yelled, lifted his neck, held his nose, put her lips over his and blew her breath into the young man.

"Midge, radio Hawaii. Tell them what we've got," Leanne yelled. "Make sure they have an ambulance waiting when we get there,"

Midge ran toward the cockpit. Maggie blew again.

Vinnie's eyes opened.

"That you, Maggie?"

"Yes. Lie still or we'll lose you. Hang on till we get to Hawaii. You are hurt real bad."

Midge remembered a sermon and the young man who delivered it as she returned. She spread her legs around Vinnie's head, grabbed his elbows, pulled them to her hips, pushed them back, then pulled again and again as she prayed and begged, "Dear Lord I didn't know what I was saying. Please forgive me. Don't let him die,"

"We won't." Maggie said.

"He won't lose him...if his lungs will hold up," Leanne said.

Maggie kept blowing in his mouth while Leanne held the gauzes to his chest and Midge kept pumping and praying. She, Maggie and

If They Were Family

Leanne worked to save the life of their passenger, yet the bubbles, gurgles, and bleeding continued.

Again and again Maggie pushed her breath into Vinnie. Leanne held the gauze tighter. Again and again Midge pulled and pushed

Maggie relieved Midge. Midge relieved Leanne. Leanne relieved Maggie. Vinnie opened his glazed eyes.

"What are you bitches doing?" Vinnie asked.

"I'm not a bitch. I'm a nurse saving your life." Leanne declared.

"You have been injured badly, Vinnie. And you're not out of the woods yet. You can still buy the farm unless we help you. Stop talking and let us get on with our work. We have to keep you alive until you get better help than we can give you," Maggie added.

"Four years of firefights and ambushes. . . Only to die on the way home. . . No way, bitch. . .No way." Vinnie mumbled.

"If you don't shut up, you will," Leanne said.

"Seems like the old days. . .in the streets back home. . . kicking ass . . . get out of my face, bitch," Vinnie said before passing out again.

Maggie pulled the mask off Vinnie's face, leaned forward, covered his mouth with her own and blew.

As he was carried off the plane Vinnie said, "I owe you a big one, Maggie. I'll look you up when I get home and repay you. You can count on that."

"Save the tough guy crap for the gang at home. You don't impress me any longer," Maggie said.

"Let's clean ourselves and change. We still have half the flight remaining. Our passengers up front don't need to see us looking this way. They've seen enough blood wasted to last them the rest of their lives," Maggie said.

Nearly three hours later, Maggie, Leanne and Midge could relax. Leanne cleaned and changed while Midge sat alone. Maggie silently questioned the meaning of Vinnie's owe you one and pay you back statements.

"I wasn't cut out for this," Midge said to Maggie.

"We all have seen too much of the wasted blood and too many wounded. I'm glad it's us working with these boys rather than someone who doesn't show compassion."

"I didn't have any compassion today."

"You had it. It just took you a little time to find it. You came through when it counted."

"You called him Vinnie. Do you know him?"

Call Me Maggie

"I was one of the girls in his gang a long time ago."

"He called you us bitches and called you a whore. He must have treated you very ugly."

"He did. He is as bad as they come. He does ugly things to people. Too ugly to talk about. Go change and try to forget Vinnie molesting you. He won't do it again."

"If he is so bad, why did you try so hard to save him?"

"He's one our young men returning from a hell hole that has changed them forever. A hell hole we can't imagine and one they will never forget."

"Was he was the one who raped you?" Leanne asked.

"Yes, one of them."

Two hours later their plane was nearing the U.S. shore. Midge still sat alone in the window seat. An endless blue sea of rolled beneath her. She was unaware as green forests replaced blue water, and then change into gray peaks with webs of white. Grays and whites soon became an fields of amber and golden brown dotted with insects of New Holland yellows, Farmall reds, and John Deere Greens. America's heartland was in harvest. Only a few days earlier one of the motorized pests had deprived Midge of sleep. Images of red bubbles rising, bursting and oozing through her hands burned upon Midge's conscience. Gurgling sounds throbbed painfully in her ears. The pain in her breast reminded Midge of the incident's onset.

A slender spire nestled upon a tower passed her window. Midge's thoughts turned to another spire and another young man who spoke of peace, love and forgiveness. His face replaced the one she had prayed over and forced her life giving breath into a few hours earlier.

Maggie belted herself into the seat by Midge.

"This was my last flight, Maggie," Midge said, tearfully.

"Get some rest when you get home. You'll change your mind."

"It wasn't what Vinnie did that makes me want to quit. I've had boys back home and guys on the plane grab me like he did, but not as hard. It was me wanting to let him die."

"We have to take care of the good, as well as the bad."

Maggie wondered whether it would be her last flight, as well. An acquaintance from her past had found her and could find her again when his wounds healed. He and his gang could also find her friends. If he harmed them, would she be capable of using the restraint then that she used today? Was she capable of preventing harm to the ones who had become a large part of her new life?

If They Were Family

Midge remained in the darkened metal cocoon while another plane load of soldiers were repatriated into homeland sunlight to spend Labor day with their girlfriends, wives and children, or parents and family. She would spend her holiday praying for forgiveness.

That night Maggie followed two red dots as Midge went homeward down U.S. 13 until she tuned in to White Horse Farm's dark lane. Maggie asked herself, would Midge find peace and happiness down the road? Would peace that had evaded her since Midge's attack, await her at the end of the lane?

A single white rose standing in a Coke bottle greeted Maggie, but it went unnoticed. She went directly upstairs and soaked in a tub of bubbles for more than an hour; an action she had not done following previous trips. The pasture glowed golden under a harvest moon as Maggie strolled silently with Norman, then had half-a-cup of tea with him and bathed again.

"Would you like to talk about your flight?" he asked when she finally joined him just as Johnny Carson said goodnight to the nation.

"No. Right now I need some time alone. It's something I must work out for myself. But I will be home each night for the next eight weeks. I'm teaching Clara's classes," she answered.

Norman knew whatever upset Maggie was monumental. She had raised her barrier around herself again. He craved a means to breach herself imposed stockade, but the key evaded him. Even Linda and Leanne's stopover didn't seem to help erase whatever was eating away at his friend, partner, and lover.

"Was her career workload finally overcoming Maggie? Has it consumed the best of her?" he asked himself.

Two days later, Maggie drove to the airport again. She would instruct, not fly. A week later Midge re-entered the 707's metal cocoon and joined Leanne on another trip to bring their boys home.

Maggie and Leanne pulled up the lane at White Horse Farm. Midge tooted her horn and continued driving south. Norman parked beside the Nash when he arrived. Maggie hugged him with one arm. The other carried her flight bag. Leanne copied Maggie although her hug was briefer. At daybreak they departed for Washington and a day with Bobby Joe. Maggie went north to instruct new stewardesses. She would not fly until the students graduated.

The following morning Norman left before nine for coffee with his father and a meeting with an art distributor. The distributor agreed with Norman. His Amish pictures would make a good calendar. He would make a printing run of them, the Pennsylvania farmhouses, Cape Henlopen seashells, and Delaware Lighthouse as calendars. Two each group would be printed into 24x36 inch posters as well as post cards. Norman left with a proud chest and fatter wallet. He drew two headshots and a New Year's Eve Ball committee group to shoot and process before a basketball game at seven o'clock. Inmates at the Greenbank Prison were having a game with Delaware State troopers in the prison gym.

Maggie and Leanne watched as technicians adjusted new metal and plastic arms on Bobby Joe. Later they sat in his classroom at nearby American University. Before leaving Maggie wrote letters for a couple of patients and read the Washington Star to another. She wore the same stewardess face a few had seen on their way to the hospital. Leanne and Bobby Joe had little time alone before joining her and patients for dinner. Bobby Joe now fed himself with his artificial arms and crab claw fingers. Leaving the hospital, crowds filled the street, locking Leanne, Maggie and the car between rioting masses shouting slurs at them. They saw rioters break storefront windows and run away with any and everything they could carry through the Washington Streets. Fires were set in some neighborhoods that consumed entire city blocks.

Norman photographed similar events when the policemen were called to control riots in Wilmington. Dr. Martin Luther King's dream and life had ended earlier that afternoon in Memphis. Anger fueled riots raged for days in many cities.

"We got caught in little messy traffic for a while. You should see Bobby Joe on a keyboard of something he calls a computer. He now writes ten or more letters a day. How was your day?" Maggie asked.

"Same old same old except I'll have four calendars and eight posters in print by the end of summer," he replied.

It was now July, 1969. The rumors had finally come true. They now flew in the large Boeing 747-400. The "Dash 400" indicated the larger plane carried four hundred seated passengers or more than a hundred stretchers.

Leanne helped Maggie remove seats and hang stretchers in the lower deck after landing in Vietnam. Eight seats were left in the rear for attendants. The seats would be flown stateside in the plane's cargo hole with black bags. The upper deck was saved for walk-on or uninjured returnees. They were grounded less than four hours to unload, remove seats, and re-load for the flight back home. About 5:30 Leanne went forward to direct walk-ons upstairs and litter bearers to the cavern below. At 6:37 A.M. the plane took off and headed east. Midge and another attendant served drinks and food to the upper section while Maggie, Leanne and four other attendants comforted their passenger in stretchers.

"It was never this bad when I was a candy stripper. I have to find a book of Miss Congeniality phrases." Leanne said.

"One of the drunken walk-ons just pinned me to the wall, asking if I knew how gorgeous I was and pleading for my phone number so he could call me later and meet him for a romantic celebration when he get back home," Leanne reported.

"Did you have any other problems with him?" Maggie asked.

"No. He passed out before I could give him the phone number I gave all the others who didn't stop; the one for The White House."

"When I began flying I thought I was hot and being a stewardess was my ticket to adventure. Guys on tourist's junkets changed that. I would get four of five propositions on each flight, numerous offers for dinner, and a few who wanted a date, and more suggestive overtures than I could count. I soon learned being a good attendant was better than being a hot one. The guys on these flights don't need glamorous attendants, they need good ones. I have been known to put a knee in more than one tourist's groin if they hurt me. Bobby Joe can tell you how I handled Vinnie. When one of my girls has a problem, I can get mean, jump in the way I did when I was in Vinnie's gang. It would have gotten nasty when he hurt Midge if you had not yelled at me," Maggie said.

"Would you have used the knife on Vinnie or let him die?" Leanne asked.

"I'll never know unless he hurts one of my stewardesses or someone in my family. Then I will get as mean as he is."

"If he hurts you again, you won't have to, I'll get mean for you." Leanne said.

"Let's talk about something more cheerful. Seen any good movies lately?" Maggie asked.

At 3 A.M. on a June morning in 1972 Kevin placed a kiss on Linda's forehead as he did five mornings each week at that time before going to check on Deanna. He kissed his daughter, adjusted her blanket, stood up, stared at her for a moment, and kissed the child again. His lips touched her brow an instant longer the second time. The night before he had promised his daughter they would pick apples for Aunt Maggie's horses when he finished work, if she would go to sleep. He turned and left Deanna's bedroom. By the time he reached the door, his mind was already on his delivery route.

Call Me Maggie

He drove from the little house he and Linda rented between his in-laws home and the bakery building. The house was near her parent's sandwich shop. Close enough to walk with the little girl.

Kevin's walk through a lot with identical Grumman vans was punctuated by fellow drivers' greeting him. He updated his route details, and assured dispatcher he would be okay on today's trip, then climbed into the delivery van. Kevin had agreed to make today's run so the route's regular driver could hunt squirrels. He had made the run the day before with the driver. Today he carried a list of the stops and a road map. It would be dark for another ninety minutes as Kevin drove across the sleeping city. Traffic would present no tie-up at that hour. Soon he was driving north on Governor Prints Boulevard with the Delaware River barely visible on his right. Once across the Schuylkill River Bridge, Kevin pulled over, turned on the light above the driver's seat, and placed a map on the engine cover that served as a make-shift desk. He read the first few lines on his list of drop sites and drove to the address of the top entry. The list contained a variety of small food businesses that could be found in any of the city's neighborhoods. Most were small operations such as the submarine shop his wife and in-laws operated.

His in-laws had frequently suggested that Kevin join them and Linda, learn the business and assume full operation of the shop with Linda when they retired. Kevin declined saying he would be happier driving a truck than putting in the long hours spent operating a "Mom and Pop" sandwich shop.

With the first stop completed, Kevin drove to the second and third and so on until just before 11 a. m. His work day would be finished within an hour and he could spend the afternoon with his daughter and perhaps Linda. He parked the van behind an old Impala near the deli door for shorter trips carrying the shop's order inside. Two men the Impala followed him in deli from leaving a female behind the wheel of the Impala. Inside the deli one man ordered three sandwiches and the other stood in a corner near the door trying to remain unnoticed. Kevin placed his packaged breads and rolls in front of the deli's cold cut case, then slipped around the woman assembling sandwiches at the bar and restocked her bin with loose rolls that would become deli-made sandwiches shortly, While the owner got the payment ready he took a drink from the refrigerator, opened the twist off top, and began drinking,. Thoughts of his wife in a shop thirty miles south making similar sandwiches mingled with images of his daughter picking apples as he waited for payment. Kevin pushed $78.00 into a shirt pocket, leaving bills visible above the

If They Were Family

pocket. He and the deli owner were still talking when one man came to the cash register station. The other moved close to Kevin and the owner. It was the first time Kevin was aware they were in the deli. He recognized the two and said nothing.

Both men pulled guns from their jackets. One pushed his pistol in the owners face. The other demanded the owner empty the cash drawer in a bag. The owner put a wad of bills in a bag, and then instinctively put the three sandwiches in with them. Kevin was facing the men as they turned from the owner. Their eyes met. One man raised his gun to within three inches of Kevin, pulled the bills from the pocket, and fired a single bullet into the center of Kevin's chest. Kevin slumped, fell backward, and murmured a few words while his blood mixed with an unfinished Pepsi on the floor.

The woman cleaned her hands before calling for an ambulance as the two men raced to the Mustang and sped away. A news team from the CBS station in Philadelphia was at the scene before the ambulance crew or police arrived. They began video-taping the scene, then recorded a few seconds of Kevin's driver's license which included his photograph. In an interview, deli owner told the television reporter that Kevin had said something as he fell. The deli owner could not be sure whether Kevin had said damn it or something close to damn it.

It was too late for Kevin when an ambulance crew rolled a gurney with him into the Temple University Hospital emergency room across the street.

At 12.00 p.m. the television began their noon hour news program. The lead story was the shooting of a young Delaware man killed while delivering bread to a Philadelphia delicatessen. One of the closing two scenes was of a hole in one of the van's windows which had passed through Kevin's chest, a store window, and then into the van window. The other was close-up of his driver's license and picture.

Kevin's father had suffered minor heart attack in May and had spent a few days at home recovering. He made himself a sandwich and turned the living room television set to Channel 10 just before twelve to watch the news. He remained stunned until just after 2 p.m. when he made a call to Norman at the newspaper office. Norman cursed and rampaged for more than fifteen minutes. The editor of the paper finally convinced Norman to go his father's home or go comfort Kevin's wife.

"Not until I make a phone call!" Norman insisted.

He got the number of WCAU-TV and called the station's news editor. For more than a quarter-hour he voiced his objections and re-

Call Me Maggie

minded the station's editor of news gathering guidelines that responsible newsmen observed. His editor took over the berating Norman started with the television man and ordered Norman to leave. Norman drove to his father's home.

John Choma was in the Reed's Submarine Shop having lunch when the broadcast began. John, Linda, her parents, and many of the lunch crowd saw the same broadcast. John convinced them to close the shop and go home. He made two quick telephone calls and was soon northbound on U.S.13 to the Philadelphia hospital with Linda and Norman. As they stood by the body, Norman's mind flashed a lifetime of memories beginning with a red-haired baby being placed in his arms one cold morning in April 1945.

Each of three identified the corpse as Kevin James Kennedy, age 27, husband of Linda Reed Kennedy, father of one daughter, Deanna. Linda signed papers to claim Kevin's body.

All the family was at the Kennedy home when Norman. John, Linda, her daughter, and her parents arrived. Many friends and neighbors joined in the loss of Pop Pop's son, Maggie was among them watching Channel 10's Six O'clock News updated version of their lead story including the interview with the deli owner. After the lead story ended, the station manager came on camera, explained the station's news policy and apologized to Mrs. Linda Kennedy and the family of the victim for their hasty noon broadcast. He also announced that station was establishing a reward fund for information on Kevin Kennedy's murderers. The fund had already reached the sum of $55,000.00. The manager apologized again.

Maggie rushed to Norman and said, "I've gotta talk to you. Now!" then took him to the rear hall of beyond the kitchen

"Kevin wasn't saying 'dam it,' he was saying 'Dominic'. And I know the Dominic he named. Drive to Philadelphia with me and bring pistol if you've got one," Maggie ordered Norman.

"Maggie, you can't do this," Norman told her.

"Oh yes I can! The SOB beat me and raped me. He's murdered your brother and my best friend's husband. Now I'm gonna make him pay as I should have years ago.

"Maggie, you can't," Norman repeated.

"I can and I will, with or without you," she said with pleading eyes. "Stay here if you like; I'm going to Philadelphia."

"I'm with you, Should I ask Lionel and Ernest to come with us?" he asked softly.

260

If They Were Family

Maggie declined taking his brothers. Once in Norman's car he handed her a large pistol. She removed some of the articles from her purse and put the pistol inside with the one she had picked up off the street the day she met Linda and Kevin.

Traveling some of the same routes Kevin traveled earlier, Maggie's anger lessened. Her plan became clearer. She directed Norman to a police station. She told the detectives of the incident outside bandstand. She could only provide Dominic's name and the names of other Impala gang members as potential suspects. She did not mention Dominic beating and raping her eight years earlier but did give them details of their activities and their leader who lead them with ruthless force and brutality. Within the hour they were in the dark canyons in the city of brotherly love searching for the ones who ended the life of Norman's brother and widowing Maggie's best friend.

Maggie put on sunglasses, put a .38 special in the pocket of her overcoat and returned the second pistol to Norman. She dropped her purse to floor of the car, got out and headed for the door of tavern. Inside she went straight to a large corner rear booth Vinnie Gambini and two other men sat in the booth. Before the men knew she was there, Maggie blocked the man on the left. Norman followed her and blocked the one on the right. Maggie held the pistol in both hands and pointed at Vinnie's forehead.

"You are going to tell me the truth for the first time since I met you. Where is Dominic?" Maggie demanded.

"Keep your hands on the table, cousin" Norman cautioned him.

"Long time no see, Maggie. Thanks again for fixing me up on my way back. What can I do for you? I said I owe you one," Vinnie replied.

"Where is Dominic?"

Two pistols cocked as she spoke.

"Freelancing. I ain't seen him in a year or more. He went on his own," Vinnie said.

"That was my brother killed in the deli this morning. Where is he? Did you see the news today?" Norman demanded.

"Yea, I saw the news. We were just talking about it."

"Dominic doesn't piss unless you say pee. Where is he?" Maggie demanded.

"I told you, I don't know. We split long ago. Now you and your new pimp get off my ass, whore," Vinnie came back.

"She's no whore!" Norman yelled.

Call Me Maggie

He had never heard anyone call Maggie a whore. He leaned across the table and placed the pistol between Vinnie's eyes.

"No, Norman. His ass is mine," Maggie said.

"Look you two. I ain't seen Dominic in a long time. I told you he went on his own. Sal, too. Doing small-time stuff. Girls can't make enough. They have to pull a stickup every day or two to support two women and four big narc problems," Vinnie reported nervously.

Vinnie's breathing hastened. His sentences hastened.

"Where can we find him?" Norman asked.

He's breaking down, Norman thought to himself. Maggie was not sure.

"Where is Dominic? I can still feel him beating me. I can feel you beating me even more. I still have nightmares of you raping me. Now tell me where the hell is Dominic?" Maggie shouted.

"Let me do some checking. I come up with him. I'll take care of his no good ass. After all, what are friends for? Give me a call Monday." Vinnie stopped short of reaching into a pocket, and asked, "May I?"

"Very slowly," Maggie warned. "And don't think I'm your friend. I should've finished you off when you got stabbed."

Vinnie pulled some business cards from his coat. The top one he held out for Maggie, the rest dropped to the tabletop.

"It's the best I can do right now. I'll take care of things for you. You can count on it. Call me Monday morning."

"I'll be back, if you don't answer my call."

Norman walked back to the door. Maggie followed Norman, sidestepping and still holding her gun on Vinnie. Norman pointed his at the bartender, the only other person remaining in the tavern besides Vinnie and his two companions.

Norman made countless turns following Maggie's directions as they weaved through the canyons to avoid being followed. After a while she read the card by light from a clip-on mirror.

"The little white card read: Vincent Gambini, Director, Special Services, International Brotherhood of Teamsters."

"That son of a bitch did go straight, almost."

"But will he find Dominic?" Norman asked.

"We'll know Monday."

Saturday afternoon countless family members, friends, and flowers filled the funeral home across the creek from the Kennedy home just as they had when Mom Mom Kennedy died. The Red Cross had found Lionel in Germany. Maggie got him a seat home on her airline.

If They Were Family

Kevin lay in a coffin at front of the room. His hands were covered by small spray of flowers. An accompanying embossed ribbon read, "Daddy." Nearby, another larger one read "Brotherhood of Teamsters." Later the crowd of well wishers watched as Pop Pop Kennedy, Kevin's widow Linda, Norman, Kevin's two brothers and his sister tossed dirt into an open grave next the one everyone called Mom Mom Kennedy.

Linda locked in Norman and Maggie's arms as they left the grave and said, "He will never know, now."

"Never know what?" Norman asked his sister-in-law.

"That I'm pregnant again," she sighed.

At the Kennedy home afterwards, older women gathered in the house while young men and young women gathered in front of the garage with the man they called Pop Pop until well past sunset.

Linda insisted that Maggie and Norman stay with her that night. She said Vinnie and Dominic might come looking for them.

Norman slept soundly, although the sleep was all too short. He went out for a Sunday paper and left Maggie to sleep on. He returned with copies of both Philadelphia Sunday newspapers.

"Maggie, wakeup! Wakeup, Maggie."

His news was urgent.

A headline in one paper read "Two Found dead, Police Suspect Underworld Link."

Maggie crowded next to Norman and both read the story below the headline and then searched the second newspaper.

"What do you think, Maggie?"

"Vinnie kept his word. He took care of things."

After Linda read the stories, Norman insisted that they take her to bakery on Monday to wrap up Kevin's affairs.

Norman opened the meeting with questions about insurance the company had on their employees and benefits for the driver's survivors.

"We don't have any, but we are offering $5,000.00 reward for information on the shooting," the bakery manager told them.

"You mean one of your drivers gets shot by two holdup men. One gets scared, turns the other one in, and he gets reward money you post while the driver's wife and family get nothing?" Maggie asked.

"That's right. But we collected $938.00 from our employees," the manager said.

Call Me Maggie

"How long can she live on that? What about union insurance policy? Did he have that?" Maggie asked.

"No. But, three men from the teamsters were in on Friday. They left this for Kevin's wife," the manager added.

He handed Linda a brown business envelope. She opened the envelope and removed two sheets of paper. One was a hand written note on Brotherhood of Teamsters, stationary. The other was a hand written check in the amount of $25,000.00. The signature on the check read Vincent Gambini.

"I'll be damned!" Norman and Maggie said in chorus.

Norman pulled a story cut from the Sunday newspaper out of his pocket and handed it to the manager, and ordered the older man: "Read this!"

Norman, Maggie and Linda waited until the manager glanced back up.

"It looks like you get to keep your reward money. Those are the two men. Did you see the name Dominic Vetri? Did you hear the deli owner say Dominic?" Maggie asked.

"And look at the name on this check. Vinnie did them in or hired the ones who did," Norman added.

"I'm sorry. That's company's policy. There's no more I can do," the manager stated.

Early on a December morning, Linda called Norman and asked him to accompany her back to the bakery. The manager had requested she come in for another meeting. Maggie called Norman just as his call from Linda finished.

"I'm going with you. Don't dream of saying I can't."

Wrapped boxes covered the bakery manager's desk and a few other employees were behind him and the desk.

"Mrs. Kennedy the gifts are from the bakers and drivers. We re-evaluated our employee guide. This is from the company," the manager said, handing an envelope to Kevin's widow.

Maggie handed Linda a second envelope marked WCAU-TV. It contained another check saying, "Pay to the order of Mary Anne Johnson, $72,000.00. Reference: Reward."

"You should have it. You will need it, raising two children," Maggie whispered.

Norman, Maggie and the Kennedy clan did their best helping Linda get through the next few weeks. Each stopped when they were in West Wilmington; Linda had visitors often. Her parents convinced her

If They Were Family

to put more effort into their sandwich shop; they would be giving it up soon. It would keep her mind busy, but she had a lot to learn before she was ready to run the business. They invited her to move back to their home and she accepted.

More than six weeks had pasted since the funeral. Maggie visited Linda between flights as she had been doing for the past nine years. Norman tried to make his visits just after the lunch rush before he went to work. The visits had been almost regular. Sometimes he took his dinner hour in the little shop as well.

On a cold January evening Linda called Norman and asked him to stop by the house after he put the paper to bed. She knew he enjoyed having companionship on lonely nights when Maggie was away and she liked having someone to talk with after putting Deanna to bed and was dressed for bed herself when he arrived.

"Norman, I want you to do something very special for me," Linda began.

"Sure, Linda, What is it?"

"Don't say sure too soon. You should hear my request first, think about it, and then decide. I don't have to know now."

"What is it Linda?" Norman asked.

"I want you to make some photographs of me."

"That is not a problem."

"It could be. I want you to photograph me for a book like you did for Maggie as I go through this pregnancy. If they turn out good enough, you will have another book you can publish."

"Of course I will. I would love to."

"Hear me out. I don't want just a shot of me in a pretty dress from the Maternity Mart, although a few like that would be nice. I've seen the ones you shot of Maggie in her dresses. Make mine like hers. I'm sure you can make a pregnant woman as attractive as you have made of her. But photograph the whole process from now until and including the baby's birth. Show the joy, the pain, the sweat and tears, and the heartbreaking loneliness without Kevin. Show me explaining the things to Deanna, with the doctors and nurses, working in the shop and all the things an expectant mother goes through and photograph me giving birth to Kevin Junior. Can you do that for me, Norman?"

"I can do that, Linda. I'll do it for you and Kevin. He's not with you any longer. I wonder if he would approve."

"He's with me. He's right in here, He'll approve."

265

Call Me Maggie

His camera fired as she lowered hands to her stomach and began rubbing.

"Why don't you catch up with me once a week and make photographs of whatever I am doing, feeding Deanna, working in the shop, taking a shower, getting an exam, or in church. Whenever you see a good picture, shoot it. I will put no restriction on you. Shot some of me nude as my stomach gets larger, even when it gets big as a barn. I will be like flower in the park while you take the pictures.

"You will be better than a flower in the park. Some could be risqué and compromise your modesty," he said.

"The hell with modesty! So you'll see a little flesh. You have already seen most it at the track and when I was nursing. Think about it. Talk it over with Maggie and get back to me."

Linda went to the sofa, lay down and opened the robe. Norman wondered if he could really make beautiful photograph of her as she massaged her swollen breasts and stomach. He shot one. A moment later he shot more.

"Linda is excited about you visiting the doctor with her. The doctor was hesitant but finally gave in. Linda told the doctor that her office would be filled with pregnant women once your pictures are seen and that brought her around," Maggie said at breakfast the next morning.

"I want to make pictures of her and the pregnancy as good as the ones I have made of you. And that's going to be tough. Your body is the only one I have photographed lately."

"Not really. By the time she gets a third bulge; you will be used to photographing her. If you're not, pretend she is me with my swollen belly sticking out."

An hour later Norman pushed the door closed behind himself as Linda rushed to Maggie with a hug. Norman waited as the two whispered and then he received a hug too.

"Mom has Deanna at her house. Dad's gonna oversee the shop. My appointment is at nine-thirty. We gotta go or we'll be late. I want to be at the shop before the lunch rush overwhelms my father."

Ten minutes later Norman was photographing Linda on a scale dressed only in an examination robe. A few minutes after that he made pictures as the doctor listened with a stethoscope pickup on Linda's bare stomach and chest.

"Everything is fine now. We will wait until February or March to make a decision on you getting back in race car. Meanwhile take it easy and get lots of rest," the doctor said.

If They Were Family

Norman photographed Linda straining to close the top button on her blouse. It remained unbuttoned with her bra showing as she left the office for the sandwich shop.

Her father finished taping a sign inside the shop window, raised his hands palm up and shrugged. Norman looked over his shoulder and read: "Champions."

During lunch Linda said, "I signed a lease yesterday to open a second shop at Price's Corner. If you can enlarge some of your pictures from the race track, Norman, we will decorate the store with them. I'd like a print of the layout you did in the newspaper the first year plus the ones Geographic printed too, please. You pick the ones you feel are best to make up the rest, but don't limit it to just shots of me. Include Kevin, Lionel, Ernest, the fans, the officials and lots of race cars. Better make four copies, we plan to open two more stores in the spring, and we will redecorate the original store. Lionel is welding legs onto tire rims for glass top tables. We are gonna use bucket seats as chairs. Everything will be racing oriented. The bar will have half a car above it. Maggie had a good idea and we are gonna use it."

Norman saw a glow in Maggie's eyes. Linda's announcement caught him off guard. Neither Maggie nor Linda had mentioned the idea to him. But Maggie usually kept ideas and plans to herself until they were completely formed. That was Maggie's way and she always had a surprise or two up her sleeve. The new stores and pictures of Linda's pregnancy were only two more examples of her secrets. Maybe she was keeping a few more in store for him, Norman told himself.

"Dad will manage the old shop as always and I will open the new one. Mom will take care of Deanna. If I can't race next year, Lionel wants to drive in my place. I don't want to wait until Junior is born to belt up again. But right now, we are going to make sure I'm up to it with the little one growing in my belly," Linda said.

"You will be up to it," Maggie assured her friend.

"I had better be. I already have sponsors committed to back me. It would be tough to resell sponsors on a new driver. They're buying into the oddity of a female driver who wins, not just a winning car with a new driver," Linda stated.

"Sounds like the Goldey-Beacom lessons are paying off for you. Racing seems like a business to you nowadays," Norman said.

"It is. Racing has to pay for itself and turn a profit, too. I'm gambling the reward money from Kevin's death and my parent's retire-

Call Me Maggie

ment savings to kick start the new stores and a new car. Plus I have to think seriously about my children's future."

"Kevin would be proud of what you are doing."

"I hope so. And I wish he could be a part of it all. I miss him a lot. And my daughter misses him even more. If you have time, stop by to see your goddaughter."

"We have a presents for her. I have some errands to run this afternoon and Norman will be at work," Maggie said.

"I will be over on my dinner hour," Norman said.

He made pictures as ribbon and paper were torn from the box.

"It's Barbie doll. Thank you Aunt Maggie," Deanna said.

"Bring your new doll with you, Honey. Mommy, Grandma, and you are going to look at a new race car."

"Uncle Norman has to go to work. Aunt Maggie has some shopping to do, too." Maggie said giving the child a hug.

Norman sat for a moment with his arm over the seat behind Maggie. He gently rubbed the back of her neck. She rubbed his leg as they watched snowflakes cover the windshield in a cold white blanket.

"Linda has some ambitious plans," Norman said.

"It's better she plans a future than mourn the past," Maggie said. "The restaurant idea is good. She plans to hang the first car from the ceiling for everyone to see. And she has applied for a liquor permit for more income. Her time in the business school was well spent and so were her races. Now it's time to cash in on both. She's got spunk."

"Lots of it!" Norman added.

"And Lionel will have a new car to tweak-out."

"And I have to get some weather pictures. They say we may get up to six inches. That may cancel your flight. You could use a few days on the ground."

"I could. Right now I have to tour the salvage yards for Champions decorations. Linda wants me to handle that. A little extra time would be helpful."

"You'll do fine. Your heart is in it, but you may get a little cold."

Norman and Maggie exchanged hugs. He went looking for weather pictures, Maggie cleaned the windshield of her Jeep and went looking for bucket seats, wheels, hubcaps and automobile paraphernalia.

Norman went looking for snow pictures. The viewfinder went dark as an exposure was made of forty-foot cedar trees with branches bending under their cold colorless load framed Old Saint James Church.

268

If They Were Family

Snow had covered the grass leaving only gray tombstones visible above their white blanket.

"That's a Christmas card, if I ever say one." Norman said.

Within two hours he had made shots of a hilltop farm, a covered bridge, Greenbank Mill, a half frozen fountain, and several of people shoveling snow for his editor to select from. Just after dark he made a shot of workmen adding red holiday lights to a pine tree atop the Hercules Tower framework. By Christmas Eve the city's tallest building would be encased in metal. At seven thirty the photo lab phone rang as Norman dried his prints and typed his captions.

"My flight is on. The snow ends down in Virginia. I'm going to Arkansas. Tell Linda the salvage yards will store my finds and deliver them, too. I've got to get going. See you in a couple days," Maggie said.

Norman delivered his prints and captions to the picture editor. The phone rang again as he re-entered the lab.

"I know it's too late to date, but is it too late for coffee and a talk?" Linda asked.

"No coffee, but I can talk all night."

"I'll put Deanna to bed and unlock the door."

Fifteen minutes later he was greeted by "Behind Closed Doors" playing on her stereo closed the Linda's front door.

"I'm back here. Bring your camera. Shoot what you see. I'll be in the tub in a minute. Shoot me in there too."

Norman dropped his parka on a chair and headed down the hallway.

"Do you think women are beautiful when they get pregnant and their belly gets bigger? I never asked him what he thought being married to an elephant before . . . before I had Deanna. I know Kevin liked my boobs when they got larger."

"Beauty comes from with the woman, not from the size of their chest or the flatness of their stomach. You won't have any problems no matter how you look outside."

Linda pushed the towel off her shoulders to reveal breasts nearly as large as they were when he listened to Deanna's heart beat six years earlier. Norman's camera clicked twelve times as Linda viewed her reflection in the mirror, then he stopped when the towel fell.

"If you get nervous, pretend I'm Maggie with a bigger belly."

"That's what she told me when I asked her about documenting your pregnancy. I'll try hard not to be nervous. You try too," he answered.

Call Me Maggie

She turned her head to face Norman, putting half her face in shadows, and asked, "Will my pictures be as beautiful as the ones you have made Maggie. If not, I will leave my clothes off until you get what you want."

"Of course they will be as good whether you are clothed or not. Maggie doesn't have to be naked to be beautiful. You don't either," he replied and raised the camera to his eye to capture her again.

Norman clicked a shot of her torso down to her waist and asked Linda to cover her pelvic area with the hand farthest from him before making a few full-lengths. Linda followed his suggestion as he moved closer and made pictures of her hand on her pelvis, stomach, breasts, and finished with a close-up of tears running down her cheeks ."Are you sure you wouldn't like to share a cup of coffee with your new subject?" Linda asked as she slipped her arms into a robe he knew was once Kevin's.

"Maybe a quick one. Maggie found some decorating items this afternoon. They will be stored and delivered when you are ready for them. You won't fail. The Kennedy's will be behind you," he replied.

"You Kennedy's have always been there for me, even when I got knocked up, and even more now that Kevin is gone. Maggie and Maddie too."

"We always will be."

"Am I crazy or what? Gambling every cent I have opening a new business, upgrading an old one that provided me an education as well as a good living for my parents, my daughter and me so I can find to fulfill a dream. Be straight with me. Don't hold back. Am I going off the deep end?" Linda questioned as he photographed her making coffee.

"Follow your gut feelings and work to make it work. Your parents are behind you. Your in-laws are with you, too. The success of the shop and your racing already proves you keep focused on your goals. Let your instincts be your guide. Failure is not the worst thing that can happen," Norman said.

"Failure is not an option although it is a big possibility. Nobody remembers driver who finish in second place," she said.

Linda went to sofa and sat on an arm with her hands nervously thumbing the pages of a racing magazine. Norman raised his camera and made three exposures of Linda sitting beneath a lighted lamp. Half way through she dropped magazine, moved to the sofa with him, curled her legs and fumbled with buttons on the robe.

"Do you ever get tempted by your models?"

270

If They Were Family

"The most tempting was a writer I worked with. But that's all it was, temptation. Maggie is the only woman I need."

"Am I tempting you now?"

"No. You're my brother's wife. You are a Kennedy now. Act like one!"

"And so is that little girl crying down the hall. For her sake, I will," Linda said.

Deanna was soon asleep. Linda followed almost immediately. Norman made a shot of his sister-in-law holding his niece to her shoulder in the near darkness, finished his coffee, covered them both, the let himself out. A solitary snowman sparkled in the streetlights as he drove away listening to "Winter Wonderland."

A snowplow moved on toward the lights of Odessa reflected in the sky of falling snow as Norman pulled into the driveway of the farmette. White tracks lead to Maggie's Jeep sitting snow-covered in front of the barn. She heard his Leica click before he laid it on a bedside table. A moment later he slipped behind her in the antique bathtub of bubbles surrounded by a dozens of lighted candles.

"The flight was canceled. I'm here till at least 6 a.m. Maybe longer if they don't get the runways cleared."

"I'm glad."

"Got a snowy farm story for your lady?" Maggie asked.

"When I was a boy back on the farm, flights a dozen and sometimes hundreds of airplanes would fly over the farm as flight crews practiced for bombing runs over Europe during World War II and wonder if they would come back. Now I look up each time a plane flies over wondering if you are on and if you are coming home after going off to the war," Norman began. "And when you come home, my heart races each time I see that you are back. It happened tonight when I saw you were not flying off in this snow storm. I know you love flying and want to fly as much as you can. It's a glamorous job for a glamorous lady."

"The glamour wore off a long time ago, Norman. It's a job that has to be done. If I had grown up like some girls and not had to be tough early, I might not have the stomach or stamina to handle the care my boys need. I had no father or brothers to learn from or to protect me from people that abused me. I realize now that my street life made me tough and able to endure what I have to see. It's very hard for me to tell a wounded soldier, sailor or marine they will be back to a normal life soon when I know they have months of rehabilitation that will be harder on them than going into the war zone. It is even more frustrating to think

Call Me Maggie

some of them will spend the rest of their lives in a hospital because parts of their bodies are shot away or in a psychiatric ward because their minds are gone. The numbers are growing and the injuries are more severe because the weapons are more gruesome."

Norman laid his hand on her shoulder and kissed her cheek.

"I'm glad you're here and not flying. The storm had me a worried," he said before realizing he was admitting concern for her safety.

"So am I. It's been a hard day and I needed to lay in this tub tonight. It would be better you joined me and shared the peacefulness of it with me."

The alarm went off at 5 a.m. Norman went to the kitchen to make coffee and then outside to warm and remove snow from Maggie's Jeep. He returned for coffee with Maggie and followed her until she turned off Route 13 at the airport. His morning was spent editing proofs. By noon Maggie was westbound from Arkansas with a plane full of young soldiers. She would make this trip and three more in snow before spring arrived and Norman would work during each one.

Early one morning when Maggie got back, Norman slipped a large box and many smaller one into the rear of the ragtop. An hour later he photographed Linda kneeling beside a red four-foot long racer with Deanna seated behind the steering wheel then photographed Linda removing her dress and slipping into a maternity top while Maggie held its Maternity Mart box.

Maggie returned to salvage yard searches when not flying. Norman often accompanied her in the mornings loading his jeep station wagon, but saying nothing while hoping Maggie's searches were good for her near breaking emotional state. Linda met with renovation people who were happy to have indoor winter work. Norman sent negatives of Linda to a lab specializing in extreme enlargements to be hung in the old and new Champions and met his newspaper assignments. He also made pictures weekly of Linda's pregnancy development and her new restaurants. By late February the Reed's sandwich became Champion's Restaurant, once doorways were cut connecting it to the building next door. Signs were hung on three sides of the Price's Corner Shopping Center and Champions II opened April first.

Norman and Maggie sat at a corner table at the opening. A three lens traffic signal light flashed above them. A starting line Christmas tree stood behind the car bar surrounded by more than a hundred patrons. Pictures, posters, magazine reprints, and oil company logos on old tin signs mixed with IRI, NHRA and NASCAR flags to decorate the

If They Were Family

walls. Portraits of racing superstars were mixed with regional heroes throughout the room that was now as much of a museum as it was a restaurant with a bar.

"I will be home every night for the next two months again. The dispatcher is having a baby too. I was requested to take her position. Can you handle seeing me every night when you get home?"

"I can handle it. But working till ten o'clock is still too late to date, unless we come here," Norman answered.

"I have another place in mind down Route 13 that's quieter and much more private."

"You have just been through a freezing hell putting these restaurants together. The dispatcher assignment came four months too late. You could have used the time home then."

"I did it, didn't I? And I totally enjoyed every minute, especially tonight seeing it all come together," Maggie said beaming with glee.

"You did it. How, I'll never know, but you did it."

May first Norman drove to Farmville and attended the wedding of Leanne and Bobby Joe. It was a combination May Day and wedding and a short vacation for both.

In June a few buds began appearing on the roses. Soon the field was full of color. Maggie broke her and Norman's father's flower guideline rule. She took hundreds of roses to the little Harrington church where Midge McGuiness became Mrs. David McGraw. The flowers filled the altar with color and the chapel with essence or roses.

Linda had ignored the doctor's request to slow down and began racing the weekend in May. By July Linda's stomach touched the steering wheel, but she kept burning rubber on the drag way and racing between restaurants. Linda raced until the pink Torino July Fourth weekend. Maddie and Lionel were always in the pits with Linda. She won twelve of her thirteen events. Her trophies were displayed at the Price's Corner Champions Two. Linda signed up for a Lemans class with Maggie was her partner. Maddie joined both in case Maggie would be away, and in case she too became pregnant. Linda gave Maddie the duties of assistant team crew chief and restaurant manager once the university classes finished. Maddie kept records of engine settings and run times as accurately as an IRS accountant and did the same at the restaurant. Both restaurants were a hit with young adults that once cruised through the Greenhill Drive-in or shared booths at the Charcoal Pit. They now lounged in Champions One and Two sipping rum or bourbon in their Cokes, guzzling Budweiser, or imported mineral water.

Call Me Maggie

Norman made pictures of the three in most of their classes. He kept three albums containing Linda's pictures in his newspaper locker which had only been shown to Judith and Maggie. The albums expanded in proportion to her stomach, and nearly as fast as Linda grew larger. One copy he would present to Linda when Kevin Junior arrived. The second was kept for his picture editor and a third for Judith Rawlins. The other he kept for himself, wondering if he would ever have another opportunity to photograph a woman awaiting a child. Linda, Maddie, and Maggie finished Le Maze classes too. Norman made more pictures. Judith sold a few stories on the classes illustrated with his pictures. Prints showing Maggie were added to her fourth album. Norman's artful figure shots of her became more seldom, but shots of her working with roses became frequent.

Clara and Bee Bee graduated four dozen replacements every three months only to have two thirds resign after a few flights tending the wounded coming back home. Norman and the picture editor stood over the editing table. Before them, sixteen photographs had been juggled into relative positions they would have once the layout was completed. All the pictures displayed a facet of sweet pea harvest from a panorama of combines creeping across the field to a box of quick frozen, ready to cook beans. Norman had spent two afternoons and one evening on the assignment with Midge's father.

Two raps came from the editor's office door.

"Linda is on her way to the hospital." Judith announced.

"You two scat. We'll finish this later," Hershel ordered both.

Ten minutes Judith parked her Camero next to Norman's Wagoneer near the St. Francis Hospital. Soon they were scrubbed and in the delivery room with Maggie, Linda and Maddie. Linda lay with bare legs in delivery table stirrups. Maggie was at her right shoulder, Maddie was at the left. All three were inhaling deeply, straining with reddened faces and puffing long exhales. Linda's legs separated a nurses and a doctor.

"Push again. Harder!" The doctor demanded.

"I am. Feels like a Peterbuilt truck is trying to come out of a one-car garage," Linda said in her usual candor.

"I see red hair. Push, push, push!" The doctor coached.

"Junior's father had red hair,"

"Relax and we'll try again. You have done this before. This time will be easier. Twice makes you a pro," the doctor assured Linda.

Norman's camera clicked again and again. Maggie mopped Linda's brow. Maddie massaged her shoulders. Judith made notes.

If They Were Family

"Two strong heartbeats," the nurse said holding a stethoscope to Linda's pelvis, then moved it to her chest.

"Good. Let's do it again." The doctor instructed.

Linda inhaled deeply. Maddie and Maggie copied Linda with equally deep inhales. Norman found himself copying them behind the clicking camera. Linda's face grimaced and reddened again. She made no other sounds or comments as a red-haired baby slipped into the doctor's waiting hands. He held the baby as the second nurse cleaned the crying baby's nose and washed its front. The doctor laid the newborn stomach to stomach on Linda and the nurse finished bathing the baby. A moment later the doctor placed the infant on Linda's chest. Maddie and Maggie sighed and relaxed. Norman tried to copy them. Judith moved closer, still making notes on a reporters pad.

"You got your wish. He is an eight pound boy," Linda heard one of the nurses say.

"I knew it! I really knew I was carrying a little Kevin this time," Linda yelled.

"Stay out of that racer for at least six weeks, Mrs. Kennedy," the doctor said.

"How about four weeks? I have some catching up to do and another mouth to feed," Linda replied.

"You've come a long way sister. You have a new mechanic to raise and train now. Listen to the doctor," Maggie whispered.

"I'll try. I'll really try," Linda promised.

Maggie leaned over and kissed Linda and the baby. Maddie did the same, making the sign of the cross over her chest and said, "That was the most wonderful thing I have ever seen. I'll be here when you have yours, Maggie."

Norman placed an album of 11x14 photographs before Linda. The doctor and nurses looked over Linda's shoulder while Norman turned the pages.

"Norman. They are beautiful. I knew you would make great pictures, but this far more than I expected. Even with the watermelon belly I look beautiful like Maggie," Linda said.

"That's a fine record of pre-natal development, Norman. I had many doubts when you approached me last fall. I don't have any now. Great job, young man," the doctor said, patting Norman's back.

"Judith may want to collaborate with you soon. She's writing the text for a book we are publishing. It should be an asset to expectant mothers and students too," he said.

Call Me Maggie

"Clinical, modest, sensitive and beautiful, too. I hope you get your book printed soon. I want a copy for each of my daughters, and so will every woman, or gynecologist in the country," the nurse said.

Norman closed the album, left it laying across Linda's stomach below Kevin Junior and kissed her forehead. A moment later Norman and Judith were invited to join Linda's Lemans partners celebrating with Kevin Junior's grandparents and Deanna. Everyone hugged everyone. Norman, Maggie, Maddie, Judith, the doctor and each nurse received a cigar from Kevin Junior's grandfather.

"Makes you want to be a parent," Maggie said to Norman.

"Yes it does! Are you trying to tell me something?"

Norman had not gotten the answer he hoped for when Maggie replied, "No, I'm just that I'm happy for Linda."

Shadowy images flickered on a black and white television as a crackling voice said: "One small step for man. A giant leap for mankind."

The carefree days of the sixties were coming to an end. One of John Kennedy's dreams had come true; America had put not one, but two men on the moon and brought them safely back home before the end of the 1960's decade, yet something more frightening was occurring back on earth; fear of a nuclear attack from the Soviet Union. Cities designated and stockpiled fallout shelters while homeowners dug pits in their yards, lined them with steel and concrete, stocked them with food and water and waited for life on earth to end under mushroom clouds.

During the winter, Lionel upgraded the racecar again. Norman shot a new poster of Linda and in April 1970, she began appearing at the tracks again each weekend. This year Linda's purses grew instead of her stomach. At the end of the season she claimed another track championship.

Maggie still moved her boys across the Pacific, yet military life for them became more difficult. Constant harassment lead many to stop wearing uniforms in public, especially when hitchhiking, fearing they would be run over by a fanatical protestor. Countless peace touting flower children passed out cheap flowers on the street, in train stations and especially in airports. Maggie could expect a dozen or more if she entered an airport terminal, yet the war continued.

In May 1970, troops were sent into Thailand, Laos and Cambodia on South Vietnams western borders. Giant B-52 bombers blasted quarter mile wide paths a mile long clear of all living organisms. Other planes sprayed defoliants on millions of acres of Vietnamese forests in

If They Were Family

an effort to eliminate the forest canopy that hid Viet Cong and North Vietnamese soldiers.

Patriotism eroded even among American servicemen and especially the South Vietnamese army. Americans soldiers adapted an antiwar song, "Where Have All the Flowers Gone?" as their song of protest.

Universities that closed in the spring of after Ohio National Guardsmen fired shots into demonstrators at Kent State reopened. War babies celebrated their thirtieth birthdays. Everything was changing.

Mod clothes replaced blue jeans. Coffee houses and folk music became passé. Disco music began replacing rock and roll. The Beatles had split and didn't regroup. Songs like "Dancing Queen," and "Play That Funky Music" replaced "American Woman" and "American Pie" on listener lists on the radio and stereo players. A group of gay men named themselves Men at Work and became a sensation singing "YMCA." Candles gave way to lava lamps as mood makers. Tieless leisure suits replaced coats, ties and blazers. Miniskirts grew shorter. Drug use became rampant. Military life had become even more difficult. Constant harassment led many airmen, soldiers, sailors, Marines, and airmen to stop wearing uniforms in public, especially when hitchhiking. GI haircuts were out of style. Long hair was allowed if didn't tough military personnel's collar. Still Maggie wrapped her hair on the back of her head, put on her flight attendants mask, stepped onto planes to accompany young boys across the Pacific. The length of hair did not matter to the wounded, shell shocked, and shattered men who needed her care on their trip home.

Maggie, Leanne, and Midge kept flying replacements to Southeast Asia as the war went on in spite of peace talks in Paris. North Vietnam prisoner of war camps became crowded, mostly with Air Force and Navy flyers. Some prisoners were held up to seven years. Most were starved, abused and beaten. Some died in the prisons. Some would survive, get themselves elected to Congress, the Senate, or the Presidency in future years and send other young men into war and harm's way.

More men were being draft each month. Some went to Canada or Mexico to avoid their two years of service. In later years later years the draft would be eliminated and the void filled by reservists, or National Guardsmen and women.

The sixties had brought a time of social change. Young women abandoned their Banlon sweaters, pointed bras and went braless, while others insisted they should be permitted to join their brothers and cousins on the battlefield. Sleeveless tank tops were the rage. Sneakers and

277

Call Me Maggie

flip-flops replaced shoes. Army shirts and field jackets replaced traditional clothes in rebellion to older morees. Young men wore their hair longer than most of the flight attendants, due in part to a fad started by singers from England. Clara had two sons and was awaiting a third while keeping her position as a flight school instructor. Birth control pills were marketed, condom sales slumped, and carefree lovemaking was rampant. Sex clubs hosted scores of patrons who could make love with as many partners as they wanted twenty four hours a day. Bars featuring topless dancers became a rage with both men and liberated women. The previous summer a "Concert for Peace and Love" had been held on a rain soaked field near Woodstock, New York. Smaller ones were conducted around the country. Some were concerts, some were peace rallies, some were drug fests, some were love-ins, and some were full blown riots demanding peace and love.

In May of 1970 Ohio National Guardsmen were called to control a protest at Kent State University with live bullets in their rifles. Nine students were killed and twenty-eight injured igniting protests on campuses across the nation. Dozens of colleges closed. Students were sent home for the spring term. Colleges and universities re-opened for summer classes, but ROTC classes were reduced or abandoned. Students like Bobby Joe and Lionel who had served in Europe or Vietnam were shunned and chastised. Lionel enrolled at the University of Delaware. Bobby Joe received GI Bill assistance and continued his Computer Science and Technology studies at Georgetown University. His new dream was to add a master's degree, earn a doctorate and return to Virginia Military Institute as Robert E. Lee had done nearly a hundred years earlier. He told Leanne, Maggie and friends he didn't need ten fingers. Everyone he knew used only two fingers on a keyboard, he would get by with metal arms and a pair of pencils to surf the computer.

Universities that closed in the spring of after Ohio National Guardsmen fired shots into demonstrators at Kent State reopened. War babies celebrated their thirtieth birthdays.

Flying to Europe and Asia plus, maintaining a friendship with Linda, Midge, and Leanne, plus training her horses and raising roses with Pop Pop left Maggie little time to view and enjoy the pictures or the ones brought from her grandparent's farm. She rarely thought of them except when house cleaning and then only briefly. On lonely evenings waiting for Norman to come home, her thoughts returned to her mother and her sister, but she never attempted to contact either.

278

8

The Girls Will Be Like You

By 1973, the war had gone on for ten years and now more half a million American young men were in Viet Nam. Military life at home became even more difficult. Constant harassment led many soldiers, sailors, Marines and airmen to stop wearing uniforms in public, especially when hitchhiking, fearing that anti-war activists might run over them. Patriotism eroded. Countess peaceniks passed out cheap flowers on the streets, at train stations and especially in airports. Maggie could expect a dozen or so if she entered a terminal.

People who had sat in line to buy gas a year earlier now drove fuel efficient little cars made in Japan or Germany. Midge now drove an English Triumph Spitfire up and down U.S. 13.

Everything was changing. Hippies had drifted away from most of their communes. Only diehards remained.

Richard Nixon had been elected president a second time. A young lawyer from Delaware not old enough to be sworn into the U. S. Senate was elected to replace the aging governor and reached the legal age before his inauguration.

Maggie established a routine of writing one letter per day to protest the war. She had half a dozen strong letters and only had to change the greetings before typing. She sometimes included dime store reprints of her photographs. Her letters never mentioned that she was an airline stewardess or flight attendant as they now wanted to be called. Stewardess and steward titles became socially incorrect. Non-gendered flight attendant covered her young women and the two males who wanted fancier titles.

Midge and Leanne continued to join Maggie and copy her methods, dedication, compassion and letter writing. Midge convinced some in the Harrington church to write as well. Leanne helped hospital pa-

279

Call Me Maggie

tients, university student, and the non visible silent majority Farmville residents to write letters. Midge established another crusade to her list; campaigning against pornographic movies. A year after its release, X-rated "Deep Throat" was still drawing record movie goers in to movie theaters. Dozens of other feature length films depicting explicit erotic behavior soon followed.

The airline added two refurbished DC-8 jets carrying twice the Connie's load to their fleet, but had trouble keeping enough attendants to fully staff their planes. Salary increases to attendants filled only part of the void.

Maggie could expect extra flights each month. Rest time on the trips was reduced to six hours off duty, twelve hours on. She returned to the farm after each flight low on energy and overcome with fatigue. Leanne anticipated her train ride to Washington when she could rest and doze for two hours. Midge's rest time was reduced by five hours driving up and down the highway. Clara and Bee Bee graduated four dozen replacements every three months only to have two thirds resign after a few flights.

Maintenance hangers at the Wilmington Airport kept twenty-four hour schedules. Much of the work was done on hanger aprons, rain or shine. More manpower was needed in Saigon and filled by Vietnamese civilians hired to refuel and reload the planes, reduce ground time and keep the planes in the air, a task they did many times a day.

As the hired assistants and flight crew readied a DC-8 for a flight home, Midge noticed an emaciated you man hobbling toward the plane between two helpers. His open gown left little doubt his body was barely more than a living skeleton.

"Wait for a stretcher," Midge yelled out.

"No stretcher! I walked into his hell hole. I am gonna walk out," he tried to demand.

Midge had corpsmen place the weak soldier near the crew area.

Later in the flight she took the seat beside her latest charge, then, asked, "Do you need anything? Juice, soft drink, or coffee?"

"No, just get me home."

"Where is home?"

"Redden Crossroads. That's in Delaware."

"I know Redden Crossroads and the state forest there. My home is just south of Georgetown."

"I went to school as Sussex High in Georgetown."

280

The Girls Will Be Like You

"So did I. Majored in elementary-ed, but took this job to get away from Dad's pea farm."

"What's your name? Mine is Rooster Peterson."

"Rooster, I'm Midge McGinnis. One of the other attendants wears your MIA bracelet. I wear one for my cousin Michael. I think you played ball with him at Vo-Tec. I'm sorry I did not recognize you. You're not in your football uniform."

"I've lost a little weight. I'm a little older too. That's probably why you didn't recognize me. Been over here five years. Spent nearly four of them dieting in a tiger pit."

"What's a tiger pit?"

"It's a pit dug into the ground with bamboo sides and top where the VC kept us prisoners out in the jungle."

"How did you survive?" she asked while trying to keep her stomach from erupting.

"Every day I counted my dad's chickens and dreamed grilling up a few. Hadn't been for the insects and rats, I would have starved like some of my other pit neighbors did. The Cong weren't generous with their food. There weren't very many Colonel Saunders or Popeye chicken stands in the jungle. When I get home I'm gonna take my back pay and open a little chicken place by the highway for travelers headed to Rehoboth or Lewes," Rooster said.

The wrenching inside Midge overpowered her. She excused herself, went to the restroom and emptied her stomach. Fifteen minutes later she returned with a Coke and two steaming chicken legs.

"It's Frank Perdue's chicken. I hope your dad raised it," Midge announced when she rejoined him.

"If it was raised on Delmarva, that's good enough for me."

Midge helped Rooster down the steps at Andrews Air Force Base to a waiting ambulance, then, gave him a long hug.

"I will be up to Redden Crossroads for some of your Sussex County roadside chicken real soon. Count on cooking up enough for me to take back to the boys still over there," she whispered between sobs,

Midge stopped at Redden Crossroads on the way home, delivered a Polaroid picture of Rooster, herself, another stewardess, and a MIA bracelet to Rooster's family, then spent the evening relaying the conversation she had with Rooster on the flight back..

The next morning she and seven other attendants readied the awaited 747-400 that had been added to their fleet. Its upper deck alone carried as many an old Connie. The lower one held four times as many.

Call Me Maggie

It could reach Vietnam with twice the passengers of a 747 or DC-8 with one refueling stop and cut the air time by a full day. It could leave at daybreak, go to Europe, and be home before dinner got cold or before Norman's newspaper was put to bed and the eleven o'clock news came on TV. One 747 plane could carry twenty eight hundred troops across the Atlantic or Pacific in one week. Today's flight would take them to Germany.

A concrete wall had replaced barbed wire in Berlin to keep East Berliners from escaping to the west. More soldiers were being sent to Europe in a tit-for-tat build-up unequaled since World War II.

"David held a wonderful gospel sing at his church Saturday night," Midge beamed as she packed for a Monday flight.

"I'm sorry I missed it. Next time let me know," Maggie said.

"The pea pickers were at it again this weekend. The singers got me wound up and the pea pickers kept me up all night," Midge yawned.

"I sold and delivered my yearling stallion. Not too exciting other than counting heron nests along the creek. Fifteen this year, down two from last summer," Maggie said.

"Bobby Joe and I went to Stratford Hall to see General Lee's birth place. We even swam in the bay a while," Leanne added.

"Tell him Cousin Norman and Cousin Maggie say hello. Never mind, we'll tell him ourselves. I'd like to see if those computers can do all the things they say can be done. If they do, maybe I will trade in my old typewriter and pick and peck on it,"

They left for a short hop to Fort Dix, New Jersey and a longer one to Germany. Four advisor-consultants were the only passengers returning on what they believed should be a flying romper room in the 747's upper deck lounge area. Each man reeked of German stout and cheap cologne. Eight flight attendants for four consultants seemed to be good odds in the men's favor for a party. One cornered Midge at the stairway.

"Bring me a drink and one for you," the man demanded.

"I don't drink and we don't carry drinks on military charters," Midge replied.

"Then I'll have myself a cute little stewardess instead," he said as he pushed Midge to the floor between seats.

Maggie and Leanne hear her scream. In the next instant Leanne relived her graduation night. Maggie felt Vinnie striking her and forcing himself upon her again. Old pains returned to both as they raced up the

The Girls Will Be Like You

stairway, two steps at a time. They found Midge beneath the man, still screaming.

Maggie pulled the man off Midge, raised her knee hard between his legs and lifted it again as he folded forward. Two others grabbed the man, and dragged him toward his companions. Four scratches ran from his temple to his chin and nose was bleeding. Maggie and Leanne lifted their flight mate. Midge's lower lip bled from a cut matching her upper teeth. He blouse was ripped and disheveled.

"Cool him down or we'll freeze his ass in the cargo hold," Maggie said.

Midge limped toward the stairs, clinging to Leanne's arm.

"I'll pull your contract for this," the bleeding man said.

"And I'll feed you your own balls for dinner," Maggie answered. "Now go back to your seat and stay there."

Descending the stairs, Maggie realized she had not said anything so vulgar since coming off the streets of Philadelphia nine years earlier. A moment later, she raced to the lavatory and vomited.

"We got to her in time. She's bruised and shaken, but she wasn't raped. Maybe a twisted ankle, as well," Leanne said when Maggie returned.

"You can't drive home tonight, Midge. Come to the farm with Leanne and me." Maggie said. "We'll take care of you. We know what a woman feels like when attacked by a man."

The next morning the farmhouse was empty, except for Norman and the parakeets. He found Maggie, Midge and Leanne having coffee on the patio while Midge soaked her foot in a bucket usually kept in the barn. Around nine he photographed them walking through the pasture with three white horses trailing as Midge limped with her arms around Maggie and Leanne.

Midge returned to the airport two weeks later when her lip and ankle had healed. Not to fly, but to resign.

The annual Memorial Day parade was canceled, but the Fourth of July air show and airport open house was held. Aerospace and jet-age were new catch phrases. A dozen astronauts had walked on the moon. The public flocked to air shows for a glimpse of space displays and new aircraft, in particular, the new Concorde passenger plane capable of carrying one hundred passengers at twice the speed of sound like many of the new fighters. Air travel had replaced passenger planes on most travel corridors where speed was essential. Fifty-five mile an hour automo-

Call Me Maggie

biles, buses, and eighty mile an hour trains were losing the race with six hundreds mile per airplanes. Only a few train and bus lines survived.

Military recruiters from all service branches substituted air shows for patriotic parades to snare recruits. Maggie, Clare and Bee Bee spent the day conducting tours of gleaning DC-8s, 707s and 747 passenger planes while recruiting new flight attendants.

"This is my home away from the farm. It's a far site from sitting on the porch of a Chester row house and watching planes come and go from Philadelphia International," Maggie told Norman.

"You've come a long way in eleven years, Maggie. You have seen more of the world than I can dream of seeing."

"Mostly I see terminals and clouds."

As the afternoon wore on and the crowd waned, Maggie was drawn to a small sleek fighter plane. A plaque said it was a P-51 Mustang. She remembered her grandfather telling her mustangs were horses born in the wild and difficult to tame. He sometimes said her father had lots of mustang spirit in him. Maggie wondered if she had some if her father's mustang spirit in her.

This Mustang stood on two tall struts with wheels under each wing raising its nose high enough in the air for its propeller to clear the ground in take offs and landings. Its tail rested low on a smaller wheel giving the plane the appearance of being ready to leap into flight even when parked. Two "Raggedy Anne" dolls had been painted on its noses. Three colored circles containing the letters "M&M" were painted under the dolls. The name "Monty Johnson" appeared under its clear bubble capped cockpit.

"Are you Monty Johnson?" Maggie asked the pilot.

"No, Miss. Monty died in Korea, but this was his plane in Europe," he answered.

"Did you know him?"

"Yes, I knew him well. I was his classmate, wingman, and best man at his wedding."

"Tell me about him and this airplane," she pressed on.

"We began flying together in Europe about the time he met his wife. He named his first plane Charlene after her. He came home had two daughters before we joined up again in Korea. He named this one M&M after his daughters. By then jets had replaced propellers. He dreamed of buying this plane when it became surplus and bringing it back home, but some MIG shot him and his jet down. I bought it and brought it home for him. Raising four daughters took all my salary and

The Girls Will Be Like You

my wife's too, so the plane sat in a Nevada hanger until last year. Now that the M&M flies again, I spend some of my free time with her. My week day job is in one of the jetliners over there. Your uniform is Intercontinental, but I haven't seen you on any of my flights. Climb up and look the M&M over."

Maggie climbed up, looked into the cockpit and saw a picture of her mother and twin girls mounted on the instrument panel. A stack of brochures containing a picture of a tall, thin man standing by the paintings lay inside. A picture identical to the one of her dresser appeared inside the brochure.

"My father was Montgomery Johnson, Junior. My mother, Charlene Windsor came from England. They met during the war, but she never talks about my father. My sister is named Madeline, I am Mary Anne Johnson, but my father called me Maggie. You can call me Maggie, too."

"Maggie, I'm Skip Snyder. Are you mother and sister here today? I haven't seen Charlene since she came to the states. I've tried dozens of phone books since I joined Intercontinental, but there was no Charlene Johnson listed," he said.

"No. They are not here," she answered.

"May I take you up for a hop in the "M&M?" Snyder asked.

"I would like that very much," she replied.

Maggie slipped on a helmet as Skip strapped her in the rear seat where radios and a fuel tank once sat. Soon the plane zoomed down the runway, leaped into the air, and headed toward the river. Leaving the river it buzzed past a lighthouse, hiccupped over fences, turned on its side and threaded one wing between two trees.

"Monty and I few low missions like this nearly two hundred times. He used to say it allowed him to stay close to the earth without having to do the chores," Snyder announced in her earphones.

The plane turned right over the marsh and few toward Odessa.

"Take that little farm between the village and the river. We would line up on it five miles out, throttle back, glide in, race the engine, scare the farmers, and be gone before anyone on the ground knew we were coming."

Maggie watched the farmette come closer and disappear beneath the Mustang's.

Within moments her flight ended. The engine silenced. Maggie unstrapped herself, but remained in the plane studying the pictures.

"Say hello to Charlene and give her a hug for me."

Call Me Maggie

"I would like to fly with you and learn more about my father," Maggie said, avoiding further mention of her mother.

"I'll request you be added to my crew."

Tuesday morning she asked Norman to take a ride with her.

"Where would you like to go?" he asked.

"First to the airport, then to Chester to see my mother."

"Is something wrong?" he asked.

"I went to see her yesterday. I cannot allow what I found to continue. She has regressed in to childhood. She is unable to provide life's most basic need for her herself. She needed me before I left and she needs me more now. She is weak, alone, and in despair. She missed my father more than I knew. She gave Madeline and me life, but her despair and broken heart prevented her from giving us the nurturing we needed. I found your family and tried to forget mine. I can't forget she is still my mother. I moved her to a nice nursing home yesterday."

Later that afternoon a few of her row house furnishings were taken to the farm. Others were stored as she had done years earlier with Grandmother Johnson's belongings. Maggie's few free evening were spent with her mother. She took fresh flowers, fruit baskets, and colorful new clothes on each visit. She would read children's books or brush her mother's hair as both counted strokes.

Norman's father had coffee at the farm many mornings before tending the rose field in what was once the south pasture. On other mornings he would train Maggie's horses to carriage harness or saddle.

A 747 circled over the farmette and headed back toward the airport while the hot summer sun burned down on Maggie, Pop Pop and their rose bushes. Norman had left around 10 a.m. to photograph the Philadelphia Phillies home game. Each wore long sleeved shirts even though the thermometer on the barn read 92 degrees and the humidity gauge read 79 percent. Pop Pop had made passes with a roto-tiller between the roses, leaving weeds close to the bushes for Maggie to cut down by hand and a goose neck hoe, a task that left scratches and blisters on their hands.

"Take it easy Pop. You're not a youngster any longer," Maggie advised him.

"I can go to meet Saint Peter from a rocking chair as easily as I can go from the field. I'd prefer to go from the rose field. My heart has always been in the soil," Pop Pop answered.

"A new crew is training in that bird. I'll be on it is less than thirty hours and we still have lots more roses to weed," Maggie said.

The Girls Will Be Like You

"We will do what we can today and tomorrow. Norman and I will finish up in the mornings when it is cooler. He can still handle a hoe. He's hoed weeds alongside me since he was six years old."

"It's roses and flowers now, not cotton or corn," Maggie stated

"Or tomatoes, cantaloupe, and cabbage as we grew the last two years we farmed. Planted two acres of each for extra money. Marketed the first pickin' and the price dropped so low it didn't cover the truck to haul the next load to the market. A year's work and income lost. I didn't even have money to move off the farm when we decided to give up."

"Wasn't there anything you could with them?"

"Rush to can as many of the tomatoes as we could. Pickle the cabbage and cantaloupe, and invite the neighbor to do the same. That way some of it was used and not wasted. Cows and mules don't take to tomatoes and melons well. But our hogs fattened up fine. Hadn't been for the tobacco crop and fat hogs, we would have starved. I still have trouble eating cantaloupe and bacon," Pop Pop said.

"That must have been difficult for you and Mom Mom."

"It was about the same as when she carried our first child full term only to have the baby die during birth."

"With the roses, we can keep them in the ground for another year. I dry their blossoms for potpourri, make lots of rose petal tea and hope the market gets better next year," Maggie said.

Midge's Triumph Spitfire pulled up the lane stopping at the rose field fence. Midge and David crawled through the fence and joined the rose tillers. Midge and Maggie embraced as the two men greeted with introductions and handshakes, as David waited for his hug from Maggie.

Pop Pop guided the tiller to the barn where it would be washed and parked in an unused stall. He opened a barrel, put grain in a bucket for the colt, and his sister to share with their mother, and then gave each a pad of hay. He washed his hands before rejoining the others. Maggie had cut more than three dozen rose buds, soaked an old feed bag, wrapped the stems and bud, and then wrapped them again in a dry bag before handing them to the couple.

"They should keep fine until you get them home or to the church," Maggie said.

"Or the nursery school we have set up the church basement. You can find her there all day since she has not been flying," her husband said.

Call Me Maggie

"There was a real need for childcare down there where everyone either farms or commutes north to work, so we started one. The community college got involved with a few courses and credit for students who work with us. We are on our way to Wilmington for a review with the city campus dean to set one up for city families. We are going to need one at home soon. David and I are going to be parents this winter," Midge said.

"That's great, congratulations," Maggie said hugging them again.

"It would be a lot easier if I weren't flying all around the world seeing the things I see. We think we are doing something good for our church members and the pea farmers too. It satisfies my need for a challenge and helps them too. But I will be flying with you a few more months and after our baby comes, too. You're not loosing me yet." Midge said.

"Good, I still need you to help with our boys. But a basement full of kids is a great challenge. I'm sure you will do as well with them as you have done with our big boys," Maggie said.

"At least the little ones won't be hitting on me! How is Norman?" Midge asked.

"As busy as ever. How about some lunch?" she replied.

Maggie serves bows of blueberries and plates of cantaloupe to the couple and Pop Pop. He only nibbled at the melon before him.

At 1:45, the couple left for their meeting in the city. Maggie and Pop Pop returned to the field, humming and singing in rhythm with their hoes striking soil until his thoughts turned to a young couple and two little boys working their crops while three toddlers played on an old quilt beneath a poplar tree at the edge of a rock filled cotton field. Maggie's thoughts wandered through her grandmother's flower garden.

Pop Pop declined dinner with Maggie insisting that he had hundreds of thirsty cuttings to be watered.

Maggie fed and watered the horses, geese and birds, then rested for a few minutes on the fence staring at the rose field before watering plants grown from seeds she had salvaged from Grandmother Johnson's garden twelve years earlier or ones Pop Pop gave her.

After a short trip to the mailbox, Maggie turned on the bathroom radio, ran water, and settled into the tub for a long soaking under mountains of bubbles. Warmth not found in the bath came over Maggie as she thought about Norman. A long lace topped white dress hung near the tub waiting for her bath to conclude. Long dresses were still her pre-

288

ference when not in uniform or denim work clothes that she wore around the farmette. After each bath she chose one from her collection that ran from the window to the corner in the large bedroom. A collection of nearly three dozen found in her grandmother's closet had been supplemented with others she found in thrift stores and yard sales. She usually wore one or sometimes a gown after her bath and during the few quiet evenings she shared with Norman before their fireplace on the patio under starlight.

Maggie would return to the tub again with Norman as they soaked by candlelight, talked and caressed each other. He was still uneasy seeing her nude unless they were making photographs, sharing a bubble bath or sleeping together. He now shot fewer nudes, but still carried a Leica his shoulder and still documented almost everything she did in his presence. Ideas came more slowly than in their first few years together, and she was gone more, too. Three albums were now dedicated to candid and clothed pictures. The original one Linda and Leanne saw now contained the collection of nearly five hundred nudes. She hoped a book of the pictures would be published someday. They were Norman's work and they showed her changing from a young girl from the streets of Philadelphia and Chester into a mature young woman. And they were a record of her life with Norman. He had photographed her with Presidents Kennedy, Johnson and Nixon, several senators, numerous local figures, firemen, farmers, Linda, Kevin, Deanna, Midge and Leanne, and countless other people she would remember viewing the album. He kept his promise and never published a picture identifying her.

She still had the same figure that she had in 1962. Her hair was a little longer now and more blonde than strawberry. Sunshine and the time spent outdoors on the farm had made her freckles darker, even though she wore a hat, long sleeved shirts, and slacks when working outside as she had today. A little "Cover Girl" hid the freckles in planned close-ups, but usually Norman's photographs were spontaneous and the freckles were visible unlike the overly airbrushed shot she saw in magazines abandoned on the plane. Posing for him still aroused amorous and sensual feeling in the body she nourished with good food, farm work, and exercise on the farm or when her plane was readied for the flight abroad or back home.

Maggie had many other achievements that made her proud of her life since driving away from American Bandstand with two strangers. Her work with the soldiers she took to war and the ones she tended coming back shared the top of her list with her relationship with Norman. She could not give up one for the other.

She was proud of an idea that brought movies to her passengers on long flights. Lionel had converted a movie projector to aircraft current and she could project movies for her passengers. When video recorders came on the market, he converted a few of those for her, too.

Her white horses sold for top dollar. Many of her plants were photographed by Norman and nearly two dozen now appeared in catalogs, and on calendars or greeting cards. Other women had school pictures and yearbooks. Maggie had calendars, greeting cards, and horse photographs to cherish along with a file of thank you letters from speeches or demonstrations she gave on life saving and flowers. Raising flowers, vegetables, and her horses satisfied the procreation instincts, she believed, yet something was still missing from the busy life she had made for herself.

She had not traveled out of the state for an anti-war demonstration since 1968 when she suffered a concussion and a few fractured ribs at the hands of Chicago policemen in Grant Park. She preferred her own methods of protest with letters and pictures, or direct contact, rather than taking part in demonstrations toting a sign in public.

Maggie had enjoyed an hour of solitude when the phone rang. "Hold any plans you have for dinner. I'm bringing ball park hotdogs. Be there by eleven," Norman said.

Before eleven Maggie lit torches on the patio and candles in the kitchen while waiting for rose tea to heat. She had planned to grill fresh red snapper, yellow squash, and green peas for their starlight patio dinner. Headlights on the barn told her Norman was driving up the lane. A moment later, she met him with a smile, a warm kiss and a lengthy embrace. She noted that his body had not changed in twelve year either except for the limp and receding hairline. His Tony Curtiss curl was receding with his hairline as middle age approached. He limped more than had usually for the past year. She assumed he had done a lot of kneeling at the game.

"I'm so happy to see you tonight." Maggie whispered.

"What makes you so happy to see me tonight?"

"I have had a wonderful day since you left and want to share it with you. I'll be leaving tomorrow and won't see you again for nearly a week," she said.

"Well it's good that your day was wonderful. Will you tell me about it over these tube steaks," he said, heading for the radar range.

The Girls Will Be Like You

Maggie knew Norman held her career, her peace efforts and her farm activities in high esteem. He had complimented herself imposed additional flights, promotions, raises, and peace initiatives. When she substituted for attendants who took vacations, went on honeymoons, or had their babies, or took up slack during personnel shortages, he let her go and filled many of her roles on the farm. He gave her time to fly, be an activist and be a friend to Linda, Maddie, Midge and Leanne as well as companion to his father. He was always there for her when she needed a sounding board.

A buzzer signaled the tea and re-warmed hot dogs were ready.

Maggie had set the farmhouse up when demands on her lessened just after they moved from the city. Little had been added besides the electronic food cooker, a programmable coffee maker that had morning coffee ready when they awoke and a Kitchen-aid that sliced, minced, or pureed vegetables more quickly than either she or Norman could do by hand. Their kitchen contained old appliances. They had two enamel stoves, one gas and the one from Grandmother Johnson's, which burned wood. Their sink had been mounted in a table rather than a cabinet. An oak ice box, newsprint type case and pie safe that served as cabinets were older than Maggie and Norman combined. A hand cranked ice cream maker still found use whenever they craved ice cream or sherbet Their kitchen was locked in time between bareness of Alabama or Chester County poverty and the modern conveniences they added did everything except plan the menu.

Maggie took a teapot and cups to the patio table. Norman followed with their hotdogs limping past two large screens holding drying petals. The petals would be sold in gift shops along with lavender she was drying on screens in the barn's lean-to. Candles were centered among floating rose petals in six white bowls surrounding an urn of long stemmed red roses on the table greeted them.

"Your father plowed the entire field today. We weeded half of it. Midge and David stopped by. They have started a day-care in the church, and are trying to get one set-up in Wilmington. They will be having a baby this winter. I took a long bath and daydreamed of you. Glad you are back. How was your day?" Maggie said between bites of onion and sauce laden hotdogs.

"Just another baseball game until Boots Powell put a line drive on my ankle. I'm not sure if the applause was for him hitting a fowl, or me crawling off the field."

Call Me Maggie

"I'm sure it was for you surviving a hit from him. Did you bring the ball home as a souvenir?"

"Heck no! The first baseman grabbed it and threw it to the plate. I should have gotten credit for an assisted out."

"We will soak it after our tea," Maggie assured him.

She knew unless he had been seriously injured, he would have kept the incident to himself, just as his father never mentioned his cuts or scrapes until someone noticed and put Band-Aids on him. Maggie told herself Norman was getting more like his father each day as she prepared warm salty water to soak his ankle under starlight. She got no squabble from when she insisted he soak it again before bedtime under a foot of bubbles.

Norman's limp had lessened when he brought coffee to Maggie as she slipped into her blazer a few minutes following a 4 a.m. alarm. A fleeting flash caught his eye as the sun reflected off a westbound 747 over the farm as he fed the animal just before daylight. It was barely noticeable as he drove to Philadelphia for another game that evening.

Thirty six hours later, Maggie momentarily froze as she was about to leave the Saigon terminal when she saw a skeletal figure in a wheelchair. Visions of Rooster Peterson flashed before her eyes. The freeze melted enough for Maggie to run and kneel before the wheelchair. The figure had strawberry blonde hair.

"Madeline?" Maggie asked with her voice trembling.

"Maggie?" came her questioning answer.

"What has happened to you, Madeline?"

Madeline did not respond. Her attendant spoke for her.

"She has been sleeping in the streets and starving," answered the attendant.

"Oh, no," Maggie cried out.

"She is a lot better than when the old Mama son brought her to our orphanage. We are sending her stateside. It's getting too dangerous here for Caucasian on the streets alone, much less one that's as helpless as she is," the attendant added.

Maggie noticed he wore twin bars on one lapel, a small cross on the other, separated by an orchid cleric's collar and black shirt.

"We've got a spot on a Hercules transport and a room in our hospice waiting for her," the chaplain said

"She's my sister, I'll take her home. My plane has nurses and she will receive great care."

The Girls Will Be Like You

"She has been off the horse nearly four weeks. Four more and she'll be on her feet again," he said. "Would you like to go with your sister, Madeline?"

Madeline remained quiet.

"Where is the hospice, Chaplain?"

"Exton, Pennsylvania," he answered.

"That's practically in my backyard. Our mother is in West Chester. I live a few miles south of Wilmington."

If Madeline knew Maggie had said West Chester instead of Chester, neither the chaplain nor Maggie could tell.

"Madeline, go with your sister. I will see you at Harmony House when I finish here. It may be a while, but when I see you, you will be well and strong."

The chaplain made the sign of the cross over Madeline' bowed head. Maggie pushed the wheelchair and her sister to the airplane. Leanne helped carry Madeline up the steps into the cabin. Madeline reclined in an attendant seat and remained silent until after the plane refueled in Anchorage.

"How is Mom?" Madeline asked.

"In a nursing home getting better. She has good days and better ones. I try to see her when I'm not flying. She gets great care. Just as great as you are going to get when we get home,"

"I guess your dream to be a stewardess came true. How long have you been one?"

"Long enough to care for passengers like you who need my help. A little over twelve years, now."

"I'm happy for you, Maggie. Are you married?"

"No just a little farmhouse and some horses instead of kids," Maggie answered.

"No husband?

"No husband. Just Norman, the man who helped me leave you and Mom and hid me from Vinnie Gambini and his gang," Maggie said.

"Vinnie took up with me after you left. He was awfully mean, forced me to become a whore like his other girls. When he got drafted, I got out of the gang and met a man working for a contractor at the navy yard, got a check from grandmother and went to Nam with the guy. He turned out to be worse than Vinnie. When my money was gone, so was he. Now, here I am with nothing left but my skin and bones," she said.

"Spare me any more details. I have enough of my own. Have any plans for yourself back home?"

Call Me Maggie

"Not yet. Just get well, get dried out and find a better way to survive. Hell, I don't even have any clothes to cover these ugly bones," Madeline said, bowing her head again.

"I have enough for both of us, but they're Raggedy Ann and Plain Jane."

"A glamorous stewardess with Plain Jane clothes? That's a lot different from the outfits you wore Bandstand or dressed in for evenings in Philadelphia," Madeline said.

"I wore those things to attract men. I earned them lying on my back with them. Now I am sorry for having gotten into that way of life. It nearly got me killed."

"Me too!"

"This is not an airline for a glamour girl stewardess taking vacationers to resorts and meeting them after them after the flight. My boys aren't looking for a Miss America in gowns and jewels or a half naked cocktail waitress. They want someone to reassure them that they will come back whole and well, not on a stretcher or a bag in the cargo hold. If they are lucky enough to ride home in a cabin seat, they want a stewardess who helps them remember the good thing they left behind. They see me and my attendants as sisters, cousins or mothers, and girlfriends back home, not as an easy pickup. Seeing a little tit or watching our butts swing is not what they are looking for. Some of them can't even see. They can't cop a feel when they have no hands, or dance with us in the aisle when they have no legs. Their eyes, hands and legs are still somewhere in Vietnam. I am a flight attendant to give them care and tenderness, not their calendar girl fantasy. Plain Jane has become a habit, even behind closed doors with Norman," Maggie said.

"Plain Jane would be best for me now. At least Plain Jane dresses won't attract guys who want to tear them off. Anything has got to be better than to keep on living as a cheap whore, or getting beat-up all the time," Madeline said.

Madeline finally faced Maggie. Maggie saw a scar above her sister's chin matching the shape of teeth, and the one Midge wore. Several others were on her face. Needle marks lined both her arms. Her strawberry blonde hair was dull and disarranged.

Maggie drove Madeline to see their mother and to Harmony House after calling Norman, saying only that she was back and would probably not be home until late in the night. It was past midnight when she passed him in the kitchen saying only, "I'm home," before running a hot bubble bath.

The Girls Will Be Like You

Norman knew Maggie's flight had not been a good one. She had receded into her stockade again. He brought her tea and remained awake more than an hour waiting for her bath to end. Around four he awoke to find Maggie pulling and packing clothes from her rack and dresser. His heart raced as never before.

"Are you leaving me?" he asked loudly.

"Leaving you? No Way! Madeline is in the hospital and needs a few things. I'm taking these to her," Maggie answered.

"Maddie or Madeline?" Norman asked.

"Madeline Johnson, my sister."

"Give me a minute to shower and get dressed. I'm going with you," he said, firmly.

Maggie had been hoping Norman would join her on the drive, but was unsure and had not awakened him. Would he accept Madeline and give her support similar to that he gave the frightened prostitute he took into his home twelve years ago rather than deliver her to a safe house or when he cleaned blood from her hair in a Chicago alley six years earlier. She wondered if he would accept Madeline sharing their lives. He would have another prostitute in his life.

"Madeline has been terribly abused and living in the streets as a worn out, used up, whore, thrown away like an unwanted kitten. She won't make a pretty picture; underweight, unattractive and unsightly," Maggie said.

"I have seen and made enough pictures of things that were not pretty to fill a book," Norman said.

Maggie knew Norman had seen the worst that life could deal some of the subjects he had photographed. He had interviewed and photographed the indigent, the neglected, and the abused in the highest income per capita state in the nation. He had photographed life's ugly side as well as the beauty he sought in pictures of her. He had pictured her in all possible situations, except with her mother and sister. She had seen his fire and accident pictures in the newspaper. He did not discuss incidents he photographed where people were abused, neglected, injured or killed. He had photographed life coming into the world and leaving it. He did not talk about the things he saw and she did not talk about the wounded or maimed she brought home from the war. Unless there was good and positive they could share, each kept their unsightly encounters hidden within themselves.

Within an hour they were on the road. Maggie snuggled close over the Wagoner's hump. He had laid three books to her right. One was

295

his study of Cape Henlopen. Another contained many of her flowers. Each bore the credit line: "Photographs by Norman Kennedy." Norman mow had seven books, dozens of magazine spreads, a few posters calendars and greeting cards with his credit line.

"You were right when you saw Madeline in Saigon. She was prostituting when the demand for escorts diminished. Her pimp left her with no way to get home when Grandmother's money ran out and life on the streets caught up with her."

"How is she health-wise?" Norman asked.

"Run down, under-nourished, under-weight and worn-out. We may be twins but we are hardly identical anymore. Selling myself didn't work for me and it certainly did not work for Madeline. She became less desirable to the men who could get a live-in Vietnamese girl and a house for a month for less what they paid her for a few hours. She had to live in the street, homeless, rejected, and alone. All through history men have kept their prostitutes in the shadows. Our standards today are still Victorian. Men still have mistresses. Some women even indiscreet lovers they keep for their manhood services. Prostitution was at its peak in Victorian Society. Men kept wives and girlfriends safely above real life to be adored like a jewel. But in the shadows, a whore waited to fulfill their sensual pleasures. It was a double standard that did not work. If it had worked, we would all have been born illegitimate bastards while Victorian wives remained childless. Madeline and I have been whores and prostitutes selling ourselves to strangers. So has our mother. I don't want to be a Victorian jewel either. I just want to be a woman who cares for and loves the people who love me regardless of what I have been in the past, or the way I live my life now, even if I am gone for days giving the best of myself to others. Madeline may not feel the way I do, but I hope she finds a better life than she had in Chester or Vietnam, even if it's only a fraction of what I have found with you and your family. I opened the door to a better life for her, but she must step through it. I gave the best care I could to our boys coming back from the war. Now I must show how much I care for both my families."

"I am sure your differences with Madeline will be resolved. Bringing her back was a big step. She will take others, if she is half the person you are."

During the winter Maggie received a Christmas card bearing a South Dakota postmark. The card read: "Been here two months working with nuns on an Indian reservation. Dry and clean for 289 days. Say hi to Norman, and give Mom a hug for me. Love, Madeline."

296

The Girls Will Be Like You

Russians sent more weapons to the Viet Cong and North Vietnam. Americans sent more men and weapons to the South. They sent men into space so often it became commonplace, but only the Americans sent men to walk on the moon. Women joined spacemen in both space races. Cold War one-up-man-ship continued.

New words, environment and ecology, became politically and socially correct. An energy crisis loomed sending gasoline, electrical and heating costs higher. Compacts replaced gas guzzling, chrome endowed, battleships on interstate highways connecting major cities from the Atlantic to the Pacific oceans and from Florida to Alaska.

Musical icons Elvis Presley, Jemi Hendricks, Janis Joplin and a fewer lesser known's ended their lives with drug overdoses. Only one Woodstock Festival was held, even though dozens of others were planned. Locals blocked future festivals fearing music fests would be drug fests. Stadiums became the choice for music concerts. American groups copied and competed with British groups making fortunes playing before thousands in stadiums and basketball arenas worldwide.

Linda became a celebrity in demand at sportsmen banquets and auto dealerships. Lionel built GM cars and tweaked Linda's Dodge. Maddie carried Little Lionel around the corner each morning to his grandmothers for babysitting. She and the big Lionel bought Pop Pop's house. Pop Pop bought more roses and a real green house.

Some American women began to receive treatment and salaries to their male counterparts. Some became military and airline pilots, as well as senators in Washington making decisions whether to send or keep their sons out of wars such as Vietnam. Maggie prided herself for having played a role in gaining women's equality, and bringing the human toll of the war into people's conscience. Little did she know that the worst was ahead of her as she made even more trips were made across the Pacific. The President announced he would bomb the North Vietnam back to the Stone Age.

Maggie was approaching her thirtieth birthday, had thousands of flying hours in her log books, and had built herself an activist's reputation but still brought wounded and dead young men home from Americans tired of TV war scenes served with their dinner. More than half a million had been wounded and fifty eight thousand had died in a war no one wanted. Viet Cong losses were at least double that without counting those not found after B-52 bombers dropped bombs that annihilated everything on one by one and a quarter mile swatches of Vietnamese land.

297

Call Me Maggie

Diplomatic envoys were sent to China in more than twenty eight years hoping to establish trade agreements, form an alliance against Russian, and lessen weapons to Vietnam. A new diplomacy was established as the two nations' volleyed white balls over ping pong tables while Chinese made weapons kept arriving in Viet Nam.

By spring of 1975, North Vietnamese artillery and tanks were approaching Saigon. Even the airport began being shelled. The war continued without ever achieving peace until Congress saw the futility of continuing and passed a bill cutting off funds and withdrawal of American forces began almost as soon as President Ford's signature dried.

All Vietnamese who had worked for the Americans knew their fate would be harsh if they did not leave their homeland before the North Vietnamese took over. Refugees left the country any way they could, especially in overloaded boats. Others walked into Cambodia, Laos and Thailand. Every available plane, large or small, old or new, civilian or military headed toward Southeast Asia. The owner of Maggie's airline personally began making rescue flights ferrying refugees out. On his first flight more than a dozen were still trying to climb dropdown steps as he began his take off roll. Maggie attempted to raise the steps and door. A Vietnamese woman chased the plane down the runway, passed her baby up the steps, waved goodbye, and fell onto the runway just before liftoff. The plane slowly got into the air with half its passengers standing where ever they found space. Its sixty seats were full of children sitting three and four upon each other.

The city was surrounded. Roads and rivers blocked. Helicopters landed in parking lots, in street intersections, on rooftops and on lawns, ferrying American and Vietnamese allies to ships offshore. Larger planes made short trips to airports in friendly nearby countries, and then returned for more refugees. Families numbering up to three dozen could be found on the flights. Maggie, Midge and Leanne made numerous flights resting only when going back for another load in the days of withdrawal and evacuation. Neither could achieve real rest. More than seven thousand persons had been airlifted out in less than a week, one overloaded plane at a time. Yet many Vietnamese families became separated and lost in miles of jungle, ocean, red tape, and by a lack of aircraft.

"I can still see the face of the woman on the stairs waving to her baby before falling. She fought to be the last one on board, before her strength and luck gave out. Her image is burned in my mind," Maggie told Leanne.

The Girls Will Be Like You

"The survival of their loved ones was more important than their own lives. When this over, I know what I'm going to do. I may never have to die for Bobby Joe, but I will live my life for him," Leanne said.

"I have never had a good family life before. I have one now and I am going to make it even better," Maggie said.

Hardly a product, fashion, or fad lasted longer than the credit card payments. Everything was disposable. Maddie and Midge bought disposable diapers. Linda bought trash compactors for each of her restaurants only to buy replacements, and later replacement for the replacements. City dumps became over filled with worn out and disposable products and packaging waste from replacements.

Jets and turbo jets that replaced propeller driven airliners soon began joining Connies, Stratocruisers and Gooneybirds in airplane graveyards. Hippies, flower children, peaceniks and draft dodgers returned to society, got jobs, had children and ran for public office. Some even got elected.

Once the evacuations were finished and the troops brought home, flight attendants, including Maggie, airline employees began losing the jobs.

"This ole girl brought us home again," the Skip Snyder said as he and Maggie left their 747.

The other pilot and attendants left half-an-hour earlier after bringing their final load of soldiers back from war horrors half way around the world.

"What are you going to do now that the fighting is over and you won't have to care for the wounded any longer?" the pilot asked.

"Raise more roses, breed more horses, enroll in the university, finish my education, and take care of my boys in the Elsmere Veterans Hospital. Both applications were accepted. I'll be a therapy aid. Next month I'll start going there each afternoon instead of coming here. I plan to ease up a little, make some changes in my family life, and in my relationship with Norman."

"Raise roses, breed horses, give therapy to your boys, go to college and have a better family life. That's easing up?"

"In my book, it will be. How about you? Any plans?"

"Build a houseboat, show M&M and keep flying jets to pay for them. Commercial aviation is growing. Pilots will be in demand. Flight attendants too. Why don't you sign on with a corporate fleet or one of the big carriers? U.S. Air is based in Philadelphia. That's close enough for you to drive rather than commute from Vegas to Dallas, like me."

Call Me Maggie

"And have passengers pinch my chest or grab my butt. No thanks. I started flying for the glamour of being a stewardess and seeing exotic places. I soon learned that I was needed for better things. A boat in the desert? You're pulling my leg."

"Sounds crazy doesn't it. My wife is a hotel manager in Las Vegas. Our kids are in college. I play drums in a band. She keeps the band booked. The weather is good, and there's a lake nearby large enough for us to find privacy."

"When you put it that way it's not crazy at all. Good luck with your boat, your drums, your family plans, and your flying."

"And don't you lose the place in your heart for the boys in the hospital. They need you attendants like you looking out for them. You have the right knack for helping the wounded survive and get better. Best of luck, Maggie."

"Thank you, Skip. I will need lots of it."

She hugged the white-haired man who had told her everything she knew about her father and checked out with her dispatcher.

The little charter airline would remain based in Wilmington for several months carrying vacationers and sightseers here, there, and everywhere. One of the flight paths was over the hospital and another over the farmette. Maggie would see the planes over the hospital when she took her boys out for sunshine and fresh air. She would see them over the farm many evenings. But she would never the farm, the rose field, or her horses from inside the planes again.

Maggie knew easing the soldiers fear and pain had been her most satisfying responsibility. She wanted to continue working with her boys. A four line newspaper help wanted ad had provided her with the answer in deciding what she would do when the war and her flights ended. She had driven past the hospital many times. It had no sign on the lawn. It looked like an apartment complex. She never knew follow-up treatment she started continued so close to home. A position on the hospital staff fit her desires to a tee. She applied and was accepted.

As Maggie drove west, the sun was setting over Basin Road and the large spaghetti bow intersection Kevin and Ernest had helped build. She could still see Kevin covered with brown dust. She remembered the many times she rode and flew with Norman as he photographed the highway. She could almost drive the interstate to Cecil County Dragway or to Washington, D.C. blindfolded.

Maggie parked her Jeep in front of the white house surrounded by a picket fence again. Pop Pop was rocking on the porch.

The Girls Will Be Like You

"You gotta see our new rose," he said before she could close the gate.

"I'd love to see it," Maggie answered.

The two headed toward the garden. The dogwood tree stood bare over a blanket of blood red leaves.

Lionel was tweaking the engine of Linda's racer. Maddie sat at the wheel. Their son slept beside her. Linda and Maddie kept the Champions restaurant-lounges operating with the same smoothness as Lionel kept Linda's racer running. Maggie saw Linda, Kevin, and Deanna as if they were there too.

"Welcome home. Linda's been calling for you all day. Give her a call when you get a chance," Maddie said.

"I'll go up there after I see Pop Pop's new rose," Maggie said.

Maggie met Pop Pop in the garden. She leaned over and sniffed the blossom he cupped. It nearly covering both his hands. A light red blush divided each white petal.

"Great fragrance," she stated.

"I think we have us a winner," Pop Pop said.

"It's a special one alright. Got a name picked yet?"

"Fairy's Blush," he answered.

Maggie remembered that Mom Mom's given name was Fairy.

"Great name and great way to remember her."

The old gardener cut an unopened bud, handed it to Maggie and said, "With this, you can remember her, too."

"I will. I'll dry it and frame it also."

The elder Kennedy removed his glasses to wipe his eyes.

"Come have dinner with me. Help me celebrate. Today's flight was my last," Maggie said to the man who had replaced her own father.

Maggie and he passed nearly a hundred people before reaching a table holding a "Reserved" sign at the Price's Corner Champions lounge.

"You guys have to come with me to California. I am appearing on the Johnny Carson next Monday night. You two need a distraction and I need some company. I'm taking the kids to Disneyland while we are there. I won't take no from you two or from Norman," Linda declared.

"Okay with me. How about you?" Maggie replied.

"I don't know. I have never been in a plane. Getting on a six-foot ladder makes me dizzy and nervous," Pop Pop said.

Call Me Maggie

"Of course you will come. You'll love it. Besides, Maggie knows how to make fliers relax and enjoy their flight."

"I'll be right beside you all the way as you have been beside me for so many years," Maggie promised.

"Well alright. I already spend more time with Johnny and Ed than I do with my family," Pop Pop said.

"Johnny will be on vacation. Phyllis Diller will be the hostess. Send her some of your roses. I'll write a letter to go with the roses," Linda said.

Maggie saw Linda's promotional skills working again as though she was selling sponsorship and promotion for her racing career. Linda made two phone calls. Norman soon joined them. Lionel and Maddie arrived after putting little Lionel to bed at her mother's home. Maddie volunteered herself and Lionel to care for the farm, water the roses, and care for the horses if she could ride the mare again. Linda left at eight to have dinner with her children. She would return to close Champions with Maddie after her children were in bed with her parents watching over them.

Pop Pop opened "The Tonight Show" Monday night presenting Mrs. Diller two dozen of his rose cultures. He said she could grow similar roses with tobacco juice and tender loving care. Mrs. Diller opted for his loving care suggestion, but declined his tobacco juice idea after tasting a pinch of Red Mule chewing tobacco. Linda closed the program telling Phyllis about drag racing, showing films of a few races, pictures from her album, and her risqué poster.

"I put my jumpsuit the same way men drivers do, except I have to use more effort when the zipper gets to my chest."

Linda got national sponsors, thanks to the appearance. Pop Pop got rose bush orders, and pride to replace long days of loneliness caring for roses that he had substituted for his wife's companionship.

After the trip Maggie brought her mother to the farm for three days in fresh country air. The remaining two weeks Maggie took relaxing strolls through the rose field, bred the philly again, and visited a housing development where her grandmother's farm one sprawled. She and Linda shopped for medical uniforms in thrift shops. Maggie chose white, but changed her mind, heeding Linda's advice for pink.

"Do you ever think about marrying again?"

"Once, after seeing Joe Jobbe a few times. I realized I didn't have time for another person in my life, boyfriend or husband, and he couldn't replace Kevin with me or the kids."

The Girls Will Be Like You

"Is he still drinking a lot?"

"No. He only drank Cokes and ate steaks subs around me. I told him with racing, running a business and raising two kids, I couldn't date often. He came back a few times with Judith Rawlins. I suppose he brought her to spite me."

"I doubt it. You created Champions as a meeting place for car buffs like Joe and Judith. They have a project car in the works. Norman is making pictures for a book on it with Judith."

"How many books is that now for them?" Linda asked.

"Five for Judith, seven for Norman not counting his layouts in American Graphic, Maggie answered.

As the second week ended, they shared chores around the farm after early morning coffee. Maggie had caught up on many of the things she had promised herself would be done, yet her list remained long. She had removed the top from her Jeep, driven for miles on country roads and to the beach, picked up her mother for a day in Amish country, and finally spend a day in Midge and David's day care, plus an evening of with them at a gospel music song fest.

A twenty-four foot lead line connected Maggie's right hand to the halter on a fifteen month philly. A shorter line moved occasionally, responding to her left arm. After a few moments, Maggie rewarded the yearling with grain in her cupped hands followed by rubbing and patting on the young horse's neck. Training then continued just as Pop Pop had taught Maggie. Soon a blanket lay across the horse's back. Later a saddle was added. Finally a small bag of grain was tied to the saddle. Satisfied with the young horses' progress, Maggie and the philly shared apples. Maggie placed her left foot in the stirrup and tested the horse's reaction. The horse stood in place. After a few more cycles in and out of the stirrup, Maggie climbed into the saddle. With pressure in her sides and a soft "Get up, Starlight" from Maggie, the horse walked the grass bare circle again. Returning to the barn, Maggie opened the stall door and led her mare into the pasture. Moments later they walked along the tree line near the creek. This time the mare trailed her foal as the nestled her head over Maggie's shoulder.

Norman stopped by the farm that afternoon and took pictures as she trained the fold to harness and surrey. Norman made more pictures as Storm and Deanna paraded a white surrey through Odessa during Colonial Home Week. Maggie rode atop Starlight.

His artful figure studies of Maggie, her hair or glamorous shots of her in long lovely dresses became seldom, but pictures of her visiting

Call Me Maggie

her mother in the nursing home, working with his father among the roses or with the horses became more frequent. Maggie's newest favorites were shots were of her rocking Kevin Junior on the patio and one of her and Deanna with the horses. She placed both on her dresser next to the soldier's picture taken from her mother's house the day she left Chester.

"Let's take the convertible for a ride," Norman suggested one Tuesday.

He lowered the top and they drove north. Half an hour later he parked. Within minutes, two submarines cruised by New Castle Wharf.

"How did you know they would be here today?"

"I can't reveal all my secrets."

"Norman, I have many secrets I have kept from you. It's now time I reveal some of mine. You share your work, your thoughts, your dreams and your family with me. I have not always shared mine with you. The promise we made the night long ago has been kept by you more than by me. You are truly a partner. I have not been yours."

"I never knew you kept anything major from me, except the horrors you saw with the boys you brought home. You had your wall of silence and kept things to yourself until you them worked out for yourself. Then you shared them with me. I did the same with you some of my assignments."

"I did not have good parents to guide me and give me assurance as you have had. I craved parents and a home I could bring friends to and he proud. I give your father the love I wish I could have given my own. We have a closeness that helps me remember my grandparents. We share the horses as my grandfather and I did before he died and the plants as my grandmother and I did," Maggie said.

"He needed you as much as you needed him. Mom accepted you as another daughter. Dad has substituted you for her in the things you and he do together. Those rings were the most precious thing he had to express his feelings for you. He wants you as part of his family as much as you wanted him as part of yours," Norman said.

"Those rings are the most precious things I will ever have unless you give me one."

"I have had one for you since the day we bought this farm when I suggested we go get married in Elkton. It's still up stairs."

"I never knew you had gotten a wedding ring. I wore your grandmothers to ward off unwanted advances for a long time. It worked; no one ever gave me trouble. We will know if you still want me to have yours when this conversation finishes. And if you still want me, too."

The Girls Will Be Like You

"I will still want you."

"In school I was the shy girl in old clothes hoping I would not be noticed. After growing up, I discovered Bandstand and wanted to be like the kids I saw there: happy, carefree, and well dressed. I got attention, but it was the wrong kind from the wrong kind of people. Trying to fit in, I did things I should not have done. I joined a crowd I should not have joined. I made choices and have had to live with them, always frightened, always ashamed, always trying to hide them, especially from you. You took in a tramp and encouraged her to be a lady. You took a whore and made her beautiful pictures of her. You tipped off a girl from the Chester slums about the airline, and I became a stewardess who tied her hair with a stretchy, put on a mask hoped men would touch me or want me. I wanted to be wanted by you and you only. I only dressed nicely for you and your pictures. It worked. Most of the time you are more like a father or a brother to me than a lover. You gave me freedom to fly away, write letters to strangers, dress like a Victorian lady and model naked as the Mona Lisa. I bet if I had burned my bra with the feminist or became a nun; you would have been there with me and put pictures in my album, too."

"Insecure, frightened, or not, you did it by yourself. You worked hard to become good at what you do. You did school alone to become the best stewardess they had. You kept working as though there was no tomorrow, taking extra trips or filling-in whenever you were needed. You stuck it out, when hundreds of others quit. You had your goals and went after them."

"No I had some bad memories and I was running away. There is a lot you don't know about. Like pulling a man off Midge so she would not have to endure the pain and scars of rape as Leanne and I have had to bear. Telling you about it would have caused you to worry that it could happen t again every time I left your sight. I can kick butt as well as any women and most men. I learned it after I started flying. I only wish I had learned it at an earlier age. If I had I would not have worried all these years whether some creep from Philadelphia might find me and destroy the life I have found with you. You have shared your life with me, but I have not shared mine with you. I want you to have all of what's left of my life. I don't have to take the job in the hospital or go to college. I can never spend half the money I earned and put away flying."

"You not changing your mind about working in the hospital, are you?"

305

Call Me Maggie

"Let's go home. I'll think about it some more. I still have one un-resolved question."

Two white horses and a foal came to the fence as Norman put the convertible away. Maggie went to them and Norman followed.

"Thank you for the ride and the submarines. I'm sorry for keeping secrets from you."

"Sometimes you build a stockade around yourself that keep you in as surely as this fence keeps your horses safely inside. I can't get in and you can't get out. You may have needed it when we met, but you don't need it any longer. We are a couple and couple share. We don't fence ourselves in or the other one out. Tear down the fence Maggie. Let yourself be free. The past is gone. You don't have to hide any secrets or fears and pain any longer. Especially from me."

"I know. You and I have done almost everything a couple should do together except hear you introduce me as your wife or have children. I breed the horses and raise flowers, but haven't had your children. I don't know how to be a wife. All my experience with men has been distasteful except with you, your brothers and your father. I have only a few memories of my own father, but many good ones of yours. He was a soldier and if someone like me had been there as I grew up, I would have grown up close to him as you have with yours. I have no brothers except your three, and thousands of others I met going back and forth to Vietnam. That's why I kept going back to Vietnam. The ones with any life left in them got the best care I could give them. In many ways, I feel like I am your wife. I'm sure your family and our friend think we got married quietly and never told anyone even though we don't wear rings and never have clung to each other like Kevin and Linda once did or Lionel and Maddie still do. I have never said I love you even though I love you more than I can ever tell you. I never felt secure enough to be a real partner and get married. I was one of the young girls living in shadows until I met you. I saw hundreds of them in restaurants near posts and even more in Saigon. I didn't want you to be married to an ex-whore.

"I have never thought of you as a whore. You told me you did not want to get married, and that was alright with me. We did everything married couples do except have babies. I felt you had your reasons and would change your mind. At first I thought it was your career and that you might find the right man flying. But you always came back to me. In time it didn't matter. You were there for me and my needs. It was of you that I did my best work, made my best pictures, and enjoyed my life

The Girls Will Be Like You

with more than anyone else. I hoped you felt the same, so being married didn't seem so important after a while."

Norman could sense a great uneasiness within that Maggie was trying to release. He had seen that internal conflict many times when she kept problems confined within her impenetrable stockade. He remembered the Mothers Day that Maggie's mother was so drunk she did not know Maggie had visited her or could share the news that she was back in school getting her diploma and becoming a stewardess. He remembered the night he told her he had seen Madeline in Saigon what Madeline was doing there. He remembered other times when she withdrew to a bubble bath after coming off a troublesome flight and did not share her problems with him. He smiled to himself recalling a young woman going head to head with a Senator on Capitol Hill or grabbing clothes for his pictures, only to discard them for more pictures of her posing nude. He remembered how pure, how innocent and how beautiful she appeared in his viewfinder with long reddish hair draped over or billowing above loose white blouses or long white dresses. It upset Norman that he had not recognized the symbolism sooner; white was the color Maggie preferred and symbolic of the purity she had lost.

"I'm not as innocent as Midge, as brazen as Linda, or as smart as Leanne, but I try to be more like each every day. Like them I want a family to come home to and share my life with you and our children."

Norman avoided her mentioning children. He hoped she would bring the question back into the conversation. If she did not, he would.

She rung her hands and one foot tapped the ground hastily. Was the stockade being reinforced or discarded? A volcano was building inside her and its outflow he could not predict. Was she preparing him so she could end their relationship or did she have something else in mind that would not surface? He silently questioned and hoped that the eruption would affirm her intent to remain with him sharing the life he had come to love with her as its center.

"There are many other things I have avoided discussing with you besides marriage. An important one is: Are you going to stay with the newspaper and turn down jobs with more prestigious publications that pay you much better? I think you turned down Samuel Brown to be with me. And if you did, thank you, but it wasn't necessary. We could have found a way to make it work. That's farther than northern New Jersey. I could have driven down here in less than two hours on the turnpike or Interstate 95. Leanne drove from Farmville, Virginia for years and still drives from the university to make her flights."

307

Call Me Maggie

"Leanne dedicated herself to Bobby Joe and his needs. She flew less. You dedicated yourself to your flying, the needs of the soldiers, and model you wanted to be when we met. You didn't need a two or three hour drive taken out of your life after a long flight. You had too many other ways to spend those hours. Like I told Samuel, there are still some pictures near here that I want to take. Working afternoons and nights is my choice. Hershel has offered me day work many times, but I turned him down each time. Most local news happens in the afternoons or evenings. I want to be available to photograph it. It's selfish of me, but I take better news pictures later in the day and my best personal ones in the morning when I freshest. Being based in the middle of the east coast is the place best for me. And it's close to our families as well as your work and the farm. Finding a farm so close to Wilmington, the airport, the train station and three major cities was a lucky break for both of us. You have to admit, we have made it work out well for both of us."

Maggie agreed out loud and then held him close.

"I came home down River Road yesterday. I found an automobile grave yard near the refinery. It has dozens of old cars and an old shack. I would like you to photograph me nude among the rusty hulks and weathered boards. When the paint is gone, the clothes are rotten and cast off, we are weathered, rusty and worn out, we are still who we made ourselves to be. We may be a little older, maybe naked, maybe alone, but we are not disposable like the things we build and use. Take a picture of a worn-out woman in the world's waste and ugliness."

"I will," Norman said.

"You have never published a picture of me. Maybe it's time we start editing the ones we've taken into a book, unless you think they are too personal, or you don't want thousands of strangers seeing pictures of your children's mother."

"I will only worry about the people in Philadelphia or the people at the hospital. The hospital people might not like them and the ones in Philadelphia might decide to look you up,"

"I would not be setting a precedent. Nurses have been in Playboy and Penthouse. I have had no contact with anyone in Philadelphia since Kevin died. I was frightened until Vinnie took care of Linda and Dominic after Kevin died. I don't fear him or his gang anymore. He's out of the picture and out of our lives. I want you to use my real name when you do. I will be proud to be Mary Anne Kennedy. But save a few pages for pictures of me pregnant. Don't wait too long. Maggie not getting any younger,"

The Girls Will Be Like You

"Neither is old Norman, Miss Johnson."

"How about some tea?"

Maggie went inside, made their tea, brought newspaper it to the patio, laid both before him and stood overlooking his shoulders. A headline read: "Union Official Found Shot, Family Fears Mob Reprisal."

"He's definitely out of the picture now," Norman said.

"He was the first one to show me attention and the one who treated me the worst. Ghosts he created have haunted me for years. They won't haunt me anymore. I made you use a condom because I feared my sons might be like Vinnie and my daughters might turn out like my mother or my sister. Madeline is going straight. Mom is getting better. Vinnie is gone. The day we bought the farm you asked me to marry you and you have stuck with me thirteen years without getting an answer. If you still want a girl who gave more time to flying and other young men than she gave you, I'll marry you, have your children, and grow old with you. I want you to have the best of what's left of my life. Let me be your partner again and model for you again even when I'm pregnant. Linda and Maddie have children we adore. Leanne and Bobby Joe adopted a little girl that we love. Midge is expecting one. I would like to have children like theirs."

"What about your new career? You have said many times, those young men need you. Don't give up on them. Take the job. Take care of your boys."

"We made it work in the past. We'll make it work in the future, even with children. If you want children, how many? The boys won't be like Vinnie. They will be like you or their grandfather."

"And the girls will be like you."

Call Me Maggie

About the Writer

Nelson Brooks moved to Wilmington, Delaware in 1952 from an Alabama farm with his parents, three brothers and a sister. He was employed at the News-Journal paper from 1957 until 1966. He worked for other publications until 1981 as photographer and editor, taking three years between 1969 and 1972 he earned a journalism degree from Southern Illinois University at Carbondale. He served five years in the armed forces reserve in the early 1960's, never seeing active duty. Being older than his student peers, he came to know and befriend many Vietnam War veterans studying at the university on the GI Bill.

A nurse who flew with Capital Airways during the Vietnam era was the inspiration for this story and for the character Maggie. She lived her remaining years dressed in Victorian or country styled long dresses. Her strawberry blonde hair turned white remained uncut for sixty two years.

The farmette house and barn in the story were torn down during the 1990's. The pasture was divided by a four-lane roadway of the Delaware Turnpike to relieve congestion on U.S. 13. through Odessa. Nelson returns to Wilmington and the Delaware beaches frequently. The drive between the city and Cape Henlopen takes him across the site.

Nelson's father died in 2000 and his home was bought by two auto buffs, much like Linda and Kevin. His mother died in 1969 while Nelson was at the university, not in Viet Nam. His great grandfather was wounded at Bull Run and his great grandmother, the midwife, did birth more than 200 babies including Nelson's father.

Nelson retired in 2003 on a small piece of land in the Virginia piedmont to garden and write.

The dirt pan drivers, Ernest, Kevin and Lionel were modeled his brothers, Elvin, and Hoyt. The character Lionel bears many of the youngest brother, Lindsey. Hoyt died in a Philadelphia robbery much as Kevin died in this story. Elvin too, has since died. Lindsey still lives in Elsmere and in his wife's first and only home.

Maggie Linda, Vinnie, Dominic, Midge, Leanne, Bobby Joe, and all the other characters are fictional except for the presidents. The pieces on President Kennedy were actual incidents he photographed.

311

Made in the USA